£1·50

CW00727338

CAUGHT IN A SINGAPORE SLING

BOB NIMMO

Copyright © Bob Nimmo 2003

First published in
New Zealand in 2003
Horizon Press
PO Box 57-202
Mana 6230
Porirua, New Zealand
Phone: +64 4 233 8204 Fax: +64 4 479 8589
E-mail: books@horizonpress.co.nz

This is a work of fiction. Names, characters and incidents are either the product of the author's imagination or used fictitiously. Although certain real persons have inspired the creation of some of the characters in this story, any complete resemblance to actual events, organisations or persons is entirely coincidental and beyond the intent of the author or publisher.

ISBN 0 9582351 4 7

Cover design by J. Elliott Freelance.

Inside pages and pre-press by Unicorn Design Studio Ltd.

Author's manuscript supplied to the publisher by Dunsford Publishing Consultants.

Printed by Hutcheson, Bowman and Stewart, Wellington.

The inks used for the printing of this book are made from vegetable oils and natural resins, are biodegradable and do not use polycyclic aromatics or volatile organic compounds. The paper is a mixture of chlorine-free pulp and pre-consumer and post-consumer waste.

DEDICATION

To Diana and George
without whose love and encouragement
this book would never have happened

Acknowledgements

In bringing a novel to the point of publication it passes through many hands and influences. I would like to thank Dr Cathie Dunsford, my publishing consultant, whose support and professional advice helped strengthen the original work. I am grateful to my publisher, Chris Mundy and his team at Horizon Press for their confidence and understanding.

I would also like to thank Dr Batia Horsky, Israeli and US adviser on military medicine, stress and suicide management, for her stimulating 'over coffee' discussions and comments on character psychology and profiling; Dr Iria Claverly, paediatrician, for allowing me to peruse her research on Asian child abuse; Mr Martin Gilmour, good friend, ex-legionnaire (French Foreign Legion) and military logistics planner, for his advice and unflagging support. I would also like to thank my special friend, Mr Tee Kai Yin, for helping me with all the Singlish dialogue.

Finally, I would like to acknowledge my many Singaporean colleagues who over fourteen years put up with the eccentricities and extravagances of a strange Caucasian visitor. In particular I would like to thank, with great affection, Ms Ruth Goss, that larger than life figure who became the inspiration for Jean Simmons.

Although I am critical of some Singaporean institutions, attitudes and ideas in this book, I remain very much in love and awe of the island state – a clean, green haven where for fourteen years I lost my heart.

About the Author

Bob Nimmo spent fourteen years working for the Singapore Ministry of Education, and *Caught in a Singapore Sling* is based largely on his experiences during this period. Prior to this he travelled extensively, working with the British army in Berlin and observing Palestinian training in Tunisia. He has written eight musical comedies and directed a number of award-winning plays. He is currently completing manuscripts for two Singapore publishing companies.

PART ONE

'Those who can do, those who can't teach and those who can't teach, teach teachers!'

Adapted from George Bernard Shaw

PROLOGUE

The moon disappears momentarily. Housing Development Block 418 is dark and silent. Across the neatly mown lawn in front of the estate, a brightly-lit hawker centre appears to be doing brisk business even at this hour, and the chatter of Chinese mixed with a volley of Indian drifts over the deserted car-park. A lone figure stumbles from the brightness and is soon sucked into the darkness beyond. It is shortly after midnight, Singapore time.

Clumps of trees surrounding the bottom of the block like lost shadows gaze skywards, seemingly in anticipation. Their wait is soon rewarded. A thick-set figure lurches over the balustrade on the tenth floor. He pauses briefly, before toppling forward and plunging heavily towards the ground like an under-rehearsed diver. As he falls he gurgles.

The body clips the trees, slows, then hits the ground with a sickening whump. More gurgling.

A head appears above the parapet, then vanishes.

The body lies still, crumpled, and apparently unnoticed.

Minutes pass. A dealer and his victim stride across the lawn in heated argument, unaware of the pair of eyes watching them from the back of the concrete refuse station.

Suddenly a police car, silent and white, slips into the car-park like a circling shark sniffing the smell of fresh blood...

CHAPTER

1

'One of your students has just lost his father!'

I stared vacantly at the principal. How could one misplace one's father? Perhaps he had run away or simply disappeared. When I thought of some of the little rascals in my form class, I could understand a father wanting to disappear. Lucky man! Still, I really needed to concentrate. My morning had begun so badly. Unable to catch a taxi, drenched in an unexpected downpour and caught sneaking into the school like a shamefaced wolfhound by the deputy principal, I thought things could not get much worse. But they could!

The principal pursed her lips, 'I'm afraid we have a rather delicate situation here.'

I found it difficult to imagine Mrs Benthusamy in a delicate situation. A large woman, she had arrived at Pleasant Park after serving in the same capacity in a smaller establishment lost somewhere on the distant fringes of the educational fraternity. She was big in size, big in voice, big in reputation, and very big in ego. Nothing delicate about her.

Unlike the rest of us, stress or indecision were never a bother, her confidence coming from the conviction that she alone knew what was best for staff, students, and parents — a belief she had often drawn to the attention of the Ministry of Education whenever they saw fit to comment critically on any of her programmes. The principal's frequent boast was that her door was always open. Unfortunately it was more open to some than others.

Luckily, she found Caucasian teachers an unusual species and this limited her mobility in my direction.

'… and the police wish to interview him, but he will not cooperate. Ah… Peter, you are not listening.' The motherly admonition shattered my reverie.

'I'm sorry, Mrs Benthusamy, my mind was elsewhere. Could you…'

'Please focus, Peter. We have a serious problem.'

Yes, I had grasped that part.

'Young Chang Yan Siang arrived for class today, but the boy shouldn't be here.'

How typically Singaporean — should not be at school, but was. Anywhere else it would have been the other way round.

'What I am about to reveal must be kept in the strictest confidence,' she whispered.

You've got no problem with me, I thought, but you had better look to your own security system.

'Early this morning, Yan Siang's father fell from the balcony outside their eleventh-floor HDB flat.'

Finally the principal had my full attention. 'Oh dear,' I offered, uncertain as to what was an appropriate response in this sort of situation and still not fully aware of what lay ahead of me.

'It's worse,' the principal continued, leaning forward. 'The boy was standing in the corridor when his father fell.'

'Oh no,' I breathed heavily.

'Naturally the police would like to speak with Yan Siang as soon as possible.'

Ah, now I had it. She wanted me to excuse him from class.

'They have asked for a staff member to accompany the boy

to the Tanglin Police Station to fill out a report, and as you are his form teacher…'

I stood up abruptly, my mouth hanging open in a bemused sort of way. 'Me? But, Madam Principal, I'm surely not the best person to accompany the boy. I don't speak Chinese and besides, I have classes.' I knew this was weak and I was grasping at straws, but I simply could not think of a better reason for avoiding my responsibilities.

'You are the boy's master teacher and no one knows him better!'

Oh dear, just like Her Graciousness to stick to protocol. Her convenient memory had obviously misplaced the conversation we had had two months earlier, when, because my class had more absentees (considerably more actually) than any other class approaching a term holiday, I was told that I was the worst form-teacher in the school with the most notorious form class. At the time I had taken this as a compliment, but now I was boxed in. I had to escort the boy. The decision had been made.

'As you wish, though I don't think I'll be of much help.'

'You'll handle the matter superbly, I'm sure,' Mrs Benthusamy beamed, pleased that the issue had been so easily resolved. After all, you never could tell with these Caucasian teachers!

I rose to leave and had reached the door when the principal added, 'Please set plenty of work for all your morning classes, Peter. We wouldn't want the periods to be wasted, would we?'

It was a pity the tag question was rhetorical. I would quite happily have let the little darlings waste the morning. Who knows, it could have proved to be one of the most educationally productive mornings of their entire year.

I walked along the corridor, straight into the deputy-principal. Twice in one morning — my luck really was bad.

'Everything all right?' she called after me, hoping it was not.
I paused and looked at her. This exceedingly skinny woman

exhibited a dress sense that would have flattered a hawker-centre bag lady. She had a smile which flashed insincerity over a face neatly sculpted and pleasantly attractive, but in her case beauty was indeed skin deep. She loved gossip, especially the sort she could share over a cup of tea tarek in the principal's office, hence her nickname 'Snake'. Now, in her tone, I could detect that edge of superciliousness which comes from knowing one has caught the other party at a disadvantage. I nodded and continued on to the staff room.

Fortunately, most of my colleagues had headed off to their duties and only Jean Simmons was still at her desk. How I loved this woman. She was truly an oasis of sanity in this desert of drudgery. Jean had originated in Scotland, but her travels had taken her to so many places around the globe that she could hardly be regarded as belonging to any one particular locality. She was a free thinker — outspoken, articulate, highly educated and tall… very tall! She wore unusual outfits which only her character could fill and was possessed of a worldly wisdom which combined just the right mix of east and west.

'Hi yah!' she chorused.

'You don't want to know!' I replied, sinking onto my customary seat. 'Bugger it!' I continued, as the catch slipped and I found myself considerably lower than I wanted to be.

'That stupid hinny Yap.' Jean rose from behind her pile of clutter. 'If she comes to me one more time aboot the corrections for her… that school magazine, I'll punch her, Pete. So help me I will!'

The thought of Jean punching somebody appealed and I burst into laughter. That is what I loved about her. She could wipe out the most irritating developments with one comment.

'It's nae joke. These people are sair stupid! No one cares about her silly little articles in that sodding magazine and we have a… a principal who wants everything written in the past tense! I ask you, Pete, is it any wonder we're all going crazy?'

'I've just been instructed to take a student to the Tanglin Police Station.'

'No! What happened?' Jean dropped everything and came over, hoping to hear about another embarrassing little episode.

'Apparently his father fell to his death early this morning and the kid saw it happen.'

'Oh, my poor dear!'

'Thanks, Jean, I'll cope.'

'Not you, the pair wee chappie. But why the polis station? Would it no be better for the wee lad to be interviewed here in familiar surroundings?'

I silently reflected that considering the number of times the wee lad had been absent, sent home or recorded as missing, the police station was probably as familiar to him as the school.

'Och, you know what it's like, Jean. The Wicked Witch of the West has made her decision and we've just got to cope with it.'

'Still, did you nae suggest it?'

'Me? Me make a suggestion? Dinny ye ken, hen, that suggestions cost money or status or something. Anyway, aren't you supposed to be in class?'

'I was… about twenty minutes ago!' She laughed, grabbed a pile of books, and sped across the room.

As she burst through the door, she collided with our mutual mini-boss, the Head of English. Profuse apologies and much scrambling later, Theresa Loh arrived at my desk.

'And why were you so late this morning?' she effected sternly and then broke into a laugh. 'Tanglin Police Station? Ha! Serves you right. Just make sure we don't have to come and bail you both out!'

Theresa with an 'h' was a class act. She dressed in outfits that would cost most teachers a month's salary and it was rumoured her husband was a multi-millionaire. I could never figure out what such a classy, attractive, elegant, rich, and superbly chassised woman was doing wasting her time in this place. Fabulous fun when caught away from educational pursuits, she possessed a great sense of humour and a heart as big as all outdoors. She was completely disinterested in the business of English teaching and I often found her missing from class. Usually she just forgot she was supposed to be there. Unfortunately, she also had an irritatingly deferential approach to the principal which occasionally cost her the respect of her fellow teachers.

'Give me a break! I'm supposed to take an extra rehearsal this afternoon and I'm way behind in my test marking!' I replied. Hell, I was beginning to sound like a rundown, overworked English teacher.

'Stop your moaning. I've got a couple of free periods, so I'll give you a ride down to Tanglin, if you like.'

'Now, that would be much appreciated. I'll go round up Yan Siang. Do you have any idea where he is?'

'Try the sick bay.'

'I'll meet you in the car park. What little wagon did you bring today?'

'The Mercedes. Don't be long.'

I left the staff room and turned back into the administration corridor. Two doors on the right was the sick bay. This pathetic little room was aptly titled. Painted a deep shade of nauseous lemon and sparsely furnished with a cot and desk, it could immediately worsen the staunchest constitution. Given that most visitors were already hovering in a limbo somewhere between hypochondria and genuine lethargy, this little haven was hardly likely to improve their physical or mental well-being. If you were not already depressed when you walked in, you sure as hell would be when you left. It was even rumoured that fifteen minutes in this place had effected a remarkable recovery in some students, who clearly preferred the rigours of the classroom. As I entered, I noticed that two cockroaches, no doubt having wandered in there by accident, had made for a distant corner, stretched out, and promptly died. Yan Siang sat curled up in the opposite corner, his head on his hands, which were wrapped around his knees in the foetal position, his back to the door. He heard me and glanced up.

'My God!' I breathed.

When the principal mentioned the name, I had vaguely remembered an irritating entry in the class register, but I could not put an image to it. Now face to face with the name, distant memories flooded back. This was the little shit who had made my life a misery umpteen times over the last few months. Most often he was absent and, as his classroom behaviour was subnormal, that would have been a blessing, if it were not for the forms and the telephone calls. When a child is absent without written support, the form teacher is required to phone the parents. This is generally unpleasant for local teachers, but it is worse for a Caucasian. In the case of Yan Siang, the phone was usually answered by his little sister or mother. The former was too young to be of any help and the latter had a hearing difficulty and could not speak much English. On one occasion I struck the grandmother and the conversation comprised such a series of grunts and wild exclamations that I felt I had caught her in the middle of Tai Chi.

When the telephone failed, the letters began. After several messages, I had achieved no more success than I had with the telephone. On top of this, on the rare occasions when he did show up, he was invariably late and this necessitated the filling out of the notorious green form, accompanied by an entry in the late-book and, on the third successive occasion, another phone call to his parents. I had become so familiar with his phone number that I had committed the damned thing to memory.

My difficulties did not end there. His behaviour in class bordered on animalistic. He had a nasty habit of spitting paper at those students he did not particularly like, which was most of the class. Consequently, he was regularly in trouble and his file was thicker than all the other students' files stacked end on end. Added to this were the three occasions he was caught smoking in the toilets (once in the girls'), the time he found a wallet which was not lost, the various occasions he had insulted teachers or argued with their decisions, and the day he put the gardener's hose through the top window of the library and successfully flushed most of the poetry section into the quad. The senior librarian had to be offered a pay rise to convince her to return to her duties.

All in all, this lad was headed for the crapper, and as far as I was concerned, the sooner he got there the better.

'Good morning, Yan Siang. I was sorry to hear... about your... ahh... father. Bad luck that. Still we must... ahh... keep going.' I prattled on, becoming more and more conscious of Yan Siang's silence and my own inanity. 'Mrs Benthusamy has asked me to take... I mean, go with you to speak to the police. Mrs Loh has offered to take us in her car... her Mercedes.' There was no reaction. 'Let's go now!' Reluctantly he stood.

We moved along the corridor and up a short flight of stairs which carried us over the administration block and gave a commanding view of the school garden, surrounded on all sides by orange-tinted plaster. This was my favourite spot and I would often stand and lean over the parapet, gazing for hours at the bougainvillea, hibiscus, and orchids — all dominated by the vibrant flame of the forest.

Yan Siang gazed blankly ahead, plodding dolefully down the stone staircase which took us out to the main entrance. The rain had faded to a light drizzle and I noticed Theresa standing, arms folded, waiting.

'I just bet you didn't leave any work for your classes,' she smiled knowingly.

'I'm afraid it slipped my mind,' I groaned.

'Don't worry, Marie will cover your first two periods and she's quite prepared to improvise.'

'Good for Marie. I just hope the class doesn't decide to improvise as well!'

I opened the rear door for Yan Siang and then climbed in the front. Theresa was a very careful driver. That did not necessarily mean she was safe, as she was easily distracted, but she treated the Mercedes with kid gloves. She slipped the automatic into reverse and slowly edged around two neighbouring vehicles, both fine cars but lacking the sheer class of the Mercedes. We nosed gently down the drive and out the main gates into light mid-morning traffic. As I sank back to enjoy the plush luxury of the trip, I glanced over my shoulder at Yan Siang.

For the first time I really noticed the boy. His desperately thin and rather spindly appearance was accentuated by a uniform which seemed at least two sizes too big. Straight black hair hung loosely, and considerably longer than school regulation length. His little knees pressed firmly together, while the rest of his body hunched forward. He looked desperately tired and sad, yet I saw a beautiful face with rich black eyes and finely moulded lips which pressed over a perfect set of young teeth.

Suddenly his eyes flickered up with a look of cold contempt. Surprised, I turned away.

'I'll drop you off outside the police station, but I can't wait. The principal is already unhappy because I'm helping you out. Perhaps I'll stop and get her a little bag of her favourite coffee from that stall near the school.'

'If you really want to cure her dyspepsia, pop a couple of spoonfuls of arsenic in for flavour,' I volunteered hopefully.

'Careful, Pete, little ears are listening.'

'Get real. The little brain behind those little ears is far too preoccupied.'

As we turned into Tanglin Road, which took us directly to the station, I began to feel sorry for the boy.

'Look, I don't know how long this is going to take, but I'll have to hang about until the police are finished.'

'Any excuse to avoid class!' Theresa teased.

The Mercedes stopped just short of the station in front of a large area of shrubbery. As I struggled out a couple of sharp pieces of bamboo poked me in a most unfriendly manner. I opened the rear door for Yan Siang, who exited in silence and stood like a little waif on the edge of the pavement.

'I'll see you later,' I called to Theresa, closing the rear door.

She leaned forward and whispered, 'Good luck.'

I grimaced and moved off, followed by my little charge.

CHAPTER

2

Tanglin Police Station is set on Tanglin Road, just before the major intersection with Orchard Road. It is a solid, white building, dating back to the war. The entrance on the ground floor exudes informality and the atmosphere is surprisingly friendly. Most of the officers are young cadets, several of whom are completing their national military service. The reception area, open on two sides and cooled by large fans, offers rather basic seating for the public.

As we walked in, I moved over to the desk where a burly Malay sergeant was explaining something in Mandarin to an elderly Chinese couple. Eventually, with much nodding and smiling, they moved over to sit on a bench against the wall. The sergeant turned to us, and in crisp, clear English thanked me for accompanying the boy. We were asked to sit until the officer in charge of the case called us.

I sank onto a wooden bench roughly padded in fading leather and glanced around the room at the thick black furnishings and the old, worn notice-boards. Bright posters railed against the evils of littering and promoted the importance of courtesy, while others advertised the virtues of police work. Soon I tired of the décor and picked up a magazine.

Yan Siang sat on my right, still gazing at his hands in silence. I flicked aimlessly through the pages of *Newsweek* until my eyes suddenly lighted on an advertisement for *Air New Zealand*. Happily I thought back to my arrival in Singapore twelve years earlier.

I had left New Zealand single and thirty-two. Warmly welcomed into the Singapore Education Service, I was offered an apartment in a new staffing block at the Ngee Ann Polytechnic situated in Bukit Timah — historically infamous as the place where Percival surrendered to the Japanese in 1942. Nowadays, this area is famous for the range of its cuisine. Along Upper Bukit Timah Road and Jalan Jurong Kechil, clusters of little hawker stalls sell delicious Asian delicacies. Here the old fragrantly blends with the new.

My first school languished on the other side of Singapore and it took an hour's bus journey to get there. This meant rising at five-thirty. In Christchurch this would have been a real challenge with the icy winters, but here the early mornings were pleasantly warm. The principal was a wonderful old, uncluttered, Chinese-educated gentleman, who had a delightfully refreshing non-grasp of English. He would stand before the school during assembly and lecture the students on a wide variety of subjects. One of his more memorable moments came when he wished to make the point that, while the girls were contributing admirably to the school culture, the boys were not. In a loud, booming voice, he announced to the assembled throng that 'The girls are showing their parts, but the boys are not showing their parts. I am most displeasing.' The gaffe was bad enough, but all the Chinese teachers nodded wisely in agreement! I had to exit quickly in the direction of the toilet to get rid of my indigestion!

Suddenly, the police sergeant informed us that they were ready to interview Yan Siang. We were shown into a small white-washed room at the end of a long corridor. Three plastic bucket seats had been placed in front of an ordinary wooden desk, behind which sat a young man in an officer's uniform. Beside him stood another man about twenty years his senior, dressed in a light suit.

As we entered, I noticed that the chair on the left was occupied by a middle-aged Chinese woman wearing slacks and a t-shirt. She rose as we moved into the room, nodded to me, and then began to berate Yan Siang in Hokkien. Yan Siang turned away and moved to the seat on the right. The woman sobbed gently to herself, shaking her head. The older man moved to help her back to her seat, but she shrugged him away and sank heavily onto the plastic.

'Please have a seat!' the young officer commanded. I complied, taking the central chair and musing about the devil and the deep blue sea.

'Thank you for coming. I hope we can sort this whole unfortunate business as quickly as possible. Do you know Mrs Chang, the boy's mother?' He motioned in the sobbing woman's direction and she offered a watery smile as I extended my hand. So this was the lady I had confronted on the telephone.

'He very bad boy… bad, bad boy,' she sniffed, again shaking her head.

I could go along with that.

Yan Siang never reacted. He still sat staring at his hands.

'Now, boy,' the officer began.

'Ah… Yan,' I interrupted.

'Pardon me?'

'His name is Yan,' I replied.

'Oh, yes, well then, Yan. This man here is Detective Ling. He would like to ask you a few questions about the accident this morning. We know it has been very hard on you, but we must fill out a report and we hope you will be able to help us. Okay?'

Yan Siang looked up, stared straight ahead, and said nothing.

At least I was not the only one singled out for the silent treatment.

'Talk! Where is your mouth?' his mother shrieked in Hokkien.

'Thank you, madam, but I think we can manage,' the officer admonished. Madam muttered away to herself in dialect, throwing threatening glances at her son.

Detective Ling began to speak to the boy in Chinese and I again interrupted, 'Please speak in English or there's no point in my being here.' The detective threw me a glance as if to say there was no point to my being there anyway.

'Sorry. But my English very little, lah. I not so good,' the detective laughed. 'Boy… ' he continued.

'Yan,' I repeated, glancing at my knees for no particular reason.

'Yan!' the detective emphasised. 'This morning, what you doing not inside but outside with your father?' There was no response. 'Why you not sleeping? Got problem?' Still no response. 'How can your father fall? Big man… where got so easy to get over concrete, lah? How?' No movement or sound from Yan Siang. 'Wah lau, come on, boy… ahhh… Yan. Why you so like that? We not going to hurt you.'

He continued in this manner, pleading, cajoling, threatening even, for another ten minutes, and then he ran his hands through his hair in frustration. The interview was going nowhere fast. Mrs Chang had begun crying again and the officer had started to drum his pencil on the empty report.

The detective knelt by the boy's chair and began to plead with him some more. 'We know your father good man. He good family man. How did he fall? Got anybody up there? Say, lah! Why you so gee-arhh? We cannot eat you one! Ah yoi!' The detective vented his frustration through an amusing mixture of Singlish, Hokkien, and broken English.

Yan Siang deliberately turned away with a rude, haughty shrug. His face in the air, he looked straight past me to a distant point on the back wall.

I had had enough of this rudeness. 'Yan Siang, you must answer the detective's questions. He only wants to find out the details so he can settle this matter. If you know anything, you must tell him.'

The detective smiled his thanks, but Yan Siang continued to stare into the distance. So much for the principal's confidence.

'Is there something you're afraid of?' asked the officer, vainly trying to break the hidden barrier. 'We're not blaming you… or your father. But we need some answers and you're the only one who can help us.'

The detective moved back and spoke to the officer, while the mother again berated her son in Chinese.

'Do you think you could leave us to speak to the boy alone for a while?' the officer asked hopefully.

Clearing my throat in a manner which suggested more confidence than I actually felt, I replied, 'I can't do that. My school insists I be present during the interview. It's a professional requirement.'

My failure to accede to the officer's request drew a scowl from the detective. He was plainly unused to this sort of stonewalling.

'Perhaps if you left for a few minutes I could speak to Yan Siang. I may be able to persuade him to tell you what he knows,' I offered.

The quickness of the detective's reply underlined his reluctance, 'I do not…'

'No, that might work,' the officer interrupted. 'Come on, Ling, let's go for coffee.'

Ling was unhappy with this arrangement, but he was outvoted. I followed them through the door and drew it shut behind me. 'Could you please take Mrs Chang for a coffee as well? The boy may feel more relaxed if his mother isn't present.'

The officer went back into the room and escorted a protesting Mrs Chang into the corridor.

'Thanks,' I muttered.

I sat down on the middle chair and faced Yan Siang, who sat with his back to me. There was a long silence while I studied the back of his neck and tried to formulate a strategic approach to the questioning.

Finally I blurted out, 'If you don't answer the officers' questions, they won't let you go home and you won't be allowed to return to school.' The absurdity of this statement hit me as soon as I had uttered it. Considering the ferocity of his mother, home was probably the last place the boy wanted to be and school certainly was not the first. There was no carrot in that offer.

'Look, Yan Siang, everyone is trying to help you. We only want what is best for you, but the officers must do their job. Can't you just tell them what you saw?' Then it occurred to me that perhaps he had not seen anything. 'You were actually on the balcony? You did see the accident?'

The boy turned and looked at me with a triumphant gleam in his eye. My heart missed a beat as I waited for his comment. Nothing! The gleam faded and he turned his back on me again.

I continued gently and then threateningly, asking him question after question, until the officers returned. With great embarrassment, I had to admit that I had achieved no more than they had. Yan Siang's mother gave me a supercilious sniff, pleased that I had done no better with her boy, but the thought of her failure as a mother levelled the score in my mind.

'I'll tell you what we'll do,' the officer suggested in a friendly voice. 'You go home and perhaps later on today you could take a piece of paper and write down anything you can remember about this morning.'

Yan Siang continued to sit motionless — no thanks, no acknowledgement. His mother again spoke harshly to him in Chinese.

The officer continued, 'Then you can mail your report to us

and we'll send you an official reply. How does that sound?' To me it sounded pretty damned generous, but the little sod continued to just stare at his hands.

I stood and the others followed my example. As we moved out into the corridor, I thanked the young officer for his understanding and told him that Yan Siang had probably been traumatised by his experience. He nodded. We parted at the reception counter, Yan Siang and his mother leaving in the direction of Orchard Road, the officer and the detective to another interview, while I wandered out into Tanglin.

The rain had gone and the sun seeped hazily through the late morning humidity. It was nearing lunchtime, so I decided to cross the road to the new Tanglin Mall where I might just beat the lunch crowd. As I waited for the traffic lights, I thought back over the interview and recalled my statement to the young officer about the traumatic effect of the accident on Yan Siang. I remembered the gleam in the boy's eye. He clearly was affected by the accident, but I was sure he knew more than he appeared to. His eyes were not the eyes of a traumatised child. He was in control and he knew that we were lost, swimming in a dark, bottomless pond. The lights changed and I crossed the road.

CHAPTER
3

Tanglin Mall is a meeting point for all ages and tastes, with its impressive exterior promising hidden magical delights. I entered from Orchard Road up a flight of steps and through glass doors into a concourse dominated by a large open space and escalators giving access to mezzanine floors above and the basement below. There is an exciting variety of shops which cater to the exotic tastes of the connoisseur and stores which offer tempting bargains in furniture, souvenirs, and clothing to the less sophisticated. One can spend hours, and a good deal of cash, browsing through a number of Aladdin's caves where the eye is dazzled and the willpower tested. Colourful hanging lamps, weirdly shaped figurines, exquisitely hand-painted vases made from a breath-taking range of materials and textures, tall dragon gods, small delicate Chinese courtesans — all flashbacks to another life and another time. Beyond these, dizzying scents from long-dead empires and fruity homeopathic remedies promise heady hours of bathing pleasure.

I made for the basement food court. As anticipated, the lunch crowd had not arrived, which meant I could wander around the various stalls at my leisure. I decided to treat myself to claypot chicken, a sumptuous dish where chicken, vegetables, and rice are cooked in a special pot. With a fresh watermelon juice, I settled down in a far corner.

I was just finishing my meal when the young police officer from the interview descended the escalator with two colleagues. I shrank a little lower, hoping he would fail to spot me. The trio ordered three drinks and sat down at a table well away from mine. Minutes passed, and I was calculating the distance between my position and the nearest exit when the officer stood up, turned around, and strode purposefully across the eating area, carefully negotiating the tangle of tables and chairs in his path. I smiled grimly as he arrived at my table.

'How are you?'

'About the same as the last time we met,' I answered coolly.

'Great. Do you mind if I sit down for a few minutes? Perhaps I could get you a coffee?'

I was about to politely decline when I realised I did fancy a cup of local coffee.

'Please,' I replied.

'Black or white?'

'White with sugar, thanks.'

He went to place the order, while I thought about the interview. I really did not want to discuss the matter any further. I was still recovering from the futility of the whole exercise.

He returned with a dark, steaming brew.

'Thanks,' I acknowledged.

There was a long pause and then he said, 'Look, I'm sorry about the interview earlier. Ling's a hard man, but he's a good detective. I think he's a little unused to dealing with school students though.' A pause followed as he squeezed his cup thoughtfully. 'It must have been hard for you, having to represent the kid, not knowing much about the accident.'

I looked into his eyes — brown, clear, with long, curling lashes. His face was deeply tanned, with flawless skin and strong sensual lips between a pair of seductive dimples. He had left his hat on the other table and his thick, soft hair, tinted light brown, fell naturally across his forehead. I admired his angular features, a strong chin, and an unusually narrow nose. Embarrassed, I suddenly realised he expected a response.

'Yes,' I muttered.

'So you don't really know about the accident?' he probed.

'The principal gave me some background, but no one seems to know much about what really happened, other than the obvious.'

'The father fell from the balcony outside the family home?' He looked at me for a long moment and then glanced away. We drank our coffee in silence.

'Still, the father was a big man and the balcony is protected by a solid, metre-high railing. It's difficult to imagine someone just pushing him over and it's hard to see him missing his footing.'

'Perhaps things were going badly for him and he… well, you know…'

'Outside his own flat, from such a difficult position, with a whole mass of trees below that could have broken his fall and made the attempt useless? He only died because he was unlucky enough to catch his head on one of the larger branches.'

I was not a detective and I was not interested. I wanted to get away from this conversation, but the guy was friendly and probably just overzealous, so I changed the subject. 'You speak excellent English.'

'I should,' he laughed. 'My father paid a fortune for me to do my BA at Cambridge. I studied Medieval History and met a wonderful professor. Actually, I loved England. I'd really like to go back when I've completed my National Service.'

'I see. And what would you like to do there?' The answer did not really interest me and I think he realised it.

There was a long pause before he looked up. 'Do you mind my asking how you came to be in Singapore?'

'Money,' I replied honestly.

'And have you made it?'

'I'm comfortable. And to be honest, I've grown to like the place.' I continued describing my background, the job and my dreams for about another ten minutes before impatience got the better of his courtesy, and he interrupted.

'Sorry, but I've got to get back. They only let me out for half an hour.'

My selfishness suddenly embarrassed me. 'I'm the one who should apologise. I hope I didn't bore you.'

'Not at all. I'll give you my number, in case that young lad remembers something or you need help or whatever…' He took out a name card and handed it over. With a firm handshake and a warm smile, he rose and rejoined his friends.

I sat there for several minutes, intrigued by the interchange. Why did he come over to speak to me? I certainly gave him no reason earlier to suppose that I was interested in his friendship. I turned his card over in my hand: *Raymond Chia, Officer Cadet.* Absentmindedly, I put the card in my shirt pocket, glanced at my watch, and stood up. Happily, I realised there was no point in returning to school, although I was supposed to conduct an afternoon rehearsal. No problem. Ronald, my assistant, would manage.

I walked down Tanglin Road, crossed at the lights, and caught Bus 75. As we meandered past the golf course and Gleaneagles Hospital, I gazed distractedly out the window, lost so deeply in thought that I almost forgot to clamber off at the Ngee Ann Polytechnic.

The lift stopped on the tenth floor and I stepped out. I gazed through the large open spaces provided in the building's superstructure, across Western Singapore. Skyscrapers dotted a leafy green canopy, bisected by gleaming silver threads. My door opened into a neat apartment with a high-ceilinged main room. Two teak elephant chairs surrounded an Italian-styled glass coffee table, with a sofa beyond. Behind these, two display cabinets featured treasures I had collected from various parts of the globe. An Iranian rug spread across the tiled floor, and the walls bore colourful scenes of the Thai countryside and Indian fishing villages, with a special place reserved for family portraits. There was a small kitchen and one ensuite bedroom.

I sank onto the sofa as Sylvester, my fluffy Himalayan cat, jumped up and sank his claws. He does not really intend to hurt, he just likes to exercise his claws on my stomach. Worse than this, he has a tendency to grab visitors round the ankles and sink his teeth. Most people do not appreciate the shock or the pain and Sylvester has caused me several embarrassing moments. Nevertheless I love him, for whatever else he lacks, Sylvester has character.

I heaved myself up and walked over to his cupboard, pulled out a rather smelly piece of fish and dropped a bit on his plate. Next I made my way into the bedroom. I dragged myself into the ensuite, threw handfuls of water at my face, and dried off. Then with the air conditioning on, I threw myself across the bed.

CHAPTER

4

Damn! What time was it? The phone drilled its way into my zone of awareness, but I could not focus. I stumbled off the bed, and then realised I wanted to pee. No, wrong way. I had to stop that ringing. I wrenched the door open, fell over Sylvester, caught my head on the side of a chair, and grabbed for the cell phone. Wrong. It must be the door! No, it was definitely a phone. I scrambled up and over to the cordless phone by the window.

'Hello!' I yelled into the receiver.

'Pete?' Ming Chuan sounded anxious.

'Yes,' I sighed.

'What's wrong?'

'Nothing. I've been asleep,' I yawned, 'and I've just woken up.'

'Oh, sorry. I won't see you tonight. I'm meeting Tze Kit. Do you mind?'

'Of course.'

'Sorry!'

'You've said that already. Actually it doesn't matter, really. I'm having dinner with Jean at Newton Circus. You can always join us later, if you'd like to.'

'No, I go home tonight. May be very late.'

'You take care and call me when you get home.'

'May be late.'

'Doesn't matter. You call. I love you.'

'I love you too.' A click and then silence, but the vision of Ming Chuan remained.

I sat back and stared dreamily out the window. So much in love at forty-four. Unbelievable. Had I been told by any man eight years before that I was going to meet a young guy and fall madly in love, I would have punched the teller. And yet it happened. Me? The guy who had broken countless female hearts and two engagements. I shivered. I was shopping in Plaza Singapura — the old version — when I tripped on the escalator and twisted my ankle. A group of young guys shot out of the lift and one of the group was so concerned he insisted on helping me out to a taxi.

Weeks later, back in the plaza, I bumped into him again. We exchanged greetings and I offered to buy him a coffee. Ultimately we ended up having lunch and discovered we both had a passion for musical comedies. Some months and several musicals passed and I slowly realised that this young twenty-two-year-old was unique. Surprisingly, it seemed perfectly natural. However, it took me a long time to admit it to myself. Slowly my life changed as I discovered a new milieu — a culture of deceit and lies. One could never be open or honest about such a relationship. Singapore, flying in the face of international human rights legislation, had outlawed homosexuality. Now that I had entered this lifestyle, I saw at first-hand the stupidity and hypocrisy of their position. Ming Chuan could not reveal his feelings to his family and because of my position, I had to live a very private life. I found this particularly difficult, as I had always been proud of the girls I dated and I loved to appear in public with my maid of the moment. Now I had to lie and all my friends wondered about this fabulous girlfriend they could never meet.

Ming never actually moved in with me. He spent half the week with his family and the other nights with me. I came to loathe the nights he was absent and I longed for a time when we could live honestly together. Still, life was great and I would never change anything. Not that Ming was breathtakingly handsome or a stunning physical specimen or a sweet, effeminate little beauty with a figure like Linda Evangelista. He was an ordinary Chinese guy, of moderate height with passable looks. Of course, he did have one hell of a smile. And, clichéd as it may sound, our chemistry worked — we understood each other. That is not to say that we were never passionate, we were! But the essence of our success was simply that we enjoyed each other.

Toilet! My physical needs brought me back to reality. I glanced at the clock as I made my way to the bathroom. It was six-thirty. Just enough time to sink into a deep, soothing mixture. A good bath is one of life's last great natural pleasures, bubbling to the brim with thick, soft, tinted foam and hot enough to make entry slow. Of course it must be accompanied by a glass of fine wine and good music.

The haze of early evening dimmed the sparkle of the distant cars streaming along the expressway. I knew a magic transformation would soon occur and the sleek money-business of day would be replaced by the glitter and sensuality of night. Like a vast dragon, the city rose and assumed a new spirituality.

I sank into my bath clutching a glass of Chateau Megyer Tokaji — a light Hungarian sherry, 1988 vintage. The mellow voice of Nat King Cole crooning about travelling around the world in a remarkably short time filtered through from the bedroom. I emerged refreshed and satisfied.

Downstairs, the grassy area surrounding the quarters had taken on an other-worldly look. Small triangular lamps lined the twisting driveway and dark shrubs dotted the lawns beneath the first-floor windows. The children's playing area was deserted, with the slides, swings, and hanging bars surrendering their bright daylight colours for deeper, more uncertain tones. Stereo babble, babies' shrieks, and homework-bound groans filtered down from open apartment windows. Night in the staffing quarters had an energy all of its own.

I walked down to the back gate — the only opening in a high green fence, topped with barbed wire. They took security very seriously in this place! Once through, I followed the footpath along the exit road from the expressway, beneath the underpass and over to Bukit Timah Plaza, which bristled with lights and sparkle. There I caught the 66 down to Newton Circus.

Hungry, I wandered past the hawker stalls. The aromas and sizzling sounds tempted as I eagerly examined the dishes under preparation. I was amazed at how comfortable the stall holders appeared, despite the heat from their cooking plates. Seeing a Caucasian, they smiled, nodded, and tried out their broken English. Tough, weatherbeaten old uncles in baggy shorts and stained singlets competed with young, energetic fellows in tight jeans and t-shirts.

'Hi yah! Over here, Pete!'

I turned round to see Jean waving at me from a far table. She was sitting with her partner, Rojan, quaffing a Carlsberg Special.

'You're early,' I laughed, approaching the table.

'Rojan finished ahead o' time so I met him here. Quick, sit ye doon. Sit ye doon! Ye'll take a drink?'

'I'm parched, but not that muck you're pouring down your gullet. I'll have a Tiger.'

Rojan called out in Malay to an old Indian woman who was rolling between tables, collecting trays and empty glasses.

'What a day!' I sighed.

'You look tired, my good man,' Rojan boomed between mouthfuls of beer.

I could never understand why he called me his good man.

He did not know me that well and I hoped the epithet was not deserved.

'It's not fatigue, Rojan, it's hunger.'

'We'd better order,' Jean boomed. 'Food and another round!' She rose a little unsteadily and cast her gaze about, rather like a soccer player assessing the weakest point of the defence.

We moved over to the stalls and chose our dishes. I had decided on beef rendang, so I headed for the Malay stall and placed my order. I requested some chicken satay on the side, since this place was famous for it. Jean chose sweet and sour fish, while Rojan ordered a dish which suggested by its colour and smell that one would be unwise to try to discover the contents. Newton Circus was equally famous for roosters' feet, pigs' intestines, and bulls' pizzle!

We returned to our table to find the drinks replenished at Rojan's expense.

'Thanks mate,' I offered, sitting.

'No worries,' he replied.

'Tell us how it went with the polis,' Jean spluttered, washing down mouthfuls of fish.

'Actually, nothing much happened. The kid wouldn't talk and the policemen accepted it. End of story.'

'Nah! Can't be, man,' Rojan shook his head. He leaned forward, brandishing a piece of foul-smelling flesh between two chopsticks. 'The police will keep at it until they get to know everything.'

'Pair wee laddie. He must have been petrified.'

'Look, honestly, Jean, the two officers were very understanding and friendly. That kid has got real problems. Even I couldn't get him to open up.'

'The father just fell from the balcony and no one knows what happened?' Jean queried, shaking her head. 'Did he jump or something?'

'No one knows. The kid saw it, but will say nothing.' I paused to chew through a tough piece of meat. 'I'm sure he knows something.'

'How come?' Jean asked.

'It was just the way he looked at me, the arrogant little sod. He had a gleam in his eye as if he enjoyed keeping us guessing.'

'Wasn't he a wee bit bothered aboot the loss o' his father?'

'Nope. Not at all. Even his mother was more interested in getting him to talk than providing any comfort. A strange family.'

'Och! They're all a wee bit queer aboot here, Pete. Fatalistic.'

'Hold on,' Rojan interrupted.

'Am nay referring to you, pet, dinna fret!' Jean smiled, patting his hand. 'Still they a' seem to accept the hand o' fate a mite too readily for ma satisfaction.'

'Anyway, it's not our concern. How was school?'

'A' dinna ken! A jist slid frae one period tae th' next and let it a' wash abin me. Am na stressing masel' oot for that place. But a gied yon hinny, Yap, the magazine articles an' told her a' would proof-read nae mair!'

'What did she say?'

'Nithing, I nivva gied her the chance. Stupid coo!'

We finished our meal in silence. I had never asked Jean how she came to meet Rojan, but they were an unlikely pair. She was strong-willed, tough, with a long Gaelic ancestry. He was comfortably fat, happy with his world, and unflappable — the epitome of your lovable chump — cuddly and generous. I really enjoyed their friendship.

'Would you like another beer?'

'Yes, but it's my turn,' I replied, signalling the old woman.

'Did you nae have some sort o' rehearsal this afternoon?' Jean asked.

'Ronald would handle it,' I replied.

'Ya nae bothered yon principal mae find oot?' Jean asked, lighting up a cigarette.

'At this point I couldn't care. She's never shown much

interest anyway.'

'Och tis nae right, she shouldna be a principal at all. She'd be better serving in one o' yon stalls.'

I burst out laughing. 'Jean, Jean! Have pity on the poor sods who would have to eat her food.' We all laughed together.

The drinks arrived and the cool amber liquid slipped easily down my throat. With each mouthful the world looked better.

'Would you like to go to a pub later?' Rojan asked.

'Better not,' I replied. 'It's been a taxing day and –'

'Taxing? What yah blethering aboot. You've been oot o' the old bitch's way for a whole day. Celebrate, man!'

'Not tonight, Jean. I really want to go back and collapse. Perhaps this weekend we could get together.'

'Say nae mair, Pete.' She blew smoke hazily into the air as we watched the cars shoot past the shrubbery fringing the pavement. They seemed quite noiseless, what with the laughter and gossip of the diners.

Jean stubbed out her cigarette. We said goodnight and headed off in different directions. I climbed the overhead bridge, having decided to walk back. It was a clear night with only a few distant stars, but there was a bright, nearly-full moon. Traffic was light and pedestrians scarce. I pulled out my cigar case — a gift from Ming Chuan — and paused to light a small café-creme. Leaving light smoke rings in my wake, I ambled along Bukit Timah Road heading for the Seven Mile.

Jean was a good friend. Her full name was Jean Simmons McCorkingdale, but she hated the surname so she dropped it. She told me that her mother was a great fan of the film star Jean Simmons, hence her inheritance.

Weary from the walk, I opened the door to my apartment and felt that warm feeling which comes from knowing that you are entering your own private world. I dropped my keys on the table, sank onto the sofa, and turned on the TV to catch the late news. It was over, so I watched the weather report.

CHAPTER

5

Again the bell jangled. I rose shakily. Who the hell could this be? Maybe Ming Chuan had changed his mind, but he had a key.

I peered through the peep-hole and blinked. It couldn't be. Yan Siang leaned against the door. This could not be happening. How did he know where I lived? Perhaps I should pretend I was out or had gone to bed. No good. He had probably seen me arrive.

Reluctantly I opened the door. 'What on earth are you doing here?' He shrugged. 'You should be home in bed, not wandering about the city at this time of night. Does your mother know you're out?'

Another shrug. I felt totally helpless, but I knew it would be unwise to continue the conversation on my doorstep.

'You'd better come in,' I fumed.

Yan Siang sauntered into my private retreat. I was furious.

'How dare you come here? Especially after humiliating me today at the police station!'

He quietly removed his shoes and sat on the floor.

'Does your mother know where you are?' He looked at me for a long moment and then shook his head. 'Oh, that's really great! Why here?'

Visions of the mother's and detectives' reactions to his visit flitted through my mind and then my brain focused on the principal. That resolved the issue.

'Well, you can't stay here. You'll have to leave.' The boy looked at me and resolutely shook his head. 'I can call security, you know. Or the police.'

The boy was unimpressed. He folded his arms around his knees and lowered his head. I stood in a daze, totally uncertain of my strength in my own space. I walked over to the window and gazed down on the dark tops of the trees.

Suddenly my initial shock and anger faded. 'Have you had anything to eat or drink?' He raised his head and looked at me. 'Are you hungry?' He nodded.

I moved to the refrigerator and took out some bacon and a couple of eggs. While these sizzled away, I made some toast and boiled the water. A good strong cup of tea might improve the situation. I took out a can of Pepsi. Again he shook his head. I returned the can and continued to fuss over the food. Soon I had bacon and eggs with toast laid out on the table.

He pulled himself into a chair and took the knife and fork I offered him.

'Thanks.'

I smiled. He had finally spoken. But beyond that, Yan Siang ignored me and attacked the food ravenously. I made myself a cup of tea and poured him a glass of water, then I sank down opposite.

'Look, I don't know why you came here, but there's nothing I can do for you.' The words echoed in my mind and I realised what little substance they had. Here was a child lost in his own world who trusted nobody, but had chosen my doorstep. Lord knows he had no reason to trust me, and I had even less reason to trust him, but here he was.

'Is there a problem at home?' I knew he had a brother in his twenties and a baby sister. Perhaps he was ignored with all the confusion surrounding his father's death.

'You must phone your mother and tell her where you are.' He stared coldly at the empty plate.

'If you don't call your mother, I'll call security.'

There was a long silence. Finally he rose slowly, walked over to the phone, and carefully dialled a number. Suddenly he burst into Chinese, harshly and loudly. At the end of the tirade, he replaced the receiver and returned to his original position on the floor.

'You told your mother where you were?' Silence. 'Look, I can't understand Chinese and I must be sure that your mother knows you are here.'

'She know,' he coughed.

At least that was something. I decided to make up a bed on my two-seater sofa. He would be more comfortable there than on the floor. I was still unhappy with the situation, but too tired to argue. This whole sorry mess would have to be resolved in the morning. I found a spare toothbrush and a towel and pointed him in the direction of the sink. Finally with a curt goodnight, I disappeared into my bedroom.

I called Ming Chuan and confirmed that everything was okay with Tze Kit. Several minutes later, I peeped around the door. Yan Siang was still sitting on the floor. Too bad. I was bloody tired and if he wanted to sit on cold, uncomfortable tiles all night, that was his choice. I turned out the light. The curtains hung wide, letting in the flickering Singapore scene. I slipped a Mantovani disk into the player and eased my naked body under the duvet.

What time was it? The music had stopped and it was still dark. I froze. Something had disturbed me. Suddenly I felt a soft form nudge my back. Sylvester? My breathing relaxed. I turned to move him gently away and found he was not there.

Horrors! Someone was in bed with me. Who? I shot up and flicked on the light, jumping so far clear of the bed that, had the window been open, I would have gone through it.

Head buried in my pillow, Yan Siang lay motionless where I had left him. How the hell did he get into the bed and how long had he been there? I saw figures moving past a window in the neighbouring block. Panicking, I reached over and turned out the light. God, what if they had seen him? This was fast turning into a nightmare. Think, think!

'Yan Siang, wake up. You can't stay here. It's… it's not decent.'

Suddenly remembering I was naked, I stepped into the bathroom and hastily wrapped a towel around my lower body. Please, dear God, take me away from this. I stumbled over my discarded slippers and leaned over the bed.

'Yan Siang, you must sleep outside, this is my bed.'

It is funny how silly and selfish one becomes in terrifying situations. The boy never moved. Too bad! I had to shift him. The thought of touching him sent shivers down my spine and yet I would be damned if I was going to surrender my bed.

'Yan Siang, if you don't move I'll drag you off the bed and lock you outside the door. I'm sick of all this nonsense. It's very late and we've both got school tomorrow.'

Well, I knew I had anyway.

There was still no movement. Time for action. I leaned over and was about to lift the little form, when I noticed he was shaking. Fear? Cold? I looked closer. The pillow was wet and he was biting the edge of the duvet. I could not believe my senses. The little thug was crying. Oh no, he was not going to pull that one. I placed my hands under his back and lifted him off the bed. He was very light and as I turned, he threw his arms around my neck and began to sob uncontrollably. I stood there, uncertain. He gripped me fiercely and sniffed loudly. I moved to the door and with each step his grip tightened. As I eased the door open, he placed his leg across the gap.

'Please can I sleep on your bed?' he pleaded.

'You can't,' I said softly, and added, 'You'd sleep in your own bed at home.'

'No I don't.'

'What do you mean? Everybody sleeps in his own bed.'

'I don't.' Then he began to sob some more.

I thought for a moment. Jean had said these families were strange. Perhaps they all slept in the same bed in his house. Still, it was ludicrous and this was not his house. Damn it all! It was three in the morning and here I was with an intruder in my bedroom, even if he was only fourteen. I cursed myself for not having called security in the first place. Why did this have to happen to me?

I gently placed the boy back on the bed, taking care to move him as far to the right as possible. He curled up and again buried his head in the pillow. For a long time I sat there staring out the window. Finally I got up, dressed in a t-shirt and shorts, and crept under the covers on the far side of the bed.

Sleep would not come, so I moved a pillow into the middle to form a barrier. I turned over and had started to drift, when I thought I heard a tiny voice whisper, 'Th-thank you.'

CHAPTER

6

I awoke before the alarm. The clock showed five-fifteen. Great!
I could lie for another 20 minutes. Gradually I grew aware of a
weight on my right side, and then I remembered — Yan Siang.
During the night, the little nuisance had shifted the pillow and
now he was using my left shoulder as a replacement. I turned
over and gently pushed him aside. He rubbed his nose and moved
against me again. I gently extricated myself. His breathing
indicated he was in deep sleep. I marvelled. Here was a boy
who had been through an experience that would have devastated
most adults, yet he lay dead to the world, seemingly secure and
safe in my apartment. Something was very wrong.

I got up, taking care not to disturb him. The kitchen still
contained the devastation from the night before. Yuk! I made
myself toast and tea, pushing the debris to one side. For ten
minutes I sat and stared at my breakfast, eating nothing. What a
mess. Yesterday my life was meandering along at a comfortable
pace. Now I was a defacto father, embroiled in… I had no idea
what I was being drawn into. Goodness only knows what his
mother would have to say about Yan Siang spending the night
in a stranger's apartment. Of course, in the strictest sense, I was
not really a stranger. There was a professional relationship.

I groaned at the absurdity of my predicament.

Quietly I prepared to leave for school. Then it struck me. Leave? How could I leave with a boy still asleep in my bed? The whole episode was beginning to sound like a perverted version of the Goldilocks story. I crept back into the room. Yan Siang lay where I had left him, sleeping peacefully. He had cast the cover aside and the top half of his body, fully clothed, lay exposed. The white, misty light of dawn illuminated his face, giving him the composure of an angel. I grimaced as I remembered his 'angelic' behaviour at school. Yet here he seemed different — young and vulnerable. He looked every bit a fourteen-year-old, ready only for the daily fun of being a kid. Still, this was not my problem.

I disappeared into the bathroom and re-emerged a few minutes later, brushed, deodorised, and perfumed, ready to face the world. Again I stared at the nuisance. I knew it was unwise to leave him in the apartment alone, but what option did I have? I took two towels from the drawer in my dresser and placed them on the foot of the bed, hoping he would take the hint. Then I pulled the duvet cover up to his chin and quietly left the room. I knew there was nothing in my apartment the boy would fancy, but I removed the six $50 bills I always kept in the bottom drawer of the TV cabinet, just in case. I was about to leave when I remembered the key. I scribbled a hasty note, instructing Yan Siang to lock the door and leave the key in my letter-box.

The sun was up and shimmering rays broke through the gaps between the large blocks in the neighbouring Housing Development Board estate, casting playful patterns over the playground and onto the tennis courts. The humidity was already high and I was grateful that I had enough time to walk leisurely through the poly. As I crossed the overhead bridge, I glanced down at the trucks and cars going into the city. In an hour, this would be a steady stream in both directions. I scampered down the far side and skipped across the tiled courtyard out onto the road.

The superbus rumbled along like a great metallic hippopotamus, rarely exceeding forty kilometres an hour. With its fresh, new air conditioning system, plush seating, and roomy capacity, the bus was great. It was the driver who was not so good. Superbuses do not necessarily come with super drivers.

I was happy to get off and join the chattering throng pushing towards the school gate. The kids always make the job worthwhile.

I walked past the office to the usual greetings and then remembered I had not signed in. This is another unique feature of education in Singapore — signing the logbook. Every teacher is expected to sign 'in' when he or she arrives and 'out' when they leave, rather like a group of factory workers. The Ministry of Education is always talking about professionalism, but in reality there is little of it in the Singapore teaching service.

My early arrival in the staff room raised a few eyebrows. I acknowledged the exclamations of surprise and moved to my table. Remembering my experience the day before, I hastily switched chairs with the young lady who sat across from me. She had only been in the school three months, but in that short time had firmly established herself as a genuine pain in the arse! Naturally sycophantic, she had latched onto the Head of Senior English — a lovable old fellow, whose only distinguishing feature was his inability to move in any forward direction. He firmly believed that the essence of English teaching was grammatical accuracy. To him, a piece of writing was a failure if the commas were misplaced or the spelling a little suspicious. He was also irritatingly punctilious. One never needed to refer to the school bell if one had a class, you simply observed old Raj Nethander. Seconds before the bell went, he would be out of his desk, books in hand, ready to advance on the enemy! However, his worst trait was easily his awe and fear of the principal. She regarded him as an English paragon, which handicapped him from the start in the eyes of the staff, and he ran about the place at her beck and call. Jean and I nicknamed him 'Neanderthal', although he could probably move faster than a dinosaur.

The sound of the school bell moved me out of the staff room and along the corridor to the parade ground. Students were piling out of doorways and streaming along corridors and walkways, like purple riverlets in full flood. From every direction, they converged on the central quadrangle and formed up in classes, resembling the phalanxes of a great ancient army. Her Graciousness, accompanied by Snake, ambled along the balcony edging the front of the hall. Wearing an outfit of some strange orange fabric, overlaid with Lincoln-green cotton, she floated down the steps to the flagpole like an over-inflated circus balloon. Snake huddled behind her left shoulder doing an award-winning impersonation of Uriah Heep.

It had been decided, in the usual unilateral fashion, that all teachers would take turns officiating at flag-raising. This meant that for some it was an opportunity to demonstrate their pomposity, while for others it was ten minutes of pure torture. This morning we had an example of the former.

'Hurry up, students!' she shrilled, raising the final syllable to a pitch that would have impressed Dame Kiri Ti Kanawa. 'In your lines, please. Clear columns between each row. Hurry up, Swee Ling. Stop talking, Jolene. Put your tie on, Rafidah.'

At this point, she paused, folded her arms beneath her ample bosom, and heaved. What effect this was supposed to achieve beat me, but it enabled her to crane her neck forward like an over-enthusiastic stork, determined to catch any untoward movement. Her performance was drawn to a close by the final bell. We all stood to attention while the bouncy, lyrical chords of the National Anthem burst through the early morning grey. Everyone was expected to sing, but as this was a regular morning ritual, most had become bored with the whole charade. Even in the background, the principal whispered to her vice behind a book. Considering her admonitions to the students, it was not a very good example. As the last chords died away, she moved forward.

'Good morning, students!' There was no response. 'Good morning, students!' the determined woman bellowed.

'Good morning, Mrs Benthusamy,' rose from the midst of the assembled mass in a gurgled, mono-syllabic rhythm, rather like a liturgical chant.

Out of the corner of my eye, I saw a resplendently clothed, but somewhat pallid figure emerge from a side corridor and move in my direction.

'Good morning, Ms Simmons,' I recited, imitating the students.

'Bugger off,' Jean snorted back.

'You don't sound very happy.'

'My head's banging fit to burst, my throat's as dry as a wooden god, and I've got 2/3 first period.'

'Lucky you,' I murmured.

Her Graciousness was addressing the assembly on the subject of impressions. Certain students had been creating bad ones outside the school! Recently, three students had been caught smoking in Orchard Road in uniform. Today they were going to be punished in public. I loved this part of the Singapore education code. It was like stepping back into *Tom Brown's School Days*.

'We will give these students, who have disgraced our community, an op-por-tu-nity to apologise to the school,' Her Graciousness concluded.

The school leaned forward en masse, eagerly anticipating some other poor little sod's suffering. When the offenders emerged from a door behind the principal, there was a wild burst of applause. The duty teacher, on the verge of an apoplectic fit, threw herself at the microphone and screamed for silence. Unfortunately, this time she miscalculated her pitch and a banshee-like shriek echoed around the courtyard, drawing guffaws of laughter from the students.

Snake slithered forward. 'There will be complete silence now or I will call the whole school back for an extra assembly this afternoon.'

The laughter petered out and the three recalcitrants stepped forward and apologised. The trio comprised two rather rough-looking boys and a spindly girl who kept giggling. The boys mumbled something about being sorry for their actions, while the girl, in a miserable, whining tone, apologised for stealing Mr Tang's cigarettes.

As I began to laugh, Jean muttered, 'Ambitious little madam! Stealing her teacher's fags!'

'Poor guy. I bet he'll live to regret his carelessness.'

'I've had enough of this farce. I'm going upstairs,' Jean whispered.

'I'll join you,' I replied, as the discipline master appeared from the right with a miserable little piece of stick that looked like it had once been the handle of a doll's umbrella.

In the staff lounge, Jean poured two cups of coffee. 'C'mon, Pete, we've gotta get oot o' here. We're losin' mair and mair brain cells every day listening to yon morons.'

'True enough,' I grinned, throwing myself into one of the armchairs and sticking my feet up on the coffee table. 'What happened to you last night?'

'It was Rojan, the big lump! He took me to a wee pub ootside Chinatown. Lawd, Pete, we kept drinking till the wee oors. One of his mates showed up and I couldna drag him away. By the time we left, I was fair buggered.'

She paused for a moment and blew on her cup.

'This coffee's rotten. Why dinna they buy decent beans.'

'Would you like some tea?' I offered.

'Naw… I've got to get on, laddie.' She pulled herself up and moved over to the sink.

'I like your outfit,' I commented, admiring the long mauve skirt, topped by a fashionably frilled cream blouse just visible beneath a deep blue jacket.

'Thank ye kindly, sir. It took me a gid deal of trouble to find it. It's no easy being so tall… in Singapore, I mean.'

'Well, you look great.' I smiled. 'You should give those two downstairs some sartorial advice.'

Jean leaned forward, lost her balance, and up-ended herself across my neighbouring armchair.

'Ooops. You okay?' I asked, moving to help her.

'Course I'm okay,' Jean bubbled with laughter, as she pulled herself upright. She leaned forward again and whispered, 'Them twa doonstairs are beyond help… totally beyond help.'

I laughed, as she continued, 'I ask ya, would you dress yoursel in your own curtain materials?' Jean pointed to the décor of the room and nodded wisely.

Suddenly, she grimaced in pain. 'Ya haven't got a Panadol, have you?'

'Try the top drawer in my desk,' I replied.

As she dragged herself into the staff working area, I looked about. She was quite right about the décor. The windows were edged in orange and green drapes which were intended to match the pink and red cushions on the light yellow chairs. The total effect was a psychedelic nightmare.

I re-entered the main room. 'I say, Jean, when are you free for some food?'

'Aboot the third period.'

'Great! I'll see you in the canteen.'

'Och, but please dinna bring that Loh woman. Am in nae mood for her blethering this morning.'

'I understand. See you.'

I watched Jean negotiate her way around the tables, heading for the door. What a woman!

The staff returned. I fossicked about trying to find my record book, wherein all one's weekly activities were expected to be recorded — another peculiarly Singaporean irritation. I finally found the millstone lying under a pile of month-old papers which I still had not marked.

'Mr Richards, your comprehensions are so interesting and your questions so clever…' Oh boy, this had to be someone on the cadge for a free period.

The sensuous tones belonged to Mrs Roberta Singh. Initially I found her friendly and attractive, but over time I had learned, to my cost, that she was deceitful, treacherous, and dishonest — a winning combination in this school and one that guaranteed she would go far. She draped herself across the edge of my desk, her sari brushing the tops of my files, while her little round bum warmed my unmarked papers.

'Could I possibly borrow a comprehension for my second-period class? Just as a practice lesson, you know how it is.' Oh, I knew how it was!

'Of course you could borrow one, Roberta, but I don't think they're here. I could have a look for you, but for the second period? That's short notice.'

'Oh?' She had not expected this answer — local teachers thought I was a soft touch. 'I see. That's a pity. I've done everything in *Clue*.'

Poor dear, that meant she would have to teach for once. Shame! She jumped lightly off my desk, sweeping her sari across my face and leaving a deep, rich scent behind her. I admired her taste in cosmetics, even if she left a lot to be desired as a colleague.

I picked up my record book and hummed my way to the first-period class. Outside the staff room the route was clear, but as I approached the stairs, I could see Snake hovering about on the second landing. No problem. I reversed and took the canteen staircase. This route was a little longer, but it kept me well away from those nasty fangs.

Arriving on the fourth floor, I turned and walked into a boisterous class of thirty-two boys and eight girls. Informal greetings rang out as I called them to order. Slowly they settled, almost to silence. This was a normal class of secondary four students, who had sat their big examination in September and were now awaiting the results. Although most of them would be attempting O-levels the following year, getting them to work at this stage was not easy. Still I tried and, after many questions, catcalls, scuffles, and delays, they were finally on task just as the bell went. 'Better luck next time,' I mumbled to myself as we all left the room.

Now I was free for two periods, so I headed down to the canteen for a drink and breakfast with Jean.

Occupying a large concreted area underneath the hall open on two sides — one opening onto the parade ground, the other providing access to the school playing fields — the canteen's stalls offer a good variety of local and Western delights. Long lines of wooden tables, gleaming in pastel shades of yellow and green, flanked benches smelling of fresh varnish.

Jean was standing at a popular Chinese stall ordering laksa, but I walked straight to the Malay vendor and ordered roti prata, signalling at the same time to the coffee vendor for two cups of the local brew. We sat on the far side, looking out over the playing fields to a distant line of trees which bordered a large estate. Though it was hazy and warm, the fan above us provided a comfortable down-draught.

'You look better,' I said positively.

'Bee Jaysus… open your eyes. I've just had 2/3. It's like open-trench warfare,' Jean spluttered.

'I was a bit late for my class, so by the time they'd settled, the period was done.'

'Congratulations!' There was a long pause while we munched away. 'You got hame all right, then? Last night I mean,' Jean enquired.

'I did. But not without incident!'

'Not again,' Jean shook her head. 'It seems to follow ya aroond.'

'I was getting ready to retire when Yan Siang turned up.'

'Yon laddie who lost his father? He nivver did!' Jean leaned forward, 'Here, that's dang'rous. You canna have kids turning up on your doorstep. How'd he ken where you lived?'

'I have no idea. I certainly never gave him my address and the school wouldn't.'

'Dinna count on that, laddie. I wouldna trust these wallies! Ha ya seen how yon twa jessies sit blethering in the office au day? Oor wee laddie coulda walked past yon pair and taken a wee keek.' Sometimes I felt I could do with a translator when Jean got carried away. However, seeing my bewilderment, she explained, 'He could have snuck into the office and read your file.'

'Or he could have followed me home.'

'No. That's creepy.'

'It gets worse. He wouldn't leave, so I let him stay.'

'Pete,' the word was more of a sigh than an enunciation, 'are you crazy, man?' The shock of my revelation brought her fully back into Oxford English.

'Wait, wait, you haven't heard the best part. Sometime in the middle of the night he crept into my bed.'

'He was in your bed?' Jean shrieked.

'Shhhh…' I breathed heavily, glancing around the canteen. Fortunately no one seemed to have heard the exclamation.

'Och, laddie, how'd ya get rid o' him?'

'I didn't. I left him sleeping in the apartment.'

Jean stared at me for a long moment, thunderstruck. 'You'd better gang hame, afore he empties ya hoose.'

'He won't. Besides there's nothing he would be interested in.'

'What ya bletherin' aboot? You've a television set, videos, dvd players, ornaments…'

'C'mon, you're over-reacting. He's too small to carry anything that big.'

'Och aye, and wha' aboot his mates? He may be part of a whole gang, a… secret society or worse. Ye ken nothin' aboot him!'

'Look, he's just a kid!'

'Och, gae on wi' ya! Dinny be a big saft tattie! If I were you, I'd gae hame this instant. Dinny fret aboot this place. You can tell them you're nae feelin' sae gid. Ya shouldna be, leaving that kid in ya hoose!'

'Jean, Jean! Stop panicking. I'll phone my neighbour and get her to look in on the apartment.'

'Ya sure ya can trust her?'

'Of course I can trust her.'

'Gid! Call her noo!'

'I will. Stop worrying.'

'If any o' yon thick-heads 'ere find oot that you had a boy in your hoose, you'll be finished, Pete.'

I laughed, 'See, every cloud does have a silver lining.'

'You've got plenty o' brass, but it's nae a jokin' matter.'

'Look, I'll make the call. Till then there's no point in tearing oor hair oot! By the way, don't forget the staff meeting this afternoon.'

'I was kinda hoping I could sneak away.'

'Don't try it!'

We drank our coffee in silence until the bell went.

CHAPTER

7

At one-thirty we made our way to the theatrette, a large room, fully insulated and air conditioned, with tiered seating. When we arrived, we discovered that all the go-getters were already comfortably ensconced and chattering away. Snake was busy setting up a laptop for a PowerPoint presentation, while the principal pretended to converse enthusiastically with the Head of Science. In reality she was glancing about like a furtive ferret, trying to determine who was absent. Jean and I smiled graciously at her as we moved into the second to back row. She just hated teachers sitting that far back!

After the usual greetings and the minutes and the matters arising, the agenda proper began. The first item dealt with the controversy surrounding the water cylinder in the staff lounge. The principal pointed out that the chairperson of the School Advisory Council had spent considerable time and effort choosing the 'refreshingly bright' décor for the new lounge. Ah, now we knew who was responsible for that disaster! However, her 'wonderfully artistic' selections had been ruined by the intrusion of that 'grey metallic tank'. Most of the staff remained silent, while one or two morons nodded in agreement. No one raised the point that it was the staff lounge and the good lady from the School Advisory Council had never been invited to spend her time and effort or the staff members' money on any selections.

The principal continued, 'That terrible grey thing simply doesn't fit with the rest of the décor.'

At this point, I chorused out, 'Believe me, there is nothing on this planet that would go with that décor!' Jean guffawed loudly, while several other teachers laughed and looked admiringly in my direction.

The principal was clearly embarrassed and angry. 'Thank you, Mr Richards, but that is not really relevant.'

'Oh, but it is,' I continued, determined now to make my point. 'The staff lounge belongs to the staff. We have to live there and surely that gives us the right to decide how it is decorated. Besides, we paid for the water heater and it is necessary.'

'Hear, hear!' Jean chorused supportively. Several other staff members nodded in agreement and uttered encouraging noises, careful to make sure that none of these wafted down to the principal whose cheeks were purpling as she realised she was losing control of the situation.

'Come now, Mr Richards, we must not be selfish. After all, what sort of impression would visitors get if they were escorted into the lounge and suddenly that grey... that grey...'

'Water heater,' I called out helpfully.

'– monstrosity... loomed into view? They would hardly leave with a very good impression.'

'If they caught sight of those curtains and cushions forget the impression, they'd be lucky to leave with their stomachs!' I countered to general laughter.

The principal ignored me and carried on, 'Nevertheless, I will report to the School Advisory Council that we will be looking into the matter.'

'You can look into it; we'll be drinking from it!'

The principal moved on and Jean and I settled back to our marking.

Two weary hours later we were able to escape.

I reached home at four-thirty to the pleasant discovery that the debris of the morning had disappeared. All the dishes and pans had been washed and put away. The bed had been made and the towels were neatly folded. I was impressed. On the table, I found the reverse side of my note covered in juvenile scrawl. The spelling and grammar were refreshingly original, which made it all the more meaningful:

Dear Teach,
Thank you for your understanding.
I cannot to tell you what happen. I cannot to tell any one.
I do pleats and make bed.
I think you good friend.

P.S. This first time I sleeped with teacher.

I shuddered at the final statement, but the rest of the message proved I was right. This boy knew more than he was telling anyone. He probably needed to talk about it to ease his own presence of mind, but I did not want to get involved any further. Jean's words were ringing in my head. I could not afford to become a father figure to some lost little soul and I was no doubt lucky to have escaped as lightly as I did.

I phoned Ming Chuan and we agreed to meet for dinner. Minutes later I was sipping a sweet sherry and puffing on a Schimmel-pfennick when I noticed Sylvester playing with a little red card. It appeared to be a packet of matches, with a rampant dragon in yellow on one side and three Chinese characters on the other. Beneath the yellow design were the words: The Flaming Dragon. Yan Siang must have dropped it, but where would a fourteen-year-old get such a packet? I thought back to the note on the table — *I cannot to tell you what happen.* I suddenly felt cold. What was it Yan Siang could not reveal? What really happened on that balcony? I looked at the little packet again. There was something strange about it. Troubled, I returned to my cigar and sherry.

For a time I sat puffing away distractedly, trying to focus on other matters, but my mind kept returning to that little yellow dragon. It would not leave me alone. I decided to discuss my discovery with a good friend, Terence, at the first opportunity.

The meal had been delicious. I related my adventures of the previous night and Ming Chuan was surprisingly understanding, but quite emphatic about my distancing myself from any further trouble. I happily agreed and draped my arm across his shoulder as we passed a shady wooded area. The traffic was light, so we could take a few risks. Once we entered the brighter section of Sunset Way, my arm dropped and we walked along like a perfectly ordinary couple. The high fence on top of a slight ridge which formed the boundary of the Military Police and Dog Handlers' Camp served to remind us of the dangers inherent in our relationship.

We crossed the road to the walkway which led down to the canal, running between Clementi Road and Commonwealth Avenue. This was our favourite place — quiet, secluded, and romantic. As we descended to the running track, two joggers puffed past.

Across the canal, car lights appeared and disappeared as vehicles entered and left the parking areas beneath the towering, white blocks. Rectangles of light, interspersed with patches of shade, formed attractive mosaics across the front of the nearest buildings, while little red beacons flickered at the highest point of each block. The evening was cool and comfortable, with a thin mist left over from the thick atmospheric conditions caused by recent Indonesian burning. It was a good night for walking, especially for lovers seeking anonymity.

Ming Chuan clutched my hand and squeezed every now and again as we exchanged glances. This was our time and space, one place we could be ourselves, beyond the touch of our usual acquaintance. We passed a bridge spanning the gaping chasm on our left. A young Chinese couple sat in semi-darkness, cuddling each other. They quickly separated as we approached. We wandered on, holding hands where the darkness and shadows allowed, until we came to a deserted bench set back from the path and shrouded by several thick shrubs.

I opened the plastic shopping bag I had carried from the restaurant and produced two diet cokes. The tops popped, we sat drinking quietly, watching the activity in the apartments opposite.

'I wonder if they can see us?' Ming mused.

'Hardly. They're silhouetted against the light from their apartments, but we're in darkness.'

'Good,' Ming smiled and leaned over, taking me in his arms and crushing our mouths together. The world tipped sideways and my eyes closed. Minutes later, we eased apart and sat back on the bench as a figure emerged from the gloom. It gradually assumed the shape of a young police officer riding a scooter. I looked at Ming and we both suppressed a laugh. The officer rode past with not so much as a glance sideways.

We remained seated for a while longer, enjoying the quiet fragrance of the night. Then we stood. Clementi Road was a string of sparkling car lights in the distance. Walking back, we passed an Indian couple, much too preoccupied to notice us. They had no problem with honesty.

'Are you coming back with me tonight?' I asked hopefully.

'I wasn't going to…'

'I'd appreciate it. Then if the boy shows up, you can deal with him.'

'Thanks a lot!' Ming snorted. 'I don't want to help with your strange little sleep-overs!'

'Ha! Ha!' I sneered.

'You're lucky I'm so understanding.'

'True, I'm very lucky.'

We passed another couple spread out across a bench. The boy was lying on top of the girl and they seemed completely entangled in their own private little paradise, unconcerned about policemen on motor-scooters. Clementi Road suddenly emerged from the gloom, the stream of cars now clearly defined. We walked up the steps. One last squeeze and we were back in the real world.

He stood slightly off the road, hidden by a phone booth. Tall, slim and young, he wore black jeans and a dark jacket, with a wide-brimmed cap, looking for all the world like a gangster or enforcer from a secret society. As he stood waiting, he pulled a cigarette, then turned to light it. The smoke curled away, betraying his position to anyone in his immediate vicinity, but there were few people about. For a while he played with the lighter, and then the belt on his jeans.

Ah, there they were. He could see the two of them approaching the edge of the canal. In a moment they would be on the road, about two hundred metres in front of him, a comfortable distance. His eyes shone earnestly. The older guy looked a little on the plump side. He walked quickly, with a determined stride. The younger man seemed slimmer and slower, with slightly hunched shoulders and a shorter gait. He watched them move off down the road. Suddenly they veered to the left and crossed the street. Damn! They must have had the lights. Now he had to cross. He looked vainly for a gap in the traffic, but there was a steady stream on his side, turning in from Pandan Way. Why had he not realised they might cross early? He moved nearer the lights, and then, seizing a dangerous opportunity, leapt between three cars. He was not worried about being hit, more about being seen. One car hooted angrily, while the other two simply slowed and swerved.

Now on the right side, he walked after the receding couple, watching them pass Sunset Way and move on up to the playground area. This was an easy tail. He knew where they were going, but he had to confirm the precise destination. The younger guy put his arm around the other's waist.

'Bloody queers,' he muttered viciously, and smiled. As he passed under a street light, the shadows turned the smile into a twisted leer. His face had been cut in two places and both wounds had healed badly. This pleased him. The effect was better and cheaper than a tattoo.

He followed his prey the length of Clementi Road and watched them turn into the Ngee Ann Polytechnic. Aware he could not walk through the main entrance without security asking unnecessary questions, he squeezed through a narrow opening he had prepared earlier in the fence. Once on the other side, he slipped quickly across a soccer field and around the back of the main block. He descended the bridge first and waited behind the lift-bay, which gave him a good view as they approached. The young one looked to be in his late twenties, with few distinguishing features. No matter. He was hardly important. It was the fatter one who held his interest. He had a podgy, white face with a balding crown, although his chin was firm, framed in a trim, white beard. Around forty, he could be considered handsome in a Western sort of way.

They entered the lift. He moved quickly to the front and counted the floors, watching as it stopped on the tenth. After making a mental note, he slipped away into the darkness.

I stepped out of the lift and opened the door. Ming Chuan hit the light switches as I went into the bedroom to strip. Generally I walked about the apartment in shorts, sometimes with a t-shirt, sometimes without. Ming Chuan was always more modest.

While I poured a couple of juices, he made a phone call.

'Do you want some chips?'

'Okay,' he replied.

I filled a bowl and carried the lot over to the television corner.

'Thanks for coming back with me. I guess sleep would have been difficult if I'd had to spend the night alone.'

'What makes you think you'll get any sleep now that you're not alone?' Ming smirked mischievously.

'That sort of distraction I can take.'

He switched on the television. Channel 8 was screening a Chinese soap opera, and even though I had to follow the action through sub-titles, I always found these programmes more convincing than the locally made English dramas. For a few minutes I watched a very beautiful, anorexic heroine weep copiously over her husband's brutal betrayal while her mother-in-law admonished her to be strong and look to her responsibilities — the great Asian ethic. Then I remembered Terence.

'Look, I've got to call Terence. We're supposed to meet for dinner tomorrow night.'

'Go ahead,' Ming said over his shoulder, his eyes glued to the unfolding drama.

I slipped into the bedroom and dialled Terence at home. There was no reply, so I tried his cell phone.

'Ell…o!' Typically Terence.

'Hi!' I answered.

'I was wondering when you were going to call? How's the play?'

'I don't know, I've had to skip a couple of rehearsals. Perhaps we could discuss it over dinner.'

'Sure. When?'

'Tomorrow night?'

'I'm working late.'

'I thought we could try Pasta Fresca.'

'Oh, well, ah… in that case, I think I could persuade the boss to let me go early.'

Terence was an easy mark. The way to his mind was via his stomach.

'I'll meet you outside the restaurant, about seven?'

'No problem. See yah!' The line went dead.

On returning to the main room I soon lost interest in the Chinese show, so I ran a bath and poured myself a glass of riesling. I watched the soapy bubbles reach the rim, and then slipped in. As I lowered myself gingerly under the frothing water, I thought about Terence. He was a good friend, with numerous contacts around the city. His finger was usually on the pulse of the night scene, and he knew most of the biggest names in the entertainment world. He was a clever cookie with a gorgeous girlfriend. I splashed around and sipped my wine, slowly sinking into that comfortable state somewhere between light-headedness and sleep. Ming Chuan arrived and undressed. His lightly tanned figure shimmered as he lowered himself on top of me. He always lay half in and half out of the water, as my baths were usually too hot for him. His smooth brown arm reached behind me for the wine and he took a mouthful. We soaped and washed each other and then he exited, leaving me to enjoy the remainder of the wine and bubbles.

Eventually I struggled out, dried myself, and slipped into bed beside him. He was soft and slender with that rich, olive sheen peculiar to Asians. Just running my hands over his body brought me to a state of arousal that no female had ever achieved. I felt strong and manly as we moved up and over each other in a completely untutored, natural way. He loved my touch, while I enjoyed his light, suggestive movements. Our climaxes were fierce and noisy, but the other party's pleasure was always paramount and the best moments were those just after. We lay back on the bed, apart, exhilarated by the sheer energy and enthusiasm we had just expended.

I gazed at the ceiling where an unused fan, shaped like a propeller, dangled superfluously. I admired the yellow curtains hanging from the poles on each side of the four-poster teak bed. This was one of our real treasures. Hand-carved in intricate detail, this exquisite king-size dream machine had been a bargain.

I turned towards the window and gazed at the dark shapes below. Despite the hour, the neighbouring blocks were still alive with activity. Ming Chuan moved closer.

CHAPTER

8

I walked into my Secondary Three English class to discover Yan Siang in bold attendance. Gone was the shy, tearful lad of a couple of days before. Here was confidence supreme, sprawled across a school chair with one foot on the desk in front.

'Good morning, class. Put your foot down, Yan Siang, please.'

He slowly complied, fiercely chomping gum to emphasise that his foot was not the only part of his body committing an offence.

'Please take out the work we were doing on the hunter's escape from the wolves.'

'Teacher, can I be excused?' I turned in the direction of the question.

'Why do you want to be excused, Yan Siang?'

'I need to go to toilet.'

'But we've just had recess.'

'I didn't need to go then, but now I really need to shit.' A burst of laughter rippled across the room.

'In that case, ask properly.'

'C'mon, teacher. I very desperate. I'll… c'mon… c'mon… please, sir.' He looked around the class for more tittering support, but nobody laughed.

I glared at him. 'I don't know why you bother coming to class, you spend most of your time outside it.' I walked up to his desk. 'You know the rules. No one is allowed out of class during periods. Why should I treat you differently?'

He looked at me defiantly, a twinkle in his evil little eyes. 'Because I can make this room very smelly!'

'Please let him go, sir. He's making a big enough stink now.' Sandra swept her hair back and looked around the class at her friends, giggling.

'You've got five minutes.' He jumped up and headed out the door. 'I mean it! Five minutes!'

The class went into groups and soon there was an attractive buzz — the sure sign that most students were on task. Wandering around, I answered questions and offered suggestions. Twenty minutes passed before I realised that the chewing-gum king had not returned.

'Carry on with your work, class. I'll be back in a few minutes. Any noise and we'll continue at one o'clock.'

'Can't! There's assembly.' Trust Ching Loong to remember assembly, as if he would attend anyway.

I disappeared along the corridor to the boys' toilet. The fragrance hit me as I entered and I held my breath. Predictably the place was empty. That little bastard! I knew I should have kept him in class. I ran up the stairs to the toilet above. The end cubicle door was locked, but the telltale smell of tobacco suggested that whatever was going on inside had little to do with personal relief.

'Out!' I shouted, banging on the door. There was a burst of activity inside, followed by the sound of the flush. A few moments later the door crept open and out stepped Yan Siang and another student from a different class.

'So, a pre-arranged rendezvous,' I gloated.

'Of course not, sir. We just met for a quiet smoke.'

I took the other boy's name and sent him back to class. He

scurried away without uttering a word. Then I grabbed Yan Siang by the scruff of the neck and threw him against the wall.

'Listen to me, you lump of shit! I've had it with you.' The boy's eyes opened wide in shock. 'I put up with all your nonsense at the police station, and I take pity on you and allow you to stay in my apartment, and what thanks do I get? You treat me like a moron!'

The boy drew himself up and glared at me. 'You... you touch me again, I'll tell my friends... to... to...'

'To what? C'mon, little man. To what?' I pushed him back against the wall. 'I don't think you've got any friends. The police don't like you. Your mother's fed up with you. The teachers are sick of you. I'm all you've got left!'

'I don't need you. I've got real friends.'

'Oh, have you? Where?'

'They're... they're... in places.'

Suddenly a youngster walked in. 'Out... get out!' I shouted.

'But... but I need to,' the kid wailed, opening his pants.

'Use the toilet downstairs... go!' I yelled.

The boy took off, leaving me facing my prize little prat.

'Bully!' Yan Siang blurted.

'Bully? Me? I haven't started yet. When I get going, I'll make your kung-fu thugs look like Little Bo Peep.' I grabbed his shirt collar again and a button fell off.

'You've torn my shirt,' he sneered contemptuously.

'Oh dear, so I have. Well, I wouldn't worry about your shirt, kid. Wait till I start on you!'

I glared at him for a long moment. He glared right back. You had to give the boy credit, he sure had balls. Once again we had a Mexican standoff. I released my hold on his shirt and let him straighten up. He unruffled his feathers and put the button in his pocket, then made to leave.

I stopped him. 'This isn't finished. I'm going to report the cigarettes to the discipline master.'

'So? Report!' He shoved his way out, leaving me alone and impotent.

I wandered out of the toilet and stood by the staircase staring out across the landscaped eco-pond, past the new condominium to the distant skyscrapers.

When I returned to class, I found Yan Siang missing and so was his bag.

'Teacher, did you really punch Yan Siang and rip off his buttons?' Adolphus Tee's face shone with admiration.

'Settle down and finish your work,' I ordered. So Yan Siang had done a little stirring before he left.

The bell rang and the class made to leave. I ordered them back to their desks and reminded them of their homework. This served to underline who was the real boss.

Worn out and fed up, I returned to the staff room. I dropped into my chair and the catch slipped again. That damned woman had swapped the chairs back.

'There has to be a better way of earning money than this,' Jean sighed, emerging from nowhere, dragging herself and a pile of books across the room.

'When you find out what it is, be sure to tell me.' I noticed the pile of books she was carrying and groaned, 'Damn! I was supposed to collect my secondary three English books.'

'You dinna sound sae guid.' Jean looked at me over her glasses.

'I've just gone three rounds with Yan Siang.'

'He's returned to class then?'

'Has he ever!'

'Och, we all have our wee crosses to bear.'

'This isn't a wee cross. It's a goddamn, gigantic bloody millstone!'

'What happened?'

'He was smoking in the toilet.'

'Och, the wee divil! Tis pleasin' ta see tho' he's recovered frae his tragic loss!'

'I'll tell you one thing for sure, I'm not making another phone call or writing another letter for that little bastard. They all know he's not functioning, but I seem to be the only one who gives a shit!'

The bell rang, announcing the final double period, sixty-five minutes of *Journey's End* — a damned good drama set in the trenches of Word War One. I enjoy this play and I can really relate to the plight of the soldiers, as I am sure they could have related to mine had we been able to swap places. A double period, and then assembly, followed by a long rehearsal! What a day.

Drama rehearsals take place in a large store room underneath the hall. It had originally been used for gym equipment, but after much flattery, coercion, and bribery, the ELDDS (English Literary, Drama and Debating Society — if ever there was a misnomer this was it!) had secured it for rehearsals. It was dusty, badly lit, and oddly shaped, but beggars cannot afford to be choosy.

I arrived clutching two sandwiches and an orange juice. We had missed so many rehearsals I had to make this one count.

'The emperor is absent, the chancellor has a sore throat, and the princess has netball practice,' Desmond, the president of the ELDDS, intoned as I sank onto a chair.

'Thank goodness the queen's okay,' I replied sarcastically.

Desmond is a wonderful lad — courteous, intelligent, and efficient, but boy, does he take himself seriously.

'Ask the second players to take over will you, Des?'

'I'm afraid Malik, Juliana, and Hannifa have Malay until four-thirty. They'll come as soon as they've finished.'

Running rehearsals for a school show is not easy. The kids have plenty of enthusiasm, but there are just too many other things going on.

It was clear this was going to be another inadequate rehearsal. The kids were still page-bound and although time was running out, I had to let them stumble around holding onto their scripts.

The struggle went on for two hours, with missed cues, back-on stances, inaudible whispers, and unconvincing gestures. Finally my patience ran out.

'That's it, thank you. We'll call it a day.'

I arrived late at the pizza restaurant, Pasta Fresca del Salvatore, on the third floor of the new Shaw Centre. It is a small, quaint pizzaria, long and narrow, with tables and chairs closely crammed together in an over-intimate fashion. However, the food is aromatic and delicious.

I could see Terence was already seated with the menu.

'You're early.'

'No, you're late,' Terence jabbed back.

'Since I'm paying, that's my privilege.'

'Whatever.' Terence dropped the menu on the table. 'Josie said she might join us later.'

'No problem,' I replied, picking up the menu.

'Can I get you something to drink?' A young Thai waiter had appeared from nowhere.

'Do you have any Lambrusco — the imported variety, not some Australasian cast-off?'

The waiter stared at me for a moment and then hurried off in the direction of the kitchen. A few moments later, one of the owners appeared.

'Xcusie sir, we have, alas, no Lambrusco tonight but we do have a very pleasant Chianti.' My disapproving glance said it all. 'So sorry, M'sieur,' the owner looked as if he were in pain. I glanced at Terence.

'I'll settle for a beer,' he offered.

'Two Tigers, thanks,' I muttered.

The owner nodded and left.

'You always make it difficult,' Terence laughed.

'Rubbish! What's the point of savouring fine Italian food if you've gotta wash it down with some cheap plonk?'

'If you say so.'

'I had a rehearsal this afternoon.'

'How was it?'

'Terrible. They don't know their lines, half the cast weren't there, and we still haven't filled some parts.'

'So, what's new?'

'It's not just the show. I've had a really bad week.' I described my experiences with Yan Siang. 'As far as I'm concerned the little prick could self-destruct, but I think he knows a lot more about his father's death than he's letting on.'

'Why should it bother you? Let him go. You don't need the aggravation.'

'Someone has to bring the kid round…'

'Maybe he doesn't want to be brought round.'

'Would you care to order?' That creepy little waiter had once again sprung from nowhere. Terence ordered fettuccini with fish, while I went for my usual Hawaiian pizza with very little cheese. As the waiter left, I excused myself and went to the toilet.

By the time I returned, the food was on the table. I sat down and got stuck in.

'I don't see what you can do to help the boy. You're not even in the picture.' Terence had obviously been considering the problem in my absence.

'But I found something,' I spluttered between munches.

'Yes?' Terence sounded bored.

'A small packet of matches. Looks like it came from a restaurant or club.'

'And?'

'What would a fourteen-year-old kid be doing with a packet of matches from some night club?'

'Plenty of things. Probably pinched them to light his cigarettes.' Terence laughed while he munched. 'All kids pick up things like that.'

'From a night club?'

'Sometimes. Did you get a good look at this packet?'

'Of course, and something about it bothered me. I couldn't see what it was until today. Here, see if you can see anything unusual.'

I pulled the packet out and handed it to Terence. He studied it for a while, taking care not to let his examination interfere with his gastronomic enjoyment.

'It looks perfectly ordinary to me.'

'Correct me if I'm wrong, but these little packets are advertising gimmicks, aren't they?'

'Usually.'

'Good! Then explain to me why this packet has no phone number or address.'

Terence turned the packet over in his fingers several times. 'Hell, you're right.'

'Of course I'm right.' By now I was leaning across my pizza and whispering. 'I thought you might be able to check it out.'

'I suppose I could ask around. No doubt I'll be wasting my time, but anything for an old mentor!' The dig reminded me that I had once taught Terence and we had worked on several plays together.

He finished his fish and was eyeing a piece of my pizza. I knew I could not eat it all, so I pushed two wedges onto his plate. He grinned appreciatively. After the meal, Terence agreed to give me a call the following day. If only I could have foreseen the trouble that little packet of matches was going to cause, I would never have let him proceed.

CHAPTER

9

How I hated Saturday mornings. Anywhere else, Saturday was a great day, eagerly anticipated and thoroughly enjoyed. But not at Pleasant Park Secondary! Saturday morning meant seven-thirty remedial classes, followed by an ELDDS meeting. The latter I did not mind, it was the former I loathed.

I had chosen my Secondary Three English class as the subject of my remedial programme for two reasons. First, it was the class which would benefit the most from some extra work, and second, I could count on most of the little souls absconding. Sure enough, when I walked into the room, only six cheery faces greeted me. I took the roll and then handed out a set of comprehension exercises. Midway through the lesson, another two little souls wandered in, raising the attendance to twenty percent.

Remedial lessons never bothered Jean, she just ignored them. Of course, the powers that be had made certain remonstrations, but after realising the futility of their efforts, they simply gave up. This meant that Jean appeared to have won, but the score would be settled when she received her confidential report. Not that Jean cared. She lived for the day when she could collect her bonus and take off.

Another rehearsal followed the remedial lesson. Again we faced absentees and late arrivals. Notwithstanding these difficulties, I was attempting to block a rather difficult fighting routine when Mrs Daisy Liew burst into the rehearsal room.

'Mr Richards, I must speak with you.'

Oh dear, the imperious voice. Daisy Liew had only two voices — the nasal whine and the overbearing, autocratic spit. I was about to suffer the latter.

'Take five, kids!' I yelled as I walked over to the visitor. 'Yes, Mrs Liew?'

'Where is Monica?'

'In the props room working on costumes, I think.'

'She is supposed to be on court five playing volleyball against a visiting team from Raffles Girls'. This is the only chance we have to beat them and our star thruster is missing.'

I had no idea what a thruster was, but apparently Monica was our best one. I also believed in helping the sports teams win as often as I could and a victory against Raffles Girls', the top school, would be something to savour.

'Monica is a member of the ELDDS and she is expected to attend our meetings.'

'Nonsense! Monica was given permission to be excused and she…'

'Permission by whom? I'm the teacher in charge of the ELDDS.'

Daisy Liew's eyes gleamed, 'The principal excused her.'

'When?'

'This morning and –'

'Well, that's a bit late.'

Daisy pushed her way past me out the door, 'I knew you wouldn't listen. I only came here out of courtesy.'

'I knew nothing of this. And you have no right storming into the middle of my rehearsal like the wild woman of Borneo.'

'That's the sort of insulting response I'd expect from you.

I'm going straight to inform the principal!'

I moved closer. 'You do that. After all, you spend so much time kissing her derriere, it would be a pity if such industry didn't show some profit.'

I turned abruptly and walked back into the room, leaving the silly old tart standing open-mouthed in the corridor.

An hour and a half later, the rehearsal over, I was heading down the administration corridor when I came face to face with Her Graciousness.

'Could I speak to you for a moment, Mr Richards?' I walked into her office and sat down. 'I am grateful to you for handling that matter with young Chang Yan Siang the other day.'

'No problem,' I muttered.

'Mrs Liew has just been to see me in a distressed state over one of her volleyball girls. Apparently she was needed in our game against Raffles Girls' Secondary. Mrs Liew found Monica in time, so not all was lost. But she felt you were very rude to her and –'

'Please, Mrs Benthusamy, let's cut to the chase.' I stood up. 'We all know Daisy Liew is one of your little bosom buddies. But let me clarify three points. Monica is not a volleyball girl, she is a bona fide member of the ELDDS. Second, I was never informed that she was needed for the volleyball match — a point of courtesy, guaranteed by the school code. Thirdly, Mrs Liew burst into my rehearsal room in a most offensive manner and I merely gave her the treatment she asked for.'

'In a school, Mr Richards, there has to be a little give and take, if things are to run smoothly.'

'True, but in this school, we always have to do the giving and it's your friends who do the taking.'

'Mr Richards, I will not let you speak to me like this.'

'Tough! Now, I'm going to enjoy what remains of my weekend. I suggest you do the same.'

I walked abruptly out of her office. This was the second

woman I had left gobsmacked in one morning — not bad going. At last I had a spring in my step and a song in my heart.

I arrived back at my apartment to the sound of the telephone.

'Hello.'

'Hi there. It's Terence. Sorry I didn't call you yesterday, but I think I've found out where your flaming dragon is located.'

'What?'

'That packet of matches… remember?'

'Of course.'

'It's not a restaurant and it's not a club. It's a flipping dive!'

'What do you mean?'

'It's a place for picking up prossies.'

'Are you sure?'

'Very sure. Josie has a friend who works for Kwah Beng Heng, the real estate developer, and rumour has it that he met his latest mistress there.'

'But how did Yan Siang get a souvenir from a place like that?'

'Beats me. And if I were you, I wouldn't try to find out. Honestly, Pete, Kwah Beng Heng lives in a world a million miles away from you and me.'

'Can't we just take a quick look at the place?'

'Have you any idea what it could cost to get in?'

'Nope. But there's no harm in asking.'

'I already have,' Terence sighed.

'Really?'

'I knew you wouldn't let it go. Josie has an acquaintance, an acquaintance mind you, not a friend, who might be able to get us in. But it'll be expensive. This acquaintance should be free, but it'll cost us fifty dollars each!'

'Fifty bucks! Bloody hell, what've they got inside this place?'

'That's only for the first drink!'

'Don't worry! At fifty bucks there won't be a second.'

'You're still going to go through with it?'

'Of course! I've never actually been to a place like this. Besides, I might be able to claim the money back from the school. After all, we are going there on official business.'

'Fat hope! If the school finds out that you're frequenting whore-houses, exclusive or not, your official business will be over before it gets started!'

'Yeah, yeah! Life's full of risks.'

'I'll try to fix it for tomorrow night.'

'Sunday?'

'Of course! They usually do their best business on Sunday nights and the more clients there are, the less likely we are to attract attention.'

'Okay. Call me later. And thanks, mate!'

'It'll cost you.'

I laughed as I heard the phone click.

CHAPTER

10

I reached Eunos Mass Rapid Transit station at eight forty-five, having enjoyed a comfortable trip on the Singapore MRT system — fully air conditioned and spotlessly clean. The station was well lit, but outside I entered the nether world where creatures of the dark emerge to mingle and enjoy. I crossed Changi Road and walked down Still Road, turning right into Joo Chiat Place. Although well lit and peopled, there was an eerie, uncanny feel to the area. Women hung round doorways which led into long corridors with rooms branching off at regular intervals. I received catcalls and invitations — the price of being alone.

After a long walk with my eyes fixed firmly in front of me, I reached the corner of Joo Chiat Road. This was the rendezvous point. I hoped it would prove one of those rare occasions when Terence would be early. It did not. Forced to stand on the corner, I tried to look inconspicuous. But a Westerner in Geylang? No chance! Eventually Terence emerged from the gloom on the other side of Joo Chiat Road. He waved me over. The nearby street lamp illuminated his companion, an attractive female in a long, green cheongsam. She was slim and elegant, light make-up on a pretty face. I was pleasantly surprised, although I was unsure what I had expected. Still, this lady looked as if she were on her way to the opera or a black tie dinner.

'Good evening,' I said, approaching them.

'This is Mai Ling. That's Pete.' Terence's idea of a formal introduction.

'Does Josie know you're out in the company of a stunning young beauty queen?'

'Yeah, yeah!' Terence sounded bored. He turned to the young lady. 'Take no notice of him. He's got a very sweet mouth.'

Mai Ling nodded and smiled shyly. No doubt she was used to receiving compliments.

Terence moved me aside. 'It's like this. Mai Ling is an escort and you've paid for her company for two hours. Believe me, that's all you can afford. Then you'll have to pay her taxi home.'

'What's this going to cost me?'

'All up, about $500. But don't worry, you can get it back from the school. You're on official business don't forget,' Terence sneered.

'Listen, mate. This could be the bloody end of a very promising friendship. Five hundred bloody dollars!'

'Shhhh… you don't want the lady to hear. She thinks you're loaded!'

'I haven't got $500.'

'Don't worry, they take credit cards!'

'Bloody hell! You can't be serious!'

Terence laughed, 'Of course I'm not, you damned fool. She's doing Josie's brother a favour. I'll explain later.'

Terence spoke to Mai Ling in Chinese and we moved off down a little side-street which I had not seen in the darkness. We crossed a deserted road and turned into a larger street, flanked on all sides by parked cars. At the end, directly ahead, I could see the frontage of an oriental-style building, topped by a huge flashing dragon, etched out in bright neon tubes of green, yellow, and red. Beneath the dragon hung a longitudinal sign displaying the four Chinese characters I remembered seeing on the little packet of matches.

We reached the entrance and Mai Ling moved forward. Two huge Chinese gentlemen in suits and ties stepped into the light. Mai Ling spoke to them in a low voice and pointed in our direction. I shivered. Suddenly she beckoned us forward.

A large, carved wooden door swung open and we entered an enormous room. The interior was red. Totally red. The walls were hung in deep red velvet. The leather couches and chairs were red and the low wooden tables were draped in red fabric. The ornately designed lanterns hanging from the ceiling cast a light red pall over the area beneath. It was as if we had entered the boudoir of an ancient Chinese princess.

Three musicians in a dimly lit corner played lightly on old Chinese instruments, their discordant plucks and strokes adding to the surreal atmosphere. Large scrolls of Chinese landscapes, depicting mountains and forests hanging in misty limbo, fell from the walls and the powerful tang of incense drifted across the guests, sitting on cushions or lolling on couches. Altogether it was the most amazingly sensual atmosphere I had ever experienced.

A young woman, swathed in a rich silk kimono, jet-black hair set up high in the Japanese fashion, skittered across to us. She bowed respectfully and showed us to a table in the centre of the room. I glanced at Terence and he directed the guide to a more discreet alcove on the other side. I was still a little concerned. Our table was a good way from the door and it would be difficult to leave in a hurry.

Another young lady arrived with a pot of tea and three small cups which she daintily set in front of us and filled.

'This is free,' Terence informed me happily.

Suddenly a far door opened and two young Chinese men appeared, exquisitely dressed in costumes I had presumed were only worn at Chinese New Year. They moved amongst the tables, bowing and greeting guests. One of them eventually reached our table.

'Would you like something a little heavier to drink?' the boy whispered in perfect English. He bent across the table and I stared at his painted eyes, heavily lined eyebrows and thick, red lipstick. He looked like a theatrical mannequin.

'Two Tiger beers and a crème de menthe,' Terence ordered, filling the gap. The boy bowed, smiled again, and rejoined his friend.

'That boy… was wearing make-up,' I breathed at Terence. Mai Ling merely smiled.

'So? Lots of boys wear make-up. Some have their ears pierced and some even put studs in their tongues.'

I accepted Terence's response in silence. Clearly I was way out of fashion. I peered cautiously around the room. There seemed to be a good number of guests, mostly male, but here and there I spotted the odd couple.

The far door opened again. Another boy entered, carrying a tray supporting two beers and a crème de menthe. More delicately made up, he looked rather pretty and could easily have been mistaken for a young girl. He smiled sweetly before moving away. We sipped our beers and listened to the distant plucking and banging. I noticed more groups of Japanese-style hostesses and Chinese page-boys moving around the tables. Sometimes one of these attendants would be invited to sit at a table, now and again surrendering their place to another. This game of musical chairs continued for some time, until the room suddenly darkened.

Without warning, the musicians went crazy and struck, banged, thumped their instruments. The volume was magnified by the darkness. Then, with an explosion of colour, a batten of baby spots flashed on, flooding the far side of the room with light. Three sections of wall had disappeared to reveal a Mandarin's garden with foliage and screens which would have done credit to any Gilbert and Sullivan operetta. Ten Chinese maidens, weaving red and yellow ribbons through the air, glided across the stage with all the elfin quality of an Asian ballet. They turned, pivoted, pirouetted, bowed, and swept across the stage to the delight of the Caucasians in the audience. Eventually they drifted away, to be replaced by a petite Chinese girl and a handsome young scholar who sang of their rapturous love in a canto-pop duet. Two muscular young drummers followed, pounding out rhythms which seemed to bounce off the walls, until I thought my head would burst. The interlude ended with a trio of young girls singing a selection of melodies from Chinese opera.

I leaned over and whispered,

'Impressive! I thought this was just a high-priced knocking shop.'

Terence laughed, 'It is!'

'What do you mean?'

'C'mon, didn't you see our little geishas making the acquaintance of the clientele? The boys are available as well!'

I sat there feeling nauseous.

'Are you all right?' Terence asked, concerned at my silence.

'Not really.'

'What? I thought you knew about all these things… being a man of the world!'

'I'd expect it in Thailand or the Philippines, but Singapore?'

'Get real. Don't tell me you believe all that rubbish put out by the PAP?'

I said nothing. My eyes fastened on the light shifting across the brocade of the boys' outfits. 'I think we should leave.'

Terence spoke briefly to Mai Ling who signalled a waiter. A short while later he returned with what looked to me like the bill. Mai Ling took a pen from her bag and wrote across the bottom of the chit.

'Shouldn't I pay?'

'It's been taken care of,' Terence murmured. 'Lucky you!'

Once outside, we caught a taxi back and I asked the driver to drop me off at Jalan Jurong Kechil. I felt like walking the last stretch.

It was a clear, cool night. Above, a few distant sparklers reminded me of my own jewelled southern skies with their dazzling displays. I sank onto the smooth cold face of a concrete bench edging a small park.

Casually I took out the little packet of matches I had taken from the night club and lit a small cigar. The packet was a replica of that left in my apartment by Yan Siang. How had it come into his possession? I refused to believe that he had been anywhere near that place, but I was haunted by the thought. Were those boys really on the make? I did not see any man leave with a waiter, although I saw some leave with hostesses. Of course, I left early. Damn! I cursed myself for going in the first place.

I finished my cigar and walked purposefully towards my Ngee Ann quarters. Tomorrow might be another day, but I had an ominous feeling that the trap my curiosity had sprung was slowly closing.

CHAPTER

11

Monday morning and the beginning of a new week. The buses were packed and I arrived at school feeling as if I had already taught four periods. I missed flag-raising — a point I would deal with later — and made my way straight to the staff lounge for a cup of coffee.

I was enjoying a quiet sip when Jean appeared.

'Hi there,' I called unenthusiastically.

'Had a bad weekend?' Jean asked, pouring herself a glass of water.

'Adventurous really. I was exploring the seamier side of Singapore... alliteratively speaking.'

Jean laughed. 'You mean Geylang?'

'Somewhere down there. I was invited to visit this high class...' I paused for emphasis and whispered, 'brothel!'

'Brothel?' Jean shrieked.

Daisy Liew had been standing at the basin desperately trying to pretend no interest, but Jean's shriek had completely blown her cover. She looked aghast and hastily disappeared into the staff room.

'For goodness sake, Jean. Why don't you just go in there, stand on a desk, and shout it out to the whole staff?'

'Shhhh… you mean one o' yon kinky wee hoorhooses?' Jean had crossed to my seat and squeezed herself over the armrest. She clutched her glass of water with such passion that I was afraid she might break it.

'Rojan took me there once. I got a wee keek doon a hall, wi' all these shameless hinnies standin' aboot.' She paused, glanced around, and whispered, 'Ye're no tellin' me that ya went in?'

Jean's eyes shone as I described The Flaming Dragon and the floor show. 'Och, ye're a dark horse!' she laughed. In her efforts to hoist herself from the seat, she spilt most of the contents of the glass over my pants. We both laughed.

'Really, Jean! What do you think the kids'll say when they see this mess!'

'Just carry an extra large pile o' books. See you later.'

My first three classes were lost in revision programmes, but after recess I had Secondary Three English and there again was Yan Siang. He behaved remarkably well and at the end of the period approached my table.

'Hi, teacher.'

'Hello, Yan Siang. You know my name is Mr Richards.'

'Sorry, Mr Richards.' There was a long pause. Finally Yan Siang glanced around to make sure we were alone. 'Can I stay with you tonight? Please?'

I stopped marking the register and looked up, uncertain as to whether I had heard him correctly.

'I cannot go back home.'

'Why?' I asked stupidly, because the reason could not possibly alter my refusal.

'I cannot and I cannot explain.'

Then, in a flamboyantly theatrical gesture, I announced, 'I visited The Flaming Dragon last night.' I watched him closely, expecting to see shock or at least surprise. There was no reaction.

'I thought you will go,' he said after a long pause.

'What?' I hissed.

'How could you?'

'I put the card on your table. I know you will go there.'

I sat back amazed.

'What possible reason could I have for going to a dump like that?'

'I don't know, but you still go.'

'All right, wise guy, how'd you get those matches?'

'I found them.'

'Great! Well let me tell you a little secret. I'm tired of your nonsense. Until you can provide a few answers, I don't want to talk to you any more!'

'Can I please stay with you tonight?'

This kid was unbelievable! I picked up my books and stormed off to the staff room.

The remainder of the day was unremarkable and I did not see Yan Siang again. I arrived back home at five o'clock and relaxed with the newspaper and a glass of wine.

At seven, I decided to wander down to Bukit Timah Plaza for dinner. With a new novel from the local book exchange, I enjoyed a meal of curried chicken and then visited the supermarket for a couple of items before making my way back to my apartment. It was a warm, clear night and the stroll allowed my food to settle.

I crossed Upper Bukit Timah Road and walked slowly up the pavement by the side of the spillway. I had almost reached the gate in the fence when two young men stepped into my path.

'Hello,' the heavier of the two breathed in a thick, chili-coated blast.

'Good evening,' I replied, trying to recognise their features. 'It's a nice evening for a walk.'

'Nice,' the other laughed.

I did not like the laugh.

'Must get on,' I smiled, pushing forward.

'Not so fast. We know you,' the heavier man breathed again.

'I… I don't think so,' I muttered, beginning to panic. Not that there was any need to. The place was brightly lit and I knew someone was bound to come along any moment.

'We know. You are the white, like prostitute, right?' I stood back and laughed. Now I knew they definitely had the wrong guy.

'Why you and your friends go to The Dragon last night?'

'Where?' I did not understand him.

'The Flaming Dragon?'

Now I understood.

'We… we… were just looking around Geylang.'

'See what? Like to see, right?' the heavier man turned away and then, without warning, swung round and hit me full-fist in the stomach. I lurched forward, bags and book flying into the bushes by the side of the path. I could not breathe.

The other man grabbed his friend,

'Eh, don't like that. This man teacher.'

'Sorry, teacher!' the other sneered and struck me hard across the face with his open hand. I had never felt such pain. It seemed as if a red-hot iron had been rammed against my cheek.

I staggered towards the road as the other man helped me back onto the path.

'Sorry, he not patient man. We want to know why you go there, do nothing. What you like? You undercover?'

'I don't… I don't know,' I spluttered, trying to understand why this was happening to me. What did they want? Undercover? Me? My mind began to wander.

'Don't know what?' the heavier man swung again and hit me full on the nose. Bells went off in my head. I grew nauseous and a misty film clouded my vision; the voices seemed to come from a long way away.

'Answer ley, why The Dragon?'

'My friend… I… wanted to… to see a show… never… I…

never been… before… First time… I… ' My mind would not focus. I stumbled over the path to the bushes and slowly sank to my knees. Everything hurt. The two men drew aside and mumbled to each other in a strange dialect. I was beyond caring. I just wanted the pain to stop.

Finally the smaller man bent over me and whispered, 'Flaming Dragon not your business… very bad place for you. You forget better… everything. You forget me and him! We know you. No police! Understand?'

I nodded, but at that moment I would have agreed to anything. The heavier man lurched over. He pushed me onto my back with his right foot and then moved away. Crazily he swung back, sinking his shoe into my right buttock. I screamed and he stomped down hard on my right arm. I rolled onto the road, anything to get away from this crazy man. Two cars shot down the spillway, hooting loudly and swerving onto the grass verge. I pulled myself back to the path and looked around for my tormentors. Gone. I was alone.

I lay there for several minutes, trying to work out which part of my body hurt the most. Blood ran freely from my nose and my arm had been gashed by the edge of the bastard's shoe. My right buttock felt as if I had just had a shot for rabies. I slowly sat up and contemplated standing for a long time before I did. Once upright, I remembered my lost purchases. I staggered around, picking up my fruit and drinks. Two bottles had been smashed and the book had disappeared. I staggered through the gate and dragged myself towards my apartment. Blood dripped everywhere. Strangely, there was no one about. I reached the lift before I walked into Vivienne, my neighbour.

'Holy moly,' she gasped when she saw me. 'Were you attacked?'

'Sort of,' I mumbled, attempting to smile.

'Did they steal anything?'

'Only my pride.'

'Let's get you up to the apartment and I'll dress those wounds, but you'll need to see a doctor.'

'Later. I just want to sit down first.'

'Okay. Okay.'

Vivienne helped me into my apartment. She wrapped me in towels and then dashed next door to get her medical kit. Upon her return, I was half-carried into the bathroom and bent over the bath. She sponged down my wounds and dressed them. There was a savage gash across my left cheek, where my attacker's ring had left its mark. After she finished, I took a shot of whisky and decided to visit the police post downstairs. Those thugs might have kicked me about, but I would be damned if they were going to get away with it.

'I'll take you. Here, put your arm over my shoulder.' Vivienne was a lot smaller than I was, but she was wiry and strong, no doubt the result of early morning runs and strenuous aerobic classes. We somehow managed the lift, but as she struggled to move me down the steps, I hit my leg on the metal hand-rail. A shaft of pure agony shot up my side and the last thing I remember was a security guard running towards us as I collapsed in a heap on the concrete.

CHAPTER

12

I awoke in a taxi on the way to the National University Hospital. The guard had secured the vehicle and helped Vivienne manoeuvre me into it. I was less than impressed, as I wanted to speak to the police, but she assured me that could come later.

As we travelled down Commonwealth Avenue, I drifted in and out of a misty fug. The pain had lessened, no doubt thanks to the Panadol Vivienne had given me, but my head still throbbed and my arm had swollen up to twice its normal size. When we arrived at the University Hospital A & E Department, Vivienne wanted to get a wheelchair, but I assured her I could walk. She guided me along a corridor to the waiting area, and the crowds of people milling around for attention dimmed my spirits. This could be a long wait. I was placed in a chair while Vivienne went up to the counter to register my arrival.

'They say they'll deal with you next. You may have to stay overnight, though, so who should we contact to bring in your things?' I gave her Ming Chuan's mobile number. Then she left.

I sat amongst the other prospective patients, waiting. A friendly old fellow, who did not speak a word of English, offered me a magazine. I smiled and shook my head. Tiredness was beginning to replace the pain and I just wanted to lie down.

I was pleased when Ming Chuan arrived.

'What? What happened to you?' he asked breathlessly.

'I thought you had classes?' I answered.

'I did, but Jason agreed to cover for me.'

'How did you get here so fast?'

'Vivienne called me and told me you were attacked. How?'

'Two men jumped on me just outside the poly.'

'Did you call the police?'

'I wanted to, but Vivienne thought I should see a doctor first.'

'Wow! Your eyes and your face!'

'Wait till you see the rest of me.'

'They attack, but why you?'

'I don't know,' I lied.

'It must be something to do with that boy.'

'Look, I'll tell you the story later, but not now… please.'

'You must be sore.'

'I am.'

Suddenly my number flashed up. Room 11.

The doctor was greying at the temples — always a good sign — and he smiled sympathetically as I sat down. 'Oh dear. You do look a mess.'

'I feel a mess.'

'I'm sure.'

He examined my nose and eyes. 'We'll have to stitch this nasty gash on your face.' Next, he softly felt my arm. 'This could be fractured. You'll need to go to x-ray. While you're there we'll do the nose. I don't think it's broken, but better safe than sorry. Do you have a Civil Service Card?' I nodded. 'Good. It'll cost you nothing. Were you hit or kicked anywhere else?' I grimaced and showed him the damage. My right buttock was a deep shade of purple tinged with yellowish blue.

He tested my vision. It was all right, but he felt it should be checked again in the morning. Then he gave me a docket for an x-ray and a trip to the surgery on the same floor. The x-ray showed that my wrist was fractured in two places, but my nose was more resilient. I was dispatched to the surgery. A while later, with my face stitched and my arm in plaster, I returned to the original doctor.

'We'd like to keep you in overnight, just to check there's no concussion or head damage. You were hit pretty hard.'

Ming Chuan left to fetch the things I would need and I was wheeled to the pharmacy for cream and tablets. By the time he returned, I was sitting in a wheelchair in a Class I ward. I had showered and changed into a regulation hospital gown, the sort that makes a good figure look bad and a bad figure even worse. With Ming Chuan's help, I donned a t-shirt and briefs and then moved onto the bed. A nurse arrived to give me a shot, which she claimed would help me sleep. Ming Chuan hated needles, so he said goodbye and disappeared. I was grateful, because I did not want to go into any more detail about the incident.

I lay for a long time staring at the darkened windows and listening to distant sounds. I tried to piece together the events of the past week, hoping to make sense of what had happened, but it was useless. Why would two strangers attack me for visiting The Flaming Dragon? It did not make sense. Clearly they thought I knew something and I was sure it was linked to Yan Siang. I was angry at my own impotence and the fact that I had been so badly beaten, yet had given back nothing on my own account. Still, pay-back time was at hand. The police could act as my vengeance!

The early morning sounds and smells of the hospital brought me round at about five-thirty. The first thing I felt was pain — a severe ache in my stomach and a throbbing in my face. Surprisingly, my head seemed okay. I turned over and tried to drift back to sleep, but the pain made it impossible.

The doctor appeared at eight-thirty and, after a thorough

examination, said I could return to my apartment once I had breakfast. The stitches would be removed in a week, but my arm could be in plaster for about six.

As he left, I had a surprise visitor — Raymond Chia, the police cadet.

'Good morning.' He moved over to the chair beside my bed.

'How are you feeling?'

'A whole lot better than I was last night.'

'Those two thugs really left their mark. I spoke to your doctor and he says you're lucky. You should be okay in about a month to six weeks.'

'That's lucky?'

'Of course. The guy who kicked you could have done serious damage if he had missed the fleshy part of your buttocks, and had he been wearing boots your arm would have been a real mess.'

'So let's all look on the bright side!' I answered sarcastically, turning away.

'C'mon, I know you're feeling lousy, but it could have been a lot worse. These guys just wanted to give you a fright.'

'How come you know so much about it?'

'Apparently one of the neighbouring families saw the whole thing and they called the Toh Yi Police Post. A bulletin was put out on the Internet and I picked your name up on my computer, so I thought I'd pay you a visit.' He moved closer. 'You see, I think this attack is linked to the case of your school student.'

'How?'

'I'm not sure, but we know you visited The Flaming Dragon the other night and I think your assailants are in some way connected to that club.'

'They are. They told me to stay away from there.'

'Why did you go to The Flaming Dragon in the first place?'

'How can I be sure if I tell you anything I won't face a

repeat of last night?'

'If you want to avoid another visit from your friends, help us catch them.'

I explained the business of Yan Siang and the matches.

The officer looked at me intently.

'We've been watching The Flaming Dragon for some time, but till now we've never been able to get a fix on the place.'

'Hell, they're running male and female prostitutes from the joint.'

'Escorts actually. We can't prove they're any more than that. It's a classy club, with classy prices and a classy clientele. We have to tread carefully or we could upset a lot of important people. We've heard plenty of stories about the place, and we know your student's father worked there for several months before he died.'

'Are you sure?' Chia nodded. 'Doing what?'

'We don't know that. And we can't move any further unless something happens. If your young friend could just tell us what –'

'He's no friend of mine!'

'I understand,' the officer laughed and moved to the curtain. 'When you're feeling better, the guys at Toh Yi would appreciate a statement. We already have a good description of your attackers from that family in Block 94, although it's unlikely we'll be able to get them.'

'Why?'

'They're probably on holiday in Thailand by now. They won't hang around after attacking a Westerner. Anyway… if you need any help, or have any more trouble, please call me. You still have my card?'

'Somewhere.'

He nodded and disappeared through the curtain.

I lay back and watched the level of activity gradually increase until breakfast arrived with Ming Chuan.

CHAPTER

13

It was great to be back in my own apartment. Sylvester gave me a particularly warm welcome, having missed me the previous night. Ming Chuan had classes, so he left as soon as he had settled me on the bed. He turned on the television and put in a video. Vivienne had left a bacon and egg pie in the microwave and shortly after I arrived back, the phone went. It was Jean, worried about my absence from school. I explained what had happened and she told me she would be around as soon as classes finished. I tried to persuade her that there was no need, but being a real brick, she insisted. Although I knew I should phone Terence, I decided to wait until later. Warmed by all the concern, I sat back to watch the video and promptly fell asleep.

Shooting and yelling from the television woke me and I looked at my watch. It was nearing noon. I kept turning over in my mind Raymond Chia's statement about Yan Siang's father. If he worked for The Flaming Dragon, then everything was linked. But how?

I went into the kitchen and poured myself a glass of water. The phone rang.

'Hello,' I answered hesitantly.

'How are you?' It was Terence.

'Terrible.'

'What happened?'

'I was jumped last night by a couple of thugs…'

'From The Flaming Dragon!'

'What do you mean?'

'Mai Ling called Josie yesterday to warn her that someone didn't agree with our little visit the other night.'

'Well, don't worry. The police are onto it.'

'No! You haven't been speaking to the police?'

'Why?'

'Hell, man! Have you got a death wish? Next time those guys won't stop at a beating.'

'C'mon, Terence, get real! This isn't some mega-thriller.'

'Listen! Something's going down at The Flaming Dragon and we're in danger of getting caught in the middle of it. I didn't tell you that Mai Ling and Josie's brother are engaged and Mai Ling went to The Flaming Dragon to pick up some money for him. We were her cover.'

'What money?'

'A lot of money. But she didn't get it. Josie's brother is out of favour and the guys who run the place grilled Mai Ling about us. They wanted to know who we were. Mai Ling spun some story about our being swau koo.'

'Swau koo?'

'Claimed we were naïve and knew nothing.'

'But we do know nothing. We just went there for a look.'

'Wake up, Pete. You went there because of that damned packet and now someone has worked out your link with that kid.'

I thought for a moment. 'Could be. The police did say his father worked at The Flaming Dragon.'

'What?' Terence shrieked.

'Steady on.'

'Steady on! Are you crazy? I wish I hadn't let you talk me into this. Now Josie's brother's disappeared.'

I laughed nervously, 'So? That's got nothing to do with us.' I could hear rapid breathing. 'Look, call me tonight. When I'm better we'll thrash this out over a meal at Spageddies.'

I hoped that the thought of dinner at his favourite restaurant would somehow calm Terence's nerves.

The room was dark, lit only by a red glow filtered through two Chinese paper lanterns. A thin Caucasian man, an expensive suit hanging off his shoulders, sat behind a heavy desk smoking an old briar pipe. He had thick white hair and a generous moustache, which gave him the air of a friendly grandfather. Behind the desk, a detailed wall screen, painstakingly carved from balsa wood, depicted an ancient Chinese battle.

'Bring the pair in,' the man whispered into an intercom. Two screens in the far wall parted and four men entered. The larger pair were from The Flaming Dragon and between them cowered the two thugs. One of the doormen placed two chairs in front of the desk, while the other manoeuvred the thugs towards them.

'Good morning, gentlemen,' the pipe-smoker rasped. 'So sorry we had to bring you here at such short notice, but my colleagues want an explanation.'

The two men in the chairs moved uneasily, flanked by the towering bully-boys. The white-haired man puffed happily on his pipe for a few moments and then continued, 'You see, we have spent three years building up our business. It has cost a great deal of money and patience.'

He sat back, his face falling into shadow. This, along with the rasping voice, gave an unnerving edge to everything he said.

'We know the police are watching us and we feed them little distractions every now and again. It's part of the game... part of the business. But we keep the public out of it. This protects our clients, you see, and our clients must always be our primary concern.' Wreathes of smoke punctuated another pause.

'I am very interested in history, gentlemen. Have you ever peered into the past?'

By the look of the pair, they were having enough trouble with the present. There was no reaction.

'You haven't? Oh, that's a pity. You see we can only understand the present if we have a good understanding of the past. And the past is littered with great ideas and great men who have failed, usually because others got clumsy. Many great men have fallen because of careless subordinates.'

He paused and puffed again on his pipe. Then he leaned forward, using the pipe as a pointer.

'That's what you are, gentlemen. Subordinates. My subordinates. You wouldn't want me to fail because of your actions now, would you?'

'But, they told us to scare that teacher, mah,' the heavier of the two thugs blurted.

'The teacher so fat, no muscle. He very weak man,' the other added.

'Dear, dear, dear! Don't you realise it's always the weak ones that are the most dangerous?'

'We already say to him if he go to police, we...'

'The police, ah... gentlemen, there's the rub. That's my very point. This fat, weak man that you describe is the sort that believes in the police. You see, he looks upon the police as his protectors. Those of us who live in the real world, well, let's just say we know better. But your good, honest citizen always turns to the police.'

'What? Then we see him again today!'

'There you go again. Not content with one mistake, you wish to compound it. Violence begets violence. It's out of date. This is the computer age, gentlemen. We don't use thuggery.' The white-haired man smiled warmly.

'Next time, I beat him until he cannot talk,' the heavier one muttered.

'I don't think so. You see, the police are now looking for you both. You have attracted attention and, what is worse, you have drawn attention to us.' The warmth had disappeared, a touch of severity crept into the rasp.

'You were instructed to retrieve our property and instead you beat up a perfect stranger for no good reason.'

'Eh, they told us to do that!'

One of the bully-boys leaned forward and, muttering something in Chinese, slapped the speaker across the right side of his head. The man squealed in pain.

'Thank you, I do not like to be interrupted.' He paused for effect. 'Your task still remains. We want our property back. However, you have presented us with a difficulty. Now you are known to the police. We will have to arrange a disguise.'

He pushed a button at the side of his desk and the screen parted again. A man and woman in white coats entered carrying towels, face-cloths, and a bowl of shaving equipment. They moved to the thugs and spread the towels around their shoulders, tucking the face-cloths beneath their chins.

'I'm a generous man. We'll begin with the hair,' the boss puffed aggressively.

The woman produced a brush and covered the heads of both men in a thick, creamy lather. Her colleague then opened a razor and removed all hair from both heads. Thin riverlets of blood ran from cuts and gashes, but neither man uttered a sound.

'Now, gentlemen, you have a choice. Eyes, nose or ears?' The two men froze. 'You can't decide? No problem.'

The white-haired man nodded at the bully-boys and they moved behind each thug to bind the legs and pin the arms, actions which brought gargles of fear from terrified throats. Then the woman moved to the man on the left and pulled a scalpel from her coat. With the practised skill of an expert, she sliced both ears from his head. The thug screamed and writhed until the man in the white coat shoved a cloth in his mouth.

The other whined like a stricken animal as the woman turned. With a beautiful smile, she whipped the scalpel across his face and gouged his right eye from its socket. The grisly ball plopped onto the towel, followed by a stream of blood as the man's head lolled loosely in a dead faint.

'Better give them a shot,' the white-haired man ordered. The woman produced a syringe and jabbed the shivering wrecks. Then, while the bully-boys carried their unconscious charges out of the room, the pair in white coats breezily cleaned up the mess.

The boss leaned back in his chair, puffing on his pipe. He studied the scene on the wall and mumbled, 'I do so hate violence.'

Shortly after one, the doorbell chimed and Jean entered. She embraced me, hastily releasing her grip when I moaned with pain.

'Och, what a nasty mess they made o' ye!'

'You think so? Well this is the improved version, you should have seen me freshly battered. 'Look, my neighbour gave me a pie. It's in the microwave. I'll put it on and you can hear all the details while we eat.'

Jean jumped up and pushed me back. 'Sit ye doon! Sit ye doon! I'll take care o' yon pie.'

After a delicious lunch, we relaxed with a smoke. I puffed a large Porto del Cuba, shaped like a torpedo, while Jean enjoyed a Marlboro and we both sipped a cream sherry.

'How can you be sure they wilna ha' a second go?'

'I've told the police and they seem to think it was a warning. They doubt there'll be a repeat.'

'The polis! Pah!'

'You don't really have much respect for our men in black, do you?'

'If ye ken what I ken about yon polis, ye'd be a mite more bothered. Ma mind wad rest mair easy if Rojan stayed over for a coupla nights.'

'That's unfair. I couldn't expect him…'

'Och, tis nae bother. Wi him aboot, those thugees'll keep their distance.'

I knew it would be pointless to remonstrate. Jean had made up her mind and I would just have to accommodate Rojan. Anyway, the presence of a 'heavy' could be an advantage.

'If it's no trouble, I would be very grateful. I've got a camp bed that I can put up for him.'

'Ye'll dae nathing o' the sort, what with yon wing in plaster. He'll handle all that hisself, dinna fret.' Jean got up to leave.

'Thanks a lot, Jean, you're a good friend.'

'Whist mon! Will ya be aboot tomorrow?'

'Unlikely. The school will just have to do without me.'

'Good for you. Be seeing ya then.'

'Cheers, Jean.'

She made her way out the door and I watched her enter the lift. As it disappeared, Vivienne emerged from the stairway access.

'What's the matter with the lift?'

'Nothing. Just part of my new exercise routine. How're you feeling?'

'Better, thanks to your pie.'

'So you tried it then?'

'Did more than try it,' I laughed.

'Glad you enjoyed it.' She turned to go into her apartment and then paused at the door. 'By the way, there was a young boy hanging around here last night. I hope you don't mind, but I called security.'

'No, that's okay. Would have done the same thing myself. I'll tell the school.'

'Take care.'

She disappeared into her apartment. I closed my door and cursed Yan Siang. I told him never to come to my apartment again, but it was like talking to a brick wall. It was time to let the school deal with the problem.

CHAPTER

14

I stayed home for the next two days, enjoying my recovery. The school panicked, especially Theresa Loh. I had three of their major examination papers. Finally on Friday I ventured forth.

When I walked into the office, the ladies were very concerned at my appearance. The cut on my face provided the most interest, but the new colouring around my eyes and nose also drew a number of tutters. Even Snake hissed out a few words of sympathy. They were all interested in the details of the attack, but were afraid to ask. That suited me.

As the bell sounded, announcing the end of flag-raising, Jean appeared and winked. 'How are yah? And how're you getting on wie yon new bodyguard?'

'He's doing a great job, I hardly see him. He arrives late and leaves early, but I'm grateful for his help, Jean.'

'Tosh! Dinna mention it. Hae ye heard aboot the latest lunacy?'

'What?'

'The principal wants us to try oot some new literature materials. There's a meeting in her office the noo.'

'No! With all the exams coming, how can we? I bet Theresa accepted this extra load on our behalf. Why is it that we're always the victims of someone else's stupidity?'

'Ah dinna ken!'

'Perhaps we're just too nice.'

'Dinny fret! Nice were yesterday, noo it's time for nasty! Am aboot to rearrange yon silly hinny's thinking!'

The principal was jiggling about impatiently when we arrived at her office. We entered silently and sat down on the four uncomfortable seats ranged in front of her desk.

'I presume Mrs Loh has given you the details of the new literature trial?' She was suddenly all smiles.

'Some,' I muttered.

'It's a wonderful opportunity for the school to be right at the cutting edge of this very important subject. Naturally, when I was asked, I knew we would all…'

'You knew *you* would. We had nothing to do with it,' I said bluntly.

'I beg your pardon, Mr Richards?'

'It's the wrong time to be trialling new materials. Our classes are all split up, preparing for their examinations.'

'And we have papers to supervise and scripts to mark. There'll no be time!' Jean added.

'The junior classes are still in session and the trials only involve the Secondary One students. They don't have examinations for another three weeks,' the principal countered.

Mrs Yap sighed and shook her head.

'I'll do the trialling with my classes, Mrs Benthusamy,' Theresa offered, oblivious to the fact that she was undercutting her three colleagues.

'Thank you, Mrs Loh. It's pleasing to see that at least one of my literature teachers is a true professional.'

'Thank you, Theresa,' I muttered sarcastically, 'you're a real gem!'

'Yah great saft tattie!' Jean bellowed at her. Theresa shrank back.

Mrs Yap sighed and shook her head some more.

I had to get out of that office before I said something I would later regret. Jean stumbled after me. We returned to the staff room without a word.

'What do yah think o' that?' Jean breathed heavily.

'I'm not surprised. You know what Theresa's like.

'Yes, but what aboot that ither stupid creature? Dithery aud coo! One o' these days she'll shake so much, yon head'll fall off.'

I laughed grimly. 'Oh, by the way, did you notice Neanderthal was missing?'

'Small loss.'

'I bet he lines up behind Theresa. He'll sneak into the Head's office later and offer his services, the sycophantic old shit!'

'He does nae have any junior lit classes!' Jean exclaimed.

'That won't stop him!' I retorted. There was a long pause. 'What really pisses me off is that we'll end up having to pilot the bloody scheme and Theresa Loh will take all the credit.'

'I'm no piloting any new scheme and that's that!'

We finished our coffee as the bell sounded the end of the first period, and the end of our unscheduled break.

Later, leaving my last class, I bumped into Yan Siang.

'Hello. I'm sorry I was out the other night when you called.' The boy looked a little sheepish. 'But what I said before still stands — you can't come to my apartment.'

'I know,' he grunted.

'That's good,' I replied, surprised by his response. I shifted the books around my good arm, trying to relieve the strain.

'I can carry your books to the staff room for you, sir.'

'That's very decent of you. Thanks.' I readily accepted, knowing it might be the only opportunity I would ever get to avail myself of his help. I handed the books over and he disappeared behind them. We walked across the landing to the stairs.

'There're a couple of things I'd like to ask you,' I continued.

'Maybe we talk outside school,' said the voice from behind the books.

'Where then?'

'Later.'

'Okay, but where?'

'Burger King in HollandVillage at two o'clock,' he breathed conspiratorially from the corner of his mouth.

'Are you sure? You're not exactly reliable.'

'Don't anyhow say, teacher, I can prove to you, you know!' he answered sternly.

I smiled at his Singlish as we arrived at the bottom of the stairs in silence. When we reached the staff room, he quickly thrust the books at me and scampered off before his friends could see him. I backed through the door, juggling the books so precariously I dropped two.

Jean stumbled across the room, swiping a wooden model of a volcanic formation off the desk of Mr Locke, the lower secondary geography master. Mr Locke did not know much about the world, but he was a dab hand with models. He was a likeable enough chap and very popular with the students, probably because he always told them what was in their geography paper shortly before the examination. His reasoning was perfectly simple — marking is easier, students get a real buzz as they all pass and no time is wasted going over the answers. Of course, when the students graduated to the upper secondary they found the real world considerably less generous.

Jean dumped her over-stuffed bag and prepared for an immediate departure.

'Lord knows how mony wee grey cells ah lost this morning. For sure ah hinny mony left!' she gasped, struggling to change her shoes.

'You off home then?'

'Aren't you?'

'I've got to check the exercises for tomorrow's remedial programme.'

'Bugger that. I'll no be takin' any damned remedial nonsense.' She pulled herself up and grabbed her handbag. 'Be seein' yah!'

'Have a good weekend.'

'Ta! Rojan'll be over a wee bit later tonight.'

'Why's that?' I grinned.

'Use your imagination, ma dear.'

'Gotcha!' I laughed as Jean bounced out the nearest door. I glanced at the clock. It was approaching one-thirty so I decided to pack up and leave for my rendezvous. Burger King... yuk! Mind you, sometimes their bacon burger was okay.

I left the 111 bus on Commonwealth Avenue and decided to walk the remainder of the way. It was a pleasant afternoon and I had ten minutes to spare. I crossed at the lights and proceeded up Holland Avenue with the towering HDB blocks on either side. Schoolchildren were heading home and youngsters played on the swings. Groups of aunties perched on the community benches beneath huge trees and talked and looked, while grey-haired men drooped and smoked.

I passed the large Holland Shopping Centre and walked on through the nauseating stench of Kentucky Fried to Burger King. It is a small restaurant with an upstairs section. I wandered in and looked around. There was no sign of Yan Siang. I climbed the stairs, but the eating floor was deserted. I returned to the main restaurant and ordered a drink. Then I positioned myself by the window so that I could see who was coming and going.

Time passed and there was still no sign of Yan Siang. I became impatient. It was imperative I got some answers from the source of all my trouble, and it looked like he was not going to show again.

Suddenly the door swung open and two Indian boys in Pleasant Park uniforms entered. They saw me and sniggered as they made their way to the counter. God, I would make Yan Siang pay for this! Having ordered their burgers, the boys crossed to my table and sat down.

'Good afternoon, teacher,' they chorused together, enjoying my discomfort.

'You not eating, teacher?' the taller boy asked.

'I'm waiting for someone.'

'Sorry, he's not coming, teacher,' the other boy spluttered, in between two bites of an enormous, over-stuffed bun.

'How do you know that?'

'Because he told me.' The boy almost choked on a rather hasty swallow.

'Why don't you finish your burgers and then tell me everything,' I suggested.

The boys chomped away happily for several minutes, while I impatiently drummed my fingers on the table.

Finally one boy wiped his mouth and grunted, 'He had to go home to visit his mother this afternoon.'

'Do you mean he hasn't been staying at home?'

'Cannot! His mother is very ill, lah!' the first boy explained earnestly.

'Crying and scolding every day. So Yan Siang go to a friend's house to stay,' the other boy contributed.

'Where?'

'Cannot say, sir!' the first boy declared.

'What do you mean you can't say? I'm his teacher, for goodness sake.'

'We know, but Yan Siang is in big, big trouble, lah!'

'Do you know what sort of trouble?'

'He cannot tell anyone. We think ha, it is something... but, sir, you cannot tell anyone. Promise? Something to do with money.'

'And sex, too! But, sir, you don't tell people we say so!' the other boy whispered nervously.

'How do you know all this?'

'We know,' they chorused together.

'Yan Siang said to us that he will see you later,' the first boy offered.

'Where?'

'Don't know.'

I was fast becoming frustrated with this pointless conversation. Clearly Yan Siang had let me down again and these two sparkling substitutes appeared to know little.

'Look, I must go. Thank you for meeting me. Go and buy yourselves a dessert.' I offered them a five dollar bill.

'Wah, thank you, teacher,' they again chorused together. As I left, I mused that with a little training those two could be a successful stage duo.

I walked out onto Holland Avenue and was halfway to the bus stop before I realised I had not had anything for lunch.

CHAPTER

15

I stopped off at Bukit Timah Plaza and had a minced pork sandwich at the Wishbone restaurant before continuing up to my apartment. My mailbox contained the usual array of bills and a letter from the folks in New Zealand, stuffed with newspaper cuttings. They loved to keep me up to date with the political situation. As I closed the box, I noticed a scrap of brown paper near the back. Scrawled across the centre in black ink were the words *You have been warned*. I was about to throw it in the rubbish bin when I decided to show it to Rojan. At least it was clear evidence that my situation was indeed real.

As I quick-stepped towards the lift, my luck turned. Around the corner, looking like a well-weathered little sparrow, shot Marilyn Farmley-Brown. No relation to the Farmley-Browns from Hawdon Lee Park, Surrey, but probably more closely connected to the Farmley-Browns of Brixton.

'Oh, oh, my dear Mr Richards. What a blessing it is to see you up and about. I was just telling Frederick… Frederick's my little pomeranian, you know, came from the same litter as Pollywog, the little daughter of the good Duchess of Devonshire, a spritely old matron who, by all accounts, gives the Duke a run for his money! It might have been the same litter, but there the similarity ends. Indeed it does. There is nothing provincial about Frederick's upbringing.' She paused for breath, placed both hands on her hips, and thrust her meagre bosom forward.

'I told Frederick about those beastly men who jumped you and how bravely you acquitted yourself against overwhelming odds.' Thank God for rumours and hyperbole! 'Gracious me, good, God-fearing Christian folk attacked by local heathens.'

She leaned forward, put an arm around my shoulder, and exhaled her foul-smelling breath directly into my face. 'It's all this gung-foo, you know, and tree-ards and such like. I told my Archibald that this is definitely his last contract! It's time we got back to civilisation.'

She patted my hand and beamed.

'But it's good to see you've recovered from your ordeal, my dear. Have you been taking soup? Bowls of soup? Good, thick steaming broth? That's the ticket.' She lunged at the steps and stumbled up two at a time. 'Tally-ho! Must get on. Nice to have had this little conversation!' Reaching the top, she disappeared into the lift.

I grabbed hold of the metal handrail and stood there for several minutes until my auditory and olfactory senses had fully recovered. While I hung there, I felt an overwhelming surge of sympathy for Archibald. According to a number of the residents, she could talk non-stop for several minutes, filling her pauses with such powerful gestures that very few listeners had ever successfully interrupted her flow. I personally believed that if anyone did get close enough to interrupt her, she would use her secret weapon and the oral contagion that struck the interruptee would render them thoroughly incapable.

After an uneventful afternoon and an early dinner, I finished a glass of chardonnay and ran a bath. I had barely slipped into the soothing water when the doorbell rang. Without question, this is definitely the worst thing that can happen to any bath-loving hedonist. I lay there hoping I had imagined the dreadful sound, but it rang again, this time with a little more urgency. I continued to lie back, hoping if I did not answer the wretched ringer would go away. It was bound to be some silly neighbour with an even sillier excuse. I continued to soak and for a few delicious moments nothing happened. Then the bell sounded a third time in one long and three short bursts. Bugger it! I would have to get out.

Seething with frustration, I donned my bathrobe and, still dripping, padded across the hall to the door. I glanced through the peephole and then staggered back against the wall with a mixture of shock, hatred, and burning wrath.

'Why, God? Why? What have I ever done to deserve this?' I glared skyward and realised the ceiling needed dusting.

Shaking, I opened the door. 'What the bloody hell are you doing here?'

Yan Siang shot under my outstretched arm into the apartment. Then pushing me to one side, he slammed the door shut and locked every bolt.

'Teacher, sorry! Some... someone's after me,' he panted heavily.

'Who's after you?'

'Two men. They follow me... all day and... and... I didn't know where... where to go. I... I...'

'So you just happened to find your way here!'

'I know... know, teacher, sorry.'

'Sorry doesn't cut it any more. I'm calling the police.'

I walked over to the phone and lifted the receiver. Suddenly there were voices outside the apartment. I dropped the phone and returned to the door where Yan Siang stood shivering. I glanced through the peephole and saw two men speaking to one of my neighbours. My God, the boy was telling the truth!

I looked at the terrified little figure and relented. 'Okay, I believe you. But there's nowhere to hide here.'

'I'm small, I can hide behind those… those windows.' He pointed across the room.

'Hell no! We're ten floors up.'

I looked around desperately. Nothing. I went into the bedroom. Still nothing. I mused at the puddle I was leaving on the tiles and my glance moved to the bathroom. Then it hit me. A couple of years before, I had returned home to find little white footprints from the bathroom, through the bedroom across to the main door. Apparently two young boys had slipped down the chute which houses the water pipes running between the floors. If they could come down it, Yan Siang might be able to clamber up the same chute.

'Listen, there is one chance.' I took him into the bathroom. Entry to the chute was via a long narrow door which I had wedged shut. I ran to the kitchen, grabbed a knife, and levered the door open.

'If you can climb up those pipes, you'll come to a door on the next floor. Hopefully, it'll be like this one and you'll be able to push it open. The tenants are nice people and I'm sure they'll let you out through their apartment, but don't scare them.'

'No problem, sir!' Yan Siang seemed calmer and more like his old self.

Suddenly the doorbell rang.

'Off you go. I'll distract the men for a while,' I said, feeling rather heroic.

Yan Siang stepped up to the cupboard. I grabbed his legs and gave him a push. He was about to move up, when he turned back, threw his arms around my neck, and breathed into my ear, 'Thank you, thank you, teacher!' He shoved a crumpled piece of paper into my hand.

'Give to Mama!'

'Get going!' I stammered.

He moved into the cupboard. I wedged the door shut and cleaned away the dust that had fallen onto the floor as someone started to thump on the door.

'Okay! Okay! Keep your hair on,' I yelled, refastening my robe.

I opened the door carefully, leaving the safety chain connected. 'What do you want?'

The two men looked as if they had just walked out of a Hong Kong gangster movie. They wore caps, pulled down over their eyes. One had a bandage around his head, while the other wore an eye-patch.

'Got see a kid?' one of the men questioned threateningly.

'What kid? There's no kid here.'

'No kid? Open the door, we want to check!'

'On whose authority? Do you have a warrant?'

One of the men leaned heavily on the door and the useless safety chain popped. I was thrown back against the wall as the pair forced their way in.

'You can't… can't just burst in here.' I stammered, sounding a lot less confident.

'Won't take long. Okay?'

I stood back, unwilling to cause any unnecessary aggravation, and watched them move about my apartment. Suddenly I realised there was something familiar about them.

'You'd better tell us where that boy, teacher!' the bandaged man called over his shoulder.

Teacher! It was them. These were the two bastards who had attacked me. I needed to get to the phone.

The man with the eye-patch moved to the kitchen cupboards, while his friend searched the bedroom. This was my chance. I stole carefully across the floor. Suddenly Eye-patch turned and saw me. He knew what I intended to do and, drawing a knife, moved to cut me off. However, he failed to see the puddle left on the floor and suddenly his feet shot from under him. With a resounding smack his bottom hit the tiles, driving the knife through his right hand. He shrieked and cursed with pain and anger as I reached the phone and called security. Drawn by the noise, his friend emerged from the bedroom.

'You'd better get lost. Security are on their way,' I announced smugly and shook the phone at them.

The pair did not hesitate. The bandaged villain helped his friend to his feet and they stumbled towards the door. I moved after them triumphantly, just as Rojan entered. The men stopped short, Rojan blocking their path. He spoke threateningly in a mixture of Chinese and Malay, but he need not have bothered. Both men shrunk visibly. They knew they were caught and, strangely, they seemed relieved. I took a cloth from the kitchen and gave it to Eye-patch to stop his cut hand pooling blood on the floor.

A security man arrived at the door and he and Rojan rough-handled the two would-be gangsters out to the lift. Suddenly I remembered Yan Siang.

I shone a torch up the chute, but there was no sign of him. He must have gotten out somehow. I secured the door and pulled the plug on my bath. My maid was coming in the next day so she could clean the rest of the mess.

I sat down for a breather and took out the piece of paper Yan Siang had given me. It was a scrappy little page, torn from a children's *little bobdog* book and covered in Chinese characters. Hardly the sort of thing you would expect a tough little nut like Yan Siang to carry about with him. Yet it seemed as if he had deliberately scratched the message down in order to pass it to me. Another bunch of trouble, no doubt. I decided to call Terence.

There was no reply from his cell phone, so I called Josie's apartment.

'Hello.'

'Hi, Terence.'

'What do you want?' he grumbled.

'Thanks very much. I'm feeling much better you'll be pleased to hear and I've got some good news.'

'What?'

'The police have caught the two thugs who beat me up.'

'How?'

I quickly explained the events of the past hour and ended with the triumphant capture of the intruders. Terence was silent.

'Are you still there?'

'Yessss!'

'I was wondering if you could do me another favour?'

'Oh, no. What?'

'I need to go to Yan Siang's flat. He gave me a message for his mother.'

'So, ask one of your teacher friends.'

'I can't do that. You know how they gossip! Look, I still owe you a trip to Spageddies. How about we visit the flat and then go on to dinner?'

'When?'

'Tomorrow night?'

'Done! Can I bring Josie?'

'Sure. Has her brother turned up yet?'

'No, and she's really worried.'

'That's no good.' I paused. 'I'll give you a call tomorrow to confirm everything.'

The phone clicked and I walked over to draw the bedroom drapes.

Far below, I saw a tiny figure frantically waving up at me. I stared, perplexed, and then realised it was Yan Siang. I waved back and the figure began to jump about, thrusting his hands in the air with V for victory gestures. I roared with laughter and excitement. The little beggar had actually escaped!

CHAPTER

16

Another Saturday morning and another rehearsal, but for once I was pleasantly surprised. My trusty deputy, Ronald Phua, had been rehearsing the cast while I was absent, and today we had a full turnout to welcome me back. All the main characters had dropped their scripts and even the weaker ones had been working hard on their parts. Perhaps we would have a credible entry after all. Ron was a bright young art teacher, with crazy, original ideas which would eventually take him to the top. A quiet type who kept his own counsel, the administration and their deficiencies never bothered him.

After lunch, Maisie Tay arrived to fit the costumes and we concluded the rehearsal mid-afternoon. I phoned Terence and made a quick get-away.

The Ang Mo Kio Interchange was packed with people and it took me a while to spot him.

'You okay? You don't look too good,' I said.

'I haven't been sleeping very well,' Terence croaked.

'It sounds as if you have a cold.'

'Probably.'

'Where's Josie?'

'She couldn't make it. Something about work.' He sneezed and coughed.

'Are you sure you're up to this?'

'No, I'm not!' he snorted. 'Let's just get it over and done with.'

We moved off to the 269 bus stop and took a bus to Avenue 6. I had written down the block number and the Chang flat was on the top floor. We went as far as we could in the lift and walked up the last flight of stairs. Flowering trees in pots, hanging lanterns, and empty bird cages cluttered the corridor, with little rows of shoes sitting outside each doorway. The Changs' apartment appeared clean and neat. Two faded rugs hung across the concrete balustrade, and to the left of the doorway a blue porcelain stool supported a basket drooping deep, scarlet orchid blooms.

'That must be where the father fell,' I whispered to Terence, indicating the rugs.

We knocked on the door. There was no response. We knocked again. Finally the door opened a fraction. I could see a pair of eyes in the gloom, but little else.

'We would like to speak to Mrs Chang, please,' I enunciated in clear, formal English. Terence repeated my request in Chinese.

'Mrs Chang no in,' an elderly voice croaked.

'This must be the grandmother. Tell her we have a note from Yan Siang.'

Terence again spoke to the old lady in Chinese. A thin, bony arm shot out and grabbed the paper from my fingers. The door closed. I shrugged at Terence and we moved off down the corridor. We had almost reached the stairway, when a cracked old voice called after us.

'She wants us to go back, I think,' Terence explained.

We returned to the old woman, who was holding a small envelope which she thrust at me as I neared her.

'What's this?' I asked, intrigued.

'For you. For you. Give you!' the old lady nodded furiously.

'You'd better read what was on that note,' I said to Terence. He asked for the paper and it was hesitantly handed over.

'*Mother, to give teacher packet from under God Statue,*' Terence translated.

'I don't want any packet.' I tried to give it back, but the old lady would have none of it. She finally slammed the door and left us stranded.

'What's in it?' Terence asked.

I opened the packet and pulled out a small computer disk.

'What the hell's that?' he whispered.

'The source of all our trouble?'

'Get rid of it!'

'Why? Don't you want to know what's on it?'

Terence moved away. 'Whatever is on that disk, it has nothing to do with us. It's absolutely none of our business.'

'How can you say that? One of my students instructed his mother to give it to me. Clearly Yan Siang wants me to know what's on it.'

'Great! Then you take it home and you have a look at it. But whatever you learn, keep it to yourself. I don't want to know about it.'

'C'mon, Terence. You know full well that I'll need a password to get into the disk and the information is probably encoded. You're the best computer whiz I know. Actually, you're the only computer whiz I know. I need you to take a look at the disk.'

'And get my head kicked in for my trouble? Are you hard of hearing? I don't want any part of that bloody thing.'

Without realising it, we had walked down six flights of stairs and now Terence stopped by the lift. We waited in silence. Finally it arrived, carrying one passenger and his bicycle. We reached the ground and walked out to Avenue 6.

He still wore black jeans and a dark jacket, but tonight no cap covered his thick, bleached hair. As he watched the two men leave the block and cross the road, he pulled out a cell phone, dialed a number, and stood rubbing his fingers on his belt while the call went through.

'They've just left that address and they're waiting for a taxi,' he grunted into the phone. 'Do you want me to follow them?' The reply was clearly in the negative. 'Done!'

He looked around, checked that no one was watching, and then mounted his motorbike, gunned the engine, and took off in the opposite direction.

'Let's taxi in to Tanglin,' I suggested.

'I don't feel like Spageddies,' Terence groaned.

'We might as well take a taxi anyway. I can drop you off at Braddell.'

'Thanks.'

It took us a while to flag down a taxi. Once on board, I sat staring at the disk in my hand. It looked quite ordinary, with no label. 'Aren't you just a little bit curious?' I tempted Terence.

'No way!' He sat with his arms folded, staring out the window. Now and again he threw me a sideways glance, but he continued to feign indifference.

'Such a challenge! Who knows what little tricks this disk could contain,' I taunted. It was like waving a bottle of whisky in front of an alcoholic. Finally Terence turned.

'Give it here!' he sighed. He turned the disk over in his fingers and shook it gently. 'It may take me a while, depends on the format. Still, it looks simple enough.'

'And you love a challenge! Thanks, mate, I owe you one!'

'You owe me a big one! No more Spageddies. Next time it's the Westin Plaza Compass Rose!'

'Done!'

'We should probably hand this to the police.'

'No way. It could contain private family information.'

'Yeah, and there goes another flying pig!'

We both laughed like two kids with a new toy. I watched the trees and iron fences flash past, gilded by the late afternoon sun. We cruised along MacRitchie Reservoir where the runners were completing their circuits. Finally, we reached Braddell and I watched him cross the road. It was good to have a friend like Terence, someone you could trust, a person who knew all your peculiarities and accepted them. He shrugged and waved as the taxi moved on.

CHAPTER

17

After all the excitement of the past few days, I needed a complete break and Sentosa was it. Ming Chuan and I caught bus 61 at our usual stop and enjoyed the ride down to the World Trade Centre. From there we caught the cable car. We had a little cabin all to ourselves, and I held my breath as the car swung out and left us suspended hundreds of feet above ships of all sizes. Below to our left was Keppel Harbour, while out to the right were ferry terminals and beyond these, Indonesia.

We left the cable car, walked past the wildly colourful dragon thrashing about just outside Cable Car Plaza, and turned down to the monorail which circles the island. After a short wait, we entered a little car with three Japanese tourists who were clearly enjoying their experience. The train traveled slowly, winding its way through lush bush, down to the edge of the sea which curled slowly over a rocky shore and up past roughly-hewn stone figures to Underwater World. It paused for disembarking passengers, then continued up a steep incline to Fort Siloso where heavy grey guns still point out towards the sea like long, dead fingers.

Our silent, snake-like progress continued down past Rasa Sentosa — the famous resort which caters to a richly discerning clientele, on to the lagoon and beaches. Here we decided to get off and walk. It was a sultry afternoon with a light wind. Out beyond the lagoon on the edge of the horizon lay dozens of ships, testimony to Singapore's reputation as one of the busiest ports in the world.

Tall palm trees rustled and the lagoon appeared tantalisingly inviting in the heat. Two lovers passed on a tandem, while youngsters shot by on rollerblades. Around the edge of the lagoon, tourists stretched out on towels and a lonely young man wearing a Corrective Work Order lazily gathered up pieces of litter. Out to our left a group of fit, young Malay boys kicked around a soccer ball, watched by a group of noisy girls seated on the grass. We wandered on.

Suddenly, shrieks and yells shattered the calm. Further along the beach, three guys were taunting a group of young girls while a distraught older woman was desperately trying to separate them. It took a while before I realised they were Pleasant Park students, and the older woman was none other than my old friend Daisy Liew. What was she doing on Sentosa?

'Give that back to me this instant,' she shrieked at one of the boys.

'Come and get it!' the boy cheekily replied.

As I got nearer, I could see the boys were taunting Mrs Liew, not the girls. They had rolled her tie-around blouse into a ball, which they were using in a game of catch.

'I'd better go over and help the old girl,' I sighed.

We crossed the road and walked down onto the beach. Upon seeing me, the boys hastily returned the blouse to Mrs Liew. I recognised them and they knew it. Two were from my form class and the third looked like one of Jean's little darlings. She would be delighted.

'Mark and Li Wei, come here!' The boys slowly walked over. 'What were you doing?'

'It was only some fun, teacher,' Li Wei muttered, trying to hide a grin.

'That's strange. Mrs Liew didn't seem to think it was very funny,' I replied.

'Sorry, sir,' Mark offered.

'I think you'd better go back and apologise to Mrs Liew.'

'Yes, teacher.'

Li Wei was a good student and although Mark could be a handful, their fun was generally harmless. However, I felt their choice of target on this occasion was unfortunate. I watched the boys approach the old harridan who stood with her back to them. As the boys apologised, she turned and hit Li Wei across the face with a blow that sent him reeling backwards onto one of his friends. Shocked, I moved swiftly across to the group.

'Hi there, Mrs Liew, fancy meeting you here,' I laughed, quickly pulling her aside.

'You can't strike a student. That's assault!' I hissed at her.

'How dare you threaten me! I know they are your students. Ever since we arrived they've followed us around, making a nuisance of themselves. I suppose you put them up to it!'

'Don't be absurd. I had no idea they were here. Besides, Jennifer is Mark's girlfriend and she probably invited him along.'

'Oh no, don't try to shift the blame onto my girls. This was a perfectly innocent outing and now it's been ruined. I'm going to tell the principal. This time she'll have to do something!'

'You can tell the principal anything you like, but you'd better pray Li Wei's parents don't make a formal complaint.'

'You haven't heard the last of this, believe me!' She stormed off in the direction of her girls. Jennifer had left the group and was attempting to console Li Wei, while Mark and the other boy adopted a threatening stance off to the right.

I walked over to them.

'It serves you right for picking on that old tigress!' I scolded Li Wei. Then I noticed the back of his head was bleeding. He must have caught it as he fell.

'She had no right to hit me, teacher,' Li Wei sobbed.

'Well you did provoke her,' I replied, trying to defend the indefensible. I walked Li Wei over to a nearby bench.

'Is he all right?' Ming Chuan whispered, joining us.

'He'll live. I think you'd better go hide in case that old bitch sees us together.'

It was at this point, when I thought things could not get much worse, that they did.

'Don't look now, but we're in trouble,' Ming Chuan warned.

'Why?' I asked, turning around.

'Guess who's just arrived!'

Then I saw them. 'Oh God, it's not!'

'I'm afraid it is.'

Strutting across the field like two perfectly preened pea-hens were Lucy and Lulu. Actually their real names were Jeremy and Anthony, and they were two of the most charming young guys Ming Chuan knew. Of course, that was when they appeared as men. Once the pair donned drag, everything changed. Their hips sashayed, their lips pouted thickly in red or purple, their hair assumed staggering colours and breathtaking proportions, and their conversation was overlayed with camp innuendo.

'Hello, darlings,' Lucy blared as she drew nearer. 'Give us a bump!' We swayed our hips together and bumped. I could see Mrs Liew in the distance, her eyes on stalks and her mouth ajar.

'Mingy, my dear, give us a kiss!' Lulu gushed and grabbed Ming Chuan in a tight embrace.

'Ooooohhhh, the boy's bleeding! What's yah been doin', Pete?' Lucy shrieked as she saw Li Wei's wound.

'Don't be such a bitch, girl!' Lulu interrupted, hitting her with her hand bag.

'Here, put this round it, dear.' Lucy removed a handkerchief from her bra and bound it around the boy's head.

'Who are these people?' Li Wei asked astonished.

I ignored the question.

'Ohhhh, my poor darling, you need to see a doctor,' Lulu gushed.

'So do you, girl,' Lucy laughed.

'Shut up, yah jealous cow!' Lulu gave Lucy such a push that she reeled over, caught her heel on a branch, and landed on her knees.

'Ah… yah… what yah done! Look at my knickers now!'

'Oooooohhhh… no one wants to look at your knickers, girl.'

I grabbed Lulu and pulled her to one side.

'Normally you guys are fun, but we've got school kids here. Before my career goes completely down the gurgler, do us a favour. Take your friend and bugger off.'

'Come on, girl,' Lulu pouted to Lucy. '"We'd better go.'

With a broken heel, Lucy hobbled off down the pavement. Suddenly she slipped and they both started to laugh. By the time they reached the main road, they were hooting hysterically and falling all over each other.

As they disappeared I turned to Ming Chuan. 'We'll have to take the boy to have his head checked. I think there's a first aid unit back at Cable Car Plaza.'

By the time we boarded the monorail, Li Wei had calmed down considerably and was enjoying all the attention. Mark was still angry about the incident and I knew I would have to reason with him before we parted. The other boy seemed to have mysteriously disappeared.

Li Wei had suffered quite a deep cut, but the clinic accepted my Civil Service Card and waved the cost of the stitches and bandaging. After the treatment, I shouted the boys coney dogs and drinks at the local A & W restaurant.

'Listen, I want you guys to forget about that business with the girls.'

'Why?'

'Because the girls will back Mrs Liew and they'll claim you were causing trouble in the first place.'

'But we were only saboing her.'

'Well, she isn't the sort of person you should sabo and when she tells the principal about it, they may call it bullying. It would be best if you said nothing.'

Reluctantly they agreed, but I was to live to regret that advice!

The boys went off to buy ferry tickets, while Ming Chuan and I walked back towards the cable car station.

A vaporous twilight enveloped the island and as the lights came on, we found ourselves in a magic wonderland.

'Let's walk down to the Merlion and see the musical fountains,' Ming Chuan suggested.

I laughed and embraced him, turning towards the avenue of flowers. When we first met, Sentosa was one of our favourite meeting places and we enjoyed many a romantic evening amongst the gardens and shrubbery.

The approach to the newly built Merlion reminds one of the gardens at Versailles. Lights colour the surrounding trees and glittering sparks thrown from the many fountains scatter across the changing shadows. Central to everything, the massive statue of the Merlion rears up in white and shoots laser beams from its dark eye sockets. With the head of a lion and the tail of a fish, this creature from Singapore's past stands as its symbol for the future.

To our left lay the amphitheatre where the musical fountains play twice nightly. The audience sits on circular stone seats and watches groups of water jets, bathed in radiant splashes of colour, dance and leap in time to popular music. Lasers, including those from the Merlion, streak across the sky and draw fiery outlines on the blackness. It is an awesome experience.

The show was halfway through when we took our seats. Youngsters shrieked, visitors marvelled, and the elderly just smiled contentedly.

'It's a great show!' The voice of Raymond Chia startled me. 'We're not bad, are we?' he beamed. 'I mean we Singaporeans!'

I turned around to face him. 'In this field, you're amongst the best in the world.' He was sitting with a very beautiful young Chinese girl. 'Do you often come to Sentosa?'

'Not a lot,' he answered. 'But when I have a day off, I like to get as far away from the centre as I can. What about you?'

'It's too expensive to come here often, though it's a great diversion now and again.'

We sat staring at the watery display for several minutes.

'How's your young student, our mutual friend?'

'Don't know,' I lied. 'I haven't seen him lately.'

'He's still said nothing about his father's accident?'

'Nothing.'

'Strange.'

'Why?'

There was no answer.

Suddenly the performance ended in a crashing crescendo of spray and sound.

'We heard two thugs had been picked up at your apartment and Ling was wondering what they were doing there.'

'Ling?' I asked, stalling for time. So they knew about the incident in my apartment, but how much did they know?

'Detective Ling. You met him at Tanglin,' Chia explained. 'What were those two after?'

'Just another threat.'

'You sure?'

'Of course I'm sure. I even found a warning note in my letterbox.'

'Funny, that. They turn up to threaten you and get arrested. A bit odd, don't you think? They're either very stupid or suicidal!' He paused as we watched the audience shrinking. 'I think there was more to it.'

'Oh yeah? You always think there's more to it!'

'One of the men, the one with the nasty eye, told us they were looking for your young student. He said the kid had been hanging out at your place.'

'Well he's a bloody liar!' I jumped up and moved off.

'Okay, okay! No need to get angry. I'm on your side, you know.' He helped his lady friend to her feet. 'But I thought you should know that the injuries those guys had were given to them by their boss. A reward for failing to follow instructions.'

'Injuries?'

'One had an eye cut out and the other lost both his ears. Nasty piece of work.' Chia leaned closer and whispered, 'If their boss is prepared to do that to his hired help, just think what he might do to a foreigner!'

Ming Chuan looked at me in horror and I smiled limply. 'Well, you've got your thugs. Get them to rat on their boss and you'll close up the whole operation. I'm out of the picture.'

'That's wishful thinking. You won't be out of the picture until your student gives us the information we need. That pair of losers won't tell us anything. Not while their noses and tongues are still attached.'

I pulled Ming Chuan along the row and walked up the steps, leaving the policeman and his lady behind. I was so angry I did not even bother to say goodnight. We walked down to the cable car station in silence. For this I was grateful. I could feel the fear emanating from Ming Chuan in waves. As we stood waiting for a cabin, he turned to me with troubled eyes.

'You must get rid of that disk.' I squeezed his hand and nodded. 'I really love you,' he said in a husky voice.

'I know you do,' I whispered, stopping the tear on his cheek with my finger.

CHAPTER

18

I was about to leave for school when Terence called. He had spent most of Sunday working on the disk, but had made little progress. As I anticipated, he loved the challenge.

The driver of bus 111 swerved to avoid a cyclist and I swung across the aisle and collided with an elderly lady who sat down on a young student. The boy was so embarrassed he immediately surrendered his seat to the old lady, who took it ungraciously. On the window above her head was a poster exhorting citizens to be courteous. How I love these little ironies. As I swung back into position, I thought over the events of the past few days. There was little doubt the disk was dangerous, but to whom? Until we had some idea of what it contained, it was unsafe to give it to anybody. If Yan Siang was at school, I would corner him and demand an explanation. But judging by my success in this area to date, it was unlikely that I would learn much.

The bus accelerated into the school bus stop and ground to a halt as Jean pulled up in a taxi. She offered me a lift, during which I outlined my adventures on Sentosa.

Throughout the day I kept an eye out for Yan Siang and finally caught him at the end of his maths period. He had failed to appear for his English lesson, but I knew he was in the school — his little friends had ratted on him. So I waited outside his maths room and grabbed his arm as he came out. I marched him up to the top floor to a quiet spot overlooking the canal which bordered the school.

'Okay, I want some answers!' The boy just glared at me coldly.

'C'mon, Yan Siang. I helped you the other night.' I paused.

'By the way, I'm pleased you got away. You'll be happy to know that those thugs are now cooling their heels in a police cell.'

'What? Police cell? Good good, teacher!' he sang happily.

'Why were those men chasing you?'

'I don't know,' he answered feebly.

'C'mon, Yan Siang, I picked up the package. Do you know what's on the disk?'

'What... what disk?'

'You mean you don't know what was in the package?'

'No.'

'How did you know it was there then?'

'My father told me he put it there. It was his.'

I suddenly felt cold. 'You mean this disk has something to do with The Flaming Dragon?' He nodded. 'Is that why those men were chasing you?'

'They are my father's friend.'

'Then your father had some very strange friends.' I stepped across to the balcony and stood beside him, staring out over the netball courts.

Finally I whispered, 'What happened the night of your father's accident?' He stiffened. 'Somebody pushed him, didn't they? A big man like your father? A high concrete barrier? He didn't just fall, did he? Why don't you tell me what you saw?'

He turned to me, his eyes glazed with tears. A hand shot up to wipe away a stray drop. How young he looked. I swallowed heavily. No one this young should have to go through what this kid was, carrying around some secret piece of knowledge that he was too afraid to speak about.

'Why can't you tell me what happened?' He looked away again. 'Does your mother know?' He shook his head. 'But you do?' Silence. 'C'mon, Yan Siang, I may be able to help you.' I put my hand on his shoulder. 'Can't we just be friends?' He shrugged my offer away.

Suddenly three girls panted up the stairs. They paused, saw us, and raced away giggling. I was so engrossed that I failed to recognise three members of Mrs Liew's damned netball team. Yan Siang sniffed heavily and began to walk towards the stairs.

'If the people at this Flaming Dragon place think you've still got the package, they'll come after you again. Next time they could hurt your mother, or your grandmother. What about your little sister? Aren't you worried about her?'

The boy paused at the top of the stairs. 'Of course. That's why I'm not staying at home.'

'They can still find you! Get real, Yan Siang, these men aren't playing games!'

He glanced at me then disappeared down the stairs, his final words bouncing off the walls, 'I know!'

CHAPTER
19

A week later, I found myself mid-morning Tuesday standing in the school hall while the Secondary Four students sat their first mathematics paper. It had been a rather uneventful week.

Terence had struggled with the disk, but was unable to break the code. Finally he persuaded a friend, whose father is a Singapore Broadcasting Corporation director, to help him get to the SBC's computers. I was still waiting to hear if they had been successful.

Yan Siang had disappeared. I asked a colleague who spoke Chinese to phone his home, but even his mother had no idea where he was.

The lit trialling had gone ahead and, true to form, Theresa kept forgetting to give her class the correct texts, so the rest of us had to cover for her. Jean was thoroughly fed up. To cap it all off, the English composition paper had been completed and we were all up to our eyeballs in marking.

The clock ticked on. Finally the examination finished and the answer scripts were collected. I headed back to more marking in the staff room. I could hear Jean grumbling from behind a huge pile of papers before I reached my desk.

'Having fun?' I called over the 'wall'.

'Ay yah! Ay've never read sich drivel!' Considering Jean had said the same thing the previous year and the year before that, the drivel had to be getting better.

I sank into my chair and looked unhappily at the pile facing me. 'What's it like having Rojan back?' Since the capture of the thugs, I had been on my own.

'Exhausting!'

'Ah yoi, yah brazen hinny!' I joked.

We laughed and reluctantly settled down to mark. I had barely read three compos before the bell went.

'Time for a coffee,' I yawned, getting up.

'Sooooory, I've got an examination,' Jean answered very seriously.

'Mr Richards, the vice-principal would like to see you,' Mr Nethander whispered as he slipped past me into the staff room. Just my luck, I thought as I changed direction.

Snake sat in her office, walls covered in laminated aphorisms and jingoistic cliches, on one of the highest-backed chairs I had ever seen. She resembled an imperial wizard in her flowing cheongsam and high hairdo.

'Come in, Richards.' Serious tone, serious business.

'Good morning, Mrs Lee. That's a very attractive shade of pink,' I ventured, sitting in one of the two vacant chairs.

'Thank you.' Although she fixed me with a steely gaze, I could not help noticing how pretty she was.

'I am a little uncertain as to how to proceed.' She rubbed her fingers nervously and proffered a smile. 'It's the first time I've had to deal with anything like this.' An uncomfortable pause. 'We'd best wait for Mrs Loh. Mr Nethander has gone to fetch her.'

Several minutes passed before a breathless Theresa panted her way into the room and stood to the right of my chair. Nethander slid in beside her.

'The reason we have asked you here... is to speak to you...

or rather to discuss several complaints we have received about certain recent… goings-on.'

'Goings-on?' I laughed. She must have heard about my assault.

'We have had a complaint from two parents and an anonymous stranger regarding your relationship with a student. A boy in your form class. Yan Siang.'

My levity evaporated.

'The accusation… I mean claim, is that this boy, Yan Siang, spent a night in your apartment.' Snake paused and smiled nervously.

I was dumbfounded. Where had this come from? That damned kid must have boasted to his bloody friends.

'As a matter of fact, he did spend a night in my apartment,' I stated openly.

'In your bed?' Snake smirked.

'Oh dear!' Theresa gasped, covering her mouth with her hand, while Nethander shifted his weight awkwardly.

I ignored the vice-principal's barb. 'The boy was tired, scared, lonely, and…'

'Vulnerable?' she offered.

'Yes, he was vulnerable,' I agreed coldly.

'So you offered him warmth and compassion. Anything else?'

I stood up, angered by the unwarranted suggestion. 'I don't appreciate the line you're taking with this.'

'Sit down, Mr Richards. I want to resolve this business amicably. We're all friends and colleagues here.'

Friends and colleagues? I looked around the room. Snake was definitely no friend. Theresa lacked any sort of stomach for this sort of thing and experience had taught me that one could never depend on her for support. And as for Nethander, he would sniff in whichever direction the principal's wind was blowing! But, where was the principal?

'Where is Mrs Benthusamy? Shouldn't she be in on this?' I asked.

'Mrs Benthusamy is in Canada on a two-week orientation course. As acting principal it falls to me to deal with this matter,' Snake answered grimly. 'Mr Richards, I appreciate these accusations are upsetting...'

'Upsetting? You're accusing me of sleeping with a young boy and...'

'No one said you were in the bed, Mr Richards,' the vice-principal smiled evenly.

Damn! If anyone was keeping the score, I was falling well behind on points!

'I refuse to discuss this matter any further, until I've had proper legal advice.'

'Legal advice? Does this really have to go that far?' the vice-principal murmured gently.

'Mrs Lee, you can't possibly believe that Peter... Mr Richards, behaved as these people suggest? He has a girlfriend and... I know he wouldn't do such a thing!' Theresa's naivete was marvellous, God bless her! She really thought she knew me.

'It's not a matter of what I do or do not believe, Mrs Loh. Complaints have been received and I have a professional duty to deal with them. If I don't, the Ministry of Education will. I invited Mr Richards in here, with witnesses, so that we could reach a friendly resolution of this unfortunate matter. It's clear I was wrong. Now I will have to inform the School Advisory Council.'

'Do what you must, but be aware these allegations border on defamation,' I warned.

'Not when they can be proved, Richards. And these are not all. We haven't touched on Mrs Liew's statement yet.' She stood up and drew a file from the metal cabinet behind her table.

'Here we are,' she said, unfolding a white sheet, '... unnaturally familiar with a young man... cavorting with two men in women's clothes... injuring a student... embracing a boy in a secluded corner of the school...'

'I refuse to listen to any more of this rubbish!' I pushed my chair back and stormed to the door. 'But a word of warning. You'd better check all these fairy tales very thoroughly. Sometimes, witch-hunts do lead to the burning of the right witches!'

'Don't threaten me, Richards! You will hear from the council in due course.'

I left the room, shaking with anger.

'Let's go for a coffee,' Theresa suggested.

Once in the canteen, I dropped onto a bench opposite Nethander while Theresa went up to get the drinks.

'Wheww… that's some list of complaints. Where did they all come from?' Nethander was obviously still getting over the shock, poor man! He still thought 'gay' was a state of well-being!

'It's a mixture of exaggeration, hearsay, and downright lies!' I replied.

Theresa returned with the coffee and a pineapple tart to cheer me up. Good old Theresa, she did have her moments.

'What are you going to do?' she asked.

'What can I do?'

'Get legal advice, and I know just the person.' Theresa pulled out a pen and pad and scrawled a name and address across the top sheet. 'I'll call her tonight.'

'Are you sure?'

'Perfectly.'

'It's very generous of you, Theresa, thanks.'

'Call and make an appointment.'

'It'll stir up a hornet's nest. The Ministry hates teachers with lawyers!' Nethander muttered. He sipped his coffee and burnt his lip.

'Tough. The Ministry is not my priority at the moment. God, what a mess!'

'I see you've had your stitches removed,' Theresa observed,

judiciously changing the subject.

'Last Friday,' I confirmed.

There was a long pause, finally broken by Nethander, 'But what's in Mrs Liew's statement?'

'C'mon, give me a break! Daisy Liew is a nasty old bitch who's been gunning for me for weeks.'

'Her netball girls will stick by her, you know what they're like,' Theresa offered unhelpfully.

'What happens when it goes to the SAC?' I asked cautiously.

Nethander looked at me. 'You'll be called to a hearing with witnesses and the matter will be examined. If they feel the allegations have merit you'll be suspended pending a fuller investigation, at the end of which they'll decide whether to make your suspension permanent.'

'And that would mean goodbye contract, goodbye Singapore!' I muttered.

'Worse, they'll bring in the police.'

'It's never going to get that far. Stop scaring him, Nethander,' Theresa scolded.

We finished our coffee and I wandered back to the staff room. I desperately wanted to get away from the bloody place, but I knew I could not leave until the exams were over. The rest of the day I dragged myself around the school. On the final bell, I returned to the staff room to find an official-looking envelope lying on top of my marking. I tore it open and discovered that I was summoned to a special meeting of the SAC at two o'clock Friday. Boy, they did not waste any time!

I reached my apartment completely bushed. Time for a glass of Lindeman's Cavarra Shiraz Cabernet 1996. I relaxed on the sofa inhaling the spicy aroma and staring into the flaming colour. Gradually I felt better. I decided to call Terence, but there was no reply.

I pulled Theresa's note from my wallet and read the scrawl:

Miss Leo Shau Wee — Toh, Lee & Jefferson,
Barristers and Solicitors
Free and fast if you quote my name

— Theresa

Suddenly the phone rang. Terence!

'I think I've… I mean we've broken the code.'

'Great! Can we meet?'

'Tonight? No way, I'm too tired! How about tomorrow night?'

'Okay, but where?'

'Josie has invited me to have dinner with her family in Clementi. How about outside that restaurant on the corner of Pandan Way, opposite the army camp?'

'I'll be there. Don't be late!'

'You should talk! Good work, by the way!'

I replaced the receiver. Finally some good news. Time for another glass of wine!

CHAPTER

20

If it had not been for Jean, I would have been unable to face school. I fancied everybody knew about the scandal, although no one mentioned it. Perhaps I was just paranoid. But Jean took me under her wing and proved a capable distraction.

At one, I took a taxi to the enormous Concourse building in Beach Road. Earning the designer an international award, this amazing construction juts out at various angles, its daring metal struts and unconventional buttressing make it an eye-catching landmark. The offices of Toh, Lee & Jefferson occupy the eastern corner of the twelfth floor and, true to form, there was nothing modest about Theresa's lawyers. Two frosted glass doors, with gold lettering featuring the partners' names, opened into an expansive reception area.

A secretary escorted me down a long corridor with clerical bays and offices off to both sides.

Miss Leo's office oozed success. A large desk, flanked by two comfortable chairs, sat before a huge, angled window which afforded one the most panoramic views of the bay area I have ever seen. Original works by Singapore artists hung on each wall. In the centre of the room a designer suite surrounded a glass table set on three small marble pillars. A tray supporting a large coffee pot and three cups had been placed on one end of the table, while two plates of dainty Chinese cookies sat temptingly on the other.

'Mr Richards, so pleased to meet you. Please take a seat over here.' Miss Leo indicated the designer sofa, but I preferred one of the plushly stuffed armchairs, fearing if I sank into the sofa I might never be able to get up again.

Miss Leo Shau Wee wore a Chanel suit with an emerald clasp pinning a Cartier scarf to her left lapel. She had flowing black hair which swept across her shoulders in a way that would have graced any shampoo advertisement. Her flawless skin, complimented by delicately applied makeup, set off dark, intelligent eyes and full lips.

'Would you like a cup of coffee?'

'I'd prefer tea,' I replied. A legal secretary left discreetly to brew my tea as Miss Leo spread herself across the sofa.

'This really is a most unfortunate matter. I find it hard to understand why the school has failed to deal with it in a more reasonable manner.' She picked up one of the plates and offered me a cookie.

'Yesterday evening Theresa phoned me and outlined your position. This morning I called the school and explained that I would be acting on your behalf.' She paused and smiled, 'I hope you don't mind my being a little proactive.'

'Not at all,' I answered, smiling to myself as I imagined Snake's face when she got the call.

'I had to move quickly because we have very little time before Friday.'

'What about your fee?'

'Oh, Mrs Loh is taking care of that. The bill will be sent to her husband's company and, believe me, it will be lost in their accounting department. They are one of our biggest clients and it's a pleasure to help one of their friends.'

Good old Theresa, so what if she was a bit strange. I began to feel guilty about suspecting her commitment in the first place. The secretary returned with my tea, plus a jug of milk and a bowl of sugar. This time she was clearly taking no chances.

'Let's get down to business. I need to hear your side of the story, Mr Richards. Please tell me everything.'

'Everything?' I asked nervously. She nodded. 'Very well. I live with a young Chinese guy for starters.'

'I take it Theresa doesn't know this? She has you down as completely straight, God-fearing, honest…'

'The God-fearing bit is right and I'm reasonably honest, I suppose.'

'Do many people know about this young Chinese man?'

'Only a few close friends.'

'Keep it that way! If the opposition finds out, it could severely damage our case.'

'I am not ashamed of my friend, Miss Leo.'

'Don't misunderstand me, Mr Richards. Your sexual orientation is no concern of mine. I am speaking purely as your lawyer. Homosexuality is still illegal in this country, and if it became known that you were involved in such a relationship, it would make the ridiculous allegations you face more believable.'

'I understand.'

'Tell me about this Yan Siang.'

'There's nothing much to tell. He's a student in my form class. He saw his father fall from their HDB balcony and naturally it's affected him rather badly.'

'You feel sorry for him?'

'I didn't initially. The little beggar has been a bloody nuisance in my class.'

'I see.' She paused. 'According to the allegations, he spent a night at your apartment, sleeping in your bed.'

'That's true, he did. But there was nothing wrong with it. It was very late. He phoned his mother and she agreed.'

'Are you sure? Did you speak to the mother?'

'Of course not, I can't speak Chinese. Why do you ask?'

Miss Leo flipped through the file she was holding and stopped at a marked page. 'Here it is. According to one of the complaints, the boy's mother knew nothing about his intention to stay at your apartment.' She paused and looked at me for a response.

'That's impossible. I was there when Yan Siang spoke to her over the phone.'

'There was no one else in your apartment? No one who could verify what you're saying?'

'Nobody,' I muttered.

'Then we have to grill the boy. Is there any reason he wouldn't tell the truth?'

'I don't think so.'

'The second complaint is from a Mrs Supraniam. Do you know her?'

'No.'

'I made some inquiries and it seems that she has two sons — Nadi and Haji, friends of Yan Siang. You gave them a treat in Burger King about ten days ago.'

'So that's who they were. Yes, you're right, I did meet them in Burger King. But why should their mother complain?'

'Could be she found out that Yan Siang stayed in your apartment and now she fears for her own kids.'

'The old bitch!'

'Mr Richards, you're dealing with very ordinary people here. They're good souls usually, but capable of doing enormous damage if they get the wrong picture.'

'How do we challenge all this?'

'Once we discredit the mother's complaint, the second one should disappear.'

'What about the stranger?'

'Oh, you mean the so-called third complaint… made over the phone by an unidentified man? I wouldn't worry about that one. Your vice-principal was a little carried away when she attached any importance to it. Unless he comes forward and makes an open statement that we can challenge, his complaint will be set aside.'

Finally some good news. This lady knew her stuff. Beneath the warm exterior I sensed a core of steel.

'Now, let's deal with Mrs Liew. Can you describe briefly what happened?'

I outlined the incident on Sentosa. The secretary took notes, while Miss Leo listened intently.

'We can discount the intimacy allegation as irrelevant. Your two friends in drag won't do our case any good, but it's more smoke than fire. However, that's the end of the good news. They have a witness who is prepared to swear that you knocked Li Wei down and injured him.'

'Me? I was nowhere near him!'

'Sim Yuan Zheng says different.'

'Who?'

'He was one of the boys at the scene apparently.'

My God! The boy I thought came from Jean's class. 'Surely the other two will discredit him?'

'I'm counting on that. Anyway, I'll handle the meeting on Friday. Hopefully your board members will have the good sense to treat the complaints with the contempt they deserve.'

'Hopefully,' I echoed. 'What happens if the SAC accepts the complaints?'

'You'll be suspended and I'll have to earn my fee. But let's cross that bridge if we come to it.'

'Thanks for your help.'

'It's nothing, believe me.' She escorted me out to the lift.

For most of the afternoon I felt depressed, embroiled in an ugly situation not of my making. However, by eight-thirty I felt a little better as I anticipated discovering the contents of the disk.

I took a bus down to the army camp and crossed the road to

the restaurant. After standing outside for about fifteen minutes, I felt so conspicuous that I decided to sit down inside with a coke. When I finished the drink, there was still no sign of Terence. I sat admiring the swinging red lanterns strung across the main restaurant, while the rich aroma of curry fish and chili crab wafted around me. Nine-thirty and there was still no sign of my friend. I began to feel uncomfortable.

I paid for the drink, then walked down Clementi Road and descended the concrete steps which lead to the running track along the edge of the canal. I wandered along reminding myself that Terence rarely arrived on time, but deep down I knew he had never been forty minutes late.

I passed the first bridge and walked on. Then I saw it — a dark bundle lying on the dry floor of the canal, slightly to the right of the bridge. Discarded rubbish? I walked to the edge for a better look. Suddenly my breath caught, blood rushed to my head, and I felt nauseous. It could not... must not be. But I knew it was. I looked around for help. There was no one. I searched frantically for a way down the steep sides of the chasm. In the distance I saw steps cut into the concrete, but they were too far away. There was nothing for it. I scrambled, slipped, and finally fell headlong down the slope, my hands ripped raw and my shoulder aching. I struggled to my feet and ran to the bundle.

Terence lay on his side, legs akimbo, left arm grotesquely twisted beneath his body. A dark fluid seeped from his nose and his face was badly cut and bruised. I bent down by his mouth to check his breathing. It was ragged and shallow. Frantic, I staggered up and looked for help. No one! Then I spotted Terence's cell phone protruding from his right pocket. Please God, let it be working. I dialled the emergency number and on the second attempt heard a female voice. Breathing in gulps, I spluttered out the details. The girl calmly asked me to repeat them. I was told to remain at the scene. An emergency vehicle was on the way.

Nervously I hunkered down and felt for Terence's pulse. It

was thready but present. For something to do I draped my jacket across the broken body.

Suddenly two figures appeared above me, their jogging outfits black against the sky. 'Are you okay down there?'

'My friend has fallen into the canal and he's badly injured,' I yelled back.

'Have you called the police?'

'I've called an ambulance.'

The pair talked urgently for a few moments and then one came down the steps while the other disappeared.

'How is it?' the young guy asked gently.

'I don't know, but he looks bad.'

'My girlfriend has gone to get the police. There's a post just over the bridge.'

'Thanks.'

The young man examined Terence with a professional air and then turned to me, 'It looks like he's been stabbed.'

'I can't understand it! I was supposed to meet him on Clementi Road.'

'His hand's very clammy. That's not good.'

'Are you a doctor?'

'A third-year medical student.'

'He's going to be all right though?'

'It'll depend on how badly he's been injured internally.'

I dropped down beside Terence and took his hand 'Hold on, Terence, hold on,' I croaked desperately.

The sound of sirens echoed off the neighbouring blocks. Finally. I watched as a metal ladder dropped and two white-clad figures clambered down to us. A man dropped down beside Terence and listened at his nose, and then tried for his pulse, while an older nurse wrapped a blood pressure cuff around Terence's arm. I stepped back. Next the man produced a penlight and checked Terence's pupils. He grunted and carefully turned the body. Suddenly he yelled at the nurse, who produced a heavy pad and bandages.

'Pressure's sixty over forty!' she announced as the man urgently padded and bandaged Terence's waist.

'Would you give us a hand?' he called to the med student as he dashed for the ladder. Meanwhile, the nurse had already started a large-bore IV line in Terence's right arm.

The men returned with a metal stretcher. They gently moved Terence onto the frame and placed a support under his head. As they turned him over, I noticed a massive gash down the side of his face.

'I'm afraid it looks like he fell on his head,' the medic muttered.

'Which means?' I asked frantically.

'A subdural haemotoma,' the med student whispered. I shuddered.

It was difficult struggling up the slope with my arm in a sling. As we reached the top, a street lamp flashed onto Terence's face. His skin was ashen.

'I want to travel to the hospital with him,' I shouted at the two medics.

'No problem,' the man answered.

I heard the nurse speaking into a radio link as I clambered into the ambulance. She was warning A&E about the need for a CT scan. I collapsed onto a metal bench, scared witless.

'You'd better tell the blood bank to cross-match eight units of packed cells. He's lost a hell of a lot of blood,' the young man instructed.

As the doors closed, two policemen ran up. The medics waved them away. If they wanted a statement, they would have to follow us to the hospital.

The ambulance pulled out into Commonwealth Avenue as he stepped out of the trees and extinguished his cigarette. His clothes were the colour of night, blending in perfectly. Along the pathway he stopped a pair of young joggers.

'That guy in the ambulance, badly injured was he?'

'I don't think he'll make it through the night,' the third-year medical student muttered.

'Pity. He must have slipped and fallen down there.'

'Doubt it. Looks like someone stabbed him first.'

'Really? Well… well. Thanks for your help.'

As they disappeared, he pulled out his cell phone. 'The subject's unlikely to survive the night, but that teacher has gone in the ambulance with him. Do you want me to follow?' There was a pause. 'Okay, then.' Another pause. 'I didn't see any disk. I'll check.' He replaced the cell phone and lit another cigarette, before moving off to his motorbike.

CHAPTER
21

The journey to Tan Tok Seng Hospital was a nightmare. With siren screaming, the vehicle swerved and lurched all over the place, while I grasped the metal seat tightly to avoid being thrown onto the floor. Terence lay motionless, the IV bag swinging above him and an oxygen mask covering most of his face. The odd times I glanced at him memories of his dry wit and eager, cooperative spirit flooded back to me and I found my emotions perilously close to running out of control. The grim-faced medics struggled to keep their patient alive and said little, while the cold, clinical interior of the ambulance added to my depression as I thought back to the events at the canal.

How could I have been so thoughtless and stupid? Terence did not deserve to be lying on that bed, it should have been me. I was the one who insisted on going to that bloody nightclub and I was the one who wanted the disk decoded. I felt terribly guilty one moment, and then bloody angry the next. How could this happen in Singapore? What right did those bastards have to inflict such pain? What the hell was on that disk? The disk! My God, where was it? Of course, his attackers would have retrieved it. That thought just made me angrier. All this pain for nothing! Still, they would pay for attacking Terence. I did not know how, but they would pay.

Leaving Terence to her colleague, the nurse moved over to me with a clinical tray. She swabbed my grazed hands and plastered the worst bits, and then she changed my sling. I smiled and nodded my gratitude.

The ambulance drew into A & E and Terence was whisked away out of sight, leaving me alone and confused. I wandered through the main entrance and sat down on a green wrought-iron bench in a long white corridor dotted with spreading palms and small shops. It did not seem like a hospital, despite the constant stream of people in white coats. Suddenly, I thought of Josie.

The phone rang for several long moments before a weak voice answered. Josie's mother. Carefully restraining myself, I asked to speak to Josie. I heard a click and then a voice I recognised.

'Hi, Josie. Look I've got some bad news. It's Terence…' I heard a disembodied sigh. 'He's been involved in an accident.'

'Is he badly hurt?'

'I'm afraid so.'

'I'll be there as soon as I can.'

'We're at Tan Tock Seng. I'll wait at the main entrance.'

Josie found me sitting on a row of seats by the taxi stand in the company of an elderly man in hospital pyjamas. She was typically brisk and self-contained.

'Where's Terence?'

'They've taken him to an operating theatre.'

'Which floor?'

'I have no idea, we'd better ask.'

Josie swept through the entrance and up to the information desk. After a brief conversation with a nurse, she rejoined me. 'He's been taken to a theatre in A & E.'

I had forgotten Josie was a nurse, specialising in eye and throat surgery. We followed the little street signs down to the area where all the emergency cases entered the hospital. Josie burst through the double doors with me in tow, only to come face to face with an officious orderly. Ignoring his remonstrations, she explained our position and politely pulled rank. A young intern appeared, drawn by the sounds of arguing. After Josie's explanation, he offered to escort us to the operating theatre where Terence was undergoing emergency surgery.

We proceeded down a brightly lit corridor with operating units branching out on either side. The intern accompanied us to an observation platform overlooking a room where an operation was in progress. I was struck by the gleaming whiteness of everything, which sharply contrasted with the green scrubs of the surgeons and nurses. Monitors flickered and tubes glistened. Then I saw the blood. A drill and saw placed in two silver dishes were coated in the thick red fluid. On the floor sat a bucket containing tufts of black hair. They were operating on Terence's head, struggling to relieve the pressure. Another team attended to a huge gash in his stomach. A rubbery mass had been removed and lay in a dish on a side bench.

'It looks like they've removed the spleen,' the intern causally clarified.

I glanced at Josie. 'It isn't good, is it?'

'No. But your friend's got the best team in the hospital working on him. He must have taken a severe bump on the head. Was he stabbed?' I nodded. 'That explains the rupture to the spleen.'

Several IV lines pumped blood into Terence's inert body and the silent intensity of the operating team underlined the gravity of his condition.

'I need to go outside for some air,' I muttered queasily.

'Not used to this sort of thing?' The intern smiled. I found his remark particularly insulting considering the circumstances.

We walked back out into the normality of the main hospital and I breathed deeply.

'You'll be suffering from delayed shock.' Josie put her arm

around my shoulders. I did feel clammy and shivery, but I was determined to hold it together.

'I'm really sorry, Josie,' I stuttered.

'For what?'

'I feel terribly responsible for getting Terence involved in… in…'

'Rot! You know Terence, he thought… I mean he thinks the world of you. And as for that disk, he loves a challenge. Wild horses wouldn't have stopped him trying to crack the code.'

'Are you sure? You're not just saying this to make me feel better?'

'Why should I? I love the guy, but I also know and understand him.'

'How can you be so… so…'

'Calm?'

'Yes… calm… when Terence is lying back there fighting for his life?' I swallowed heavily.

'Panicking and screaming won't help him. Deep down I'm burning up and it's not easy pretending I'm in control, but I have to… for him!'

I marvelled at her strength and struggled with my own weakness. We arrived at the cafeteria, which looked as clinical as the rest of the hospital. Clearly they needed a staff member with a sense of humour. I walked up to the counter and ordered two coffees, and then returned to Josie and persuaded her to sit in a little indoor garden, off to one side of the main café.

I glanced at my watch. It was approaching one o'clock. In all the excitement I'd totally forgotten to phone Ming Chuan.

'This has been a really bad day for me.'

'How come?'

I explained the business with the SAC and my visit to the lawyer. Josie was very supportive, but she acknowledged the seriousness of my position. We were interrupted by the sound of an unfortunately familiar voice.

'Good evening, Mr Richards and… ?'

'Josie,' I muttered.

'… and Josie. May we sit down?'

'Look, we're not in the mood to answer questions.' Josie looked at me enquiringly. 'Oh, this is Raymond Chia and Detective Ling, from Tanglin Police Station.'

The policemen nodded and Josie stood up. 'I'll go and phone Terence's father. Does Ming Chuan know?'

I shook my head. 'Try to get him at my place first. Thanks.' As Josie left, I turned to face the intruders.

'Why is it whenever something goes wrong, you show up?'

'Coincidence?' Raymond Chia smiled.

'Bullshit. You can't be the only two policemen on active duty in this city?'

'No, but we're the only two assigned to this case.'

'Mal de mer! How unfortunate,' I muttered.

Ling leaned across and grunted, 'Hey, very late now, we want to go home. You shut up and listen to the officer. See what he say.'

I really disliked Ling. 'There's no call to be so bloody rude!'

'Sorry! But I think Detective Ling's getting a little fed up with the way you keep witholding information.'

I did not like the edge to Chia's voice. 'What information?'

'A certain computer disk that you obtained over a week ago.'

'How the hell do you know about that?' There was no answer. My eyes narrowed, 'Are you tailing me?'

'Just let's say we know a lot more than you realise. Where's the disk?'

'How the hell should I know? Why do you think my friend's lying in here with the crap kicked out of him?'

'Calm down, calm down.' My agitation bothered Chia.

'No, I won't calm down. I'm sick of this. You're supposed to be the police. You're supposed to protect innocent citizens and catch the bloody crooks. I was attacked, now Terence is lying in an operating theatre near death and you're talking to me about disks.'

My voice had risen and I was attracting a good deal of attention. I was badly tired and frustrated. 'Why the hell don't you get off your bloody arses and go and catch the bastards who almost killed my friend?'

The garden was now deserted.

'I think we take him back to police station for further questioning,' Ling said glowering at me from embarrassment and anger.

Chia smiled, unruffled, 'Give him a chance, he's been under a lot of pressure. Poor guy's friend's been bashed and his career's on the line.'

My career on the line? How the hell did he know I had trouble at school? Was this a veiled threat? My mind started to swim. I could not handle this. I began to hyperventilate, gasping for air. The policemen looked astonished, unsure what to do.

Suddenly Josie returned. She saw me shaking and pushed me forward. Unceremoniously, she thumped my back.

'What have you been saying to him? Can't you see he's in shock?'

'Sorry, Miss, but it's vital we learn who attacked his friend,' Chia stammered.

'How would he know?'

I started to calm down and my breathing returned to normal. I glared at the pair.

Chia moved back uncomfortably. 'We'll leave an officer at reception in case you think of something. By the way, did you or your friend tell anyone where you were going this evening?'

'Not as far as I know,' I growled.

'Then how did his attackers know where to find him?'

I looked at Chia coldly, and then Josie spoke, 'What are you suggesting?'

'It could be that your phone is tapped.' There was a long

silence.

'Bloody beautiful! What next!' I threw my arms in the air and hooted with laughter.

'Shhh, Pete,' Josie scolded. 'Is there any way of checking?'

'We can send a technician around tomorrow to look at his phone. What time will he be back?'

'Three o'clock,' I volunteered.

'Three o'clock it is then.' Chia turned back to Josie. 'You'd better get him home, Miss, I think he's over-tired.'

'No way. I'm staying until Terence comes round.'

Chia cast Josie a sympathetic glance and Ling shook his head as they walked away.

I grinned at Josie, 'Didn't handle that too well, did I?'

'Let's just say they expected too much,' Josie replied. 'But I think they're right about your being over-tired.'

'I meant what I said. I'm not leaving until I know Terence is all right.'

'We all want that, but it's not going to happen quickly. He has to come through a very difficult operation. He's young and fit, but he has a tough fight ahead of him. Your hanging around here feeling grumpy and tired won't help.' I looked away. I knew she was right. 'Besides, I couldn't get hold of Ming Chuan.'

'What about Terence's father?'

'He's on his way. I'll meet him and take him to see Terence after the operation. I imagine the two of us will see out the rest of the morning. You go home, get some sleep, and come back in tomorrow. By then we'll have a better idea how he is.'

Josie walked me out to a taxi and I gave her a big hug before I stepped into the vehicle. 'If Terence wakes up, please call me immediately.'

'Don't worry, I will.'

I slumped back in the seat as the hospital lights disappeared behind me.

CHAPTER

22

I had never felt so rotten. My head seemed about to explode, my throat was as dry as Ayers Rock, and my stomach threatened to disgorge its contents every few seconds. I stumbled out of bed and looked at the clock. Eight. Damn! I had slept through both alarms and I was now very late for school. School? I uttered a dry laugh and my headache grew worse.

Leaving Ming Chuan in bed, I staggered across the floor and swung into the main room. Sylvester looked at me unsympathetically, but I had to get a couple of Panadol as my head was unbearable.

As I swallowed the tablets, I remembered the nightmare of the previous evening. Ming Chuan had given me a comfortable shoulder to cry on and cry I did, more for myself than Terence. I was promptly packed off to bed, but I could not sleep. I struggled up and sat in the main room polishing off six cans of Tiger beer, hence my present condition.

School! I had to call in before they thought I had taken the day off for spite.

'Pleasant Park? This is Mr Richards. I'm quite ill and I won't be in today. Yes, I know it's rather late… What?… What's wrong with me? I've got a severe headache… stomach cramps… and

… and morning sickness! Tell the VP I'm probably pregnant!' I slammed down the receiver.

Ming Chuan appeared and groggily walked across the room.

'Who'd you call?'

'The school.'

'Good! What they say?'

'Not a lot.'

'Go back to bed. I'll cook something.'

I grimaced. 'Nothing for me, please.'

'What's wrong?'

'I feel bloody terrible.'

'You take a Panadol?'

'I took four!'

'Ah yoi, you'll kill yourself.'

'The way I feel that'd be an improvement.' I staggered back into the bedroom and plunged beneath the duvet.

I awoke five hours later with Ming Chuan whispering musically, 'What you like for lunch?'

'Roti prata,' I mumbled, still half-asleep.

'I go and see if I can get it,' he sang pleasantly.

Fortunately he could and we sat and ate roti prata with coffee while I explained everything that had happened. He was happy I had seen a lawyer, and even happier when he learned it was going to cost us nothing.

'That technician will be here soon. Watch him, will you?'

'Why? Where you going?'

'In to see Terence.'

'Not by yourself!' Ming Chuan came over and threw his arms around me. He planted a delicious, curry-filled kiss, and then drew back and smiled. I laughed and gave him a wild bear hug. God, how I loved this man!

'Ay, almost forget,' he said separating. 'You know that VP woman call back and she says she wants you back tomorrow.'

'She would!'

Ming Chuan laughed. 'So bitchy that woman! She said the teachers would like to know, as soon as possible, something about a boy or a girl!' He looked at me quizzically as I fell about laughing.

The technician arrived at two, examined the telephone, and found a little round metal disk stuck to one of the connectors. That was it.

The ride to the hospital was mercifully uneventful, but I was nervous. We had heard nothing of Terence's condition and I could only suppose that Josie was too tired to call. Of course, it could be that she was reluctant to burden me with more bad news. As we walked up to the main entrance, I saw A & E in the basement. It looked different in daylight. Then the horrors of the previous night rushed in and I stood for a few moments with my eyes tightly shut.

'C'mon, Pete,' Ming Chuan urged, 'not far to go.'

We scrambled up the rough, dirt path worn across a grassy embankment and pulled ourselves onto the sweeping roadway that fronts the hospital. I asked at the information desk if it was possible to visit Terence Wang. The duty nurse looked through a long registry on her computer and for several terrible moments I feared he might not have survived the night. Finally the nurse found his name. He was in intensive care and we could only see him for a few minutes.

Terence lay in a cubicle beside an enormous window which looked out over the city.

'Wahhhh… so beautiful view,' Ming Chuan murmured positively.

Josie was sitting beside the bed. 'Hi, guys.'

'How's he doing?'

She shrugged. 'He got through the operation okay. Now he's just got to wake up.'

Terence was stretched out on a metal bed, his head wrapped in layers of sterile gauze. A clear plastic endotracheal tube stuck out of his mouth. Monitors attached to various parts of his body measured his blood pressure while ECG leads took his heartbeat. His urine dripped down a plastic catheter into a collecting bag fixed beneath the bed. The covering sheet had slipped, revealing a large surgical dressing over his stomach. Smaller bandages and tape covered his face and left ear.

'What a mess!' I shuddered, turning away.

'Go in and squeeze his hand,' Josie urged.

I hesitated.

'Go on. Squeeze his hand and he'll know you're here.'

I stumbled into the room and drew up a chair. At close quarters I could smell that horrible antiseptic odour that usually accompanies death. Terence lay inert. Only the machine assisting his breathing indicated that he was actually still alive.

I took his left hand and squeezed very lightly. 'Hang in there, Terence, mate! Can't let the buggers win.' A lump rose in my throat and I started to burble. 'I need your help with the play. If we get past the selections, we'll need a good set to win a gold. The kids are keen, but they haven't a clue when it comes to knocking a couple of bits of wood together.'

Josie had joined me and I began to feel self-conscious. 'I don't know if he can hear me, but I… just had…'

'It's okay,' Josie soothed, 'I'm sure he knows we're here. Let's go outside a moment. Ming Chuan can stay with him till we get back.'

Josie guided me out of the intensive care unit and across to a little balcony overlooking the car park. We sat down on two rattan chairs facing each other.

'It's going to take a long time for Terence to come round, if he comes around.'

'If… what do you mean?' That cold finger reached for my heart again.

'We've got to face it, Pete. He's badly hurt. The doctors are struggling to maintain his blood pressure and it's a constant battle to keep him breathing. There... there could be brain damage. We don't know how long he lay at the bottom of that canal.'

'Couldn't have been too long. I set out to search for him straight away when he didn't show.'

'No one's blaming you, Pete, you did the best you could. But now we've got to focus our energies and do what we can for Terence. Whatever happens to him, the people who did this must be caught.'

Good old Bodicea Josie. 'Where in the hell do you get your strength?'

Josie looked at me squarely and then cast her eyes upwards, 'Faith. The old fella up there's never failed me yet.'

'Have you been here all night?'

'No, I left shortly after you. Terence's father sat with him.'

I looked out across the car park towards a nearby hill, dotted with expensive homes. 'How could this happen? Why Terence?'

'Because he had the disk.'

'Damn that disk! We don't even know what was on it.'

Josie beamed, 'Oh, yes we do!'

'What are you talking about? The disk disappeared.'

'The one Terence was bringing to you disappeared. But last night it occurred to me that Terence might have made a copy, so I checked the hard disk in his main computer.'

'And?'

She leaned forward. 'Good old, sweet, innocent Terence did all the figuring on his hard disk and never erased anything. I made a copy of the decoded information.'

'Where is it?'

'Well hidden. And as a precaution, I cleared the hard disk. Now there is no record of anything.'

'Brilliant. But what was on that damned disk?'

Josie reached into her pocket and pulled out a folded A4

sheet. 'This is part of the first section.' She handed me the sheet.

I was staring at five columns. There were no headings, keys or any explanation. The first was a list of colourful misters — Mr Blue, Mr Magenta, Mr Violet, and so on, twenty-plus names. The second was filled with numbers, separated by dividers, and each set ending in rd, st, pl, or av. The third listed one of the last three letters in the alphabet. The fourth contained animals, while the fifth was a combination of the letters A − J.

Mr Magenta   *167/ 564-12st/898-10; 555-9Y bunny BEJJFJ*
Mr Seagreen   *28/140-33av/898-10;555-9Y squirrel CJJEEJ*
Mr Burgundy   *368/836-47cres/823-7;1074-9Y vixen CJJJJJ*
Mr Peachred   *604/450-43st/299-24;317-32Z gazelle CJJHJJ*

I stared at the printout in amazement. It could be a coded list of drug couriers, prostitutes, money launderers, anything. Terence had done a fine job in breaking the computer code, but we were left with another puzzle and no key.

'It's like a shopping list for the Singapore Zoo,' I groaned.

Josie laughed.

'Don't be so miserable! I've already spotted a couple of things. Notice the letters st, av, cres, rd, etc, in the middle column.'

'Abbreviations for streets or roads?'

'Exactly. That suggests a list of addresses.' She paused and glanced at me. 'Now look at the final column. See how often J is used? I worked on this for a while and tried to substitute other letters, but nothing worked. Then it occurred to me that these letters may stand for numbers. J could be 0. Notice the letters used range from A to J. That is 10 letters in all. What if A stood for 1, B for 2, and so on. This would give you a figure in the thousands, which is just about the amount of money these guys would be working with.'

'Well done, and…' I said hopefully.

'I'm afraid that's as far as my thinking's taken me. But it's a start.'

'Of course,' I said trying to sound cheerful.

Suddenly Ming Chuan reached over my shoulder and grabbed the paper from my hands.

'What's this?'

'Shhhh… keep your voice down,' I breathed. 'It's a printout from the disk.'

'What disk?'

'The one Terence was decoding. It may help us identify his attackers.'

'Us? No way, too dangerous! Hand this to the police. It is their job not ours.'

'We'll think about it,' I said, retrieving Josie's sheet. 'In the meantime I'd like to spend a bit of time with Terence. You two can go and get a coffee.'

'Thanks!' Josie stood. 'Oh, my brother phoned me from Thailand. He wouldn't say what he was doing, but he sounded relaxed and cheerful.'

'Relaxed and cheerful,' I thought to myself. Poor old Josie. With our luck, her brother was probably up there procuring drugs for The Flaming Dragon! But at least she would no longer be worrying about him.

Ming Chuan and Josie went down to the canteen while I remained with Terence. Fifteen minutes later, Josie rushed up to me holding out her cell phone. 'It's your lawyer, and she doesn't sound too happy!'

'This is Mr Richards, I…'

'Finally! Pete, I've been calling everywhere. We have a problem.'

'I'm listening.'

'It seems your student, Yan Siang, has disappeared.'

My heart sank.

'I've called his home, the school, his friends… and no one has seen him.'

'Can we get by without him?'

'It'll be difficult. He's our crucial witness. Without his

155

testimony, the complaints may stand.'

'What should we do?'

'You could try phoning his home or checking again with your school. Someone must know something.'

'Leave it to me,' I sighed.

I returned the cell phone.

Ming Chuan looked anxious, 'Something wrong?'

'Fraid so. Yan Siang's disappeared. I need to speak to his family. Trouble is, they can't speak much English.'

'Want me to come with you?'

'That would be a big help.'

Josie looked concerned. 'I'd offer to come, but…'

'No, you're needed here. We'll call you later.' I gave her a peck on the cheek and turned to Ming Chuan. 'Let's go.'

The room was still bathed in an eerie, red glow. A different suit, a different pipe, but the same shrunken shoulders and white hair hunched in the same atmosphere, heavily laced with the sweet smell of briar tobacco. Two Europeans in business suits sat facing the older man. One had a long angular face with exceedingly thin lips, the other looked more jovial with ruddy jowls and a bulbous nose.

The white-haired man lowered his pipe. 'You can't be serious! How could a boy outsmart you?'

'We did recover the disk,' the more jovial of the visitors offered hopefully.

'But not cheaply, you fool, not cheaply!'

'That hacker won't survive. He's barely alive now.'

'But he is alive!' the older voice hissed.

The thin-faced man leaned forward. 'So? I'm sure he has no idea what hit him and the police have no clue either.'

'Loose ends and more loose ends. This is terribly unfortunate. Loose ends have an unfortunate habit of coming back neatly tied up in a hangman's noose. Have you never studied history?'

'I prefer to stick to the present,' the thin man answered brusquely. 'That disk is not really a problem, but the missing boy is! Where the hell did he get to? We've had six men out looking and the kid's not been spotted.'

The ruddy jowls shook and the bulbous nose twitched. 'We could always tackle the mother or grandmother. Perhaps lift the kid's sister.'

The white-haired man sent smoke billowing into the air. 'No violence! Absolutely no violence! If we handle this whole business discreetly, then we attract no attention. That way we survive!'

'You survive! It's of no consequence to us! We're under contract to tidy up the mess you've gotten the organisation into.'

Shaking with anger, the older man crashed his fist onto the table. 'I told them not to ship the goods through Singapore. Rank stupidity! We're the management end, not a delivery station.'

'If you were such able managers, then we wouldn't be here,' the thin lips whispered. More white clouds shot towards the ceiling. 'What happened to your two defectors?'

The gnarled hand pushed a button on the intercom and a young Chinese man entered.

'Did you contact our friend at Queensway Prison?'

'This morning, sir. The goods have been dispatched.'

The young man left.

'Does that answer your question, gentlemen?'

Suddenly the ruddy jowls drooped lower. 'How do we get this kid then?'

The pipe wavered, 'The only link we have is his teacher.'

'You mean the one beaten up by your men?' Again the pale lips were drawn into a fine, thin line.

'Unfortunately they were a little over-zealous and they have paid for it.'

'If we trouble that teacher again we run the risk of an international incident.'

The pipe shook. 'Not trouble, dear me, no. There'll be no need for any trouble.'

'Good.'

'You see, this teacher has gotten himself into a spot of bother with the school authorities. Unfortunate for him, fortunate for us.'

'Explain that.'

'It seems this naughty fellow has been playing around with his students.'

'Sounds like he should be one of your clients!' The jowls shook as their owner chortled.

The white-haired man smiled benignly, 'And as chance would have it, one of the students involved is our little friend.'

'I see,' said the thin-faced man.

'I don't!' said his partner.

'There is to be a hearing of the matter at the school. All you need do is stake out the meeting until this little fellow shows, and then grab him… quietly!'

'How do we know he'll show?'

'Because he is the teacher's only hope of beating the charge.' The white-haired man smiled and sat back. 'I've made certain of that.'

'When's this meeting?'

'Tomorrow. Two o'clock.'

The men stood. 'Let us hope tomorrow will see this matter happily resolved.'

'I'm sure it will, gentlemen, I'm sure it will. But for tonight, you must relax. I have two delightful young ladies eagerly awaiting your instructions.'

The jowls shook as the lips smacked.

'We'll see,' the other man answered without a smile. He turned and strode out, his partner flapping in his wake.

The white-haired gentleman relit his pipe and turned to admire the battle scene on the wall behind. Suddenly he swung back and hit the intercom button.

'Send in the other two,' he coughed.

The screens slid apart and the unhappy pair slunk in, still sporting an eye-patch and head bandages.

'Welcome back, gentlemen. I trust you appreciate your early release.' The pair huddled in frozen silence. 'To date, your work has been rather disappointing, but I'm going to give you one final chance to redeem yourselves.'

The pair visibly shrank and a sigh slipped out like an embarrassing burst of flatulence.

'You are to follow your friend, the teacher, until he leads you to that clever little fellow who gave you the slip the other night.'

'Can't other person do this?'

'Why? You have all the experience.' The rasping voice hardened. 'You're surely not forgetting how much you owe me?' There was a deliberate pause. 'I want that boy brought here… unharmed.' The old man drew on his pipe then leaned forward, 'Another two men are also interested in this boy… '

'Ala mah! So dangerous. We're not professionals.'

'Unfortunately you're not, as you have so clearly demonstrated. Nevertheless, you have a head start. The two gentlemen I have just mentioned believe the boy will be appearing at his school tomorrow, but I know for a fact he has left the country. The teacher will learn this and go after him. All you need do is follow him. Quite simple.'

The two men groaned as the young Chinese man reappeared.

'Show these gentlemen out, thank you.' The trio made to leave. 'By the by, gentlemen, it is generally believed that you are no longer part of this mortal coil.'

'Wh… what?' the heavier man stuttered.

'Some people think you are dead. So search carefully or we

may have to make that thought a reality. Good day!'

At the first knock there was no response, so we knocked louder. The door opened a fraction and an eye and nose appeared.

'What you want?' gasped an elderly voice.

Ming Chuan asked to speak to the mother and the door closed. A few moments later it opened fully and Mrs Chang appeared. She was very grey and seemed thinner than when I first saw her at Tanglin Police Station.

'Ah, teacher, Yan Siang no here… ' She burst into tears and then spluttered forth in Chinese.

Ming Chuan translated. 'She says men came here looking for her son. She thinks they were loan sharks.'

There was a pause while noses were blown and eyes wiped. Then the grandmother started yelling. She held up her walking-stick and pointed it furiously at a photograph on the wall screaming,

'Huai ren! Huai ren! Huai ren!' Finally she sagged, turned to Ming Chuan and spoke tearfully.

'The grandmother says that Yan Siang very close to his father. She says the father was bad man, but not to Yan Siang. He loved his father.'

I noticed heads poking out from neighbouring apartments. Our conversation was beginning to attract attention.

The mother took over again. 'Yan Siang did chores for his father and he helped at his work,' Ming Chuan translated.

'Does she have any idea where Yan Siang is now?'

Ming Chuan smiled and spoke gently to the two distressed women.

'They say uncle took him up to Malaysia, they think Malacca. Uncle would not tell the address.'

'Is this a blood uncle or just a friend?'

'Real uncle… father's brother. He very good man. Very good,' the mother blurted out.

I looked at the distressed woman and spoke gently, 'Mrs Chang,

I'm very sorry about your son. I have been trying to help him.'

'I know… you good man. Yan Siang… he like you very much. He say you good teacher… best teacher.' She sighed. 'First time I see you, I know you good man.' My recollection of our first meeting did not quite tally with that.

'Big men and that woman, they huai! They don't know you. I know you and you good to Ah Yan.'

Ming Chuan looked puzzled. 'What men?' he asked in Chinese.

The mother answered with great gestures and wild, explosive language.

'She says two men made her sign the complaint about you. She didn't believe, but they very convincing. They said a woman… Mrs Supraniam… had also complained, but Mrs Chang says she don't know this woman.'

Ming Chuan's eyes sparkled, 'Pete, this can help tomorrow. You must go back and call the lawyer right away.'

I looked over Ming's shoulder at the two women hunched together beyond the open door. Suddenly they were joined by a pretty little girl, an oriental Dresden doll.

'But Ming, Yan Siang loved his father and he saw who killed him. He's told no one because he knows the information is lethal. We've got to find him!'

Ming Chuan glared at me. 'Pete! You got big, big trouble. You could lose your job, your home, get in trouble with police… What about us?'

'Nothing can hurt us, you know that, Ming. But I couldn't live with Yan Siang on my conscience, not after what happened to Terence… and…'

Ming Chuan knew me too well. 'Ah yoi! Tomorrow go to meeting and after we look for Yan Siang… together!' I threw my arms around him and he quickly shrugged me off. 'The family… they're looking!'

I did not care. I embraced him again and squeezed tightly. Beyond us, the family smiled and softly closed the door.

CHAPTER

23

The conference room was ready. The round table, usually the focus of the room, had been removed and in its place stood a row of desks and beyond, five chairs. A select quintet had been chosen from the School Advisory Council to hear my case. Ironically, the posters depicting a skein of geese gracing a northern sky above the words: *Strive for What Lies Beyond*, *Let's Rise Together* and *The Best is Yet to Come* were still hanging in their usual places. A side table had been introduced to support a huge bowl of flowers, no doubt to help colour proceedings. The struggle to find a cloth big enough to cover the whole of the top row of desks had clearly stretched the Home Economics Department beyond its capacity. They had eventually settled for two pieces of material of almost the same colour and pattern, but this near-miss merely emphasised their original failure. Three rows of plastic bucket seats, divided by a central aisle, formed a V-shape in front of the desks.

I had slept surprisingly well the night before and had arrived in time to teach my full morning programme. When Jean asked me why I was displaying such diligence under threat of sacking, I answered that it could well be my final morning teaching in Singapore and I wanted to make the most of it. Jean was entirely on my side, as were a good number of teachers, but I advised her that 'punching the VP's lights out' would hardly help my case.

I knew that every effort had been made to keep the matter away from the students, but there was no denying the efficacy of the school grapevine. I walked into classrooms to find messages of support scrawled across the blackboards.

'We Love Mr Richerds' and 'Mr Richards for Principle' were endearing, if rather poor reflections of my success as an English teacher. That the pupils clearly knew something was up was evident in the quality of their behaviour and the warm smiles I received from even the most recalcitrant little villains. All of it served to remind me how much I would miss if the SAC found against me.

I had a brief coffee with my lawyer, during which I explained my visit to the Chang's apartment and my failure to locate Yan Siang. Shau Wee was surprised at the mother's admission and assured me that she would pursue the matter if the council's decision made it necessary. At two o'clock we entered the lions' den.

The first people I spotted were two clerks from the Foreign Recruitment Section of the Ministry of Education. No one had warned me that they would be gracing the proceedings. Of course, this was hardly surprising as they had never taken any interest in anything I had done in the previous ten years anyway.

I followed Shau Wee to the front row and sat down in a bucket on the right. Already occupying the front seats on the left were Theresa Loh and Marjorie Sim, the Head of P.E., in the company of a school clerk. Behind these sat Daisy Liew, dressed as if she were going to a circus, in the company of a gentleman I did not recognise. Behind my lawyer and myself, the seats were empty. Although I had been advised this was not a trial, it still looked strangely adversarial.

At ten minutes past two, the five members of the SAC entered, accompanied by the vice-principal. Snake had gone to great lengths to build out her meagre figure and the designer suit she sported looked classy. I felt flattered that she had gone to such expense on my account. The chosen quintet took their seats while Snake and her little factotum, Margorie Sim, fussed around them. A carafe of water appeared and five glasses were promptly filled and placed.

At first glance, my inquisitors did not seem particularly threatening. There was our noble chairperson, Mrs Teo, the lady responsible for the garish decoration of the staff lounge. She had begun her professional life rather modestly as a Public Utilities Board clerk. However, good friends, good luck and, most importantly, a good marriage, had enabled her to rise volcanically. Plump, with a florid round face, the students affectionately referred to her as 'Strawberry'.

On her right sat the staff representative, Tong Say How, a good friend. On his right was a complete stranger, whom I took to be a parent. The other two members were Wang Beng Hin, a businessman who had always enjoyed my plays and the games I organised for the Teachers' Day dinners, and Penny Tee, a wealthy woman who had donated vast sums of money to the school and had a distinct aversion for foreigners. On balance, possibly a 3 to 2 line-up in my favour. I felt more positive.

Mrs Teo called the gathering to order and outlined the agenda. The vice-principal would begin by reading out the complaints, followed by a statement from Mrs Liew. Next my lawyer would have a chance to present my side and finally the council would ask questions. No interruptions would be tolerated during the reading of the complaints or the presentation of the statements. We were reminded that this was not a court, merely a gathering to appraise the validity of certain matters. As I glanced around the said gathering, this reassurance brought me little comfort.

The vice-principal walked quietly forward.

'Mr Richards has been on the staff of Pleasant Park Secondary

School for the past four years and he has acquitted himself well. He is a highly competent teacher, professional in all his dealings with staff and pupils and diligent and resourceful in the execution of his duties. He possesses considerable talent and natural ability, especially in the areas of drama and literature.'

I quietly wondered to myself if this were true, why were we all here?

She continued, 'It came as a considerable shock to me to receive these complaints.' She paused and for effect, held up a sheaf of papers. 'Naturally, my first thought was to place the accusations before Mr Richards so we could quickly put the whole business to rest. No one was more disappointed than I when Mr Richards failed to address the issues and instead refused even to discuss them.'

Shocked and disappointed? It seemed to me that Snake was savouring every delicious moment.

'Mr Richards seems to have forgotten the civil service code which governs the behaviour of all teachers. None of us is above the regulations and, when our judgement or actions are questioned, we have a duty to address the allegations. Mr Richards cannot even use the excuse that he is a foreigner and is therefore unaware of our regulations, as he has been teaching in Singapore for many years now.'

Penny Tee straightened. The word foreigner had struck its target.

'As acting principal and Mr Richard's supervisor, I was naturally sympathetic to his position, but when Mr Richards refused to settle these matters I had no alternative but to bring them to the attention of the SAC.'

She turned to the heads of department, 'I will now ask Mrs Loh, the HoD of English, to read out the complaints.'

At this point, Mrs Teo intervened. 'That will not be necessary, Mrs Loh, thank you. The members of the SAC have read the complaints. We feel it would be better to give Mr Richards an opportunity to speak to these matters before we proceed further.'

Well, you certainly had to give Her Honour, Madam Chair, credit. She no doubt believed I could answer the charges and the proceedings would be abandoned, thus avoiding any further embarrassment. Miss Leo stood up.

'Thank you, Madam Chairperson, I appreciate this opportunity to speak on Mr Richards' behalf. The panel may wonder why Mr Richards isn't speaking for himself. The answer is simple. As his lawyer, I have advised him not to address these issues personally since they are emotional and distressing. It is important they be dealt with quite dispassionately. I am sure you will agree.'

'To begin with, neither Mr Richards nor myself has seen the complaints referred to. Consequently, we find ourselves unable to deliver an explanation since we do not fully understand what we are expected to explain.'

There was a stunned silence. Good for Miss Leo! Strike one to our side!

Mrs Teo turned to Snake, who looked supremely uncomfortable. 'Is this true?'

The vice-principal stood slowly and turned to Marjorie Sim. After a few moments of hissing and wild gesticulations, she turned back to the panel. 'I find Miss Leo's claim rather extraordinary. I spoke to her myself on the phone and…' She paused to grab a paper proffered by the clerk. 'This is the fax detailing the complaints which was dispatched to Miss Leo's office.'

'When was that faxed?'

Snake flustered about and found a date. 'Yesterday.'

'Yesterday? Late in the afternoon, no doubt. The fax arrived so late I was unable to read it, let alone deal with it. Why was the fax not sent earlier?'

Snake whipped back, 'No one knew Mr Richards was going to engage a lawyer.'

Miss Leo sat and we exchanged words, and then she continued, 'Mr Richards says he made it quite clear at the meeting on Tuesday that he was going to seek legal advice.'

'Legal advice,' the vice-principal smiled, 'but whose? There are many legal firms in Singapore. I am not clairvoyant!'

Miss Leo was unfazed. 'Was Mr Richards given a copy of each complaint?'

'He never asked for one.'

'Mr Richards didn't need to ask in a case of this gravity. It is accepted practice to give any accused person complete details of the accusations against him.'

'That may well be the case in the courts and places which you inhabit, but we are not lawyers. This is an educational institution. We have no time to waste on such niceties!'

'Such niceties?' Miss Leo repeated scornfully. 'It is a matter of natural justice. Not only did you fail to inform Mr Richards of the full nature of the complaints, you scheduled this hearing –'

'Meeting!' Mrs Teo hastily corrected.

'You scheduled this meeting with such speed it gave him no time to investigate the nature of the matters to be discussed.'

'The scheduling was entirely for Mr Richards' benefit. If this matter drags on, rumours will begin to circulate and irrespective of the outcome his reputation could suffer.'

'Your concern is remarkably touching, but if you were so concerned about Mr Richards' reputation, why did you not confront him with his accusers in the first place?'

'We cannot bring parents and strangers into the school to accuse a teacher.'

'Why not?'

'Because it just isn't done.'

'I see, this school inhabits a different planet, does it?'

'The parents would refuse.'

'They cannot refuse. In a matter of this gravity, the most

sensible thing would have been to allow Mr Richards to confront his accusers.'

'Legal language again! This is not a court, we are a school.'

'If this matter is not settled satisfactorily, school or not, you will end up in a court when Mr Richards brings legal proceedings against you.'

At the mention of legal proceedings, a shudder ran through the panel. The chairperson leaned over and spoke briefly to the stranger on her right, who eventually cleared his throat.

'Thank you, vice-principal and Miss Leo. We are grateful for your explorations, but I must, on behalf of my fellow members, remind all parties to these proceedings this is not a court. Legal language has no place here and Miss Leo should confine herself to speaking on Mr Richards' behalf. I am surprised she does not realise that I am well aware of the legal position. Moreover, the panel will not tolerate any threats, legal or otherwise. We have been called here to determine the merits of certain complaints and our authority is clearly laid down in the Education Act.'

Snake cast a supercilious sneer in our direction as Miss Leo rose again.

'I beg the council's pardon. I did not intend to be presumptuous. I would also like to apologise to His Honour, Mr Justice Tang. My failure to recognise such a worthy jurist compounds my other shortcomings. However, I feel I had to make it clear that we were not fully apprised of the nature of the complaints.'

'And you were right to do so, Miss Leo.' The worthy jurist turned to the vice-principal. 'I view with considerable disquiet the school's failure to provide adequate briefing and time for preparation of these matters. Miss Leo's comments on natural justice are quite valid.'

Snake seemed to grow visibly smaller.

The panel conferred briefly, and then Mrs Teo spoke. 'We appreciate that the school failed to give Mr Richards reasonable warning and we will consider this in our deliberations later. However, we must proceed. For the benefit of Mr Richards and Miss Leo, we will now hear a summary of the complaints, please.'

As an unhappy Theresa Loh got to her feet, my spirits sagged — strike two to their side! Theresa looked in our direction and gave me a soft smile. Her summary was mercifully brief and most of the juicier bits were omitted.

We already knew the facts, so the first two complaints contained few surprises. However, I was intrigued when Mrs Chang made no mention of Yan Siang's phone call.

Mrs Supraniam's complaint was a duplicate of the first with the addition of 'my enticing her sons to Burger King and offering them money'. Neither of these facts was true. But how to prove it?

The third complaint was from a stranger who claimed to have seen what went on in my apartment from a neighbouring HDB block. His descriptions were lurid, but woefully inaccurate.

At the end of her unpleasant duty, Theresa slipped back to her seat. There was a brief pause before Mrs Teo invited Shau Wee to respond.

'Let me say at the outset that Mr Richards totally refutes any suggestion that there is an improper relationship between him and the boy at the centre of these three bizarre allegations.'

'Oh, there is a relationship, but it is a thoroughly professional, caring relationship. The sort of relationship that our government is constantly calling for between teachers and students, and parents and their children. Mr Richards is Yan Siang's form teacher. With no warning, he was asked to escort this boy to Tanglin Police Station and give him follow-up counselling. Was any assistance provided by the school? Oh, dear me, no. Did the vice-principal offer to take this vulnerable young boy under her wing? Did Mr Richards' head of department offer him any advice or assistance? No! A Caucasian teacher, new to our culture, was expected to look after this young Chinese boy — a boy who had recently witnessed his father's death and is at odds with his own identity.'

'Let us examine the complaints more fully. The first is from the boy's mother. It may surprise the SAC members to know that the mother never wrote the complaint.' This drew angry glances from the panel, most of them thrown in Snake's direction. 'No, indeed. She may have signed it, but just yesterday she told Mr Richards and another witness that she didn't believe the complaint.' More glances.

'In addition, Mr Richards insisted that Yan Siang phone his mother to tell her where he was on the night in question. No mention is made of this phone call in the complaint — a fact the mother knew, but nobody else would have.

As for the second complaint, Mr Richards was in Burger King to meet Yan Siang. He had no idea the two Supraniam boys were going to appear. There was no pre-arranged meeting with these boys and Mr Richards did not give them money, he merely bought them dessert.'

'The third complaint is easily dispatched. Mr Richards' apartment only faces the HDB blocks on one side — the main kitchen-room side. Mr Richards' bedroom is totally hidden from these blocks. How then did this anonymous stranger get such a good view? Either he is a contortionist who can peer round corners or he is a liar. I know which of these I'd put my money on.'

'In summary, what do we have? A questionable complaint which will be retracted, a duplicate which is factually wrong, and a third complaint from someone who couldn't possibly have seen what he claims to have seen.'

Miss Leo resumed her seat. The panel buzzed together, and Snake looked decidedly sick. Mrs Teo called on Mrs Liew to read out her statement. If what we had heard up till now was implausible, what we were about to hear was downright ridiculous.

In a tremulous voice, Mrs Liew outlined how she came to

be on Sentosa. She described the outing, the behaviour of her girls and the intrusion of that 'wicked little trio'. Up to this point her story had the whiff of veracity, but suddenly things changed. She described how I came on the scene, hugging and cuddling this younger man. I insulted her by arguing in front of her girls and I openly encouraged the boys, one of whom started to fool with me. Consequently, I knocked this boy backwards and he cut his head. This drew more glances from the panel, all cast in my direction.

Mrs Liew then described her shock and that of her innocent young girls when two men dressed as women arrived. Scantily clad and behaving in the most embarrassing manner, this pair canoodled with the young boys before we all went off together. She ended her woeful tale adding that one of the boys would support her story as would all her girls, three of whom, on a later occasion, had come upon Yan Siang and myself 'involved in unnatural intimacy'.

The chairperson nodded to Miss Leo, who rose slowly. She looked at Mrs Liew, shook her head sadly then turned to the panel.

'What we have here is a sorry tale of professional jealousy.'

Mrs Liew leapt to her feet and was about to speak, when Mrs Teo stopped her.

'Sit down, Mrs Liew! You had your chance, now Miss Leo is entitled to be heard uninterrupted. Carry on please, Miss Leo.'

'As I was saying, professional jealousy.' She carefully emphasised the last two words.

'For some time, Mrs Liew has resented Mr Richards' popularity with the students and his ability to engender their loyalty. On the day in question, when Mr Richards appeared with his young friend, 'that wicked little trio', to use Mrs Liew's own words, were behaving inappropriately and it was Mr Richards who called them off. It was Mrs Liew who caused the boy to fall and cut his head, not…'

'How dare you!' screamed Daisy Liew, leaping to her feet once more.

'Mrs Liew, you have been warned. Another outburst like that and you will leave the room!' Mrs Teo was in military mode and she left Daisy Liew standing, gaping open-mouthed like a landed fish gulping for air.

'With regard to the hugging and cuddling, we can produce witnesses who will dispute this and I won't waste your valuable time by dignifying the rest of Mrs Liew's allegations with a response. Suffice it to say that the men were old friends and cross-dressing is not an offence in this country. In fact, any child can see drag queens on popular SBC shows in prime time.'

'I am sorry Mrs Liew had an unpleasant Sunday afternoon, but it is hardly fair to blame Mr Richards for that.'

Miss Leo returned to her bucket.

There was a short conference, and then Mrs Teo announced that the committee members would retire to examine the information laid before them. We were all advised to go and enjoy a drink in the school canteen. Shau Wee and I walked out to the main entrance.

'Nasty business,' Shau Wee observed.

'Unfortunately. What do you think of our chances?'

'I think the council is pretty much on your side, but they have to lay this matter to rest comprehensively. Imagine if they dismiss the allegations and the other side trot along to the news media. They only have to produce one student who swears Mrs Liew is telling the truth and... well... the resulting damage doesn't bear thinking about. The SAC would be humiliated and the school badly embarrassed.'

I leaned against Shau Wee's Mercedes and gazed out across the fields leading down to the meandering road which wound up to the school. It produced a comfortable feeling and teaching here was a comfortable job. I did not want to lose either.

I looked back at Shau Wee. 'How did you know the HDB

blocks don't face my bedroom?'

'I didn't. Call it legal licence.'

I looked away again, lost in distant thoughts.

Shau Wee put her arm on my shoulder and whispered, 'C'mon, we're not beaten yet. If we lose this round, we start playing hard ball.'

I sighed. Suddenly Marjorie Sim appeared on the balcony and signalled that we were needed. We re-entered the conference room to find everyone seated, waiting.

Mrs Teo leaned forward and coughed. 'We have decided that the allegations laid against Mr Richards in the three initial complaints lack substance and foundation. We fully accept Mr Richards' explanation and we believe that the testimony of Yan Siang will satisfy the complainants' concerns. Further, we would like to record our gratitude to Miss Leo for her careful and succinct evaluation of the issues raised.'

'Thank the Lord,' I sighed.

Mrs Teo continued, 'However, we feel that the allegations made by Mrs Liew, clearly supported by student testimony, must be examined more closely. Consequently, we will reconvene here next Friday, at which time we will hear fuller testimony and examine witnesses.'

'Until that date, it is with the deepest regret and totally against our wishes, that we must suspend Mr Richards from all teaching duties at this school. That is all. Thank you!'

Chapter

24

It took me some time to comprehend the shock of the council's decision. I staggered out of the conference room into the arms of Jean, who had stayed back to hear the result. Shau Wee muttered that from now on the gloves were off! Theresa Loh buzzed around the three of us like a blue-arsed blowfly, twittering inanities about silly fools and stupid decisions, but I just wanted to get away from the place. I would never forget the smirk on Snake's face and the supercilious thrust of Daisy Liew's chin. I felt so utterly defeated.

Jean and I retreated to the nearest watering hole in Holland Village and I proceeded to get thoroughly plastered. It was an expensive process — nothing comes cheaply in Holland Village. At around six, Jean suggested I head home but I was nowhere near finished. This was one objective I was determined to accomplish and by seven I had succeeded. Jean bundled me into a taxi and took me back to Kismis Avenue.

Ming Chuan was badly shaken by the news. He thanked Jean and helped me up to the apartment.

I groaned awake the following morning with a blinding headache. At first nothing made sense. While Ming Chuan cooked breakfast and I dressed, he filled me in on the disasters of the previous day. Fortunately, my mind was still sufficiently in limbo for me to miss most of the details, but I felt terrible. Especially when Josie phoned to tell us that Terence's condition was unchanged.

After breakfast, I told Ming Chuan that I had promised to conduct the dress rehearsal of the school play and it was a promise I intended to keep. Reluctantly he helped me down to a taxi after I agreed to meet him for dinner. I got out at the rear entrance to the school and crept across to the canteen like a thief.

Ronald had worked the cast hard and it showed. Their movements were fluid, their dialogue convincing and their cues spot on. I felt better. After three runs through the play we had the timing right and I let the little thespians break for lunch. The play looked good and I had the feeling we might squeak into the finals.

I walked down to the nearest hawker centre alone and chose a remote table overlooking a small pond. A skinny Malay boy took my order for a plate of beef rendang, while a sour-faced waitress poured me a coffee. Two boys from school sat at a far table and when I glanced at them they waved. This made me feel worse. I had let them all down.

The food arrived and I ate it slowly, gazing out across the pond where red and gold carp shimmied through blue-green depths. A light breeze ruffled the surface, and whispering reeds bent and washed themselves in the water. I relaxed and my mood became reflective. What really happened that fateful night when Yan Siang lost his father? Why had the boy left the country? What could he possibly still have to fear? And why was that bloody disk so important? Terence and I were hardly threats to whoever owned the thing, yet they had attacked me and almost killed him. Now they were trying to have me kicked out of the country.

I finished the rendang and pushed the plate aside. It was clear these questions were never going to be answered until the code on the disk was broken and Yan Siang found. For this I needed Ming Chuan and Josie. We would have to meet and decide how best to proceed. Thus resolved, I paid for my lunch and walked back to the school.

The afternoon passed quickly and by the time we finished, the pace was cracking along. The cast decided to meet at nine o'clock on Monday morning for a quick run through the play before we left for the auditorium where the presentations were being held.

I locked the room and called Josie. Terence continued to show no improvement. She sounded tearful. I sensed that her strong façade was starting to crumble, so I invited her to meet Ming Chuan and me in Clarke Quay at nine that night for a drink. As I left the staff room I noticed the latest pile of literature trialling papers on my desk. I scooped up the lot and threw them in the nearest rubbish tin. 'Bugger the bastards!'

Stretching along one side of the Singapore River, Clarke Quay bubbles with bumboats and floating eateries. On land there are dozens of restaurants offering a wide range of dishes from Italian to Egyptian, through to Moroccan. Circles of umbrella-shaded tables line the water's edge and crazy young waiters, laden with steaming dishes and jugs of beer, zigzag their way through a poly-linguistic gaggle. It is a fascinating place with its clashing music and garish night bazaar quality, mixing lightly-clad tourists with the sartorially incongruous ring-in-the-nose set. The trendiest mix with the bendiest, and it is not unusual to find yourself rubbing shoulders with local media stars.

We found a table, recently vacated by three bleary-eyed tourists, and then settled to wait for Josie. I ordered a jug of lime juice for the others and a Tiger beer for myself from a giggling waitress who wriggled her way back into a wild-looking pub.

Eventually we spotted Josie struggling through the mass of people. We called out and waved, and she gratefully threw herself down beside us.

'Whew! That was a battle!'

'Here, have a glass of lime juice. That'll put a zing in your whistle,' I laughed, splashing juice from the jug into a glass and over the table.

'Steady on,' Josie shrieked, wiping her knees.

'What's a little juice between friends,' I chortled.

'You're in a good mood, considering.'

I looked at her and winked. 'No point in sitting around feeling sorry for myself!' I ordered another beer. 'How's Terence?' After I asked the question I realised it was a mistake.

'Not very good. There's been no change,' Josie muttered.

'None at all?'

'Nope.'

'Did the doctors say anything?'

'Nothing new.' She looked out at the passing traffic. 'Why did you invite me here anyway?'

'I thought you needed cheering up,' I replied lamely.

'Something tells me your motive was not that transparent.'

'You're right. I thought we should discuss what we're going to do next.'

'Go to the police!' Ming Chuan offered.

'Why? They haven't really done very much so far,' Josie grumbled.

I nodded. 'Exactly. And I don't think they'll do much unless we galvanise them into action.'

'How?'

'Look, I've got a week before that council meets again to end my career. I've got to find Yan Siang. He's the only one who can destroy the allegations and help me discredit Daisy Liew.'

'You don't know where he is!'

'We know he's staying somewhere in Malacca with an uncle called Chang.'

'Why not just go straight to the police?' Ming Chuan pleaded.

'With what? We have a sheet of paper which means nothing and no idea who's after us. The police probably know a lot more than we do.'

There was an uncomfortable pause. Suddenly I saw Raymond Chia emerge from a nearby restaurant with two female friends. I slid down in my chair and motioned to Ming Chuan, who promptly stood up for a better look. Within seconds we were spotted. The trio pushed through the crowd towards us.

'Good evening,' Chia smiled. 'We still haven't got that report.'

'If I were you, I wouldn't hold my breath waiting for it,' I muttered.

Why was it every time we tried to get away, this fellow showed up like the proverbial bad penny? Half-heartedly I introduced Ming Chuan and Chia presented two ladies with the sort of fabulous figures that usually decorate cat-walks.

He drew up three chairs and signalled to a waiter, who cast him a despairing glance.

'How is your friend?' he asked with apparent concern.

'Just the same,' Josie murmured.

'I am sorry. But if it's any consolation, we do have a couple of suspects.'

'Really?' I asked unimpressed. 'And how long before you arrest them?'

'We have one in custody for questioning at the moment,' Chia replied, waving at another waiter. 'It's a pity that disk was lost. I don't suppose your friend made a copy?'

My heart missed a beat, but I recovered quickly, kicking Ming Chuan under the table and glancing at Josie.

'Why would he? I don't think he had any idea what was on the disk,' Josie answered quite truthfully.

'I wonder why they beat him up so badly then?' Chia

reflected, munching nuts he had taken from the bowl sitting in the centre of our table.

'Your guess is as good as mine,' I replied.

'I heard your young student suddenly disappeared? Left you in the lurch, did he?'

'What do you mean?' I blustered.

'You've been suspended, haven't you?'

'It's none of your bloody business!'

'Language, please. There are ladies present,' Chia mocked.

'I think you'd better go!' Ming Chuan looked squarely at Chia.

'Why? Your big friend going to hit me?'

'He won't have to. Because if you're still here in three seconds, I will!' Josie threatened.

'Wahh... tough girl! Watch out, guys! Let's go, girls.' He stood up, grabbed another handful of nuts and moved off into the crowd.

'I don't like him, he knows too much,' Josie grumbled.

She had a point. Every time we turned around Chia was there and he certainly seemed to have an uncanny network of informants. His manner had also changed. Where once he was all friendly and warm fuzzies, now he was supercilious.

'I thought the business at the SAC meeting was confidential,' I mused.

'Should be,' Josie agreed.

'Then how come he knows what happened?'

No one answered my question, but they knew what I was thinking.

I changed the subject. 'We must go up to Malacca, find Yan Siang and bring him back.'

'Malacca?' Josie sounded shocked.

'You don't have to come, if you'd rather stay with Terence.'

'He won't be going anywhere for a while and I could use the distraction.'

'So we're agreed then?

Ming Chuan nodded reluctantly.

We left Clarke Quay just before midnight, totally unaware of the two pairs of eyes that had been silently watching us.

CHAPTER
25

There is nothing in the world quite like preparing to go on stage — the cautious optimism and nail-biting anticipation as everyone wonders what the audience will be like, the vigorous enthusiasm, the loyalty and whispered encouragement from the support crew. I love the beaming little faces, the nervous twittering like fledglings preparing for their first flight and the sense of achievement and pride afterwards.

We left school for the Singapore Youth Festival Drama Competition at ten forty-five. No one from the school administration showed up to farewell us. I was unsurprised, although disappointed for the kids' sake.

The trip to the venue was tense. Everyone knew the moment we had been preparing for was at hand. Ronald sat in silence and I said little, lost in my own thoughts. The highway, shopping malls and HDB blocks flashed past unnoticed. We arrived at the auditorium with plenty of time to prepare, but the students raced to the dressing-rooms to change and put on make-up.

Finally our turn came to move into position. We were given thirty minutes maximum to set up, present our play and strike. Any over-run and we would lose points. As the play ahead of us finished, our crew moved swiftly to place the screens, tables, chairs, bushes and properties that constituted our setting. Then, with a final blessing, the cast took up their positions. Lights, curtain, action!

The pace never flagged. From the moment the curtain rose, the actors threw everything into it. The dialogue crackled, the comedy was sharp and brought guffaws from the audience and giggles from the judges, and everyone marvelled at the colour and accuracy of the sets and costumes. When the curtain finally dropped, the cast collapsed in spent heaps, thrilling to the congratulations and appreciation of two very grateful producers. Ronald and I were ecstatic. Never in our wildest dreams could we have supposed the presentation would have gone so well. It was a real task ushering the exhausted students back to dressing rooms, which had to be vacated within ten minutes.

A delirious cast and crew returned to the school to be welcomed by a smiling vice-principal and several HODs. Snake's spies were obviously on the ball and the good news had been delivered. Naturally I was ignored, until Theresa Loh appeared and dragged me aside.

'Snake's over the moon,' she beamed.

'Good! I hope she stays up there!' I quipped.

'C'mon, Pete, the play was a knock-out by all accounts. I bet the witch is having second thoughts about that whole SAC drama.'

'Really? Well, it's a bit late.'

'We're missing you. The lit trial's been a disaster and we still haven't finished setting all the examination papers for the lower second.'

'Tough! Those are all your problems now.'

'Jean isn't even speaking to me,' Theresa sighed sadly.

'Perhaps you should look to your loyalties, my dear!' Then I relented, 'Thanks for your help with Shau Wee.'

'You don't deserve it!'

'Probably not, but thanks anyway.'

I strode out the main entrance and down the road to the bus stop.

When I got home, I called Shau Wee.

'I expected your call earlier than this. We haven't much time, you know.'

'Sorry, but I've been trying to refocus and it hasn't been easy,' I answered.

'I managed to reason with Mrs Teo and she's agreed to postpone the second hearing until Tuesday next week.'

'That's good news.'

'Only if we get hold of Yan Siang.'

'I'm working on it.'

'We need him to discount the girls' cuddling accusation.'

'They're talking rubbish.'

'Of course, but we still have to show it's rubbish!'

'I thought a guy was innocent until proven guilty?'

'Only in a court of law, and this isn't one! You should talk to the two boys involved in the incident at Sentosa and make sure their stories are correct.'

'Is that really necessary?'

'Do you want to be reinstated or permanently struck off?'

'Sorry!'

The door buzzer startled me. 'I must go.'

'I'll call you tomorrow, so don't disappear.'

'Of course…' There was a click and she was gone.

I walked over to the door and looked out to discover Ming Chuan and Josie leaning against the wall and door respectively.

'What are you two doing here?'

Ming Chuan beamed, 'We go see Mrs Chang, lah!'

Josie handed me a slip of paper. 'It's a Malacca number. One of Chang's contacts who may help us get in touch with Yan Siang's uncle.'

'Yan Siang's mother gave you this?'

Josie nodded.

'That's marvellous,' I gushed. 'What made you go there?'

'A hunch. How was the play?'

'Not bad. I think we'll make the final.'

'Well done. Sooo… when do we leave for Malacca?'

'Tomorrow… by bus. Are you sure you want to leave Terence? What happens when he comes to?'

Josie shook her head. 'That's not likely. The doctors say it could be weeks before he shows any signs of improvement. I'm off to visit him now. I'll see you two tomorrow!'

As I watched her walk to the lift, I quietly admired her strength. She did not seem quite as strong as before, and I wondered if she could survive the hell she was going through. I looked back at Ming Chuan and shuddered.

PART TWO

'Oh, East is East and West is West and never the twain shall meet,
Till Earth and Sky stand presently at God's great judgement seat;
But there is neither East nor West, Border nor Breed, nor Birth,
When two strong men stand face to face, though they come from the ends of the earth!'

Rudyard Kipling

CHAPTER

26

We caught the bus at the Boon Lay Shopping Centre just before eight the following morning. After a straight run through to the Woodlands Checkpoint, we disembarked and strolled through Singapore Customs. No problem. Within five minutes we were on the other side and back on the bus.

The northern link between Singapore and Malaysia is the famous causeway — the access which the allies blew up to prevent the Japanese crossing the Straits during their assault on Singapore in February 1942. Of course, as history has recorded to the embarrassment of the allies, the Japanese simply waited for low tide and walked across. Once off the causeway, we disembarked again to join the long queues struggling to enter Malaysia. Actually there were no queues initially, just a mass of people pushing their way in one general direction, but after twenty minutes of heaving and sweating, queues emerged like long lines of tangled dreadlocks. Unlike Singapore, the sign-posting is appalling and you have to guess which line you should be in. Considering the amount of money the Malaysian government spends annually exhorting people to visit the bloody place, their facilities should be a hell of a lot better!

Finally, hot, sweaty, tired, and generally pissed off, we arrived at the immigration counter. A surly-faced Muslim woman grabbed my passport, banged on a stamp, tore away part of the form, grunted twice and then tossed it back at me. Welcome to Johore!

We returned to the security of our vehicle and settled down for the rest of the trip. The bus trundled its way out into the main thoroughfare of Johore Bahru, an interesting city at the foot of Peninsular Malaysia, which presents a wealth of opportunities to the keen bargain-hunter. A dirty canal runs through the centre of the downtown area, its slimy grey sludge offering a foul-smelling welcome to all visitors. Litter lines the narrow, cramped streets with their dingy little eateries and money shops, while traffic is fast and nondescript, with older-model cars screeching a zig-zag route at crazy speeds. Taxis are infamous, totally unregulated, and likely to charge any fare they think they can safely rip off an unsuspecting foreigner.

Slowly the bus pulled its way up through the inner suburbs with their quaint bungalow houses and out onto the main highway, where the wide, open lanes gave the gleaming beast a chance to flex its muscles and show what it could do. We powered out into the country, industrial blocks giving way to scattered kampongs and wide stretches of open grassland.

As the kilometres sped past, rubber plantations replaced the grasslands. The sun splashed across the wet surface of the road still recovering from the previous night's tropical downpour. Tinkling little sparklers dripped from the tall, colourful bougainvillea framing the car repair businesses and little coffee shops, which sprung out of nowhere and disappeared just as quickly.

Around noon, the bus turned off the motorway and looped down a side road, finally drawing into a petrol station bordered by a large concrete building which housed a restaurant. Judging by the number of customers, most buses stopped there. We were advised we had twenty minutes to fill our stomachs and empty our bowels. However, one look at the fare offered in this establishment and I felt I could empty both parts of my anatomy in five!

Apart from the swarms of flies which tap-danced across most of the food, the greasy consistency of the curries and the brittle jackets encasing the chicken drumsticks severely dampened my appetite. Josie did not bother looking — she had obviously travelled this way before, and even Ming Chuan with his cast iron stomach decided to give the meal a miss.

Luckily, he had packed some savouries and sandwiches, along with bottles of juice, and the three of us decided to nip back to the bus to eat alone.

Malaysia is a beautiful country, and the last section of the trip into Malacca was a fine example. Once we left the motorway, tropical rainforest, aglow with the brilliant flame of the forest, reached down to the edge of the road. Sprawling pockets of atap houses scattered down side roads and up neighbouring hillsides like clusters of land crabs, and the larger villages boasted traditional Malay structures with huge sloping roofs and intricately decorated façades.

We reached Malacca mid-afternoon and the bus pulled into the interchange, bordered on three sides by a car park and office buildings, and on the other by the river which ran through the town. We decided to take a taxi to the hotel Ming Chuan had booked, and while I stood at a respectable distance, Josie and Ming Chuan haggled with the drivers. Finally a price was agreed and we piled on board as the driver let out the clutch. The vehicle hopped across the potholed parking area in a series of violent jerks, rather like a hiccuping kangaroo, before settling into a more regular motion.

With the driver laughing and apologising, we screeched around the first corner on two wheels. He had barely brought all four back in contact with the road, when he swung the opposite way on the other pair, sending his passengers and luggage bouncing around the vehicle like bean bags. The driver explained that he was not deliberately taking the longest route, but due to the one-way system, he had to travel in a complete circle to bring us to the front of our hotel, a Balinese building Ming Chuan had seen on an earlier visit.

It fronted onto one of the narrower thoroughfares, and although over two hundred years old, had recently been refurbished and redecorated. The building was three storeys high, with dark green facings and primrose trimmings, and a central balcony hung out over the road rather like the bulging pocket on a builder's apron. Beneath, a wide verandah shaded large, drooping palms in terracotta pots and two suites of rattan furniture had been placed on either side of a carved wooden doorway. Visitors, entering through two half-doors rather like those seen in the entrances to wild-west saloons, found themselves in a small atrium. Here a huge Balinese statue, surrounded by greenery, reached up towards a distant skylight through which the sun scattered dainty patterns up and down a curved marble staircase.

Wooden carvings of Balinese dancers, grotesque masks of mythical figures and exquisitely framed Batik pieces lined the walls, while antique sofas, reclining teak easy chairs draped in expensive antimacassars and hand-carved tables offered guests the opportunity to enjoy a quiet coffee in cool comfort away from the dust and noise of the street. It was as if one had stepped back in time, and I half expected Rudyard Kipling or Somerset Maugham to descend the staircase as we approached the front desk to check in.

After a welcoming drink, a young man in the hotel livery took our key and carried our bags to the lift. We squeezed into the tiny cabin and held our collective breath as it ground upwards.

The rooms on the top floor branched off either side of one

long corridor which ended in a wide balcony with an impressive view. Out over the roof-tops of several old shop-houses, beyond Chinatown, one could gaze across the heavily silted Malacca river where rows of flat boats lay side by side like slats in a window curtain, even as far as Dutch Square with its delightful, salmon-pink colonial buildings.

Our room was spacious and graciously restored. The high ceiling had been retained, as had the quaint shutters on the windows and the original facings and cornices, but thankfully the beds and facilities were up to date. Josie had a single room next door, which had been similarly refurbished.

We settled in, and then decided to make the all-important phone call. On the first attempt there was no reply. We waited five minutes and tried again. Eventually a male voice answered, and in Chinese, Josie explained our position. There was a short answer before she replaced the receiver and sank onto the side of my bed.

'This is the situation. Yan Siang is staying with his uncle, a wealthy farmer, somewhere outside Malacca. The uncle doesn't want him to return to Singapore until the police have finished investigating his father's death.'

'Really? He's the only one who knows who killed his father. How can the police –'

'I haven't finished yet,' Josie said.

'Sorry.'

'When I explained your predicament, the man at the other end said he would pass the information on to the uncle and later this evening, about nine o'clock, he'll call us back.'

'So we wait here… till nine o'clock.'

Josie looked surprised. 'Why? It's only four-fifteen. We've got time to go out and have a look at the town.'

I sighed and lay back. 'You go. I'd rather just lie here and wait.'

'No way. A walk will do us good. Help take our minds off things.'

There was no arguing with Josie. We grabbed our wallets and headed for the lift. Outside the air was warm and sultry, so we each carried a face-cloth to deal with perspiration. Surrounding the hotel were several fascinating little streets full of quaint antique shops and art galleries which radiated out like spokes in a wheel. We chose to walk down the widest road which ran from the right of the main entrance, stopping to peer through greyish windows at teak and mahogany furniture dating back to the colonial era. At the end of the street, we crossed into a main thoroughfare which wound its way around several ancient buildings, finally leading onto a bridge over the river. Beyond, we turned past the clock tower into Dutch Square. Beautifully landscaped and dominated by richly textured colonial buildings, this spot is one of the most famous landmarks in Asia. Just to pause and gaze about is to breathe in the very stuff history is made of, but it is not for everyone. My friends bounced past me and headed directly for the little market stalls.

I was still drinking in the atmosphere when I noticed a movement on my left. I remained gazing ahead, letting my eyes strain sideways. In the shadows beneath the left arch of Christ Church, stood an odd figure. My heart thumped as I recognised the distinctive eye-patch and cap.

Eager not to betray my agitation, I strolled over to the other two.

'Don't look round now,' I cautioned, 'but hiding in the entrance to the red church behind us is our old eye-patch friend.'

'Who?' asked Josie swinging round.

'Don't look now!' I hissed.

'What eye-patch friend?' asked Ming Chuan.

'When someone kicks the shit out of you, you don't forget them in a hurry.'

Ming Chuan broke away and ambled across to the motorbikes parked outside the church. He paused to examine the tyres on one, and then ambled back.

'There's no one with eye-patch, lah.'

'I tell you I saw him distinctly.'

'But you said they'd both been jailed!' Josie whispered.

'I thought they had. Perhaps they've been released… or… look, I don't know why he's here, but it's certainly not to take in the sights.'

Suddenly I realised that in my panic I had begun examining women's batik-patterned underwear, much to the disquiet of the lady managing the stall. I hastily dropped the garments and moved out into the sunlight.

'Let's get away from here,' I muttered.

The sun had disappeared behind the late afternoon haze and evening was approaching. We left the square and crossed the large padang where ancient bullock carts ploughed through their final rounds. I knew the general direction of our hotel but I wanted to check whether we were being followed, so turning into a busy main road I walked past a bank and into a little nonya coffee shop. We chose a table directly across from the main window, which gave us a good view of the street without the risk of being seen.

I ordered three coffees and then, remembering Ming Chuan didn't like coffee, changed the third to a glass of water.

'If we're being followed, we're going to have to be very careful how we get back to Singapore.'

'Why?' asked Ming Chuan.

'Because those men are after the boy.'

'I don't see any men!' he muttered.

'Suit yourself. You don't have to believe me. But I think we'd be best to return by taxi.'

'What, the taxi?' Ming Chuan spat water all over the table. 'No, it'll be expensive!'

'A taxi would give us total control. We can go where we like and stop when we like.'

Two men entered the restaurant. One was gaunt, the other

had curiously drooping jowls rather like an old basset hound. They stood out more because they wore business suits than because they were Caucasian.

'Let's get back to the hotel and wait for that phone call.'

'I also need to phone Singapore to check on Terence.'

'No problem, I've got to call my lawyer.'

We gulped down the coffee and nodded to the owner, leaving more than enough Malaysian money on the table to cover our bill. I led the way out the door, followed by Ming Chuan.

Josie caught us. 'I don't wish to appear paranoid, but don't you think it strange that those two Europeans never ordered anything in that place? They just sat there.'

'Why should that be strange? They might be slow readers. Or perhaps they didn't like what the place had to offer.'

'What?'

'Don't look now, but they've just walked out and they're coming in our direction.'

We walked faster. I turned a corner, crossed the road and shot into a flower shop. We all stood sniffing, selecting and sighing for about ten minutes, but no one passed the shop. When we emerged, there was no sign of the two strangers. I looked at Josie, who shrugged, while Ming Chuan grumbled and headed off towards our hotel.

An hour later, Josie knocked on our door. She had just received a call from Yan Siang's uncle. We were to meet him and Yan Siang the following morning at Bukit China.

'Where?' I asked.

'It's a Chinese cemetery,' Josie replied.

'But isn't it unlucky to meet in a cemetery?'

Josie shrugged, 'That's the deal. The uncle won't come any further into Malacca as he thinks it's too dangerous. He also warned me to check we weren't being followed.'

'Do you know how to get to this cemetery?'

'We can take a taxi…'

'And continue straight on… back to Singapore?'

'If we can find a cabby who'll travel that far.'

'For the right price, these guys will take you to hell and back!' I retorted.

We dressed and showered in preparation for dinner. Josie knew a pleasant little restaurant which overlooked the sea and was famous for its seafood and Western cuisine.

The evening was pleasantly cool. A salty sea breeze tickled the tops of the coconut palms and gently slapped an advertising banner. We enjoyed the meal. I had fried Kway Teow while the others had a seafood platter, accompanied by soft Malay music and the distant boom of the waves. Amply satiated, we returned to our hotel at about ten-thirty to discover our room had been ransacked. I stormed down to reception, and moments later an extremely worried manager stood surveying the damage. The police duly arrived and took a rather thin statement from each of us. We could hardly tell the constable much, as nothing was missing, and although we could theorise as to why our room had been visited, we did not want to give the police any reason for delaying our departure. Finally, with many apologies and assurances that this sort of thing just did not happen in Malacca, the manager left with the police.

Josie looked puzzled, 'What were they looking for?'

'Nothing!' I replied.

'Then it's a pity they didn't find it sooner!'

'What? Nothing? Ming Chuan groaned, gathering up the scattered clothing and repacking the books, toiletries and other articles that lay tossed about the room.

'Think about it. If they'd really been looking for something, do you think they'd have advertised the fact by leaving this mess? We've just been given a little advance warning. Someone is after us and they want us to know it.'

'Why?' Ming Chuan asked nervously.

'They hope we'll panic… make mistakes…'

Josie looked troubled. 'This means they're very sure of themselves.' She returned to her room.

With the shutters open, night streamed in, exotic and romantic. Normally this would have been a great time for making love, but after a few perfunctory cuddles and kisses we felt too weighed down by recent events and moved to our separate beds. As the hours passed I tossed and turned, throwing off the covers, only to clutch them back again as my body grew cold.

'Can't sleep?' a little voice whispered.

'Nope,' I replied.

'We stay awake together.'

A moment later, Ming Chuan was cuddled up beside me.

CHAPTER

27

Just after nine, we met Josie in the restaurant for breakfast. During our halal meal, the manager came to our table with more apologies for the troubles of the previous evening and an assurance that our bill would be halved as a show of good faith. This generous gesture excited my digestive juices and increased my enjoyment of the meal.

We returned to our rooms, packed, and then met at reception to clear the bill. I paid while Josie and Ming Chuan went out to find a taxi. The manager was as good as his word and our accommodation proved very cheap. I walked outside just as a taxi rattled round the corner. Recognising my friends in the back, I hastily threw the bags in the boot and clambered on board. Once again, no meter. Josie had haggled for the best price she could get and almost lost the taxi in the process.

Once at Bukit China, we scrambled out and asked the driver to wait while we looked for our contact. He grumbled and shook his head but agreed when Josie upped the ante. A late-model Proton drew up and a surprisingly young, good-looking Chinese businessman stepped out of the driver's side and shook hands with each of us.

'Were you followed?'

'We didn't see anyone, but that doesn't mean we weren't,' I replied.

'You're Mr Richards?'

'I am.'

'Good. Put those bags in the back and get in.'

We did as instructed, then turned to pay off the taxi driver. However, he wanted more than we had agreed. Our new friend spoke to him fiercely in Malay, whereupon he took off without another word. The uncle nudged the Proton out into Jalan Puteri Hang and then put his foot down.

'My name's Chang… Eugene Chang. Yan Siang's father was my brother.'

'Oh, I'm sorry,' I offered.

'Don't be! The man was a bastard. Please excuse my bluntness. I have one child, but I've always taken an interest in my brother's kids. I know Yan Siang could do well in his studies if he had more encouragement at home and better discipline generally.'

'He's a bright boy,' I agreed.

'I took him away from Singapore to give him a chance, but the poor kid misses his family. He's keen to go back there, even though he knows it's dangerous. Up till now I wouldn't consider letting him. That is, until you called.'

Chang steered the car down a side road. 'You know the boy admires you?'

I was amused. 'His mother said he liked me.'

'Oh, he doesn't like you, he worships you. Talks about you all the time — this fun teacher with the farm in New Zealand and lots of money.'

I blushed. 'Well he's right about the farm.'

'Your young lady friend said you were in some trouble?'

I briefly outlined the situation and Chang listened intently. I could tell by his worried glances that he believed every word, and I was flattered.

'Your nephew has been a very difficult student. However, you're right about his ability. He has a lot of talent, but it won't get him very far unless the people behind his father's murder are put away.'

'Are you sure you can look after him, if he goes back with you? His family can't handle him and I don't want him wandering about the city staying with friends.'

Josie leaned forward. 'He can stay with my family.'

'That's generous of you. Thanks!' the uncle sounded relieved.

We drove on in silence for several minutes, admiring the change in scenery. The little houses and shanties on the edge of the town had disappeared, and now we were surrounded by large, palatial homes — a Malaccan millionaires' row. The Proton turned into a sweeping driveway through a pair of large wrought-iron gates, which swung open automatically, and swept past a landscaped garden with a pond full of jumping koi, up to a large neo-colonial portico.

'Wow…' Josie whispered.

Chang looked at me intently. 'Do you know what my brother was involved in?'

'No idea,' I answered.

A pretty, young Chinese girl came running down the steps. 'This is my daughter, Jasmine.'

'Pleased to meet you,' I offered my hand.

'Hi, hello,' Ming Chuan said as he shook hands and Josie gave her a peck on the cheek.

'Welcome! Happy to see you!' the vivacious girl sparkled.

Suddenly a little figure shot through the door and shrieked, 'Mr Richards… Mr Richards… teacher!' He jumped the final three steps and almost landed on top of me. 'Thank you… thank you…' He threw his arms around my waist and threatened to crack some ribs.

'Hi, Yan Siang,' I gasped, overpowered by this extraordinary welcome.

'Oh, teacher!' He made to grab me again, but I held him at arm's length.

'You've got a lot of explaining to do.'

'Teacher, I know, but I change... sure... I have!' His eyes sparkled in competition with his teeth as a stray lock of hair fell across his face.

Looking at him, I suddenly knew why I had come. My career, my name, my future were hardly the reasons. It was all for him. Somewhere behind those eyes was a spirit that is part of all of us. It was not selfless. I loved this kid as every father should love his son or daughter and, more importantly, I believed in him.

'You'd better take your teacher inside and offer him a drink,' Eugene Chang laughed and winked at me.

'That's a generous offer, but we'd rather be on our way.'

'Are you sure?'

'Perfectly. Could you help us find another taxi?'

'No need,' Chang smiled.

'I beg your pardon?'

'You can take my Mercedes, it'll easily seat six people.'

'Six? But there're only four of us.'

'Six, including Boong-boong and my driver.'

'Boon-boong? Who's Boong-boong?'

'Wait, I show you.'Yan Siang bounded back up the steps.

Josie joined me and whispered, 'Boy, you've got a number one fan there.'

I smiled and draped my arm over Ming Chuan's shoulder.

'Let's move to my garage,' Chang suggested, guiding us around the side of the building into the shade of a large jacaranda tree.

'That's it?' I gasped.

Parked in the driveway, gleaming in the sun, was a maroon Mercedes — a connoisseur's dream. Ming Chuan ran up to it and marvelled. Josie just uttered a silent prayer, thanking the Lord for good people. Standing by the driver's door was a short, casually dressed young Indian, teeth flashing in a smile which suggested high spirits and impishness.

I didn't know what to say. 'This… it's very generous of you.'

'Not at all. I want the boy to be safe. If you travel in my car, you can contact me at any time if there's a problem. The car has two-way radio and a cell phone. As for the driver, you'll love him. He trained in New York, and anyone who can handle that traffic can handle anything.'

'It's very good of you to drive us,' I gushed.

'No way man!' He looked at Chang and laughed, 'He pays an' I's plays!'

Chang gave him a friendly cuff on the ear. 'This is Lincoln, as in the president!'

'No, as in da Continental!' The young man's eyes flashed.

Suddenly Yan Siang reappeared in the company of a dark-skinned boy who seemed remarkably shy.

Chang introduced him. 'This is Boong-boong. He's Thai.' The boy bowed gracefully, clasping his hands together in the traditional Thai manner. Knowing the protocol, I reciprocated.

'He speaks very little English. Yan brought him here.' I noticed that Chang's eyes had darkened.

Josie made the traditional Thai greeting, 'Pleased to meet you, Boong-boong.'

'Name Tortoise,' the boy replied.

'No, your name is Boong-boong,' Chang corrected firmly.

The boy hung his head and there was a long silence. Then he and Yan Siang ran back round the house.

Suddenly Josie looked at me in astonishment. 'Tortoise! Don't you see what that means?' she hissed.

I shook my head.

'Remember the list. Mr Magenta… an address… a letter… and a sum of money?'

It hit me. '… and an animal.'

'Exactly! I bet Boong-boong is one of those animals… tortoise.'

Chang sighed, 'So you know?'

'Know what?' I replied stupidly.

'About The Flaming Dragon?'

'Not really.'

Chang looked grim. 'This boy was brought down from Thailand. His parents sold him to an Australian and he was used as a courier. It took me hours of coaxing to get that much out of him and he refuses to say any more. Fortunately I speak a little Thai, which helped. He claims he has friends in Singapore, but they're all mixed up in that Flaming Dragon place.'

'What about Yan Siang? Has he told you anything about his father's death?'

'No, and I haven't asked him. I know he loved his father, but my brother was worthless, always moving from one shady deal to the next. I'm not surprised someone killed him and, to be honest, I'm not interested in how it happened.'

'Aren't you worried that someone might find out you're hiding the boys?'

'Up here? Not likely. I have too many friends in this district.' He laughed. 'Malaysia is as corrupt as hell. Here money speaks every language and it really shouts in Bahasa Melayu.'

The two boys returned with our bags and Chang held the back door open. We piled into the gleaming machine, boys in the front and the rest of us in the back. Josie asked if she could use the cell phone to call Singapore. Chang grinned and nodded.

He leaned down to my window and whispered, 'Good luck with your SAC.'

'You're well informed.'

'I make it my business to check out everyone I'm having dealings with, no offence intended.'

'None taken!'

'I also took the liberty of giving Yan Siang some advice on how to conduct himself, I hope you don't mind.'

'Not at all, it was very good of you.'

'He won't let you down.'

I was still to be convinced!

We prepared to leave, with no news from Tan Tock Seng.

'I think you should take this.' Chang passed a black piece of metal, wrapped in an oily cloth, through the window and I shrank back.

'It's a revolver. I've had it for a while, but I've kept it in good condition. It's registered in Singapore and Malaysia in my name, so be careful who you shoot.'

'I can't take that… I wouldn't know how to use it.'

'Just slip the safety catch,' he showed me how, 'then point it and pull the trigger. I should warn you, though, it comes with only two bullets.' He dropped the package in my lap and stood back. 'Have a good trip!'

I slipped the gun under the seat, intending to leave it there. The car accelerated smoothly and we disappeared down the drive.

CHAPTER

28

The car purred along the main road to Kuala Lumpur like a sleek cheetah. The boys in the front chattered away in a mix of Thai and Singlish, while I reclined in the comfort of plush leather, thinking back over all Chang had told us. Pieces of the jigsaw were beginning to fit, but several big bits were still missing. Boong-boong had been a real surprise.

I leaned back and accidentally pushed a button beneath the arm rest. A carved walnut case swung outwards from the back of the front passenger's seat to reveal a mini-bar. Before me spread a dazzling array of mixes, liqueurs, wines and classic beers.

I beamed. 'Now, what would everyone like to drink?'

'Tiger beer, please,' a little voice piped up from the front.

I pulled out a bottle, emptied it into two glasses and handed them over the seat. 'Orange juice coming up!'

Josie leaned over. 'I'll have the same.'

I poured Ming Chuan a glass of water and popped the top off a bottle of Fosters for myself. We settled back with packets of crisps, peanuts and Indian crackers.

'This sort of life I could easily fit into,' I cackled, munching crisps and sipping beer. The boys had discovered the secret to the stereo system and soon heavy rock was bouncing around the inside of the car. Fortunately, Lincoln had suffered this before and he quickly locked the system into a local Malay radio station.

Chang had suggested that we travel down the coast. It would take longer, but was more scenic and there was less traffic. Paddy fields and grasslands swept away to our left, with the marshy expanse of low tide sloping down towards a distant glimmer of blue on our right. Closer in, huge mangroves sunk their long, thick tentacles deep into the fluid soil, like lines of woody octopi. At intervals, sarong-wrapped mamas sat under palm trees singing and preparing coconut balls encased in palm leaves, while tiny, scantily-clad figures dashed across the shimmering horizon.

'It's so peaceful,' Josie mused. I smiled and nodded.

As the kilometres passed, I began to wonder about lunch. As if reading my mind, Lincoln said, 'We'll stop soon for food. 'Sides, I have to get some gas.'

'Sounds good,' I replied.

We filled the car in Muar, an attractive little town perched on a river delta. Once beyond the town, Lincoln turned down a beach road which brought us out onto a small headland. Below us the sea swirled and splashed around groups of rocks sticking out of the water like giant, jagged fangs. The windows lowered, allowing a faint breeze to waft through the car, scented by frangipani and jasmine. Lincoln pushed several more buttons and arm rests were transformed into small side-tables, seats repositioned to allow more space, and the air conditioning was adjusted to deal with the change in temperature. I marvelled at the technical wonders man had created and the number of them money could buy.

A large luncheon hamper appeared from beneath the driver's seat. Chang had thought of everything — the decision to give us the car was clearly not spontaneous. Once opened, the hamper proved a treat for all five senses: crisp, fresh vegetables in a tempting salad, steamed fish and tasty deep-fried chicken wings, ikan bilis steeped in thick chili sauce, fragrant coconut rice topped with fried eggs, half a dozen soft, white pao and an assortment of delicious nonya cookies. With tissues at the ready and cool drinks to wash down the flavours, we tucked into the feast. What a party! Good company, a natural ambiance and food fit for a king. Sea birds wheeled above us and the ocean softly keened below. Who could possibly ask for more?

I was admiring the bouquet of a delicate Malaysian wine when we got company. A dark-coloured Proton drew up further along the road just beyond the headland. I was not unduly bothered. The wine bubbled deliciously and my second chicken wing tasted just as scrumptious as the first.

Lincoln nudged me and pointed, 'Friends of yours?'

I followed his finger. The two strangers had left their vehicle and were heading in our direction.

Josie gasped, 'Those are the two from the restaurant.'

'Time we left,' I said urgently.

Lincoln shoved the pao he was enjoying back into the hamper, adjusted his seat and gunned the engine. The car shot backwards. I lurched forwards and found myself wearing the bouquet I had so recently been admiring. Ming Chuan grumbled as ikan bilis shot all over his pants, and Josie was searching for a rambutan that had cheekily disappeared down her cleavage. The boys shrieked with excitement.

Lincoln spun the wheel and accelerated, driving the car straight at the two strangers. They bravely stood their ground until they saw we meant business. Then one leapt sideways into a patch of reedy grass and wild orchids while the other shot straight into a mango bush. We reached the main road and sped away south. No one spoke. We were much too busy trying to anticipate the bumps which threatened to bounce our heads off the top of the car. Lincoln swerved in all directions hoping to avoid the worst of the dips, but the more he avoided, the more he seemed to hit.

'I don't think they're following us,' I gasped, trying to juggle the remainder of my meal while fiercely gripping the door handle and looking out the rear window.

'They will!' countered Lincoln.

'So what if they do? A Merc can outrun a Proton.'

'Under normal conditions, sure. But on this sort of road?'

As if to underline the point, we reached the top of a hill, shot out into space and landed with a withering bang which shook the car off into the grass verge. It took all of Lincoln's skill to return it to the centre of the road. We bounced and shook for another ten kilometres before we finally reached a comfortably flat, well-sealed stretch of bitumen.

'Awesome! This should take us into Batu Pahat,' Lincoln enthused.

Suddenly Yan Siang, who had been focusing all his attention on the rearview mirror, shrieked, 'It's them… those…!'

I spun round and saw the black Proton lurching along behind us. Lincoln pursed his lips and placed his foot on the floor. The Mercedes sprang forward, speedo needle heading for 140 kph, and the Proton disappeared in a cloud of dust. The boys cheered, but it was short-lived. Ahead of us, flashing lights and plastic orange-coloured boards warned of road works. The sigh was unanimous as Lincoln drastically reduced speed.

A brightly-clad road worker waved a stop sign and we slowed to allow two cars to pass. As the sign changed, Lincoln stuck his head out the window and thrust a hundred ringgit bill at the man, accompanied by an instruction in Malay. The road worker laughed and nodded. We drove on. Our pursuers were met with a red stop sign and three burly road workers to back it up. The gap between us quickly widened. Everybody cheered. I leaned forward and whispered to Lincoln, 'That's got to be worth a hefty bonus!' He smiled, but his eyes never left the road.

It was early afternoon, and a light mist descended across the jungle which had replaced the grasslands and rice paddies on our left. The sea had moved further away, and now a ridge of wild fern and stunted bushes ran alongside the road. We passed a sign which said Batu Pahat 35 kilometres. The roadworks ended and we returned to the well-worn, bumpy surface which made comfortable travel difficult. After the excitement, everyone gradually settled, although the boys still maintained a tense vigil.

'Wah lau… they're back again.'

We all screwed round, and sure enough a dark-coloured car was swaying and lurching far behind us, throwing up an enormous dust cloud.

'Can we make Batu Pahat before they catch us?' I asked nervously.

'I'd like to, man, but that bump we hit earlier shook the old girl around a bit and I don't want to gun her too much in case something's loose, you know what I'm saying?'

That was not the sort of answer I had hoped for, and as I glanced in the rearview mirror I regretted my earlier comments about the respective qualities of Mercedes versus Protons. The dark shape was definitely getting closer and as Lincoln asked the Mercedes for more speed, we began to swing dangerously all over the road.

Suddenly the road improved and Lincoln hit the accelerator hard. The car powered forwards. The Proton was again left in the distance and everybody heaved a sigh of relief. However, within a few kilometres the road deteriorated and all eyes returned to the dark dot slowly gaining on us once more. I held my breath as the Proton crept closer and still closer. Everyone prayed for another stretch of good road, but it did not come. We thundered along as the lethal black shape moved in behind us. Lincoln hit a large bump and the Mercedes shot to the left, giving the Proton its chance. The driver accelerated and drew alongside. For a frightening moment I saw a heavily jowled face leer out of the window and then I glimpsed the gun.

'Look out,' I yelled as three shots peppered the side of our car.

'Friccussie, that dude's sporting a piece!' Lincoln shrieked.

The boys' heads shot up for a quick look, but Lincoln pushed them down with his left arm. He was now hunched over the wheel, while Josie, Ming Chuan and I crouched on the floor at the rear. More shots rang out and I heard Boong-boong yelp in pain.

'The kid's been hit,' Lincoln groaned as he swung the car all over the road, forcing the Proton to drop back.

I clambered halfway over the front seat to check the boys as Lincoln swerved dangerously. My head shot forward between the boys' legs and crashed against the dashboard as my feet swung up and smashed against the roof of the car. With my good arm trying to gain purchase on something solid, my shoulder hit the steering wheel and Lincoln screamed in pain as my plaster-cast smashed against his inner thigh. Josie pulled on my legs and swung me upright. My head ached, but I had seen blood streaming across Boong-boong's chest and Yan Siang had vomited all over the floor and was now in a dead faint.

I collapsed into the back, mumbling, 'Blood… all over Boong-boong.'

Josie scrambled over the seat and examined the wound. Helpfully, Lincoln slowed the car and again the Proton moved up, this time trying to squeeze through on our left.

'I'm getting real mad!' Lincoln muttered. 'We're bigger than he is.'

He let the driver slip the Proton right alongside us, and just as the gun reappeared, he swung the Mercedes savagely left. With a nightmarish grinding and wrenching the two cars met and melded. For a split second we raced along together and then shot apart. The driver of the Proton, taken completely by surprise, found his car headed straight for a road sign. He swerved to avoid the obstruction, miscalculated and rocketed straight into the jungle.

'He won't bother us for a while,' Lincoln cooed in triumph.

'Is everybody okay?'

'Boong-boong's been shot in the arm. It's not deep, but it's bleeding badly and will need to be bandaged,' Josie replied.

'Is the bullet still in the arm?'

'I don't know.' She grinned wryly at me. 'How's your head?'

'Bloody awful. It's banging like a pair of bongo drums.' I looked hopefully at Lincoln. 'Can we stop for a while?' He nodded.

We drove on for about a kilometre, and then turned off onto a little jungle path. The car rolled to a stop under a large Malayan oak. I opened the door and stumbled out.

Lincoln pulled the boot lid and in seconds had set up three folding chairs and placed Yan Siang in the nearest. Ming Chuan offered him a glass of water. Josie and I carried Boong-boong across to the other chairs and sat him in one with his feet up on the other, while Lincoln fetched the first-aid kit from the back. He handed me a bottle of mineral water and a piece of tinfoil.

'Three Panadol, take 'em all!'

Next he turned to Ming Chuan. 'Walk down the path a ways, will you, and check those clowns don't catch us napping.'

Josie had carefully examined Boong-boong's injury and found that the bullet had gone straight through the side of the arm. She dressed the wound and bound it tightly.

I looked at her.

'Still glad you came?'

'Wouldn't have missed it for the world!'

Lincoln joined us. 'We'd better not hang around too long. Those other dudes'll be on our tail pretty quick, you know what I'm saying?'

'Okay, Lincoln. Look, we really appreciate all your help.'

'Ahh… it's nothing. 'Sides, I like you guys. Now let's get back in the car.'

We placed Boong-boong on the back seat with Ming Chuan at his head and Josie supporting his feet. I sat in the front with

Yan Siang. Lincoln had flushed out the floor and lit a jasmine stick. The car smelt and felt a lot better. We slipped out of the jungle back onto the coast road, although the sea was now merely a distant sigh. Lincoln drove slowly as the surface had not improved, and we were worried about Boong-boong. Within a few minutes, everyone was nodding off.

Suddenly something pulled me awake. I looked in the rearview mirror. The black Proton was steaming up behind us and we were swaying all over the road.

'Lincoln,' I screamed.

'What?' he mumbled, coming awake.

'Look out!'

It was too late. The Proton had drawn level and with our speed so low, Heavy Jowls had a perfect shot. I swung the wheel as his gun went off. A bullet ricocheted off the chrome, clipping two of Lincoln's fingers as it spun away and holed the windscreen. Lincoln swore. Again our cars collided, but this time the other driver was ready. He shot ahead and we merely grazed his back bumper. Lincoln wrapped some cloth around his fingers and left the wheel to me. The Proton slowed in front, forcing us to drop our speed. Again I swung the wheel and shot past him. But this time I totally miscalculated. We were too far right. As I struggled to correct, Lincoln panicked and pushed the wheel against my movement. The car swung crazily all over the road. Again the Proton tried to pass on the inside, but he chose his moment badly. Our sideways lurch struck him full force. He jumped a ditch and again disappeared into the jungle undergrowth.

'Leave the bloody wheel to me,' I yelled, steering to the right, as our tyres bounced over reeds and ferns on the left of the road. Lincoln let go of the wheel just as I pulled and we shot wildly further right. I could see the ridge rearing towards us.

'Look out!' I yelled as we shot crazily up the bank, hit the top and paused for one terrifying moment before flipping over and diving spectacularly towards the beach.

We landed on our left side with a sickening crunch, shattering the front windscreen and driving soft sand into the car. For several seconds no one moved, and then Lincoln forced his door up and struggled out. Yan Siang lay squashed between me and the door. I could hear Ming Chuan groaning in the back, but nothing from the other two. Once out, Lincoln opened the rear door and helped Ming Chuan pull himself up. By then I had clambered out, leaving Yan Siang unconscious against the door. I helped the others lift Boong-boong clear. Miraculously, apart from the arm, he was uninjured and in no further pain. Josie stumbled out on her own. Lincoln climbed back into the car to rescue Yan Siang. He lifted the thin little figure and passed him to me. My heart dropped. It would be a cruel blow to lose the little fellow now. I clutched him to my chest as we sank onto the sand, and Josie took his pulse and heartbeat.

'It's all right. He's just been knocked out,' she smiled.

Lincoln surveyed the damage and shook his head. His two injured fingers did not seem to bother him.

'We ain't going to be going anywhere in this here vehicle for a while,' he announced.

'What's Chang going to say when he hears we've trashed his Mercedes?' I moaned.

'Not much. He's got another three, and a Porsche. An' then there's the Daimler and the Audi.'

'What it is to be poor!' Josie remarked wryly.

'Focus, friends. This ain't no birthday party! First, we need to move away from the car and cover our tracks.'

Yan Siang uttered a groan and Josie gave him some water. He slowly stirred and tried to stand.

'Stay there,' I ordered.

'Yes, teacher,' he whimpered, closing his eyes and drifting away again.

'You'll have to wake him, man,' Lincoln ordered. 'We cain't hang around here,'

'I'll carry him,' I replied.

Lincoln looked over at Ming Chuan. 'You can move?' Ming Chuan nodded. 'Josie?'

'I think so, I'm just a bit shaken…'

'… but not stirred,' I quipped.

Unimpressed, she replied tersely, 'I can move, okay?'

'Great! So if Mingy Thingy gives her a hand with Boong-boong, you can manage Yan Siang?'

'No problem,' I replied.

'Right, let's clear the car and disappear!'

Following Lincoln's instructions, we struggled up the bank while he collected the first-aid kit and a survival box. Yan Siang came to as we reached the summit and struggled to stand on his own.

'Now what do we do?' I asked nervously.

Lincoln patted me on the back and grinned, 'Never fear, Lincoln's here!'

'How can you joke when we're in such a bloody mess?'

'Chill out, man, chill out! There's a little village not far from here and the head dude will help us.'

'Why should he?'

'Cos he works for Mr Chang.'

That sounded like a good answer, but I looked at our sorry little group and despaired, 'These people can't travel.'

'C'mon, Pete! What choice do we have? We can't just sit here and wait till those men return.'

Once again, Josie was right.

'OK. Let's go,' I sighed.

With my arm round Yan Siang's shoulder and Josie and Ming Chuan shepherding Boong-boong, Lincoln led our strange little party into the jungle as the sun dipped further towards the sea.

CHAPTER
29

Half an hour into the bush, we reached a clearing and Lincoln allowed us to pause for a rest. Considering our debilitated condition, we were progressing well. Ming Chuan had hurt his shoulder and I feared it could be dislocated. Boong-boong was obviously in pain, but he put a brave face on it, nursing his arm gingerly as Josie helped him move. Yan Siang clung to me and whimpered pitifully every now and again. His head had been caught between the frame of the door and the cast on my arm, and he was still very groggy. I was worried that he might be concussed. He looked pale and the journey was clearly taking its toll. Lincoln had almost forgotten about his fingers, but my left wrist, pulled in the struggle with the steering wheel, had come out in sympathy with my throbbing head. Josie was the only one of us who had emerged from this whole sorry episode unscathed.

We sat on upended tree stumps and clumps of fern, and polished off the remainder of the lunch. Lincoln had brought a couple of cans of beer which were now lukewarm and, mindful of my injuries, I shook my head when he offered me one. We all stuck to water, unsure how far we still had to march. The two-way radio had been wrecked in the smash, but Lincoln hoped to use the cell phone once the jungle thinned out a bit.

Somewhat replenished, we packed everything away and prepared to move on. The jungle rose up on all sides like a tall, green wall. Huge, gnarled trunks twisted above us, festooned with a variety of hanging creepers and flowering lianas. The undergrowth was thicker than anything I had seen previously, and thorny bushes fought for space with fern fronds and fat, bulbous orchids. The noise was deafening. Dozens of clicking insects and shrieking birds competed with the cries of long-tailed macaques and the chatter of other cheekier monkeys, some of which delighted in swinging down in front of us.

Initially Lincoln hacked a path out of the twisting vines and thick, short bushes with a parang he had found in the survival box. Luckily, not far into the jungle, we came upon an established track. As we prepared to move off, I suddenly realised that I had left Ming Chuan's small black bag containing my wallet and our passports in the car.

'So far away, lah,' begged Ming Chuan.

'If you guys continue on, I'll double back and catch up with you later.'

'I come with you,' Ming Chuan stated flatly.

I put my arm around his shoulder and said just as flatly, 'You can't. Someone has to help Yan Siang.'

'Help him? How about you?'

'I'll be all right!'

Reluctantly I headed off, leaving my friends to struggle further into the green depths. I retraced my steps quickly, and emerged into the sunlight slightly north of the point where the car had left the road. After glancing about carefully and making certain no one was around, I scrambled down the bank.

The bag was not in the front, so I struggled into the back and had just located it when I heard voices. I froze. My face was close to the floor and I could see nothing.

Suddenly the voices stopped and I heard someone coming

down the bank. I grabbed rattan rugs and Boong-boong's shirt and covered myself up as the approaching stranger landed with a dull thud on the sand behind the car. Carefully I pushed myself down hard against the left-hand door.

'There's nothing here,' a man shouted as he peered into the car. 'Wait a moment. There's a bundle of… something… down…' He struggled to reach into the back of the vehicle, placing his body weight across the rear right-hand door. He was within inches of my behind, when his size upset the car's balance and it started to swing drunkenly.

The man jumped clear, landing backwards in the sand.

'Bloody hell!'

'What happened?'

'Nothing,' came the disgusted reply. I heard him move away. 'They've all bloody gone.'

After two minutes of scrambling and cursing, there was silence. I remained cramped in unbearable agony for a further five minutes before twisting around to find a more comfortable position. Ten minutes later, I decided it would be safe enough to venture out. There was no sign of anybody. Clutching the bag and the gun, which I had decided to take for insurance, I clambered up the bank. The men had gone. Softly, I headed after my little band.

No one was happy that I had left. As they struggled ever deeper into the greenery, the mosqitoes and flies became more persistent and daring. Everyone began to wish for some hint of civilisation. An hour passed, and friendly green plants began to assume other, unworldly shapes. Raucous sounds of day gave way to the eerie calls of bats and other nocturnal creatures. The little group huddled together, their progress slowing to a faltering walk.

'Ah yoi, that stupid black bag,' Ming Chuan muttered.

'Forget it, man. Pete'll be okay.' Lincoln turned to his right and took a mighty swing at a protruding piece of vine just as a heavily sweating, slightly overweight European stepped out in front of him. The man held a gun. Lincoln raised the blade in surprise.

'Drop it,' the man ordered.

Lincoln did.

Another gaunt-faced European walked up the path from behind, swinging a knobbly bamboo cane. 'Isn't this nice. Just out for a little jungle stroll, are we?'

Boong-boong huddled closer to Josie. The man swung the bamboo cane and pointed to the ground. 'Sit!' he barked.

Josie stood her ground. 'These boys are injured and they need medical attention.'

The man glowered at her. 'That's what happens when you have valuable cargo and you don't drive carefully.' He swung his cane idly. 'Which of you was driving?'

The jungle sounds suddenly increased as they all held their breath, and then Lincoln stepped forward. 'I was,' he admitted.

The thin-faced man turned and smiled. He strolled over to the little Indian and struck him hard across the face with the bamboo rod.

'That's for the damage to my car and...' He swept the cane back and brought it crashing down on Lincoln's left shoulder, '... that's for the inconvenience.'

Lincoln winced with pain. Boong-boong gave a soft sigh and slumped to the ground. Josie knelt beside him.

'I told you this boy needs urgent medical help!' she declared, looking up at the two men.

'And he'll get it, my dear. Our car is parked a short distance down the road. Of course we can't take you all, but we'll be only too happy to look after the children, won't we?' He turned to his fat friend, who licked his lips and nodded enthusiastically.

'If you'd all be so good as to remain where you are, we'll leave with the children and once we're out of sight you can continue on your merry way.' He smiled thinly.

'That won't be necessary,' I called, walking up the path.

Ming Chuan yelled, 'Careful, the fat one's got a gun!'

'Drop it or I'll put a bullet clean through your skinny friend,' I ordered, feeling totally in control. I had released the safety catch on Chang's gun and checked the bullets were in place before I showed myself. It felt particularly good to have a chance to turn the tables on those who had been responsible for our recent pain.

The two strangers were taken completely by surprise.

'Why didn't you check for the teacher?' the gaunt-faced man grunted.

'Hurry up, drop the gun,' I repeated, waving my weapon about and enjoying the moment. In my enthusiasm my finger curled round the trigger and the gun went off. The bullet shot past the gaunt man and struck a woody branch behind him. In his confusion he leapt sideways, straight into the path of a splinter which pierced his left ear. He howled in pain. Heavy Jowls promptly threw down his gun and Lincoln jumped past Ming Chuan to grab the weapon and the cane.

'Awesome, man, you can sure pop out of nowhere. Ain't that something!' Lincoln laughed as he walked over to the gaunt stranger and slashed him twice around the legs with the cane. 'Now we're quits!'

The weight of the gun in my hand and the full import of the risks I had just taken brought me to my senses. 'Here, Lincoln, you'd better take over. I don't feel too good.' I sank to my knees and vomited.

'We'd better move,' Lincoln decided.

Josie pulled Boong-Boong to his feet. 'How? These boys have had it. They can't walk another step.'

Lincoln smiled, 'No sweat. We'll take their car.'

'Where is it?' I asked wearily.

'I'm sure our friends will show us.' He advanced on the dispirited pair, but they showed no signs of cooperation. 'We haven't time to waste, man. You'd better answer.' Lincoln looked fearsome with the sharp red welt across his cheek. He waved the gun threateningly, but the strangers still seemed unconvinced.

'That's it then!' Lincoln spun round in a circle like a break-dancer, firing two shots in rapid succession. One spun harmlessly off into the jungle, the other hit Heavy Jowls in the foot. He screamed in pain and fell about the jungle floor scrambling and writhing. Blood oozed through his leather boot and Josie looked at Lincoln in horror.

'Oops! Sorry about that, man. Now, do we get a little help here or do I have to try some more target practice?'

'You didn't have to shoot him,' Josie hissed angrily.

'Stay out of it, lady. If these two dudes don't cooperate pretty soon, Fatso there'll be doing the Mexican hat dance!'

'Pete, do something before somebody gets killed!'

I knelt on the ground, utterly impotent. For several dangerous moments nothing happened, and then Yan Siang started to cry.

That was the last straw. I pulled myself up, stumbled over to the gaunt-faced man and spat, 'Listen, you lump of shit, these kids are seriously ill.'

I grabbed the gun from Lincoln and turned back to the stranger. 'Believe me, I don't care diddly about you two. So if I don't have clear directions to that car in the next three seconds, I'll start shooting chunks off your miserable carcass.' I stuck the gun between Gaunt-face's legs. 'Starting down here.'

We stood glaring at each other and still nothing happened. I savagely thrust the heavy piece of metal upwards and pulled the trigger. The bullet zinged away harmlessly, but the heat and retort of the gun were enough. There was a squelchy sound like a foot in a patch of bog and the resulting odour clearly indicated that Gaunt-face had got the message.

White-faced and moving as if he had just jumped a barbed wire fence and missed, he sidled off down the track.

'Josie, you'd better bandage the other guy's foot.'

'Tightly!' Lincoln sneered and Josie threw him a smouldering glance.

I lifted Yan Siang and followed our guide, keeping as far down-wind as possible. My good hand held the gun directed squarely at his back so he stuck to his task. We walked for several minutes then turned off the track at a point where the jungle thinned out into a small patch of rubber trees. Bordering this clearing, a fence staggered out to a jungle road on the edge of which stood a severely battered Proton.

I placed Yan Siang in the back of the car while Lincoln watched Gaunt-face.

'Let's tie him to the fence,' I suggested. Lincoln secured Gaunt-face while I walked back to the others.

Josie had bound Heavy Jowls' foot and I helped him over to a tree. Meanwhile, Josie put her arms round Boong-boong's waist and with Ming Chuan's help carried him out to the car, escorted by Lincoln.

Once they had disappeared, Heavy Jowls looked at me. 'Why don't you just hand the kids over to us?' he pleaded.

I ignored him.

'Even if you get away, we'll catch up with you sometime and then my mate'll kill you all very slowly.'

I still said nothing.

Heavy Jowls returned to his moaning.

Night was falling fast as Lincoln emerged from the darkness. Together we helped Heavy Jowls out to the car. He was not badly injured. The bullet had merely grazed his ankle. Lincoln tied him beside his partner, then turned to me, 'Give us a hand, Pete, me man! Loosen their belts, will you!'

Intrigued, I did as instructed and Lincoln pulled the trousers clean off each man, revealing disappointingly ordinary-looking briefs, one pair severely stained. He held his nose and threw the pants into the boot. Then, with everybody as comfortably settled in the car as possible, we slowly trundled off down the jungle track.

'Where're we headed?'

'Same village,' Lincoln answered. 'Those guys will head for Batu Pahat once they're freed. Hopefully that won't be till tomorrow morning when the rubber workers check the trees. That gives us a few hours head start.'

CHAPTER

30

We abandoned the car and entered the village on foot. It was hardly a village at all, just a collection of atap huts gathered around a central compound. Groups of children scattered the dust in front of the houses. Sepak takraw, Malayan volleyball played without the hands, sent them jumping, kicking, lunging and flipping in all directions. Grimy little faces smiled and laughed as we stumbled into their backyard looking lost.

A tall Malay man wrapped in a sarong emerged from a coffee shop. Wisdom and experience had carved their lines deep into his face and weighty responsibilities had whitened once-thick hair. Although his callussed hands indicated he had worked in the fields most of his life, his back was straight and his carriage bore the unmistakable stamp of authority. He nodded to me when I stood and stepped down to greet him.

'Selamat,' I smiled.

'Selamat datang,' he returned in a strong yet subdued voice, casting his eyes warily behind me and noting the condition of our group. He turned to Lincoln and for several moments spoke rapidly in Malay.

Finally Lincoln explained, 'The headman says we are welcome. However, there have been problems with bands of robbers on the run from the police in Klang and that's why he was a little nervous when he saw how roughed up we were.'

'I can understand that. Did you ask him about a doctor?'

Lincoln turned back to the old man and repeated my question in Malay. The man smiled and replied, gesturing simply with his hands.

'The old guy says the nearest doctor operates a little clinic a few miles down the road. He'll send one of the village kids to fetch him. Otherwise, there's the local bomoh.'

'No thanks,' I replied hastily. I had heard of these village bomohs, most of them little more than local witch-doctors. I turned to the headman and nodded, 'Terimah Kasih.'

The old man talked further with Lincoln, then abruptly walked away.

'He says while the doctor's being fetched, he'll take us to his house where we'll spend the night. I know these places, so don't expect too much. They haven't much to give, but what they've got we'll be welcome to.'

I was embarrassed that Lincoln felt the need to excuse the quality of the hospitality. 'We will be grateful for any comfort we're shown.'

Lincoln nodded and helped Josie move Boong-boong. I lifted Yan Siang off the bench and carried him. Ming Chuan smiled bleakly and followed.

The headman's house was set on the side of a small rise and built in the traditional style. We were greeted by three large, smiling ladies — the wife and two daughters. They made us very welcome and while the wife hurried away to prepare food, the daughters showed us to two rooms at the rear of the building. The smaller of the two was simple, but tastefully furnished. A large mosquito net shrouded the bed, which sported a stunning batik quilt.

'Your room?' I asked.

Both girls burst into fits of giggles, and then one blushed,

'Tonight, I sleep with her.' Excessive giggling followed.

The other room was more basic. Two mattresses lay on the polished floor, each draped in mosquito netting. Various carved objects lined the walls and a simple, antique washstand supported a hand-painted jug in a porcelain basin. Both were cracked. However, the room was clean and homely and, after all we had been through, positively luxurious. When the wife arrived with towels, soap, toothbrushes, tooth powder and long nightshirts, I realised that Lincoln had indeed explained our situation in considerable detail. I thanked her profusely. She simply nodded her head and smiled. Finally, we were shown a simple bathroom with a shower.

Boong-boong's dressing badly needed changing and we were alarmed when we noticed how much blood had seeped through the linen. I lay Yan Siang down on one of the mattresses and bunched two pillows up behind him. He was very white and refused to take his arms from around my neck. I gently eased them free.

Josie had a shower, followed by Ming Chuan. Both dressed in the nightshirts, which Josie drew in around the middle with the belt from her jeans. She looked rather chic. My headache had eased and my arm felt much better so I stripped and showered, and then donned a nightshirt.

Lincoln arrived to inform us that dinner would be served in the rooms and the daughters duly arrived with bowls laden with steaming, aromatic meat dishes and platters of fruit. The food was every bit as delicious as it smelt, and by the time the headman returned in the company of an elderly Chinese gentleman, we had finished the main course and were savouring succulent mangoes, juicy watermelon and rich, ripe papaya.

Josie took the doctor to examine Boong-boong. Sometime later she returned and sat beside me.

'Boong-boong has a fever. The doctor cleaned and stitched the bullet wound, then applied another dressing. He gave him an injection and left some antibiotics. However, he thinks the boy should get to a hospital as soon as possible.'

I nodded. 'Could he have a look at Yan Siang?'

Josie fetched the doctor, who helped Yan Siang to his feet and gave him a careful examination. After a few words, the doctor left, refusing any payment.

I poured Josie a lime juice.

'Thanks,' she murmured dropping onto a chair. 'The doctor says he'll be all right. He took a bad knock, but he isn't concussed.'

Yan Siang looked up at me and winked. After dinner I put him to bed. He was not very happy being left alone with Boong-boong, but I promised I would be back soon.

The headman insisted we join him for a beer and, after sharing several cans, we were allowed to retire. Josie took the smaller room on her own, while Ming Chuan and I crept into the other. We had just settled onto the far mattress, when Yan Siang woke. He sat up, fell off the bed and became entangled in the mosquito netting. After struggling clear, he hobbled over to my side of the mattress, pushed me onto Ming Chuan and climbed in.

'Push him out, lah,' Ming Chuan growled.

'Don't be so heartless. You'd better go over and share Boong-boong's mattress.'

'You want me out, leaving that little shit on this bed?'

'He's a fairly important little shit!'

I grabbed Ming Chuan as he sat up and kissed him wildly, pulling him back towards the mattress.

'Go away! Go back to your important little shit!' he flared.

I kissed him again before he grumpily stumbled over to the other bed, leaving me with the warm little body. If only Daisy Liew could see us now!

I could not sleep. I had expected the alcohol in conjunction with the Panadol to knock me out, but it failed. As the darkness deepened, I became hotter and stickier, finally pushing the sheet aside.

Yan Siang moved about restlessly, moaning softly, and crooning in some unintelligible language, 'Wes… ler… wes… we… west… ter… web… ter… wester… web… er… web… ster… ster… web…' This litany continued for several minutes before he groaned and turned over.

I thought back over the day's events and shuddered when I remembered how I had almost shot a man. Gradually I began to drift.

Suddenly Yan Siang started again. This time he kept repeating the same words over and over, 'Webster … check … webster … check … webster …' They made no sense.

I silently prayed for him to stop and gradually his whispering faded.

Certain Yan Siang was asleep, I crept across to the other mattress. Softly I pushed in beside Ming Chuan.

We awoke early to the raucous squawking of the local rooster and the clamour of an awakening household. I struggled up and made for the shower, eager to be ready before anyone else. I was to be disappointed. Lincoln had been up for over an hour. He had phoned Mr Chang the previous night and arrangements had been made for us to pick up another vehicle in Batu Pahat. Chang had also dispatched a group of men to take care of the thugs.

Breakfast was nasi lemak with locally caught fish. Everyone looked better for a night's sleep and Yan Siang was once again full of cheek, despite the nasty gash on his head. Boong-boong was smiling. Ming Chuan was still having trouble with his shoulder, but the headman's wife produced a poultice which she applied with great ceremony and he was forced to appear improved. I had a dull throbbing in the back of my head but I knew that was the drink, so I had enough sense not to complain about it.

During breakfast we were disturbed by the arrival of two

vehicles, the first driven by a burly young Malay.

'Hey, Rabul! Oh, Rabul!' Yan Siang sang out.

'Who's Rabul?' I asked suspiciously.

'Rabul works for Uncle Eugene.' Yan Siang jumped out of his chair before I could reply and swaggered up to Rabul as if he were a big hotshot greeting an important business acquaintance. They hit hands and Yan Siang regaled Rabul with all our adventures, no doubt exaggerating the part he had played in the action.

I laughed to the others, 'Guess he's fully recovered.'

'Looks like it,' Josie grinned. 'Do you think I could call Singapore?'

'Sure. There's a phone inside, and these people won't mind.'

Lincoln spoke to Rabul at length and then walked up to me. 'There's been a bit of a change. We've got two sets of wheels.'

'What?' I replied, choking on a mouthful of rice.

'Mr Chang has rigged up two cars. You'll have to drive one.'

'But I haven't got a Malaysian licence.'

'No problem, man, that's been taken care of. Mr Chang checked your licence status in New Zealand and a special permit's been issued.'

We walked over to the cars. 'Which one do I get?'

'The Corona. The other sleek little beauty's all mine.' I followed his gaze and spotted a gleaming Audi.

We split our group in half. Josie and Boong-boong went with Lincoln, who led the way out of the yard and Ming Chuan and Yan Siang came with me. Again the cars had been well-stocked with refreshments.

The goodbyes were effusive and sincere. We owed the headman and his family a great deal. The boys hung out the windows and screamed at the lithe little bodies running alongside as the cars sped down the jungle track. We found the main road and swung right, out towards the highway and away from the coastal route which had proved so costly.

It was a clear run down to Johore. I was keen to get home and I knew Josie desperately wanted to see Terence. His condition seemed to have stabilised. We streaked along, just breasting the speed limit, enjoying the cool morning air and anticipating Singapore, until we spotted a small Daihatsu truck. It had come from a long way behind, passing car after car, finally creeping in behind the Toyota. I smelt trouble.

'Yan Siang, check out the car on our tail, will you? Do it discreetly.'

'What?'

'Don't let them see you.'

Yan Siang crept up and peered over the back seat. 'Same men, but another man driving.'

'So how? What you going to do?' Ming Chuan quavered.

'Nothing I can do. We'll just have to sit tight and wait for them to move.'

We travelled on several kilometres and nothing happened.

Then, just before a hairpin bend, the Daihatsu pulled out and shot past the Toyota. Once alongside the Audi, the left rear window opened and a hand with a gun appeared. Fortunately at that moment, two cars careered round the corner and I dropped back to let the Daihatsu in.

He played his little game of car and mouse several times before I decided to strike. I waited for the next corner and this time when the Daihatsu pulled out I closed the gap, leaving him nowhere to go. The driver was too intent on the action with the Audi to see the fifteen-ton truck bearing down on him, and when he did it was too late. He jammed on his brakes and so did I. Left with nowhere to go he shot across the median, while the truck swung wildly from side to side trying to miss him. He almost made it, and then the truck tore into his rear bumper and the little wagon flipped. It cartwheeled spectacularly along the right-hand side of the road, finally spinning into the centre and smashing into another truck, two behind the first.

There was a dreadful screaming of tyres and a dull thwump as the truck crushed the front of the Daihatsu, before throwing it off the road completely.

I swung to the left and braked on the shoulder of the road, parking behind Lincoln.

'What's that fellow, crazy?' he yelled.

'We'd better see what's happened.'

'You mosey on back and have a look, and we'll wait here for you.'

Once back in the Toyota I waited for a break in the traffic, and then spun the vehicle round.

The Daihatsu was lying in an irrigation canal, thoroughly masticated. One glance and I knew instantly that no one could possibly have walked away from it alive. I looked about as people started to gather and I watched a couple of road workers clamber down to the smashed vehicle. Then I noticed the remains of a body lying sprawled on the edge of the canal. It was a mess — savagely disfigured and bloodied, twisted and broken like a pulverised puppet. What fascinated me was the head. Where two ears should have been were two dark holes and the scalp was covered in little clumps of black stubble. As realisation dawned, I staggered back to the Toyota and vomited.

CHAPTER
31

Deep down I had been happy when the Daihatsu crashed, believing that the vicious devils of the previous night had got their just desserts. Now I knew I had spotted Eye-patch and his friend in Malacca and strange as it seemed, I was sorry they had died in such a terrible way. They were really just a pair of misfits, easily dealt with. Gaunt-face and his fat friend were quite a different species.

'Teacher, teacher, they all dead?'

I looked down at Yan Siang and nodded. 'I think so.'

I had never been so pleased to reach Johore Bahru. Lincoln had arranged with Chang to drop the Toyota off at the Putri Pan Pacific Hotel, so we could all pass through the checkpoint together. He suggested we have a coffee and something to eat before we crossed, so we parked near the Kotaraya Shopping Complex and found a little coffee shop which sold fried chicken and chips.

Lincoln munched crackers and looked at me quizzically. 'Hey man, if I had as many hoods after my scalp as you have, I think I'd find myself another country!'

I did not answer, but I knew Josie and Ming Chuan were staring at me.

'You know what I'm saying?'

'I know what you're saying.'

I glared at him pointedly, but Lincoln was not easily put off.

'Those dudes in that little toy truck, they wasn't the dudes we roped up yesserday.'

'Is that right, Pete?' Josie asked anxiously.

I was starting to develop a real dislike for this pompous little ass with his 'dudes' and 'hey, mans'.

'I'm afraid so. I told you I spotted Eye-patch and his partner in Malacca.'

'Ah yoi, too many to face, lah!' Ming Chuan groaned.

I was about to reply when help came from a completely unexpected quarter.

A loud raucous scream echoed across the plaza followed by a bevy of giggles and the click of heavy heels.

'Ay told yah, girl, yah don't suit red. No one ay knows suits red, apart from moi!'

Round the corner, dressed to the nines, flapped Lucy and Lulu.

'Hi, girls!' I yelled.

'Pete, what are you doing here? Mingy, my darlin'… Oh!' She stumbled down the escalator and threw herself at Ming Chuan.

Then Lulu spotted Lincoln.

'Oh, my, who's this gorgeous creature?'

'He's too much for you, yah old tart,' Lucy interrupted, pushing Lulu out of the way. 'I bet you're a right little dynamo… an' I'm just the girl to spark your circuits.'

Seeing Lincoln succumb to the flattery, I leaned over and whispered in his ear, 'Believe me, what's under those skirts will short you out completely.' Lincoln went bright red.

I stood.

'Sorry, girls, we've got to get down to the checkpoint. We'll catch you later.'

I walked off, giving them no chance to answer.

Lincoln drove down to the immigration point and dropped us while he took the car through. Once again we lined up and once again we waited... and waited. Suddenly, I saw Gaunt-face and his friend pushing their way through the mass of people. So much for Chang's men! In the foreigners' queue, I was too far away from the others to do anything. I yelled across to Ming Chuan, but it was too late — Gaunt-face had already sidled up to Yan Siang.

Then, miracle of miracles, Lulu flounced across the concrete towards the queues, catching her heel and stumbling. I prayed she would see Yan Siang, but he saw her first and called out. Gaunt-face tried to gag him with one hand while forcing him backwards with the other, but Lulu was alerted. She stamped over and grabbed the struggling boy. Gaunt-face shoved her aside. That was a fatal mistake!

Lulu's voice carried clear out onto the causeway, 'Rape. Oh, this disgusting creature just tried to touch me.'

She took off her right shoe and began hitting Gaunt-face with such enthusiasm he released Yan Siang and cowered back. Two policemen appeared and grabbed hold of Lulu. 'Not me, officer... this man... he touched me... he's a prevert...'

'Pervert, dear,' Lucy corrected, having appeared from nowhere. She walked up to the police, nodded at Gaunt-face and, shoving her left hand down her cleavage, yelled, 'He tried to grab her tits!'

Several old aunties in the nearby queues raised their hands in horror, shocked at the performance, but keeping close enough to catch every delicious detail.

One of the policemen grabbed Gaunt-face and snapped on a pair of handcuffs.

Then, as Lulu rearranged her skirt and composure, Lucy

turned and pointed at Heavy Jowls. 'And him… he pinched my bum… go on… take him…'

Poor old Heavy Jowls had no chance. The other constable strode over, grabbed him by the neck and threw him out of the complex.

Once through customs and immigration, Lincoln drove Ming Chuan and me to Kismis Avenue. Yan Siang wanted to stay with us, but Josie insisted the boys accompany her to Tan Tock Seng where Boong-boong's injury could be checked.

I put a call through to my lawyer. She seemed okay but said she had a lot to discuss, so I agreed to an appointment in her office at ten the following morning. Apparently there had been some new developments and she asked me to bring Yan Siang to the meeting. Josie phoned soon after with the news that Terence's condition was about the same and Boong-boong had been admitted for observation. I was settling down with a glass of Stoneleigh Marlborough Chardonnay 1999 when the phone rang again.

'Yes?'

'Welcome back. I hope you had a pleasant break in Malacca.'

'Officer Chia, what an unpleasant surprise!'

'Don't be like that. I phoned to give you advance warning before we move.'

'What are you talking about?'

'Your new-found little friend, Boong-boong Tharangapourri, entered the country on a passport that has some suspicious irregularities. Do you have any idea how it came to be stamped?'

'How would I? As you just intimated, I barely know the boy!'

'That's unfortunate, since you were the adult accompanying him.'

Another veiled threat. 'Look, I know nothing about his passport. According to what I was told he was returning to

Singapore, so I supposed…'

'No need to panic. If you bring the boy in to Tanglin, I'm sure it can all be sorted out quite easily.'

'Boong-boong is not with me at present.'

'Injured in the crash, was he?'

My pulse raced. 'What crash was that?'

'I heard you forced a truck off the road. Tut… tut!'

The speed at which this man received information was unsettling. What possible interest could he have in Eye-patch's accident?

'Anyway, I won't be seeing Boong-boong for a while.'

'That's a pity, because I don't know how long I can hold off the immigration authorities.'

'Well, you'll have to do your best. When I check with the boy and my lawyer, we'll be in touch.'

I knew this was just another ruse to get to Yan Siang, but I was annoyed with myself for not checking into Boong-boong's background. Who was really responsible for the boy? As I mulled over these difficulties, I realised that it would not be possible for the boys to stay with Josie. She had her hands full with Terence. Then I thought of Jean.

Ming Chuan had gone down to the plaza to buy a few things, so I had the main room to myself. I dialed Jean at home and got her on the first ring.

'Hello?'

'Hi, Jean!'

'Pete! Where've yah bin? Och, yer sairly missed. The school is like a morgue withoot ye!'

'Thanks, Jean. Look, I can't talk now… I've rung to ask a favour. You wouldn't be able to look after a couple of little rascals for a few days, would you?'

'Ah dinna see why not. I take it they widna be safe where you stay?'

'I can't risk it, Jean. I just thought with Rojan there it…'

'Say na mair! It's done. When will ma guests be arriving?'

'I'll give you a call, if that's all right.'

'Just when yer ready. I'm looking forward to hearin' aboot all yer adventures.'

'Sure thing, Jean, but later. I must go.'

I was contemplating a bath when Ming Chuan returned from the shops, his arms full of goodies. He did not seem very happy.

I crossed the room and took some of the parcels.

'It looks like you've been busy.'

'No bread, no meat, no milk… Ah yoi, somebody has got to go to the shop. I wonder who!' There was an edge to his voice. 'Say this, say that. In the end, do nothing.'

I looked at Ming Chuan as he put the groceries away. I knew he blamed me for all the trouble. 'Why don't we sit down and discuss what's bothering you?'

'Talk! Talk! Talk! What's the use?'

I moved him across to the sofa. Through the window I could see that our bougainvillea were drooping badly and needed water.

'I never asked for any of this nightmare, Ming, you know that. But Terence is seriously ill, Josie's unhappy and lonely, Yan Siang is in danger and I need all of them to get me out of the mess at school. I thought we were in this together?'

Ming Chuan stared at the floor, seemingly lost in his own little world. Suddenly he looked up at me, 'Check Webster… check dictionary!'

'What?'

'At school, teacher always said, "Got problem with English word, check dictionary!"'

'You heard what Yan Siang called out last night?'

'Of course! "Check Webster!" My English teacher said the same, "Check dictionary!"'

At first I could see no connection, and then I did. 'Of course! The perfect key to a code — a dictionary! Ming, you're brilliant… you're bloody brilliant. Let's check that sheet of paper.'

I took out the crumpled printout and placed it on the table. If the Webster Dictionary had anything to do with the code, it could only relate to the second column — the list of addresses. But what was the connection? We both stared at the page for a long time before an idea occurred to me.

'When I used the index of the Collier's Encyclopaedia at home, they always referred me to a page and each page was divided into four parts: a, b, c, d. Is it possible that the first number in each group is the page and the second number the word on that page?'

'Don't know,' Ming Chuan answered.

'We'll need to go to the library tomorrow and check.' I looked at the sheet again and then at him. 'I love you!'

He beamed.

Evening was approaching when we arrived at the hospital. I went in to see Terence for a few moments. He looked just the same. Josie was tired, her usual sparkle muted. She took us to another ward to see Boong-boong. He was in a bright, open area with murals on the walls and cutouts of McDonald's characters spread around to remind visitors who had contributed to the décor of the ward. A paediatrician told us that our young friend would be released the following day.

Over a chicken dinner, we told Josie about our discovery and she brightened up a little. We agreed to meet the next day at one at the Queenstown Library to check out our theory.

CHAPTER

32

When the taxi turned into Beach Road, he suspected he knew where it would stop and he was right — outside the Concourse. He drew into the bushes at the base of an overhead walkway a short distance from the building and watched two passengers alight.

'They've arrived at the lawyer's office. Do you want me to tail them when they leave? Very well.'

He replaced the cell phone, balanced his helmet on the bike, and then walked into the little coffee shop. He knew he had plenty of time for a drink before the next part of the assignment.

The offices of Toh, Lee & Jefferson seemed even busier than the last time. Clerks bustled about carrying piles of briefing papers, and I had to wait some time before Miss Leo appeared and ushered the pair of us into her office. The view was still as dazzling and the furnishings as sumptuous, but today heaps of bound legal papers were stacked against the walls. Yan Siang and I insinuated ourselves into the sofa near the coffee table.

'Thank you for coming, this shouldn't take long. We are up to our ears in work, thanks to a big breach of trust case.'

She turned to Yan Siang smiling, 'This must be Chang Yan

Siang.'

Yan Siang stood, did a little bow and said in crisp, clear English, 'I am very pleased to meet you.' I was impressed. Chang had schooled him well.

Shau Wee smiled and acknowledged the boy's greeting, then turned back to me. 'Mrs Chang has agreed to drop her complaint. I also took the liberty of photographing the angle of your apartment from the neighbouring HDB blocks. However, I'm afraid we've had some problems with Mrs Supraniam.' I noticed Yan Siang wince. 'She refuses to withdraw her complaint.'

'Why?' I asked anxiously.

'That's the problem. I don't know and we're unlikely to find out because I can't speak to her two boys.'

Again Yan Siang moved uneasily.

I looked at him. 'You know these boys, why would they be prepared to lie?' Yan Siang shrugged. My heart sank. It looked like we were back to the no-speak syndrome. 'Yan Siang! It's very important that we find out why Mrs Supraniam is not prepared to drop her complaint.'

'I don't know,' he answered testily.

'Perhaps if Yan Siang and I talk privately for a while, it might be easier,' Shau Wee offered.

'Good luck.' I stood and Yan Siang jumped up. He threw his arms around me and pulled me back onto the sofa. Shau Wee looked startled and then amused, while I blushed heavily. I struggled to my feet again, placing Yan Siang firmly to one side.

I moved out to the reception area where I lost myself in the latest edition of *Peak* magazine, a publication detailing the antics of Singaporean high society. Eventually, Shau Wee appeared and shook her head. She sank into one of the Baumer reclining chairs and grimaced.

'He's a very, very troubled young man. It's clear he knows a great deal, but he's not prepared to reveal any of it.' She poured herself a glass of water. 'He's very attached to you, though.'

'I'd really like to help him, but I can't until he shares whatever it is he's trying to bury.'

'I can tell you one thing. There's something going on between him and the Supraniam kids. He's very edgy whenever they're mentioned.'

I placed my cup on the table. 'I'm sure it's to do with his father's death, but what?'

'That boy is never going to get well until he faces his demons, and to do that somebody has to unlock the door for him.'

'Have you any suggestions? Is there any other way we can find out about the accident?'

'I suppose you haven't seen the police report or the autopsy on his father?'

'Of course not. How could I get access to those documents?'

'I thought you said you had friends in the police post at Tanglin.'

I laughed loudly. 'Hardly friends.' Then I thought about it. 'Still, it's worth a try. Even if I don't learn all the answers, I could glean enough information to give me an edge with Yan Siang. Where is he by the way?'

'I sent him down with my secretary for an ice cream.'

'Where?'

'Just below our offices… there's a Baskin Robbins outlet.'

'I'd better go down and get him. Is there anything else?'

'My clerk has been working on the Daisy Liew angle and she's uncovered some interesting details.'

'Great.' I strode out to the lift.

One was arriving, and as the doors opened a very distressed young lady rushed out. Instantly I recognised Shau Wee's secretary.

'What's the matter?'

'Oh, Mr Richards, I'm so sorry. But I couldn't do anything.' She staggered and I caught her.

'Please… what happened?'

She sank into a chair. 'Two men… terrible men… said they

were police and … and… they took the boy…'

I could feel myself choking as Shau Wee arrived. 'They… they took him?'

The secretary stared past me vacantly, her eyes filling with tears.

Shau Wee moved back. 'I'll call the police.'

'Thanks! Detective Ling at Tanglin.' I began to focus.

The call went through and I waited in agony while Ling was sought.

'Detective Ling?' I heard the familiar grunt and though I hated the man, I felt better knowing he and Chia would be on the case. They wanted Yan Siang almost as much as I did. 'The boy, Yan Siang, has been kidnapped.'

I gave him a description of the men and warned that they may try to leave the country. He assured me the police would send a car immediately, but he had a fair idea where the men were headed. Suddenly, he began to lecture me on how all this could have been avoided if… I hung up at that point and fell into a chair.

'Is this nightmare ever going to end?'

Shau Wee moved me into her office. 'Settle down. This is an island, don't forget. The police will get them.'

'You don't know these men,' I groaned.

A cup of tea calmed my nerves, and I was allowed to leave to meet the others at Queenstown library.

When I reached the greenish building just along from the infamous Queensway Remand Prison, I spotted Josie and Ming Chuan standing at the entrance.

'I've got some bad news. Yan Siang's been taken by two men.'

'What? Which two men?'

'I don't know, but probably the pair we had trouble with outside Malacca.'

Josie was silent for a while, then she asked, 'Have you any

idea where they've taken him?'

'None. The police have been told, so let's hope they find him.'

We walked into the library and headed straight for the reference section. Unfortunately, there were several Webster dictionaries. We worked our way through each until I struck gold with *Webster's New Encyclopedic Dictionary*.

Mr Magenta had an address — 167/ 564-12st/ 898-10; 555-9. 167 had to be the street number and on page 564 the twelfth word down was — *lark* — therefore 167 Lark Street. On page 898 the tenth word was *said* and on page 555 the ninth word was *knee* — therefore *said/knee* or Sydney. While I tackled the second name, Ming Chuan raced away to find a map of Sydney.

The second name on our sheet had an address — 28/ 140-33av/ 898-10; 555-9. Again we assumed that 28 was the street number and this meant 140-33 = *canary* — therefore 28 Canary Avenue, again in Sydney.

Finally I decoded the third address — 368/ 836-47 cres/ 823-7; 1074-9. Accepting that 368 was the house number, I discovered that 836-47 = *rainbow* — therefore 368 Rainbow Crescent. 823-7 = *purr* and 1074-9 = *the* — therefore *purr/the* or Perth.

My excitement started to get the better of me, and by the time Ming Chuan returned with the atlas and confirmed that all these streets existed in their respective cities, Josie and I had worked our way down two full pages of names. We left the library, buoyant. Opposite was a food court, so we stopped for lunch. As we ate, my thoughts returned to Yan Siang. I described my meeting with the lawyer and mumbled on about the police report and the autopsy.

Suddenly Josie interrupted my babble.

'I have a friend who works in the coroner's office. Perhaps she could get hold of that autopsy report.'

'Really?' She smiled. 'Boy, did Terence strike gold when he

found you!'

Ming Chuan interrupted, 'What about the disk?'

'Simple, my dear! Now we give it straight to the cops, and they can handle it from here.'

'Why not try to offer it in exchange for their file on Yan Siang and his father's death?'

'Of course, they'll probably doctor — pardon the pun — any report they hand over to us, but it's still worth a try. I'll phone Chia. I want to know what they're doing about Yan Siang anyway.'

I used Josie's cell phone. Unfortunately Chia was unavailable and I had to speak to Ling, which dampened my enthusiasm somewhat.

The detective was pleased to learn that we had discovered a copy of the disk and had broken part of the code. He was less ebullient when I made my request.

'Why you want to see the file? You not detectives. We catch the bad people, not you!'

'As you wish. But in that case you'll have to find your own copy of the disk.'

'You keep this disk and I throw you in jail for obstruct.'

'You can threaten as much as you like.'

There was silence for a while, and then I heard a sigh and two grunts.

'I let you see file in your house and no more, you understand?'

'That's better. Have you located Yan Siang?'

'No, not yet, but we know where is this boy. It will not happen if you have not left him with your Scottish girl. You should give us the boy for police protection.'

'Sure... sure! You find him and then I'll believe your protective custody is worth something. I thought the two thugs who assaulted me were in your protective custody?'

'Yes.'

'Then how come I saw them in Malaysia?'

'Cannot be.'

'Believe me, I saw them. Now when do you want the disk?'

'This afternoon. I come to your place to get it.'

'What time?'

'Four o'clock.'

I cut the connection and handed the phone back to Josie. 'Anyone for another coffee?'

Josie stood up. 'I'll get it.'

'Wait a cotton-pickin' moment!' I thundered. 'How did Ling know about Jean?'

Ming Chuan stared at me puzzled, 'What?'

'He said that I had left Yan Siang with my Scottish girl. How did he know?'

'You must have told Chia,' Josie offered.

'I did not! I know I told no one because the boys never stayed with Jean. Boong-boong's been in hospital and Yan Siang was with you. The only person I discussed the matter with was Jean… on the phone.'

'You mean…'

'Exactly! The police have bugged my bloody phone. My God, I bet you that phone was never bugged in the first place. Chia just wanted an excuse to put a tap on us.'

'Whatever for? It doesn't make sense.'

'So? Nothing in this whole damned business has made sense. Think laterally. Someone in that bloody police station wants to know everything we do.'

'Why?'

'Perhaps they're in league with the crowd at The Flaming Dragon. How should I know?'

Ming Chuan shook his head savagely, 'The police? No, they will not do such thing.'

'All right then, you explain to me how Ling found out about Jean?'

Ming Chuan looked fearful, his face a mask of pain. 'But it will not happen here in Singapore.'

'Oh, you mean like guys getting bashed up and hospitalised, disks getting stolen, boys·getting kidnapped?'

Ming Chuan stood up and walked away.

Josie placed her hand on mine and whispered, 'He's been through a lot, you know.'

'I suppose. Damn!'

Her gaze bored into me as I stared sadly at the departing figure. We sat there for a long, long time.

CHAPTER

33

Ling arrived promptly at four and handed me a manila folder. I gave him the printout with our notations and decoding attached. His hand remained extended and I reluctantly handed over the disk. There was still no news of Yan Siang. Josie had gone to Tan Tock Seng and Ming Chuan had failed to call.

Sorely tempted to challenge Ling about the phone tap, I thought better of it. I offered him a coffee and sat down to look through the file. As I suspected, it contained very little. There was a medical report detailing the condition of the body and a set of interviews with neighbours and family. According to these reports, this was a remarkably quiet neighbourhood where everybody minded their own business. No one seemed to have seen anything. I knew that was hardly true. Interestingly, the accident had been reported by Mrs Chang soon after it happened. Even more curious was the revelation that although both Chia and Ling investigated the call, only Ling conducted the interviews.

The medical report had several photographs attached. These showed a man in reasonable physical condition lying face down. There was a large pool of dark liquid under his head and his left side. One photograph showed him turned over, but there was no injury to the front of his head and this troubled me.

According to the report, death was caused by massive brain and chest trauma, consistent with having fallen from a great height, but it was noted by the medical examiner that all injuries to the head were at the rear of the skull.

There were another two forms in the file. One detailed the time of death and recorded other peripheral details such as a description of the neighbourhood and the position of the body and so on. The other form outlined the progress of the body through the hands of the medical examiner and the detectives up to its ultimate delivery to the morgue. I looked through the photographs and the medical report again, but that nagging doubt remained.

Ling finished his coffee, took the folder and left. I turned to my computer and keyed in as much as I could remember of what I had seen and read. Then I needed a walk to give myself time to think.

Once out on Jalan Jurong Kechil, I headed in the direction of Bukit Batok Nature Park. The place was nearly deserted. I ambled through the native shrubbery along carefully laid paths which eventually brought me out near a disused quarry. Now an ornamental lake, this was one of those special places where the natural environment and man's creativity combine to offer a haven of solitude and serenity. I slipped onto a warm, concrete bench. I have no idea how long I sat there, but my reverie was interrupted by an urgent voice.

'Pete! Pete!' I turned to see Ming Chuan panting down the pathway. Instinctively I stood. He ran up and collapsed in my arms. I turned his face towards me, amazed at this dramatic reconciliation.

'Pete, it's… it's…' He gasped and looked away. A strange premonition gripped me. 'It's Terence.' My heart stopped. 'He's… he's dead!'

The whole world spun. I saw the dying rays of the sun tint the distant trees red and purple, the rippling surface of the lake heaved and sighed, and faraway bird-song rose and fell. Night came in short, dark stabs of pain.

'What?' I choked.

'Terence died… about… about an hour ago…' Ming Chuan began to cry. At first little sobs and then great, body-wracking spasms. I held him, still uncomprehending. Pathway lamps flickered on, catching the bushes and trees in their distended colour. A man passed with a little shih tzu, the dog snuffling and yelping as happy little dogs do.

Nothing had changed, yet nothing would ever be the same again. I turned to face the now black expanse that stretched out to cutaway cliffs like a dark, oily blanket. Trees, topped in drifting sunset pastels, formed a grotesque tiara above the savage granite face. I released Ming Chuan and stepped down to the water's edge. Peace… peace and serenity… merciful oblivion. So many problems, so much trouble and such inviting blackness.

'Pete, no! No!' Ming Chuan's voice rang through the air and bounced off the water. The blackness was suddenly dark and threatening, the distant cliffs stern and admonishing.

I turned to the pathway lined with soft lights. 'We had better get back. I need to phone… to phone…' There had to be someone to phone, if only I could remember who.

We stumbled back together, lost in our own worlds, I not knowing how to cry and Ming Chuan unable to stop.

At the apartment we found Jean and Rojan waiting. Josie had called Jean, knowing I would be unable to cope with Terence's death. Even with her heart torn in two, Josie worried for others. As I entered, Jean grabbed me. Her eyes were red and her cheeks were wet, but she cried some more. Rojan shook with grief for a guy he had only met once and a friend he worshipped. Finally, I cried. I shook, I howled, and I clung to Jean, but I finally cried.

Jean and Rojan took me back to their place and they insisted on fetching Boong-boong, knowing that Josie would have her hands full. Ming Chuan came with us. I was grateful to get away from my apartment with its bugged telephone and memories.

We spent most of the night talking and drinking. Jean had decided to give school a miss for a couple of days to look after the boys. She was sure the police would find Yan Siang, a confidence which intrigued me, considering how critical she had been earlier. Eventually the wine and worry combined to floor me and I was carried off to bed at about three o'clock.

The next morning the reality of Terence's death sank in and I was morose and sullen. I rang the lawyer to fill her in on what had happened. We arranged to meet on Monday morning at ten.

Over breakfast I had a jerky conversation with Boong-boong. His arm was still in a sling, although the wound was healing nicely. During the course of our talk, I learned that he intended to go to Australia with someone he kept calling Uncle Trevor.

'Where is Uncle Trevor now?' I asked.

Boong-boong shrugged and laughed, 'Now I have Uncle Pete… same same!'

I was not quite sure what he meant and I was not very keen to find out. He told me he had a lot of young friends in Singapore and he wanted to introduce them.

Josie called just before lunch and asked me to meet her at two in St Andrew's Cathedral opposite Raffles City. She sounded remarkably calm and self-contained, but then, knowing her as I did, this was hardly surprising.

Shortly after noon, I prepared to leave. I thanked Jean for all her kindness and when she insisted I return and spend the night there, I said I would think about it. I left Boong-boong fiercely fighting space invaders. Ming Chuan came with me as he needed to go back home to collect a few things.

Once I accepted Terence's death, I decided to phone Chia. I was desperate to find out if they had any information on Yan Siang. This time I was put straight through to the man.

'Pete, how are you?'

'So-so,' I replied.

'I realise you have a lot on your mind, but those immigration guys are getting rather impatient.'

'That's the least of my worries. Have you found Yan Siang?'

'We've found him, but we can't get to him without taking risks.'

'So what do you intend to do? Wait until they throw his dead body into the street?'

'We'll watch and move when we think it's right. Of course, if we had your little Thai friend, we might be persuaded to move faster.'

'Boong-boong is not long out of hospital. Besides, he will only talk to you with Yan Siang present. So you figure it out!' I replaced the receiver angrily.

St Andrew's Cathedral, an imposing wooden building, stands in spacious grounds in the centre of Singapore City. Opposite is the large, modern Raffles City complex with boutique shopping sandwiched between the Westin Plaza Hotel and the Sogo Department Store. I entered the cathedral and paused for a moment to spot Josie. She was sitting alone. I moved quietly down the aisle and slipped into the pew beside her. Without glancing up, she took my hand gently and squeezed. Her eyes were tightly closed and her lips moved soundlessly. I followed her example and bowed my head.

Finally she whispered, 'Thank you for coming.'

We stood quietly and walked out into the sun. I headed her in the direction of Raffles City, where there is an ultra-modern café on the first floor. I had cried enough and now I wanted the protection of a public place.

Once seated, I ordered a fruit juice while Josie had coffee.

'How are…' we spoke simultaneously, and then burst into laughter.

'You first,' I offered.

'I just wondered how you were.'

'Better than I was last night. Oh God, Josie, why did he have to die?'

'I guess the decision wasn't his to make.' The drinks arrived. 'C'mon, Pete. We both knew his chance of recovery was slim.'

She clasped and unclasped her hands around the coffee mug. 'I only knew him for about sixteen months, but that was enough. I really loved him, I know that now. It's not that I didn't know it before, but death has a savage way of focusing things.' She paused. 'You knew him for a lot longer.'

'Nine years. It isn't the loss that tears me up, it's the bloody, useless waste. God, I'm just so angry.'

Her eyes showed she understood my hurt. She pulled two sheets of paper out of her hip pocket. 'This is a copy of the post-mortem. Chang's post-mortem. You'd better get ready for a few surprises.'

'What do you mean?'

'Listen. Death was from severe trauma to the base of the skull. There was also a serious injury to the lower right abdomen, which seems to have been caused by a sharp object, probably a rock, since several stone particles were found in the wound. It is assumed the body fell onto a rock. There is a whole section here describing the state of various organs and details of the injuries in medical jargon. Those don't really interest us, but the contents of the stomach do. Apparently Mr Chang swallowed several barbiturates and a good deal of beer shortly before he fell and that probably accounts for the absence of any broken limbs...'

'Not necessarily, the ground would account for that.'

'Why?'

'He landed on grass.'

'What makes you think...'

'I saw photographs of the body in the police file, taken shortly after the fall. Chang was lying spread-eagled, face-down on a large patch of grass.'

'Then where did the rock come from?'

'Exactly. And since the body was lying on its front, how did the base of the skull get caved in?'

'Perhaps the body hit an obstruction as it fell.'

'That's it. That's what I couldn't remember!'

'What?'

'Raymond Chia told me at our first meeting that the body struck several trees and that's what bugged me when I saw the frontal photographs.'

'Yes?'

'There were no injuries to the face. If the body fell into trees, surely the face would have been scratched?'

'Not if the body somersaulted.'

'Is that usual?'

'No, but it can happen. Yet even if the back of the head struck trees, the branches couldn't have caused the fatal injury.'

'Why?'

'Because, according to this report, the injury to the base of the skull was caused by an upwards stroke.'

I stared blankly at Josie. Then the lightbulb flashed. 'You mean someone struck Chang before he fell?'

'Bingo! And since it was an upwards blow with considerable force, it must have been delivered by a fairly strong someone.'

'You're good, Josie, you should be a detective.' I felt better. No doubt whoever killed Yan Siang's father had a hand in Terence's death. We were slowly getting closer to the bastard.

'Perhaps we should tell the police what we've worked out.'

'Better not. Since Terence's death, the case has been upgraded to a murder investigation and a new team has been assigned to it.'

'Not Chia and Ling?'

'They weren't the officers who spoke to me.'

'Great! Now we might see some results.' I stood up. 'Shall

we go?'

Josie smiled, 'Sit down! I haven't delivered the best bit yet. Guess what they found on the soles of Mr Chang's feet?'

'What?' She handed me the sheets. Midway down the second page were the words — *Check Webster.*

'Hells bells!' I gasped.

'No,' she laughed. 'Check Webster!'

'How?'

She pointed to the page. 'It says here one word was written downwards on each foot.'

'But how did Yan Siang get to see the soles of his father's feet?'

'Your guess is as good as mine, although remember you said he screamed the words out during a nightmare. Perhaps he saw them…'

'The night his father fell?'

'That'd be my guess.'

'So he must know who killed his father.'

'We'd better go.'

I walked over to the counter and paid.

'They'll have to perform a post-mortem on Terence, and that means the funeral won't be for a few days. How's Ming Chuan?'

'Better. He's been great since Terence died.'

'If I were you, I'd take him out to a film show… tonight… it'll be good for both of you.'

'Would you like to join us?'

Josie smiled bravely. 'Not tonight. I can't.'

We parted at the MRT. I crossed the road to catch the 171 bus and Josie disappeared into the underground.

Entering the Ngee Ann grounds, I was greeted by a security man. 'We found something that belongs to you, Mr Richards. Found it in the bushes.'

Yan Siang shot out from the security post. 'Hello, teacher,' he grinned.

'Yan Siang?' I gave him a crushing bear hug. 'Thanks,' I burbled to the security officer, swinging the little figure over my shoulder and heading towards the lift.

Once in the security of my apartment, I debriefed him.

'That man, you know, the thin-face… shit himself in Malaysia, catch me outside lawyer office. They force me to The Flaming Dragon… locked me in a little room.'

'Did they harm you?'

'A bit here and there.' He pushed up his sleeves and lifted his jeans to reveal heavy, dark bruises on his arms and legs. 'They kicked me as well.'

'Do you want to see a doctor?'

'Haven't.'

'How did you escape?'

'A man come into the room and very quickly took me. He put me on his motorbike and fetch me here.'

'Didn't he tell you who he was?'

'No, I'm too scared to ask.'

'What about the other two men?'

'I did not see them.'

'Look you go in and have a shower while I arrange for some dinner. What would you like?'

'Maybe Kentucky Fried Chicken?'

'That figures!' I watched him head for the bathroom.

When he reached the door, I called out, 'C'mon back here.' He returned and I swung him up in my arms and hugged him hard. 'From now on I'm not going to let you out of my sight. Understand?'

'Yes, teacher. Tomorrow you phone the lawyer, I talk to her.'

'Are you sure?'

'Sure!'

'Anything you want to tell me?'

He shook his head and walked back through to the bathroom.

CHAPTER
34

We had not been to a movie in weeks and it was a great show. Ming and I were still bubbling as we stumbled out of the Boon Lay Complex into the interchange.

We turned to cross to the central island when I was grabbed from behind and pushed up against a plate glass window. I swivelled round to find myself staring into the distorted face of Detective Ling. He swung me round to face Raymond Chia.

'What the hell do you think you're doing?' I yelled at Chia, attracting the attention of several filmgoers who quickly disappeared into the bus depot.

Chia thrust his face so close to mine that I could smell the chili crab he had eaten for dinner. 'You tell us, smart arse!'

I began to seethe. This really was the last straw! 'You can't grab me like this!'

'Oh, but we can. We're arresting you for obstruction of justice!'

'Arresting me? Obstruction of justice? You're crazy!'

Ming Chuan stood off to one side, unable to comprehend what was happening.

'Are we? Crazy you say. We faxed that sheet you gave us to the New South Wales police and they swooped on all those addresses you decoded. He emphasised the last word with a contemptuous sneer. And guess what?'

'What?'

'Every address was bogus. Oh, they found the houses all right… some belonged to church organisations, one belonged to a women's refuge group, another belonged to two elderly men and one even belonged to a woman of ninety-three who had a heart attack when the police arrived and is still undergoing treatment in a Sydney hospital.'

Chia's voice had now risen to a shout. 'Four of your so-called addresses were vacant lots!'

I could feel a rising tide of nausea as I realised we'd been set up. 'How… were… we to know that…'

Chia struggled to regain his natural aplomb. 'From the beginning you've obstructed this investigation. I've got a dozen charges I'd love to throw at you, but for tonight…' He glanced at his watch. 'I mean this morning, obstruction will do.'

He clapped a pair of handcuffs on my wrists and marched me out to a plainclothes police car like a common criminal. I yelled to Ming Chuan to get hold of Shau Wee as soon as possible and to warn Josie.

The drive to Tanglin was as discourteous as the arrest. Terrible thoughts tumbled through my mind as I realised how we had been played for suckers. We should have known that the owners of that bloody disk would never have encoded a list so simply that a bunch of amateurs could break it.

When we reached the police station, I was bundled up to a reception counter where I had to suffer the indignity of emptying my pockets and signing an arrest docket. I refused to give any statement until I had legal representation. Ling seemed somewhat uneasy at my predicament, but Chia enjoyed it.

Finally I was marched along a corridor and locked in a little room with a bed, plastic chair and table. There was no toilet or wash basin and if I wanted to go to the little boy's room, I had to suffer the further indignity of calling the duty officer. For the first few hours I massaged my anger with thoughts of law suits, criminal actions, large penalties and even larger damages, but as the night wore on anxiety replaced wrath.

I slept fitfully, distant noises drifting in and out of my consciousness, and I was really grateful to see Monday filter its way through the louvred window. At about six o'clock, I was escorted to a bathroom and given soap and a towel. After a quick shower, my escort returned and I was taken down to the canteen for breakfast. At first I was too hungry to think about this generosity, but after a good meal it occurred to me that this was not the sort of treatment one expected in jail. I was returned to my room.

Shau Wee arrived just before nine with a sleepy young Indian and a constable. She motioned for me to say nothing and, after a thorough examination, my possessions were returned. Chia and Ling were nowhere in sight.

Once on the street, the Indian doctor shook hands and left. Shau Wee led me to her Porsche and as we pulled out into Orchard Road, I uttered a sigh of relief.

She grinned, 'I trust you had a comfortable night?'

'Great!' I sneered.

'When your friend called me, I simply phoned Mr Justice Chan. He's an old friend and belongs to the same championship ballroom dancing team as Theresa. On his authority I phoned Tanglin and informed them that I would be seeking your release into my custody this morning and I expected the package to be in good working order.'

'Thank you for acting so quickly.'

'It's all part of the service.' She slowed down to let a turning truck pass. 'You must have really upset them though.'

Infuriated, I explained what had happened, concluding, 'I've a good mind to sue them.'

'I wouldn't.

255

'Why not? Obstruction of justice, indeed!'

'You did give them misleading information.'

'Not deliberately.'

'That's not the way they see it.'

We turned out of Scotts Road towards Bukit Timah.

'I met Yan Siang for lunch yesterday.'

'Did he say anything about his father's death?'

'No, but he did give me the information I need to dismiss Supraniam's complaint.'

I waited for more details, but Shau Wee remained tight-lipped. We drove up Bukit Timah Road and past the plaza.

'You can drop me off here,' I offered.

Shau Wee stopped the Porsche and looked at me pointedly. 'Go and relax, but make sure you're ready for tomorrow.'

I found a little reception committee waiting in my apartment. Ming Chuan wore a pained mixture of anger and relief, but seemed to have recovered from his ordeal. Josie looked pleased to see me and Boong-boong sat nursing his arm. We made a great pair. Yan Siang sat silently in one corner. He smiled as I looked over at him, and then turned away. After I had outlined my experiences in the lockup, Josie called a council of war. She went back over everything that had happened and we decided that Yan Siang and Boong-boong would go nowhere unaccompanied.

Finally, Josie announced, 'I'm expecting a visitor any moment and he's going to help us solve the mystery of that disk.'

'How?' I asked.

'We're going to break into The Flaming Dragon… tonight!'

There was a stunned silence. 'Have you completely lost your marbles?'

'We have no choice. Both Yan Siang and Boong-boong are in danger. You face disciplinary action and a police prosecution.' Her lip quavered a little. 'And Terence is dead because of that disk. I want those people to pay.'

'We all do,' I interrupted, 'but to break into a nightclub? Josie, my dear, you're a nurse and I'm a high school teacher…'

'Who couldn't fire a gun, as I recall, but that didn't stop you in Malaysia.'

'This is different. We can't burglarise a nightclub. We don't know the layout…'

'I do!' Boong-boong's eyes shone with enthusiasm.

I looked at him sceptically. 'What do you know?'

'Like he said, he knows the layout.' I spun round as the door clanged shut and Josie's visitor moved into the room. 'Hi! I'm Matthew Yang.'

'Welcome, Matt.' She introduced everybody and I fetched a round of fruit drinks.

'Matt is Terence's friend,' Josie paused.

'Yes, I'm the one who broke the code.'

'Thanks a million,' I muttered.

Josie hastily explained my recent difficulties.

'Sorry, Pete. It seems we were all fooled. But I'm not surprised.'

'You're not?' I scoffed.

'No,' the visitor continued, 'Terence thought the first code was too straight forward. The password seemed too easy.'

I was unimpressed. 'Why have such an easy code? Isn't that a waste of time?'

'It's a delay tactic. You see if anybody without authority found the disk, it would give the organisation time to warn people and change things before the real code was broken.'

'You mean the disk really does mean something?'

'I'd bet on it.'

Josie entered the conversation. 'That's why we have to visit The Flaming Dragon. We need to access the main database to locate the real information on that disk.'

'Can't we just forget about the disk and cut our losses?' I ventured hopefully, and for the first time Ming Chuan looked supportive.

'Is that what you really want?' Josie smiled.

'No,' I groaned.

'Then let's plan.'

Ming Chuan stood up, 'I have to go home.' He walked out to the landing.

I followed him, closing the door quietly behind me. 'Whatever happened to together?'

He looked at me sadly, 'There's no point. You have Josie and the new man. I'm scared of all this disk business. I want to be out of it!'

'You think I'm not scared? I did what you wanted and gave that sheet to the police. Now look at the mess I'm in.'

'It's all my fault…'

'Rubbish!'

'I need to go home anyway.'

'Fair enough, but can I count on your support?'

The lift door opened and he sagged into it. I watched the numbers descend, and then hung out over the balcony and watched him leave the block. I felt so empty. Suddenly he turned and waved vigorously before disappearing up the steps to the bridge.

I returned to the meeting. Boong-boong was drawing a rough diagram of the rear section of The Flaming Dragon. It was a typical, old-fashioned shophouse with three floors. Our target was an office on the second floor. Boong-boong had never been inside the office, but he knew it contained the computer files simply by explaining away all the rooms around it, which he had been into.

On the ground floor at the rear was a kitchen which gave out onto a small back lane. We could enter through the kitchen, make our way along a corridor, up the stairs and back along another corridor to the office. I was concerned at the urgency.

'Why tonight?'

Josie's answer was simple. 'Matt leaves for England on

Wednesday, Terence's funeral begins on Thursday and the police are already searching for Boong-boong. Time is not on our side!'

Yan Siang got up and dragged himself into the bedroom.

I looked at Matthew. 'How long will it take to break the code on that disk?'

He shrugged. 'Don't know. But I've got a couple of ideas which may shorten the process.'

'This is so bloody dangerous. The police are already watching me. How do we get past them?'

'Good point. There are also those men who kidnapped Yan Siang.'

I sat staring into space for a while, and then I walked over to the phone. I dialed the school and left a message for Jean, telling her that we'd be turning up at her place for drinks around nine o'clock.

'How can?' Matthew asked.

'We're not all going, just enough of us to mislead the police and other interested parties. You see, my phone is tapped, so hopefully they'll suppose we're all heading to Jean's.'

'Good thinking. Who's really going to Jean's?' Josie asked.

'Ming Chuan, Yan Siang and me, I s'pose.'

Matthew shook his head. 'No can do! I need you with me in case I have to move anything. Besides, a Caucasian man will look a lot less suspicious.'

'But this Caucasian man has been seen there before.'

Josie sniffed. 'Only once. Don't flatter yourself. You're not that memorable! I'll go to Jean's with Ming Chuan and Yan Siang, while you go with Matt and Boong-boong.'

'With his arm in a sling?'

'You manage, I manage!' Boong-boong boomed.

Josie glared at me then got up to leave. 'We'll see you tonight. Let's all meet down at the plaza outside Pizza Hut, say eight-thirty?'

'Agreed.'

The pair left with Boong-boong and I wandered into the bedroom. Yan Siang was lying on the bed staring at the ceiling with Sylvester draped across his chest. He never moved or commented, so I quietly closed the door and returned to the main room.

The phone rang. It was Chia.

'Good afternoon.' The pleasant tone was seductive.

'Yes,' I replied curtly. 'Please don't bother apologising for last night, it would be a complete waste…'

'I didn't call to apologise… I was simply doing my job.'

'Really? That's what Hitler's henchmen said.'

He ignored the barb. 'Your little Thai friend has still failed to have his immigration problem fixed.'

'What is this immigration problem exactly?'

'According to his passport he never left the country. So how could he re-enter, if he never left in the first place?'

There must be some mistake. Perhaps your immigration people forgot to stamp his passport as he left.'

'That sort of thing might happen in Malaysia, but not in Singapore.'

'C'mon, get real! How could he just walk out of the country without being stopped? It's ridiculous!'

'Not if he were travelling in the boot of a car or under someone else's passport.'

I did not like the sound of this, so I decided to bluff my way through. 'Anyway, it's not my problem.'

'Oh, but it is. According to our information he was entrusted to you by a Mr Eugene Chang. That makes it very much your problem.'

My headache was returning. I was fast getting to the point where I could not handle any more bullshit.

Chia eased off, 'Look, Pete, it's not such a big problem. I'm sure we can find an exit stamp if we look hard enough, but we can't do it without the cooperation of Yan Siang.'

There it was again — that insidious sliver of blackmail.

'I'm seeing my friends tonight at Jean's — that's my Scottish lady friend. I am no longer responsible for the well-being of the two boys, but I'll pass your message on to those who are.'

'Remember, Pete, we can settle this whole business very quickly with a little sensible cooperation from all parties. Do stress this to your friends.'

'Yes,' I muttered and replaced the receiver.

CHAPTER
35

I left the apartment at ten. Yan Siang and Boong-boong had left earlier with plenty of noise, but I suspected the police would not be so easily fooled. I walked the long way out via Toh Yi Drive and caught a cab on Upper Bukit Timah Road. As far as I could see there was nobody following. Our little change of plan seemed to have worked. Traffic was light and I dropped the taxi a short way from the meeting point. It was a clear night with little haze and a thin new moon.

He had remained hidden on the bridge above the polytechnic for over an hour. His position gave him the perfect view of the bottom of the block. Although dying for a cigarette, he knew a light in this sort of darkness would act like a beacon. Still he was comfortable. His bike was safely parked at the service station below.

Action! Two figures emerged from the block and strolled off towards the side gate. He saw immediately they were kids. The boss had been insistent — follow Richards — so he settled back and waited some more. About ten minutes later, Richards wandered out. He paused and looked up at the block before doing a casual circuit of the base. Although he tried to appear relaxed, the trained eye could spot anxiety in his movements. Finally, satisfied no one was around, he walked off towards the main gate. The man in black cursed — an unexpected departure from what he had anticipated. He had surmised the subject would be unlikely to find a cab in Kismis Avenue, and therefore he would have to walk out to Toh Yi Drive. This would have given him a small margin to retrieve his bike and whip round to Jurong Kechil to catch the taxi. He raced down the steps to the bridge, across the car park and plunged under the hole he had made earlier in the fence. Now he had a direct route through the neighbouring housing estate to the service station. He grabbed his bike and shot out into the main road, almost colliding with a large truck and narrowly missing two parked cars.

As he had figured, his quarry was boarding a taxi at the bottom of Toh Yi Drive, but he himself was held fast by a set of red lights. The cab shot past him. Once the lights changed, he swept around and set off in pursuit. The tailing was easy and when the pursued arrived at his destination, the pursuer unclipped his cell phone and called in. Told to wait and watch, he sat back to enjoy a quiet puff.

The coffee shop hummed with gaggles of old aunties cutting up vegetables and gangs of elderly men eating noodles and knocking back bottles of Tiger beer. I was the second to arrive and Matt poured me a drink. I needed it. We waited anxiously for Boong-boong, who arrived twenty-four minutes late. He explained that he had quickly reconnoitred the club to avoid any unpleasant surprises and had found a good deal of activity out front, but all quiet at the rear.

We moved into the small, narrow lane that ran behind the shop houses. The darkness was broken occasionally by odd rectangles of light thrown across our path from open doorways. At the rear of our objective, we paused for a quick briefing. It was decided Boong-boong should enter first, as he had lived in the building and anyone seeing him was likely to treat his presence with less suspicion. Once through the open rear door, we entered the kitchen. I received a number of strange glances from the kitchen-hands, and one even gave me directions to the reception area. The floor was wet and slippery, with baskets of vegetables piled up beneath long, steel benches. Cooked ducks and chickens dripped from hooks above, and chefs in bloodied aprons hacked up beef and lamb for the huge pots simmering on flaming gas cookers. A strong smell of herbs and spices mingled with the raw odour of blood and disinfectant.

The kitchen gave onto a narrow corridor where a rickety wooden stairway creaked up to the second level. Here we hit our first problem — Boong-boong could not recognise the layout. We had no choice but to work our way down the hall, checking each room and apologising profusely to any startled occupants. We lucked out and decided to move up to the top. Here, Boong-boong quickly recognised the room. We tried the door and found it locked, so Matt produced his skeleton keys, but after struggling for five minutes he gave up. Boong-boong tried the neighbouring door and found a bedroom. We all entered and stood in the darkness for a few minutes, listening to the sounds of our mutual panting.

'We can't get into that room through the door,' Matt whispered.

'You don't say,' I sneered.

Boong-boong moved across to the window and called us over.

'Look.' He pointed down to a balcony which ran the length of the building. Although partitioned off at the end of each set of windows, it seemed to offer access to the neighbouring room.

'Good work,' Matt enthused. 'If we climb over that brickwork, we can reach the window.' The brickwork he was referring to was a waist-high partition about a foot thick.

'Climb over that? Aren't you forgetting something?' I waved my plastered arm. 'We can't climb over that!'

'I can,' Boong-boong chirruped. I glared at him threateningly.

Matt shrugged. 'We have to, if we're to get to the database.'

He parted the shutters, raised the window and climbed through, followed by Boong-boong. I watched nervously. Traversing the partition looked far from simple. There was a metre gap between the barrier and the next balcony, but Matt swung across it with ease. When Boong-boong followed suit, I had to give it a go. Reluctantly I climbed out into the warm night air and moved up to the partition. I stretched a leg across, heaved myself up and caught the lining of my pants on the rough concrete edge. In an effort to free my pants, I thrust off the other side of the block and found myself dangling over the road, fifty feet up. Matt reached down and grabbed my feet. But when he pulled them in, I was left spread-eagled across the metre gap like a sagging trapeze artist. I hung there terrified. Realising he had worsened my position, Matt looked around for something to lever me over. He found an old chair which he placed under my chest and, with Boong-boong on the other side, pulled me harshly upright, forcing my fingers to release the partition.

Shattered and shaken, I stood on the neighbouring balcony shivering.

'Get a grip, we've a lot of work to do,' Matt ordered as I hung about looking miserable.

Then another obstacle — the window was locked. Casually, like a professional, Matt wrapped his hand in his jacket and broke the glass. We waited for a full minute to see if anybody had heard, and then Matt reached in and opened the latch. Once inside, we made another nasty discovery. Again Boong-boong had got it wrong. This was another bedroom. He had remembered the bloody layout the wrong way around. The office was on the other side of the corridor. We opened the door and left the room quickly. Boong-boong found the correct door on the opposite side, and this time Matt's skeleton keys worked. I shot inside and crouched in the half-light, sucking in great lungfuls of air. A glance around revealed a cramped little office with walls lined in shelves containing videos, disks, and files. A wooden table ran the length of the far wall beneath a curtained window. Two keyboards sat in front of monitors, one of which glowed dully.

'That was very good of someone,' Matt whispered, slipping into a chair in front of the monitor. 'We don't even need to find the password.'

His fingers played over the keyboard like those of a concert pianist, and rows of figures danced across the screen. Suddenly he slipped a disk into the drive and within minutes the familiar list of colourful gentlemen flashed up. I stood there transfixed, while Boong-boong peered through a hairline crack in the door to make sure we were not disturbed.

Breaking the main code was difficult, but Matt persisted. He tried different combinations, and eventually typed the whole first line of the disk printout into the computer's hard drive. The screen flashed empty, and then bingo! A main file popped up. On the left of the screen was a passport-size photograph of a middle-aged man, beneath which were typed his name and address in Sydney, Australia. To the right of the photograph was a six digit number. The second line of the printout produced the same result, likewise the third and fourth. When we reached the final name, the screen went blank.

'Great! Now we have a set of files with no clue as to what they mean,' I muttered.

'We're not finished yet,' Matt whispered.

Suddenly, Boong-boong gasped, 'Men come. Quick, quick!'

Matt removed the disk and cleared the screen. Then he jumped across to the door and slipped his key in the lock. We crouched in the shadows, fearfully glancing at each other as the men arrived at the door and turned the handle. One of the visitors tried to push a key into the lock, but Matt held his own key firmly in place. I could feel myself on the verge of hyperventilating as perspiration trickled down my back. There was a further plethora of cursing and grumbling, amidst exclamations of surprise, before the men gave up. Once the lock was released, Boong-boong peered out and gave us the all-clear.

Matt went back to his task. He tried to key in the file numbers, but nothing happened. Then I had an inspiration.

'Try Check Webster,' I whispered excitedly. That did it. The screen lit up with names and figures.

At first I did not understand what was in front of me, and then the sickening horror struck. On the screen were the names and ages of young Thai boys and girls, and beside each was the name of the monster who had bought them. The Flaming Dragon had nothing to do with drugs or prostitution, it was the centre of a paedophile distribution ring! Mainly Australian, but some New Zealand and German names were lined up with coded youngsters and the enormous sums of money that had been paid for these kids.

'What's this?' Matt whispered, pointing to the letters RAC in the bottom corner of each page.

'Beats me!' I answered.

'See… see… Mr Trevor!' Unnoticed, Boong-boong had come up behind us and was gleefully pointing out Mr Trevor's name and the sum of money the sod had paid for him.

I shuddered, shocked by our discovery and appalled that Boong-boong did not seem to realise the enormity of what he was part of.

'I show you more… I can!' Boong-boong enthused.

Matt pushed his disk back into the computer and downloaded the information. Now the police would really have to sit up and take notice!

More noises in the corridor. The men were back with a waiter. Again Matt secured the door, but we had to get out. Boong-boong moved to the window and released the shutters.

'We go…' he pointed out the window.

'Oh, no, we don't!' I shook my head. 'I'm not going out that way. I'll take my chances with the guys outside.'

Matt grabbed my arm. 'Okay, we can bluff our way through the door, but he can't. Let's give Boong-boong the disk and he can use the window.'

'With that bad arm?'

'He's managed pretty well so far.'

Boong-boong pocketed the disk and climbed out onto the ledge.

'We'll meet in a few minutes in the coffee shop,' Matt whispered, but the little figure had gone.

He turned to me. 'I hope you can think fast.' He removed his key and opened the door. I stepped out onto the strangers.

'Good evening,' I beamed.

'A very good system you have here. I feel very sure my principals will be quite interested in a little investment.'

Passive faces glared back.

'Who are you?'

'You haven't been told? I guess the boss must operate on a need-to-know basis, and you don't need to know!' I stepped between the men and turned to Matt. 'Of course, we'd have to be certain your security was tight.' Matt just nodded.

The two men stared after us as we strode down the corridor, but the waiter began to follow.

'You… I… you wanted…' the waiter stammered.

'Drinks later,' I replied. 'I must phone my superiors immediately.' We left the waiter standing open-mouthed in the centre of the hallway.

Once through the kitchen, we made our way out into the lane and across to the coffee shop.

'What was up with that waiter?' Matt asked.

'He served us the night I was there with Terence. Trust me to meet the one bloody waiter with a good memory!'

'Do you think he's dangerous?'

'How should I know? But I'm not hanging around to find out.'

Boong-boong was waiting for us, all smiles. Matt took charge of the disk and we prepared to leave.

'Can't… can't!' Boong-boong howled, 'Still must show… must show…'

'What's he going on about?'.

Matt grinned, 'Must be something else he wants us to see.'

'Bugger it! I'm not going back in there!'

I strode off down the street. Boong-boong crossed in front of me and began to push me backwards.

'He's crazy!' I yelled. 'Stop him, Matt, before I punch him!'

Matt tried to separate the pair of us, but Boong-boong burst into tears. 'Must show! Must show!'

'Okay!' I yelled. 'Why not? I thought I'd seen it all until tonight, but I guess I can take a little more!'

Matt grabbed me. 'Cool it, Pete, or you'll wake the whole neighbourhood. We'll take a quick look at whatever it is Boong-boong wants to show us, and then we're off.'

Boong-boong smiled a watery grin and led us back in the direction we had just come. However, instead of stopping at the rear of The Flaming Dragon, he crept up to the next building and slipped down a wrought iron staircase to the basement. He knocked twice on a heavily weathered door. It opened a fraction and I heard voices, and then a young man stepped outside. He was obviously astonished to see Boong-boong and quickly ushered the three of us into the damp interior. There was a terrible smell of rotting garbage, human excrement and stagnant water. We followed our guide down a warm, fetid corridor and up some old wooden steps. This place had clearly been unused for years and I dreaded what Boong-boong wanted to show us.

At street level, we passed a securely boarded-up main entrance, and then crossed a cracked and stained parquet surface to a recently installed metal gate. Boong-boong's friend forced it open and unlocked the door beyond. We were struck by a blast of overpowering, stuffy air. Recovering, we peered into the semi-darkness. Shapes and shadows gradually emerged as we entered a room lined with short narrow boards such as one would find in a library storeroom for holding books. Crammed onto these shelves were dozens of young, dark-skinned children. They clung onto their bare perches like monkeys in a zoo. Some slept, others sat in a variety of crooked positions, dazed. In the centre of the room, a table held pots of rice and vegetables and two large buckets of water surrounded by plastic cups. Several older children stood to one side, their eyes a mixture of fear and surprise.

'Who are these?' Matt asked, amazed.

'Like me, have farang friends!' Boong-boong beamed.

'You mean all these children have been bought by foreigners?' I asked incredulously.

'Same same,' the young Thai boomed happily.

Boong-boong's enthusiasm took my breath away. I looked at Matt and he shook his head. Neither of us could quite deal with what we were seeing.

'Let's go,' he suggested.

We returned the stinking way we had entered, holding our breath until we escaped into the street. I felt sick but was unable to vomit. It seemed the world had turned completely upside down.

We walked through Geylang in silence.

Finally I stopped.

'How the hell do they get away with it?'

Matt shrugged,

'Speed, I suppose. They smuggle the kids in for pre-arranged customers, attend to all the paperwork here... adoption... student passes, etc., and then get rid of them fast.'

Once out on Joo Chiat Road, we stopped a taxi and headed

back to Bukit Timah. I looked at Boong-boong, and then turned to Matt. 'I wonder how he gets to stay outside that place?'

'Maybe those security guys are his friends and they cover for him.'

The bright lights of Geylang flashed past as we sped down Paya Lebar Road towards the Pan Island Expressway. My mind was in overdrive — too many sacred cows had been slaughtered in too short a time.

'That's why he had no stamp in his passport,' I realised suddenly.

'Who?' Matt asked absentmindedly.

'Boong-boong! They must have brought him in legitimately intending to dispatch him to Australia within days. Perhaps there was a hitch and that gave Eugene Chang the chance to smuggle him out to Malaysia. Once we brought him back in legitimately, customs discovered the two entry stamps.'

Matt stared into the darkness.

'What are we going to do with the disk? Hand it over to the police?'

'That was my first thought, but what's the point? They never believed me last time, why should they believe me now?'

'There's also that roomful of kids. Giving the disk to the police puts them at risk.'

'You're not serious! Nobody could dispose of that many children.'

'Don't be so sure. This is Asia and there's a lot of money at stake. It would take the cops at least twelve hours to get a search warrant and that would allow plenty of time for those youngsters to disappear.'

'What do you suggest then?'

'I don't know. I'll talk it over with Josie and see what she says.' He glanced at the sleeping boy. 'How could anyone treat kids like that?'

'How indeed!'

CHAPTER

36

Only ten days had passed since I last sat in the conference room, and yet it seemed a lifetime. So much had changed. Events in Malaysia, Terence's death and the discoveries at The Flaming Dragon had all taken their toll. I now knew the real world. The images of Boong-boong's childish innocence and Yan Siang's calculating courage haunted my imaginings. But Shau Wee was supremely confident. I knew she had worked hard to build a strong counter-argument to the allegations and innuendo, but this session was bound to be tougher.

The conference room remained unchanged, although someone had failed to remove a desktop computer which had been unceremoniously dumped in a far corner. The battle-lines were drawn, with Daisy Liew and Marjorie Sim on the left and Shau Wee, Jean and myself on the right. Jean had insisted on attending and no one had the balls to stop her. Shau Wee cautioned her about outbursts which could swing the SAC against us. As Yan Siang would be called later, he was waiting in the principal's office with Josie.

Again, shortly after two o'clock, Snake led the SAC members into the room. I noted there was one change in the line-up. The staff rep, Tong Say How, had been replaced with an elderly ex-staff member, Mrs Poon Kay Hui. I had never met this woman before, but judging by her demeanour and the frequent eye twinkles at Daisy Liew, she was definitely not on my side. That was unfortunate, as it turned a 3-2 for into a 3-2 against. Still, it would not be over until the fat lady sang and she had not even warmed up yet.

Mrs Teo endeavoured to establish a warm, friendly atmosphere with a down-to-earth welcome in which she expressed the hope that matters would be discussed amicably and the outstanding issues resolved quickly. The committee had carefully considered all previous statements and now wished to hear key testimony.

Theresa Loh stood and, with a smile in our direction, read out a retraction of the original complaint from Mrs Chang and an apology. Next came the Supraniam issue, but as neither the mother nor either boy was present, Shau Wee moved that the complaint be dismissed. Snake objected strongly, assuring the meeting that mother and sons were on their way. The council agreed to hear their statements later. The stranger responsible for the third complaint had failed to respond or appear, so that complaint was dismissed.

All attention now shifted to Daisy Liew's allegations. She moved to a chair placed in front and slightly to the left of the council members and repeated her version of events that day at Sentosa. Gone was the nasal whine, firmly replaced by the supercilious sneer! I shook my head as she told how I had primed the three boys to sabotage her outing with the girls, how I had mocked her attempts to retain control, and finally how I had fought with Li Wei and knocked him over. She even repeated her description of my behaviour with Ming Chuan, embellishing the story sufficiently to give it an extra-salacious gloss.

Once she finished, Shau Wee rose to challenge her. 'Mrs Liew, I have only one question. Are you completely sure that the events you have just related occurred in the order in which you placed them?'

'Absolutely sure, thank you.'

'Think carefully, please. Everything occurred just as you have detailed it?'

'Precisely!'

'Thank you.'

As Daisy Liew returned to her seat I glanced at Shau Wee anxiously. 'Is that all you're going to ask her?' Shau Wee simply smiled. Jean coughed politely and nudged me.

Mrs Teo then read into the record the statements of Li Wei and his friend, which completely contradicted Mrs Liew's version of events. Shau Wee had been very thorough, but Daisy Liew remained unperturbed.

There was a short pause while the SAC secretary typed the statements into her laptop.

Next, Mrs Teo explained that the third boy would be called to give his statement.

She pointed out that it was highly unusual to have a student testify in front of a group of adults in this sort of hearing. However, as this young man's account differed markedly from the other two boys, Miss Leo had requested the opportunity to question him. The school clerk left the room and returned with a confident, pleasant-looking youth whom I vaguely recognised.

'Good afternoon, Yan Zheng,' Mrs Teo chorused invitingly. 'This is not a courtroom, so you can relax. You are not going to be punished for anything you say, but you must tell the truth. Do you understand?'

'Yes, yes,' the boy chirruped.

'Good. Now we would like you to tell us exactly what occurred that afternoon on Sentosa. You do remember the afternoon I am referring to?'

'Of course I know!'

The boy relaxed in the chair and looked around the room confidently. 'We want to go Sentosa for swimming at the beach and…'

'Who is the we?' Miss Teo interrupted pleasantly.

'Ah… Li Wei, me and one more guy.'

'Thank you.'

'We went to the beach first, but too many people there and we decide to go to Volcano-land and later come back. Then we see that woman with many girls. Li Wei said his form teacher tell him that old woman was very kapo and we should sabo her. I was quite boring at that time so I think it will be very fun. We take her scarf and play it in the air. We are not going to hurt her.'

'Then what happened?' Mrs Teo asked.

'Two men come behind us and join us.'

'Do you know who these men were?'

The boy pointed in my direction and sneered, 'Teacher there was one of them.'

'Are you quite sure?'

The boy nodded.

'Continue.'

'The woman was very unhappy and she go to the man and scold him. He just laugh and call us to his side. Then he tell us jokes about what happened. I am embarrassed. I think what we do was bad and I told that man. He start to push me a bit and then Li Wei was knocked and he cut his head.'

'What happened after the incident?'

'They take Li Wei to a first-aid place for help.'

'Anything else?'

The boy shook his head.

'Would you like anything clarified, Miss Leo?'

'May I ask the young man a few questions?'

Mrs Teo turned to the boy, 'You understand this lady is acting for Mr Richards and she would like to ask you to explain a few points?'

'Of course! I know. I watch *The Practice* all the time,' the boy answered proudly.

'That's not quite the same. This is not a courtroom.' The boy nodded and Mrs Teo looked firmly at Shau Wee. 'Remember, no cross-examination.'

'Understood.' Shau Wee sat back in her chair and smiled at the young man in front of her. He looked at the ground.

'Yan Zheng, isn't it?' The boy nodded. 'You don't go to this school, do you?'

'No,' he answered hesitantly.

'Which school do you attend?'

'St Puriri's… sometimes.'

'Isn't St Puriri's Boys' School in Johore?'

'Yes.'

'How did you get to know Li Wei and the other boy… What was his name?'

There was an embarrassing silence, and then Yan Zheng muttered, 'I cannot remember.'

'I see. Do you normally forget the names of your good friends?' There was no reply. 'I'll repeat my question. How did you get to know Li Wei and Mark?'

'I've… I've seen them.'

'Then you're not really close friends, just acquaintances?' The boy shrugged. 'You said that you arranged to meet Li Wei and Mark at Sentosa.' The boy nodded. 'How?'

'I do not understand.'

'Well if you go to different schools in different cities, how did you arrange to meet up with them?'

'I… I… cannot remember… I think we talk over cell phone.'

'I see. So you arranged to meet at Sentosa at the lagoon and then you walked up the beach to where Mrs Liew and her girls were?'

'Yes.'

'You're quite sure that's what happened?'

Yan Zheng's confidence began to return. 'Of course!'

Suddenly Shau Wee removed a photograph from her file.

She handed it to Yan Zheng, while I distributed several copies to the SAC members.

'Perhaps you could look at this photograph, Yan Zheng. Who is the figure in the striped yellow t–shirt?'

There was an awkward silence while Yan Zheng considered his position. 'Ahhh… it's me,' he stated finally.

'And what are you doing?'

'Playing soccer with my… ahh… Malay boys.'

'Where do your fellow soccer players come from?'

'Johore!'

'So these boys are your friends?'

'Yah… they are.'

'But I thought you said you were at the lagoon with Li Wei and Mark?'

'I was.'

'Then why are they not playing soccer in this photograph?'

Yan Zheng started to move about uncomfortably. 'I not sure. Maybe they are at the other side.'

'I have another photograph here. Perhaps we could look at this one.' Shau Wee handed a copy to Yan Zheng.

'What do you think is happening here?'

'Don't know.'

'That's all right, I'll help you. Three boys are playing with a piece of clothing while a group of girls watch and a very angry lady is standing near the three boys. Notice one of the boys has fallen over and look at the position of his head.'

Yan Zheng and all five SAC members studied their photographs.

'Where is the boy's head?'

Yan Zheng pouted, 'On the floor.'

'No it's not. It's near the other boy's shoe. Who is the other boy?'

There was an unintelligible whimper.

'Louder please.'

'Don't know.'

'Oh, I think you do. Look again, please.'

Yan Zheng stared at the floor. 'Me,' he muttered reluctantly.

'Was there something odd about your shoes that day?'

'No.'

'Think harder.'

'I cannot remember.'

'Really.' Shau Wee reached into her file and brought out a set of enlargements.

'You've been busy!' I whispered.

The enlargements were handed around. They showed Yan Zheng's shoe beneath Li Wei's head and the foot was clearly off the ground in a kicking position. But more important were the spiked stars embellishing the lace-up pattern on the face of each shoe. There was a gasp from the SAC bench and Yan Zheng's face darkened in an angry scowl.

'Not only did your shoes have dangerous pieces of metal attached, you actually kicked Li Wei in the head, didn't you?'

'No, no! I did not!'

Shau Wee turned to the SAC members. 'I have here a police report from Johore in which Sim Yan Zheng is described as a thief, a liar and a bully. He never knew Li Wei or Mark. He was at Sentosa on a day-trip with his Malay friends, but spotting a chance for some fun, joined in the teasing of Mrs Liew. If you check the statements of Tan Li Wei and Mark Ling, you will see that nowhere do they say much about this boy and he left as suddenly as he appeared. I am not defending Li Wei and Mark's behaviour in any way, and neither did Mr Richards. Their statements clearly demonstrate that they acted alone in a childish prank which got out of hand. Mr Richards came upon the scene and sprang to Mrs Liew's defence as any supportive colleague would.'

She turned and glared witheringly at Yan Zheng. 'I leave the council members to decide just how much truth there is in your story.'

'It is true! They are all liars!' Yan Zheng shrieked.

'The wee divil,' Jean hissed.

Mrs Teo asked Marjorie Sim to remove the boy.

'Well done,' I whispered. 'But why did the boy offer to make a statement in the first place?'

'Conceit. He's a show-off!'

Mrs Teo looked in our direction. 'Is there anything further?'

'Just a few more questions for Mrs Liew, thank you.'

'I thought I had already been questioned,' the good lady spluttered, looking decidedly uncomfortable as she returned to the hot seat.

Shau Wee withdrew another set of photos from her file and again these were handed out. Each set comprised seven photographs which showed the correct sequence of events. Mrs Teo looked up from the photographs. 'Who took these and how did you obtain them?'

'Quite by chance, actually. I remembered how as a schoolgirl I always took my camera on class trips, and I thought some of Mrs Liew's girls might have had cameras with them on this occasion. My initial requests brought no results, but then young Li Wei delivered a roll of film to my office. He wouldn't say who shot it.'

Mrs Teo looked concerned. 'How can we be sure it hasn't been interfered with?'

'I had a government laboratory carefully process and check the film and I have their certificate of authenticity in my file.'

'Thank you.' Mrs Teo sat back and nodded at her fellow SAC members.

Daisy Liew, heartened by Mrs Teo's questions, sneered, 'These prove nothing!'

Shau Wee smiled.

'Oh, but they do, Mrs Liew, they do. You see, I have arranged these photographs in order. At the base of each photograph is the date and time it was taken. If you follow through from the time on the print of Mr Richard's arrival and the time on the print of the appearance of the men dressed as women, you will notice that about five minutes elapse and Mr Richards only appears in two of those photographs. How then did he have time for all the planning and strategies for which you give him credit?'

There was no response.

'How did he fit in all the laughing, encouragement, insults and horseplay that you referred to in your statement?'

Still no response.

'In fact, these photographs clearly show that the taunting of the boys stopped with Mr Richard's arrival.'

Daisy Liew was unfazed. 'It is very obvious, Miss Leo, that you have removed the photographs that don't fit your version of events.'

'Have I really?' Again the file was opened. 'Here are the negatives which completely corroborate my sequence.'

'Legal tricks.' Daisy Liew was now struggling. 'That man made a fool of me.'

'Correction, you made a fool of yourself, Mrs Liew.'

'How dare you!'

'As I have shown, Mr Richards had nothing to do with Li Wei's injury. You see, these photographs clearly show that your version of what happened is, shall we say, incomplete.' Shau Wee picked up a photograph. 'For instance, why is your hand raised to Li Wei just before he falls?'

'Where?' Daisy Liew peered nervously at the photograph in question. 'I... I...'

'Let me help you. At Mr Richard's insistence the boys returned to apologise, but you were already overwrought and you struck Li Wei the blow which caused his fall, didn't you?'

'I... I don't... have to... I...' As she sank back in the chair, the photograph slipped from her fingers and wafted across the floor.

Shau Wee turned to the SAC members. 'I submit that Mrs Liew's allegations are no more credible than those of Sim Yan Zheng.'

There was a general murmuring among the SAC members as Snake rose slowly to her feet.

'Bravo!' She began to slow-clap. 'We have all just watched an amazing show. Indeed, an extremely accomplished performance by all accounts. But no one here is fooled by the antics of a trained, highly experienced barrister against a young boy and an elderly teacher, both unused to courtroom dramas and clever legal tricks. Truly a case of two Davids against a legal Goliath.'

Shau Wee smiled sweetly, 'Or two Philistines against a Solomon!'

'You really do have a high opinion of yourself!' Snake sneered.

Shau Wee smiled again and turned to the SAC members. 'I appreciate the praise of the vice-principal, but I hasten to point out that I cannot be held responsible for what a camera reveals.'

Snake lashed back,

'Let us see how your camera deals with the rest of the allegations!'

'That's enough!' Mrs Teo was clearly not prepared to allow the session to degenerate into a slanging match.

Yan Siang was called and entered the room with Josie who sat down beside Jean. He moved to the front and convincingly explained the truth of our friendship. As he finished, a large Indian lady dressed in a garishly coloured sari stumbled in with the two boys I had met in Holland Village. The clerk immediately moved across and, much to the mother's consternation, whisked the boys out of the room.

There was a pause for the secretary to adjust her laptop, and then Mrs Supraniam was invited forward. She was a loud, aggressive woman used to getting her own way and as she sashayed up to the front seat, she threw me a withering glance.

Her statement began with a miserable wailing over the plight of her two boys, who had been brought up in the traditional ways and were healthy and attentive until just over a year before, when the older boy started to show signs of stress. He began wetting his bed and having bad thoughts. He fought with his younger brother and was easily upset, often appearing nervous when he had to go to school. A doctor who examined the boy felt he could be the victim of sexual abuse, but the mother had no idea how or who until my name was linked with Yan Siang and then it all fell into place. When questioned, her son admitted the abuse.

I glanced at the SAC members. They were clearly disturbed by this poor woman's story and yet in the dealings I had had with the boys they seemed perfectly well adjusted and healthy. However, Shau Wee was unperturbed and when Mrs Supraniam finished, she looked at her sympathetically.

'I'm sorry your son is so miserable, Mrs Supraniam, and I hope the police catch the man responsible soon.' There was a long silence and the poor woman looked fixedly at the floor.

'You have informed the police?'

There was a suppressed hiss, like steam escaping from a leaky valve.

'Yessss.'

'And they're investigating the case?' Mrs Supraniam looked up and shook her head.

'They're not investigating? Why is that?'

Again the poor woman looked at the floor. Finally she breathed, 'Not enough evidence.'

'Your son's behaviour indicates he is a victim of sexual abuse, but the police feel there is insufficient evidence to proceed?' The large woman nodded. 'Why then are you so sure Mr Richards was involved?'

Black eyes flashed in my direction. 'Who else?'

'But there is no evidence to support your allegation, is there?' The dark head drooped once again.

It was clear that the SAC members were very uncomfortable with the direction proceedings had taken. They had never imagined when appointed to the panel that they would be called upon to travel down such a sordid avenue.

Mrs Teo coughed nervously.

'Thank you, Mrs Supraniam.' The large lady, tears in her eyes, quickly left the room.

Mrs Teo continued, 'That concludes the hearing this afternoon. We have now heard as much as we need.' She glanced at her fellow SAC members and they nodded. 'It will not be necessary for Mr Richards to make a statement or produce character witnesses.'

'Excuse me, Madam Chairperson, but there is one more person you should call.'

The SAC members looked surprised.

'Miss Leo?'

'We must hear from the Supraniam boy at the centre of the allegation against Mr Richards.'

To a person the SAC disapproved of this suggestion. I leaned across to Shau Wee and whispered, 'Is this really necessary?' She ignored me.

Mrs Teo looked decidedly unhappy. 'Why, Miss Leo? It will make no difference to our decision.'

'Mrs Supraniam has failed to dispel the haze of innuendo and suspicion surrounding my client and I cannot allow anyone to leave this room under the impression that Mr Richards might have misled her boy. The only way to lay the matter to rest is to hear from the lad himself.'

There was a general rumbling of discontent along the SAC row. I found myself praying that Shau Wee knew what she was doing, as her intransigence looked like costing me all the sympathy she had fought so hard to wring from the members.

After a hurried consultation, Mrs Teo turned back to Shau Wee. 'We will allow the young man to speak briefly on two conditions: I will question the boy and if he appears upset, we will stop proceedings immediately.'

Shau Wee looked disappointed, but at least she had won her point. 'I accept that.'

The clerk disappeared once again and returned with two very nervous Indian boys, one of whom had obviously been crying. They were placed in the front row.

Mrs Teo smiled benevolently. 'You are Nadi and Haji?' The boys nodded.

'You understand that whatever you say here will not be discussed outside this room and you will not be punished?' Again the boys nodded. 'That's good. Now don't feel embarrassed or uncomfortable. This is not a court, it is simply a committee meeting. You understand?' There was more head-nodding.

'It has been suggested by your mother that one of you might have been touched by a man in a very bad way.'

There was no response. I was beginning to develop a real respect for Mrs Teo. This was a very difficult business and she was handling it admirably.

'Does that mean neither of you had this bad experience?'

The younger of the boys looked at the other then muttered, 'He did.'

There was a gasp from the main body of the room. Everyone focused on the young Indian boy at the centre of the questioning, everyone except Yan Siang. He sat bolt upright beside me, absolutely still.

Mrs Teo leaned forward and looked at the elder boy, 'Is this true?'

The boy nodded.

'Do you remember who touched you?'

Several eyes fell on me but were quickly averted.

Again the boy nodded.

Mrs Teo steadied herself and asked the $64,000 question. 'Who was it?'

The young lad looked around. His gaze fell on me and he quickly looked away. Then he whispered a name. No one heard it.

'Who?' Mrs Teo repeated gently.

'Mr Chang.'

I felt like someone had hit me with a club. I turned to Yan Siang, who glared up at me, his eyes a mixture of hatred and fear.

'Who?' I repeated aloud without thinking as Yan Siang stood up, stumbled over Jean, and shot out the door.

'His father! Mr Chang!' the young Indian lad shouted, removing any doubt as he pointed at the departing figure.

What followed was pandemonium. Jean rushed forward and took the two little boys under her wing as their mother shoved her way to the front. Josie ran out after Yan Siang. Daisy Liew and Snake huddled over to one side with Marjorie Sim. The SAC members stood, some staring, others grouped in animated discussion.

I looked at Shau Wee and sighed, 'Did you know the boy was going to say that?'

'Of course not! I thought he was a little prima donna and hadn't been molested at all.'

Suddenly a voice rang out across the room. 'I would like to address this meeting.'

Every head turned. Unannounced, the principal had entered the room. How long she had been there nobody knew, but she barrelled her way to the front and greeted the SAC members. This was a day for surprises.

Mrs Benthusamy stood to the left and leaned on the empty chair. 'I had no idea this meeting was in progress until I heard from Mrs Supraniam on the telephone. As I have just returned from Canada, I am in no position to comment on the rights or wrongs of the case. However, I must say that I am astonished these allegations have been taken seriously. With all due respect to my vice-principal, I cannot believe Mr Richards would behave in the manner suggested. He is forthright, stubborn, argumentative, lacks discipline and needs to improve his record book, but is nevertheless a fine teacher, devoted to his students. I strongly urge the SAC to end this embarrassing farce now.'

For a moment I thought I had stumbled into Wonderland and, like the white rabbit, had fallen down a deep tunnel into the realm of unbirthdays.

Jean came up to me and shook my hand, 'The ultimate blessing. If I were you, I'd hang oot for a raise and a promotion.'

Mrs Teo coughed again and everyone settled. 'The council had decided matters before this meeting began and proceedings this afternoon have only strengthened our resolve. On behalf of the whole School Advisory Council, we would like to apologise profusely to Mr Richards for the inconvenience and embarrassment of these hearings. It is our earnest wish and request that he resume his duties at Pleasant Park immediately. The council would also like to place on record their appreciation of the valuable assistance given by Miss Leo.'

No unnecessary elaboration or grovelling — how Singaporean! I thanked the council for their support and accepted their request.

Jean had abandoned the boys to their mother. 'Let's get oot o' here and find a drink.'

'Good idea.' I turned to Shau Wee. 'Will you join us?'

'Can't, I'm going to a hen party.'

'Pity. Thanks so much for all the hard work.'

'Don't mention it. It was fun. Tomorrow it's back to covenants and financial fraud. Yuck!'

As we left, Theresa swept up with her eyes full of congratulations and her brain full of silliness. The last comment I heard was something about missing lit trial records.

We walked down the corridor straight into Her Graciousness.

I nodded. 'Thanks for the kind words.'

'Just doing my job. I'd welcome you back, but as far as I'm concerned, you never left.' She strode off towards her office.

As I watched her disappear, I wondered what was going through her mind. Having to speak up for a foreigner? Hanging onto a headache like me? But then again, you never could tell with Caucasians!

CHAPTER
37

'Where is Yan Siang?'

Josie's question echoed off the columns bordering the main entrance to the school and stopped us in our tracks. In the excitement at the principal's surprise appearance, we had forgotten the boy.

'I thought you went out after him.'

Josie descended the stairs. 'I did, but he'd disappeared.'

'Och, the pair wee laddie will have gone off to hide some place. It must've been awful hearing that said aboot his faither.'

But 'pair wee laddie' or not, nothing could put Jean off her stride. 'Noo where're we going for that celebrat-or-rary drink?'

My thoughts were with Yan Siang. 'Look, I'll give it a miss today. Perhaps tomorrow.'

'Och, what's gotten into yer?'

'I'd like to find out what happened to Yan Siang.'

'Half an hour willna make much difference.'

I looked at Josie and shrugged. It was obvious Jean was determined to raise our spirits with a burst of conviviality, despite the fact that Josie and I did not feel very convivial. To make a refusal more difficult, Theresa offered to drive us to Holland Village in her Mercedes. I had no strength to argue further.

During the journey Josie called Ming Chuan, who was delighted with the result and agreed to meet us at the pub.

Theresa parked in the public car park and we walked over to the little watering-hole Jean and I had visited previously. Even though the result of the hearing was different, my spirits were low. Ming Chuan rose to greet us and guided us to a little table he had reserved at the back. The atmosphere was smoky, largely because the place was frequented by fag-totting Europeans whom the cigarette police chose to ignore. Jean lit up immediately and added to the general fug, while Theresa ordered the first round of drinks. By the third round we had relived the whole SAC session, pouring scorn on Snake and Daisy Liew and extolling the virtues of Shau Wee and the enormous intelligence of the SAC members. As I downed my third Fosters I began to feel much better, but Josie's orange juices kept her alarmingly sober. The clock behind the bar moved towards six and Josie began to nudge me with her right knee. Finally I took the hint.

The atmosphere was tense. Gaunt-face sat stiffly in one uncomfortable wooden chair while Heavy Jowls spread across another. The pipe puffed angrily. Normally the white-haired gentleman would have enjoyed having the upper hand, but in the present case it was a pyrrhic victory — the incompetence of the pair before him had endangered them all.

'Where do we go from here?' he rasped.

Gaunt-face coolly examined his fingers and Heavy Jowls slumped.

'Let's review our position. We have no idea how much the boy knows and we still haven't found that missing Thai youngster. We've had a break-in and we don't know how many of our files have been compromised, and we have succeeded in alerting the police to what was a quiet, simple operation.'

The others moved uncomfortably.

'Speak, damn you! I never invited you here, they sent you. So what do they intend to do now?'

Gaunt-face leaned forward, 'We did as you suggested and followed them to Malacca, but we were misinformed about their backing and support.'

'And how did that misinformation cause you to end up being handcuffed to a fence and arrested by the Malaysian police for molesting transvestites?'

Gaunt-face shrunk sheepishly, Heavy Jowls continued to slump.

'I'm not waiting for another midnight visit. This operation is going to quietly disappear.'

Gaunt-face looked up. 'You can't do that.'

'Just watch me! You go back and tell your bosses it's over.'

Heavy Jowls struggled upright for the first time. The instruction to go back to their bosses alerted him to the fact that they had nothing to go back with, and the consequences of that did not bear thinking about.

Gaunt-face licked his lips nervously, 'Give us a couple of days to find out just how much of your operation is blown. Then you can make an informed decision. There's no sense in panicking.'

'Panicking? I'm not panicking, you bloody fool. I have a comfortable life here and I've worked at it for over forty years. I have no intention of seeing that come to an abrupt end. But this little place is only one small fragment of my investment. I will not allow it to jeopardise the rest. You've got until I have the files and records checked, and then I'm closing the lot.'

Gaunt-face could see it was pointless to argue. They had little enough time as it was. He stood up, nodded and left. Heavy Jowls stumbled after him.

The white-haired man swung round to savour his favourite piece of art. The battle scene always renewed his confidence. He smiled, but the clouds of smoke circling above him still pumped from an agitated chimney.

We arrived back at Kismis Avenue an hour later and while I freshened up, Josie phoned home to see if Yan Siang had turned up to see Boong-boong. No luck. We decided to dine at Pizza Hut since Tuesday night was their eat-all-you-can special, and that would give us a chance to work out where Yan Siang might be. But the phone went first and solved that problem for us.

The voice at the other end was unintelligible, so I handed the phone to Josie, who explained the call.

'That was Mrs Chang. Yan Siang is sitting on the edge of the roof and will speak to nobody. She wants you to come and talk to him.'

I grabbed my bag. 'Let's go.'

The lift took forever to arrive and we finally chose to race down the stairs. We ran through the grounds and down to the plaza. Panting and wheezing, we crossed Anak Bukit and hailed a taxi. My heart banged painfully but my mind was surprisingly clear. Finally the pieces were falling into place.

Josie looked across at me. 'Are you thinking what I'm thinking?'

'Probably.'

'You finally realise who killed Mr Chang?'

'I hate to say it, but it looks like…'

'Yan Siang?'

Ming Chuan sat up, shocked. 'How can?'

Josie gritted her teeth grimly. 'Look at the facts! Mr Chang's body was full of drugs and drink. We know that Yan Siang saw the writing on his father's feet and now we also know that Mr Chang was sexually interfering with Yan Siang's friend. I don't think Mr Chang's death had anything to do with The Flaming Dragon. Yan Siang found out about the abuse. Devastated, he plied his father with drugs and drink and arranged the fall.'

'But how did a boy of his size push Chang off the balcony?'

'It wasn't one boy of his size, but three! Your innocent little fellow conspired with his two friends.'

'And those thugs from The Flaming Dragon?'

'They probably think that someone killed Chang for the disk.'

'Well done, Sherlock. You've tied it up.'

'Perhaps.'

'What do you mean perhaps?'

'We still have to explain the injury to the back of Chang's head.'

'Accidentally banged on the door, floor... edge of the balcony... who knows!'

'Maybe...'

I was annoyed that Josie sounded unconvinced. Her scenario seemed perfectly logical.

The taxi drew up outside the Chang's block and while Josie paid, Ming Chuan and I raced up to the flat.

Two elderly neighbours were trying to comfort a highly agitated Mrs Chang and while Ming Chuan struggled to find out where Yan Siang was, I looked around and glimpsed a pair of feet dangling from the far corner of the floor above. I ran back to the stairs and leapt up two at a time. The next floor was very dark. As my eyes adjusted to the blackness, I made out a little figure on the far side of the large, open, void deck. A huddle of men and several young children from the neighbourhood crouched in front, and now and again someone called out to Yan Siang in Chinese. One man saw me and announced my arrival. Yan Siang turned briefly, then looked away again. Ming Chuan and I moved up to the group.

'Tell these people to stay back, will you. They're going to scare him if they get any closer.'

Ming Chuan repeated my concern and everybody moved back. I crept over to Yan Siang and sat down beside him.

My counselling attempts began with a lie. 'We've been

looking for you everywhere, you know. I wanted to thank you for the statement you read to the SAC members. That tipped the balance in my favour. You saved me.'

Yan Siang shrugged. 'If not because of me you wouldn't be in trouble with the school.'

I was relieved to find the boy was still on this planet.

Yan Siang smiled sadly at Ming Chuan. 'I know you two lovers. You so lucky to have someone.'

'But you've got friends… family… Uncle Eugene… Josie… me…'

As my voice drifted, I glanced out into the night. Sparkling specks glittered far off into the distance. Ironically, it was one of the few nights with no haze, and one could see clearly out across the city to the purpling ocean with its black silhouettes of tankers and fishing boats. A light wind stirred the chalky dust, billowing little puffs of it out beyond the edge of the roof.

'Look, I've had nothing to eat and we were going to get a pizza. Why don't you join us?'

'Leave me alone.'

'Why? Are you worried about what happened to your father?'

'You don't know what happened to my father.'

'I can guess. You found out that he was…'

Yan Siang twisted precariously on the edge of the roof. 'I don't want you to say about… about that,' he yelled.

'Okay… okay…' I panicked.

Yan Siang stood up, his little figure cut out against the dark blue canvas. 'You don't understand. No one can never understand.'

'Okay… you're right. Please move away from there.'

'No.' He wavered on the edge of the roof. I felt sick.

Suddenly I heard voices behind me and instantly recognised Chia and Ling. Damn! Mrs Chang must have phoned the police. I glanced around. Chia was advancing, flashing a torch.

'Stay back! Stay back!' I yelled.

I was too late. Yan Siang saw Chia and for a brief second his little face caught the torchlight. An image in a horror film, I was struck by the deathly pale skin and the haunting eyes — dark caverns of fear. He bent forward dazzled by the bright light and momentarily lost concentration. One foot twisted backwards and like a video replay in slow motion, he slipped off the edge. I threw myself forward and grabbed a flailing arm as the young boy's terrified shriek disappeared downwards.

The little body banged against the building, and I held on grimly. For a small boy he weighed a lot. Chia threw himself down beside me, but my arm was fully stretched and he was unable to reach my fingers. Horrified, I realised it was my cast arm.

'Call an ambulance, for hell's sake, and spread some mattresses below!' I screamed, struggling to hold on, blotting out the pressure and the pain. I could feel my hand weakening as the weight threatened to pull my arm out of its socket, but I had to hold. Ming Chuan reached over from the other side and, while Chia held my body, grabbed my arm. This relieved the pressure a little.

I called down frantically.

'You must reach up with your other hand, Yan Siang.' But the panic-stricken boy was too busy trying to hold onto the wall.

'Give me your other hand,' I pleaded desperately.

A plaintive little voice drifted back, 'Hold ... hold... hold, please...'

I turned to Chia. 'I can't hold on much longer!' Pain filled my eyes.

'Ling's sent for a rope. We'll loop it round his body,' Chia urged.

'I bloody can't hold him.'

The little figure began to swing and I again begged for his other hand. With Chia holding me, I stretched my free arm across the cast but was unable to reach the fingers, now wet with perspiration. I prayed for the strength to hold on just a fraction longer, but I could feel the greasy little fingers beginning to slip.

'Oh, no,' I muttered, 'Please, God, no.' I turned to Ming Chuan. 'He's going to fall.'

And then my fingers were empty.

With a heart-wrenching scream the little body plummeted towards the ground. I sagged onto the roof, gasping fit to burst.

Ming Chuan put his arms round me. Chia said nothing.

We lay there for a long time and then I thought of Terence. I pulled myself up and headed for the stairs. The others followed. We bounded down the steps three at a time, brushing people out of our way. I kept telling myself over and over that everything would be all right.

When we reached the ground, two guys in white were placing a stretcher in an ambulance. The mother and grandmother stood off to one side, crying. I had to find out how he was but all anyone would say was that he was unconscious. He had fallen into a group of trees, and these broke his fall.

The ambulance slipped away.

'I must go to the hospital.'

'Why? What good can you do?' It was Josie. She had been talking to the mother and grandmother when Yan Siang fell, and she had helped them down to the ground.

'His leg's broken and I think his face has been gashed.'

I stormed off to find a taxi. Ming Chuan and Josie ran after and caught me just as I flagged down a cab.

'Leave it to the family, Pete. They need the time and space. You can do no more for the boy at this moment.'

'I… I let him fall… I have to know he's going to make it. I couldn't stand having another… another death… like…'

Josie put her arm around my shoulders. 'I know. I know.'

We moved over to a bench near a children's playground. I watched the crowd disperse. Ming Chuan's arm had replaced Josie's and I began to relax a little.

'What a family! Father pushed to his death, mother sees it and says nothing and now the son falls off the same roof. If he survives he'll probably face a murder charge!'

No one commented. We continued staring ahead like three ancient Chinese gods.

My eyes caught the trees where Yan Siang had landed. They stretched around the corner of the block and meandered in a line across the grass frontage. I stood up unsteadily and walked over to where they ended in a clump. From the end of the trees, I had a good view of the whole block and I could see the edge of the roof where Yan Siang had been sitting. It was directly above, but a good twenty feet further along from the place where we supposed his father had dropped. At that point the trees stood away from the block, so his father's body must have travelled some distance outwards to hit them.

I walked to the area where the body had landed. The police pegs had been removed but the holes remained. Although the area was trampled and disturbed, the body had landed on a relatively flat stretch of thick grass which was clean, litter-free and devoid of any rocks, gravel or obviously sharp objects. I was intrigued. Carefully, I moved around the perimeter.

'What are you looking for?' Ming Chuan called out.

'I think I know.' Josie walked over in my direction, then turned off to the left, disappearing into the shadows near the local hawker centre. Suddenly she called out, 'Over here.' I hurried across.

'Is this what you're after?'

Josie pointed to a pile of broken concrete paving stones lying against the wall of a mee siam stall. I scrambled around the heap, examining the stones carefully. They were coated in dust and other rubbish. Nothing appeared unusual.

'Look here,' Josie indicated with her foot. At the outer edge of the pile, beneath several rotting rice bags, some pieces had been disturbed. I bent down and touched the material. Nothing moved. Then I saw the hole. One piece had been extracted.

Josie checked my discovery. 'It seems Yan Siang may not have killed his father after all.'

'What makes you say that?' I asked hopefully.

'I think he was alive when he hit the ground.'

'Then how did he die?'

'Someone saw him fall. Someone who wanted him dead...'

'... and that someone came over here, picked out a rock and went back and finished the job...'

'Trying to make it look like the fall killed him.'

'Clever, very clever.'

'Not really. I'd bet it was a spur of the moment thing. The killer probably couldn't believe his luck... being at the right place at the right time.'

'Great, but how to prove it? We've got no rock and no idea who was down here.'

'True. But I think we've got something better.'

'What?'

'An eye-witness.'

I stared at Josie gob-smacked. 'Who?'

'I'm not saying till I'm completely sure.'

We walked back to Ming Chuan.

'What should we do first?' I asked impatiently.

'Go and have something to eat!'

CHAPTER
38

I had to admit it was good to be back at school, although I had had no sleep the previous night. In the early hours of the morning, I lived and relived those last dreadful moments when Yan Siang slipped away.

Flag-raising was at its usual tedious best, and to make me feel truly at home, Jean arrived late and flustered. She, along with most of the staff, was happy to see me back, but Daisy Liew's little group huddled together and whispered, throwing nasty glances in my direction every chance they got. It did not bother me — after all, victory does tend to make one magnanimous. Snake had applied for a transfer and Her Graciousness had agreed.

The students were fabulous, several groups offering little posies and cards to welcome me back. It was an opportunity for much sentimentality and mischief. Most of the senior examination scripts had been marked and analysed, although the junior papers still lay ahead of us. Theresa welcomed my return with a panic-stricken countenance and agitated pleadings for some lit trial results. I happily told her that during my absence they had disappeared. After a post-recess cup of coffee and an hilarious update on all the recent gossip, I drifted off to my final three classes, leaving Jean mumbling to herself behind a huge wall of marking.

At the end of the morning session, the ELDDS had a special rehearsal in preparation for their appearance at the Drama Festival Finals on Saturday night. Eight schools had been chosen, but only one gold, one silver and two bronze medals would be awarded to the best four plays. It promised to be a long evening. I knew the finalists included three of the country's top schools and although we were in with a chance, I did not expect much.

At four o'clock I called it a day and prepared to head home, tired and desperate to find out about Yan Siang.

Halfway to the bus stop, a maroon sedan pulled up alongside me. Heavy Jowls leaped out, thrust what I took to be a gun into my side and prodded me into the back seat. I was too surprised to yell, and as the road was nearly deserted it would have done little good. The car swept into the main steam of traffic and headed towards the city. Eventually we drew into a hotel car park. It was a sleazy, cheap, Geylang backpackers' place. Gaunt-face obtained the key, while Heavy Jowls shoved me roughly up a rear staircase. A gun can be very persuasive.

I was thrown into a room on the third floor which overlooked the car park. Gaunt-face kicked me hard in the thigh, and it hurt. Then, shaking with laughter, Heavy Jowls unzipped his pants and urinated all over me. I was able to roll out of the way of most of it, but he was sufficiently on target to seriously alter the tone of my aftershave. Clearly this was pay-back time. Handcuffs appeared, and they manacled me to the bed.

Gaunt-face leered down. 'After all the fucking trouble you've given us, I'd like to take you apart piece by piece and if time permits, I may just do it, but business first.'

Heavy Jowls released a gigantic burst of flatulence which bounced off the walls and hit my nasal cavities with a strength that could have felled an ox. For one horrible moment I thought I might be on the receiving end of a heavier dose of his incontinence, but then Gaunt-face continued, 'You've caused some friends of mine a good deal of fucking inconvenience. So I'm going to give you a chance to put things right!'

Heavy Jowls moved over to the window and released another burst. This guy really had a problem and, judging by the smell, an appetite for very cheap food.

I glared at Gaunt-face. 'What do you want?'

'How much do you know about The Flaming Dragon?'

'Very little. Why?'

Gaunt-face nodded to Heavy Jowls who crossed to the bed. 'Not a good answer.' The gaseous subordinate took a small black object out of his inside pocket. It looked like a cell phone but was fifty times more lethal. Gaunt-face turned on a battered radio which scratched and cackled like a chorus of tortured cats. 'Try again,' he commanded.

I pulled myself upright. 'I'm telling you the truth. What could I possibly know about The Flaming Dragon?'

'Oh dear,' Gaunt-face nodded at Heavy Jowls, who stuck the object against my right calf. A savage charge of electricity belted through my leg which shot out reflexively and kicked the charger from my tormentor's hand. While he stumbled across the room to pick it up, Gaunt-face smiled and tied my feet together with a piece of cord.

'What… what the hell was that?' I screeched, finally waking up to the cold reality of my situation.

'Just a little toy my friend picked up in Malaysia. Now back to business. Why did you break into the club?'

'What… what do you mean?' I stuttered.

Gaunt-face nodded again at the fat man and he advanced on my leg.

'Nooooo…' I yelped, like a stricken dog. This time the charge was sharper and the pain shot clean up my body to my neck. Both arms began to tingle.

'We… we went there to… to check a disk.'

'What disk?'

'Bugger it, you know what disk!'

'Bad answer!' Again Heavy Jowls thrust the charger against my leg and I screamed in pain.

Now I was beginning to get real angry. 'If you touch me with that bloody thing again, I'll say nothing.'

Gaunt-face laughed. 'Oh, but you will. You'll be singing like a fuckin' canary when we're through. Now, once again, what disk?'

I lay back and stared at the cornices on the ceiling. It was obviously an old building, probably pre-war. My mind began to wander. I wondered if this was what it felt like to be tortured by the Japanese. I contemplated yelling as loudly as I could, but what with the radio and the sorts of sounds that usually emanated from this place, I was sure nobody would take any notice and these two wallies would only further reduce my comfort zone with a gag.

Again a savage bolt shot through my body. I went completely rigid before sagging into beautiful black oblivion. However, my relief was short-lived. A bowl of soapy water brought me back to the uncomfortable present.

Gaunt-face was sitting by the bed, drawing designs in the air above my face with a stiletto. 'Just tell us about that disk and your visit to The Flaming Dragon.'

Suddenly it occurred to me that I had nothing to lose. What could they do if I told them the truth? They could hardly kill me, over a dozen people had seen them bringing me into the hotel. Upon reflection, I now realise I had remarkable faith in the capacity of strangers to mind other people's business. However, the deciding factor was my incredibly low pain threshold.

'Okay, we know the disk list the names… the names of men who deal in children,' I squealed.

'Who is the we?'

'Does it really matter?'

'Maybe, and then maybe not. Did you copy any files?'

'What would be the point?' Cramp began to seize my left leg. 'Could you release these handcuffs? I want to change my position.'

'Uncomfortable is it?' Gaunt-face thrust his head into my face. 'You should try sitting chained to a fuckin' fence all night.'

Heavy Jowls reappeared from the bathroom and crossed to the bed. 'Yeah!' he sneered, giving me another bolt from his wicked little weapon.

'Owwww!' I howled.

'Did you make a copy of anything?'

'Only some faces and files.'

'Damn!' Gaunt-face moved Heavy Jowls over to the window and they whispered animatedly for a few minutes.

'Okay, we're going to leave you now.' He sniffed. 'Phewww... smells like you need a bath!'

Laughing at his own wit, he undid the cuffs and grabbed my feet. Heavy Jowls looped his arms around my upper torso and together they swung me into the bathroom, where they laid me face-down in the large tub. My hands were manacled behind me and Heavy Jowls produced a length of rope which he looped under my armpits. He tied one end to the cold faucet and the other to the shower fixture above the head of the bath.

'Bonzer, teacher, we're going. Enjoy your swim.' With a laugh he kicked the hot faucet above the bath and water gushed into the plugged receptacle.

As I swayed above the rising current, my head just beyond water level, I heard the pair leave and lock the door. My body began to sag and I knew any heavy movement would pull the shower-head from the wall and plunge my face under the steaming surface. I tried to think of a way out of my predicament, but I was no Sean Connery. Hot water splashed my face and dizziness sapped my strength.

Suddenly the door crashed open and two policemen rushed

through the bedroom and grabbed me. They cut the rope and laid me on the floor. I was groggy, my face scalded in two places.

'Put him on the bed,' a familiar voice commanded. I forced my scalded eyelids open and briefly saw a blurred vision of Chia, before drifting back into a semi-conscious state.

Fragments of conversation ebbed in and out on a tide of nausea. 'His face... scalded... need treatment... in shock.' I rolled over and vomited onto a sward of fraying green. A cutter arrived and the handcuffs were removed.

Suddenly I was roughly shaken and base vowel sounds hammered my eardrums.

'Peter! Peter, we need to move you out of here.' I slowly came round, my face on fire and my body tingling.

Chia's handsome head gradually achieved definition and I smiled inanely. 'My angel...' The young policeman hastily stepped back.

A pair of arms roughly pulled me upright and a strong blast of ammonia pinched my nostrils. I was offered a glass of water mixed with a milky substance. My eyes focused and the dizziness cleared.

Chia moved closer to the bed. 'We're going to take you to Tanglin. You need to be checked out by a doctor and we need to take a statement. Do you think you can move?'

I nodded.

'Good. Don't worry about your two friends, we picked them up as we arrived and they're on their way to Central.'

I left the room, supported by two officers. Admiring the shattered door dangling from twisted hinges, I mumbled, 'That'll cost you.'

'The landlord couldn't make up his mind whether or not to give us the keys, so we took the initiative. It's lucky for you we did. If we'd arrived any later you'd have been well-boiled.'

This time the ride to Tanglin was more promising than my last. I looked at Chia and grinned, 'How'd you know I was trapped in that room?'

'We received an anonymous tip from some guy who saw three of you go in and only two of you come out.'

I marvelled, 'What a responsible citizen!'

'Hardly. I think you were being tailed.'

'By whom?'

'We don't know, but watch your back.'

After a medical check-up, I gave a detailed statement to the police over coffee and biscuits, taking care to avoid any reference to Josie and her suspicions, although I did mention the children. Chia knew all about Yan Siang and the allegations of the young Indian boy, but I was very surprised when he informed me that the police had closed the file on Chang's death.

'Won't you prosecute the boys?'

'That's up to the lawyers, but it's very messy. The public don't like children being charged with the death of an adult, especially an adult with AIDS.'

I was stunned. 'AIDS?'

'That's right. And there are other extenuating circumstances. Don't forget Chang allegedly abused that Indian boy.'

'Do you know if Yan Siang's okay?' I asked anxiously.

'He's still unconscious, I believe.'

I thanked Chia and his men for all their help and availed myself of their offer to drop me home in a squad car.

CHAPTER

39

I arrived home to a steaming bath and special dinner. The doctor had rubbed a special salve into the burns on my face and I gleamed like a buttered turkey. Ming Chuan was desperate to learn about my ordeal, but I was hungry and refused to explain what had happened until I had eaten.

The meal of sweet and sour was delicious, washed down by a nippy little chardonnay. In between mouthfuls, I told Ming Chuan about my kidnapping and subsequent escape. However, once over his initial shock, he was angry that I had not foreseen that the thugs could have come after us at any time. Still, he was relieved to know that the pair were now cooling their heels in a prison cell.

I stripped and sank into a cauldron of fizzing bubbles. Within minutes I was renewed, revitalised and reactivated by the misty warmth and a particularly cheeky little cocktail of cointreau, bitters and some other exotic ingredient. Once dried and dressed, I was ready again to face the world. It was eight o'clock and really too late to visit Yan Siang, but I phoned the hospital on the off-chance that they might let me in, as they had with Terence. No joy.

While Ming Chuan watched a Channel 8 comedy, I mused

over the newspaper, but my mind kept returning to the mysterious Chang murderer. Josie's suspicions were well founded. Why, then, were the police content to close the case?

Ming Chuan and I both took time off work to attend Terence's wake. The wreaths were arranged on stands at one side of the open space beneath the apartment block where Terence's father lived. The coffin was placed on a cloth-draped catafalque in front of a colourful Buddhist altar. To one side, a group of nuns recited verses from the Buddhist scriptures, while on the other side various mourners intoned at intervals. A strange assortment of elderly men and instruments formed a band further back, and every now and again this group would burst into a rhythmic, eastern funeral dirge, with a heavy gong and percussion base.

Tables draped in white stood at intervals the length of the block, and tea and peanuts were served to visitors at each. Some tables supported groups of old aunties playing mahjong. Josie had asked us to attend on the first day in order to greet Terence's father and pass on our condolences. He was amazingly self-contained and genuinely pleased to see the pair of us. We had ordered a large wreath which took pride of place amongst the others.

After sipping tea for just over an hour we took our leave, Ming Chuan reminding me to take a red string off the peanut plate for good luck. Once out of the block we moved quickly. I was eager to get to the hospital to see Yan Siang. It had been almost two days since his accident, and I was still to visit him. He was in the children's ward at Singapore General, occupying a private room. We found him with little difficulty. Flat, breathing shallowly but regularly, he lay with his right leg heavily bandaged and resting in a metal sling. Two drips ran into his body, one disappearing into a bag hidden under the bed-frame. His pale little face, eyes closed, matched the sheets. Surprisingly, there were only a few scratches on his forehead, otherwise his face was unmarked. His arms lay exposed at his sides and his right wrist was bandaged.

The room was airy and light, with vases of flowers on a dresser at the foot of the bed and a line of cards above, many of them from his friends at Pleasant Park Secondary. We sat flanking the bed. Remembering Josie's advice when I visited Terence, I began to talk. I discussed our adventures in Malaysia and all the fun we had had since returning. I talked quietly about the recent problems and told him that nothing had changed between us. Ming Chuan left the ward to find a drink. As I spoke to the prone little figure it occurred to me that ever since I took him to Tanglin I had been trying to find out the facts surrounding his father's death. Now, having learned the details, I mused blackly that the truth seldom sets you free.

I felt a hand on my shoulder and looked up into the eyes of Mrs Chang. She smiled warmly and introduced me to her eldest son, a tall, strapping young weight-lifter who thanked me for my help and support. This seemed a good moment to leave. I turned, squeezed Yan Siang's hand and walked out into the corridor. Ming Chuan met me with two cokes as I reached the main vestibule, and we headed out to catch a bus into the city. However when the bus arrived, I decided to return to school, leaving Ming Chuan to bus to Orchard Road.

I was surprised to find the staff room deserted. My desk was still groaning under the weight of unmarked scripts and there was no sign of Jean or Theresa. I called Josie, but her mother informed me that she would be spending the day with Terence's family. I fully understood. Obviously I would have to wait till the following day to learn how her detective work was progressing. I walked out of the staff room and headed for the bus stop. A group of students tailed me and I paused to give them a chance to talk. The school had told them not to visit the hospital and they were eager to find out about Yan Siang.

'Hi, teacher!' two girls chorused as they neared me. 'Have

you been to see Yan Siang?' I nodded and they all gathered around. 'How is he?'

'Comfortable… but seriously injured and it will take him some time to get better.' There was a collective sigh. 'However, I'm certain he'll get better,' I added hastily.

John, Yan Siang's little friend, shot to the front. 'Sir, people say he jump down his block.'

'Don't be silly,' one girl retorted. 'He slipped and Mr Richards tried to save him. His arm was pulled out of its socket.'

A combined 'wahhhhh' rose above the group as they stared awe-struck, first at me and then both my arms. Clearly some had learned of Yan Siang's fall, but fact had mixed with fiction as the message did the rounds.

'Awe… some!' a duo gasped somewhere on my right.

One girl stood on her tiptoes and called out, 'Teacher, could you take some gifts up to Yan Siang for us?'

'Please,' echoed another young voice. 'We're not allowed to see him.'

'Okay,' I replied.

Two girls pushed their way through the bunch, a large shopping bag swinging between them. I gasped as I realised these were the gifts. Hefting the bag on my shoulder, I received a cheer from the group.

One young joker quipped, 'With that bag and your beard, you look like Santa Claus.'

There was a loud burst of laughter.

'I hope you still think I'm Santa Claus when I return your exam papers!' I quipped back.

'No worries, teacher!' the joker replied, swinging along beside me.

CHAPTER
40

Saturday, the night of the Drama Competition Finals, arrived too quickly. I had not seen Josie for two days, but she had promised to meet me at the Victoria Theatre. I waited outside until the final bell. When she failed to appear, I left her ticket at the box office and made my way inside. The uniforms of students from the competing schools turned the auditorium into a vast checkerboard. This, combined with the babble of hundreds of excited voices and the constant switching of seats, gave visitors the impression they had entered a far-eastern bazaar. Our seats were conveniently situated in the middle of the theatre and I had arranged the placings so that Josie and I were on one end of the row, with Mrs Benthusamy, Snake and their clique on the other. In between, a group of prefects provided a buffer zone.

Ronald had offered to stage-manage our presentation which freed me to sit, like all good producers, in the audience. I knew our group would deliver a fine performance, but when I saw the size and sound of the supporting groups from the two most favoured schools, the thought of winning a medal slipped to the back of my mind. Four schools had presented their plays the previous night, and we were one of the four presenting tonight. After the performances, four plays would receive medals and four would receive participating certificates.

The house lights dimmed and the excited babble fell to a hush. A spotlight burst upon two young presenters who had slipped through the curtain and we were welcomed, along with the special guests.

The first play was a mythical tale set in Cambodia, involving colourful costumes and ethnic dancing. There was very little dialogue, which was rather strange, as a principal requirement of the competition was that students demonstrate their mastery of English. Nevertheless, the play was well received.

The second presentation was an adaptation of one of Catherine Lim's short stories and the comedy was well acted, with the students displaying an amazing understanding of adult mannerisms and prejudices.

I spent the interval searching for Josie, with no luck.

We were the first play after the break and the production was flawless. Our students acted as if their lives depended on it and every nuance, aside and facial distortion hammered the absurd story home. The audience rocked with laughter, clapping twice in the middle. Her Graciousness shone like an embarrassed cherub and even Snake shook her head in wonder.

The final performance was a tragic story of lost love, betrayal and suicide. However, the audience found this play rather uncomfortable and they lost interest long before the end.

The judges retired to discuss their verdict and the audience were invited to stretch their legs. I wandered outside, trying to figure why Josie had failed to appear. It was so totally out of character. My concern faded when we were called back into a seething hot-pot of excitement.

The chairman of the judging panel, a white-haired gentleman with a rasping voice, was welcomed onto the stage and gave a short critique of what we had just seen. Then he turned to the awards. He began by announcing the four plays which had earned participation certificates, and these included the drama on

Cambodia. Next he moved to the two bronze medals. One was given to a play performed the previous night, the second was awarded to the Catherine Lim comedy. This left two plays: the tragedy and ours. I held my breath.

The judge awarded the silver medal to Pleasant Park Secondary. I sat there stunned, pleased we had won the silver, but shocked that we were beaten by a play which had failed to hold its audience. We received some compensation when one of our supporting actors was presented with the best actor award. However, the principal and vice were exhilarated. Basking in the adulation of all her fellow principals, Mrs Benthusamy glowed like an over-gassed neon light and at one point I felt she looked dangerously close to exploding.

As she swept passed me she inclined her head and beamed, 'That's what comes from good administrative support!'

'Indubitably,' I muttered, heading backstage to congratulate the cast.

Afterwards, I crossed the large cantilever bridge and walked along the river towards Clarke Quay where I caught the 61 bus.

As soon as I entered my apartment I put a call through to Josie's cell phone, but there was no reply. I called her home. A sleepy voice informed me that Josie had not been there all day. Worried, I sank onto the sofa and took out a cigar.

Suddenly I felt like food. Fear often has this effect on me. Two pieces of roti prata would fit the bill nicely. I slipped on my shoes, opened the door and walked straight into Josie — a dirty, dishevelled Josie, her face twisted in pain.

'What happened to you?'

Before she could reply, a figure stumbled out from the stairwell. Astonished, I recognised my old adversary with the eye-patch. His face was badly cut and blood had congealed across the scabs. With his left leg in plaster, his clothes torn and filthy and his hands shaking uncontrollably, he looked like he had just wandered in off the set of *Friday the 13th*. I stood, paralysed.

'Inside!' the phantasm croaked.

The door closed quietly and we all staggered into the main room.

'Get me a drink!'

I obeyed while Josie sank onto an elephant chair, tears streaming down her cheeks.

'Would you… you like something?' I asked her.

'No!' The thug answered with a sneer.

'What's going on?' I whispered at her as I handed the misshapen form a drink. He grabbed the glass and greedily gulped down two mouthfuls, and then turned savagely and spat the contents onto the floor.

'What, water? I want beer!'

I returned to the refrigerator and pulled out a bottle of Tiger. Within seconds he had drained the contents and indicated he wanted another. I obliged, appreciating the time this gave me to refocus. My mind was doing somersaults. How did this guy survive that horrific crash in Malaysia? Why had he grabbed Josie and why was he here?

'Sit!' he commanded. I sat on the edge of the elephant chair, hoping to give Josie some moral support.

'More! he croaked, finishing the second bottle. This was good. At the rate he was knocking back the bottles he would soon be blind drunk and easier to handle, although his injuries suggested it would not be difficult to overpower him as he was. However, when I returned with the third bottle, he was holding a knife.

The phone rang. I hesitated, but when he nodded his permission I crossed the room and picked up the receiver. It was Ming Chuan.

'Hi!' I breathed nervously into the phone. 'I got back okay. We came second. Yes, I heard from Josie. By the way, Tweety's purring away on the ironing-board.'

Eye-patch sat up and motioned with the knife that my conversation was over.

'I must go… Tweety says bye.' I replaced the receiver.

Eye-patch drank the third bottle more leisurely, bleary-eyed and sloppy. He did not seem to want to move anywhere in a hurry. I looked at Josie who gave me a watery smile.

With no warning, Eye-patch staggered up, fell back, and then pulled himself clumsily to his feet. 'Up!' he ordered. I thought he was telling us to stand, but the word meant much more than that. He shepherded us out the door and into the stairwell. With a sinking feeling I realised that 'up' meant the roof.

'Why're we going up there?' I asked Josie.

She shrugged, and then chortled crazily, 'Maybe he fancies a breath of night air.'

'He can't seriously think we're going to jump or fall? Not two of us?'

'If he wants to throw me off the roof, he'll get little resistance. I'm past caring.'

'Come on, Josie. We're not going to give up now. Besides, you haven't figured out who killed Chang yet!'

'Says who?'

'You mean you have?'

'Shut up!' Eye-patch pushed us through the last door. We had reached the top floor. Egress to the roof of the building was prevented by a heavy gate fastened with a padlock.

'Now let's see our hero get through that.' I murmured.

Shuffling and swaying, our tormentor eased up to the obstruction and with a few twists of his knife opened the padlock. Beyond was a flight of stairs and purple darkness… darkness which started to crowd me in. I began to fervently hope that Ming Chuan had figured out my message or an over-zealous guard would do an extra round of the building.

CHAPTER

41

As we stumbled up the final set of steps, I glanced back at Eye-patch. He seemed befuddled — an easy target.

On the top step I fell backwards, digging my elbow hard into his ribs as I crunched into his body. His reaction was alarmingly swift. He sank the knife into my arm and the blade scrapped agonisingly along the plaster, finally sinking into my wrist. His other hand grabbed my free arm, and with a sickening wrench he threw me forward painfully onto the steps below. Josie bent over and pulled me to my feet.

'The bastard!' I groaned.

'Don't underestimate him. He's been knocking me about all afternoon.'

'He didn't…?'

'No, but he came close a couple of times.'

We moved onto the roof. I could see we were so high that anyone on the ground would be unlikely to notice us even if they glanced upwards. Eye-patch motioned us nearer the far edge. We complied. The evening air had revitalised Josie and she was more alert, more like her usual self. I sat painfully and wound some tissues around my wrist. Eye-patch hung a short distance away.

'What do you think he's going to do?'

'I have no idea and I don't think he has either.'

'So you've worked out who killed Chang?'

'Almost, but I need to check your summary of the police report first. I was on my way to get it when this madman waylaid me at Bukit Timah Plaza. He forced me down to Beauty World and we've spent most of the afternoon sitting like this on a deserted void deck.'

Suddenly a cool voice drifted from the far stairs. 'Well isn't this a pretty picture?'

'Inspector Chia?'

As he stepped out of the shadows, I noticed the regulation police revolver with the heavy, round silencer attached to the business end. I struggled to my feet as Eye-patch tottered to his.

'You certainly arrive at the damnedest moments.'

Josie remained on the deck. 'Sit down, Pete.'

'What?'

'Sit down!'

'Chia? I don't understand.' Clearly I was missing something, but my instincts tingled ominously.

'Chang's killer,' Josie rasped hollowly.

'Him? It couldn't be.'

Then all the little details slotted into place.

'I see,' I breathed, wishing I had done so a lot earlier.

'But… the other day… you… saved…'

Chia smiled. 'Come now, surely as a literary buff you appreciate the irony of that little gesture!' He turned to Josie. 'Life always seems to get curiouser and curiouser, don't you agree, Alice?'

Eye-patch tottered backwards and forwards, gesturing with his knife, 'They're here… like you wanted.'

Eye-patch in league with Chia? So that's how Chia knew about the accident in Malaysia.

'Well done, old friend,' Chia enthused, moving over to pat

Eye-patch on the back. He swung the sagging figure around and gave him a gentle push. Eye-patch swayed on the edge of the roof eerily, undulating like a disco dancer, before toppling soundlessly into space. I stared at the recently vacated spot in disbelief.

'Painless and swift, that's the best way to leave this world.' Chia moved towards us. 'If you had delivered the boy to me and left everything else to the police, we could have parted friends. But, then, life is never simple.'

'You killed Chang?' I asked, still unconvinced.

'Let's say I took advantage of the situation. He was almost dead anyway.'

'You don't know that,' Josie growled.

'Move over here,' Chia ordered.

We moved dangerously close to the edge.

'A pity we have to do this. But I can't leave you to spoil things. Your girlfriend's even got Ling suspicious, though he's so stupid even with all the clues he couldn't figure it out.'

'Why kill Chang?'

'Business! He was a disgusting bastard, with his little boys. That sickened me. Then he got greedy.'

He took a metal box from his back pocket, opened it and extracted a full syringe. 'This is joy juice, friends. Guaranteed to help you fly. You're welcome to take a shot.'

I shuddered.

'No thanks, I'll fly on an empty tank.'

Chia waved the syringe. 'It's your choice!'

His revolver shook threateningly, and then someone moved out of the light in the stairwell.

'Throw your weapon over here!' The slim, black-clad shadow stepped around the deck towards Chia. He also carried a gun, firmly cocked.

'Tony!' Josie screamed. 'It's my brother!'

The brief distraction was all Chia needed. Quick as a panther, he charged the stranger, knocking the gun sideways. Tony's body was borne backwards into the stairwell. With a sickening crash, the pair tumbled down the first flight of stairs, bouncing painfully over the metal-edged concrete steps.

Tony hit the landing with Chia entangled in his feet and before the police officer could recover, he thrust savagely upwards with his legs. Chia rose raggedly through the air, hung in space for a moment, and then sailed over the half-wall at the rear of the landing. We heard a fearful cry, a thunderous crash, and then silence.

Josie and I stumbled across the roof to the stairwell.

'Where's Chia?' I panted.

'Where he belongs!'

I looked over the wall and spotted a crumpled figure stretched across three garbage cans in a little rubbish alcove far below.

Josie threw herself into her brother's arms. 'Tony, Tony! Where did you come from? Thailand?'

'Not likely. I've been trailing your friend there.'

I looked surprised. 'Me?' Then the penny dropped. 'You rescued Yan Siang and… and called the police in Geylang!'

'Correct.' He moved into the light and I noticed his severely scarred face.

'But why?'

'We suspected Chia was somehow involved with The Flaming Dragon, but we couldn't prove it. Apparently for months he's been blackmailing their clients… over the Internet, would you believe.'

'Where'd he get his information?'

'Chang supplied it.'

'How do you know all this?'

'The disk.'

'What?'

I was lost completely, and then Josie intervened, 'Matt gave the other detectives the disk he copied before he left the country.'

Tony continued, 'They gave it to me. The disk had the letters RAC on certain files — Raymond Andrew Chia!'

'Of course,' I confirmed.

Josie looked at him fiercely. 'But why couldn't you tell Mum and me that you were back in Singapore?'

'How could I? I've been working for the Internal Security Department for several months now.'

I admired his black leather outfit and riding goggles. 'Is this standard uniform for the ISD?'

Tony grinned and pulled out a cigarette.

In the taxi on the way back I grilled Josie.

'When did you suspect Chia?'

'Early on. There were a number of small things. Why would the police bug your phone? How come Chia was always one step ahead of us? And think back, he gave you a real clue.'

I thought for a while then smiled, 'You mean the trees?'

'Of course. How did he know that Chang hit the trees? There were no marks on the body. Obviously he saw the man fall.'

'Why did you want to check the police report?'

'To see who conducted the interviews that night.'

'Ling did.'

'I thought as much. You see they were both called to the scene, but Chia sent Ling up to the flat while he checked the body. When he found that Chang was still alive, he looked around for the rock and finished him off.'

'But you said there was an eye-witness.'

'I was only guessing, but I think Chia thought there was.'

'Who?'

'Yan Siang, of course! That's why Chia kept pressing to find out how much the boy knew.'

'And why the other boys weren't prosecuted.' I shook my head. 'I still can't see a motive.'

'Give me a break. I'm only a nurse, not Jessica Fletcher. Perhaps Chang pinched the disk to go into business by himself. Who knows?'

'So young, with his whole career ahead of him. What a waste! Where's Boong-boong?'

Josie stared at me appalled. 'Goodness, I forgot all about him. I left him to visit his friends at The Flaming Dragon.'

I leaned forward and said in a controlled voice, 'Driver, change of plan. Take us to Geylang.'

'Wah lau! So late… no can, changing shift. Get another taxi!'

Josie was used to this sort of nonsense. 'We have no time for that, a boy is in danger. If you want to be paid, take us to Geylang… now!'

We arrived at The Flaming Dragon to find police cars with lights flashing ranged along the pavement and officers moving in and out of the nightclub. I led Josie around the back of the main building, but we found the room deserted. The fetid smell of decay still hung in the air, but all signs of recent human habitation had vanished. Even the shelves had been removed.

'Are you sure this is the right place?' Josie queried.

'Perfectly,' I replied.

'How could they have disappeared so fast?'

'I have no idea, but they were here!'

We made our way back out onto the street as Tony emerged from the club. Anxiously, we explained the situation with Boong-boong and Tony put a call through to Central.

'He's in custody. Something about a passport.'

'Is the boy going to be charged?'

'I don't know, but they intend to hold him there overnight.'

'Thanks.' I turned back to Josie. 'At least he's safe.'

'I suppose you've rounded up the gang?'

'Nope. We've only got a few of the pawns. The big pieces have disappeared into the woodwork.'

'But you will get them all?' I asked anxiously.

'Probably not.'

'What about the files on those guys in Australia?'

'After the first fiasco, I'm not sure we'll risk another embarrassment.'

'And the kids?'

'They're with immigration.'

Josie interrupted. 'At least that's good news. We thought they'd been taken away by the hoods who ran this place.'

'Hardly hoods, Jos,' Tony laughed. 'The guys who set up this organisation were amongst the best in the business.'

'What will happen to the children?'

'They'll be returned to Thailand.'

'To what?'

'Orphanages probably.'

I shook my head. 'Then they'll likely end up back in the brothels of Bangkok.'

'Probably.' Tony glanced back at his colleagues. 'Let's get out of here.'

We crossed the road to a semi-deserted café downwind of The Flaming Dragon. I ordered coffees all round.

Tony stared out at the Singapore skyline and murmured absentmindedly, 'I love this city. Children can grow up, get an education and stand to inherit a strong economy.'

'Did you say you worked for the ISD or the PAP?' I quipped rudely.

'It's true,' he replied, lighting a cigarette. 'But in Thailand it's completely different. A few lucky kids with wealthy parents get a good start, while the rest have to scrape out a living as best they can. Young girls and boys work like slaves in the factory sweatshops of Bangkok or prostitute themselves in go-go bars and private clubs, and they're not all forced into it. Many love the opportunity to earn big bucks and make new friends. They come to enjoy being flattered and spoilt by European men. This lifestyle is now so common, it's almost become an accepted part of their culture. A lot of these young people make good money, return to their villages and buy land or a business, and then settle down to enjoy the rest of their lives prosperously.'

He casually blew three smoke rings into the air and we watched them drift away.

'Recently, a lot of do-gooders from the West have gone in with the best of intentions and their own exclusive moral codes, but they don't understand the culture of the country.'

I was appalled. 'You don't mean you think that all this child sex is okay?'

'Me? Hell, I even think that gays are perverts!'

Josie was embarrassed. I steeled myself and looked away.

'Of course I don't agree with it. But until there is a complete change in the mind-set of these people, you'll never stamp it out.'

I glared at him, 'But surely if you outlaw paedophilia world-wide and enable prosecutions to take place in countries where paedophiles are caught, you must eventually have a dramatic effect on the practice.'

'You really think so? Take your little friend Boong-boong. I bet he's heartbroken that he's returning to Thailand when he had his heart set on a trip to Australia with his sugar daddy. Why should some self-righteous do-gooder take away the only chance this kid has for a decent life?'

'How can you call it a decent life?'

'You think the alternative is better? In Australia most of these kids get well looked after. True, some get misused, but that's a risk they're prepared to take. Better than catching AIDS in a brothel or choking to death in a sweatshop.'

'C'mon, we do them few favours letting foreigners exploit them.'

'Well you needn't worry. The kids that were here will all be returned to the very families who sold them or the institutions they ran away from.'

Josie intervened, 'It's late and we're all tired. You coming home, big brother?'

'Later.' He drained his coffee and stood up. 'By the way, I've some more bad news. I wasn't going to tell you this, but what the hell! We've got nothing solid on Chia. It seems he covered his arse pretty carefully.'

'What about his confession on the roof?'

'What confession? It's all circumstantial. There's no murder weapon, no witness, only your suspicions! Worst of all, they'll probably charge the kids with manslaughter.' He shrugged and walked back to The Flaming Dragon.

'I don't believe it! All that hard work and those thugs'll get away with it.'

'And Chia comes out a hero. Slipped and died in the line of duty!'

'What should we do about Boong-boong?'

'What can we do about Boong-boong?'

'We could ask Jean…'

'To adopt a young Thai boy?'

'Or board him so he can be educated here.'

Josie smiled, 'I'll phone her. It'll sound better coming from me.'

We lapsed into silence once more.

CHAPTER

42

The three of us met at the Central Police Station after lunch the following day. Ming Chuan still did not understand the significance of Tweety — favourite meal of Sylvester, the cat. It was fortunate we had not needed his help.

We discovered a very nervous Boong-boong, but the police were reluctant to release him into our custody. Detective Ling, still recovering from Chia's strange death, viewed us suspiciously. He asked for a statement, but I refused to make any comment until Boong-boong's problem was settled. The police thanked us for our help in closing the Chang file, but I wondered how much Ling actually knew. He revealed that they had conclusive proof that Terence was murdered by Gaunt-face and Heavy Jowls. Josie took the news calmly.

We explained everything to Ming Chuan on the way to the hospital to see Yan Siang, and he was predictably bitter about Chia's duplicity. The Changs were at Yan Siang's bedside so we did not stay long. I had delivered the students' bag of goodies the previous Friday and Yan Siang's little sister had arranged them around the room.

'Won't Yan be surprised when he wakes up!' she bubbled.

Mrs Chang smiled and nodded tearfully.

I silently prayed that he would have a chance to be surprised. The rest of the afternoon I went back over the evidence we had collected, but as Tony said, it was mostly circumstantial.

Monday morning. I crawled out of bed, leaving Ming Chuan asleep. I marvelled at how much we had learned about each other over the past couple of weeks. I thought back to Tony's remark two nights earlier, and I understood it. Once I would have felt indignant and angry, but now it did not bother me. What Ming Chuan and I had, many married couples, with all their social advantages, would never have.

I arrived at school in time to catch the end of flag-raising. The principal congratulated the cast and the teachers involved in the drama competition on winning a silver medal. Jean was especially happy for me and we agreed to meet later to celebrate over a cup of coffee.

At recess I returned to the staff room to find a polite little note in my pigeon-hole informing me that I had been granted an audience with Her Graciousness. I expected she wanted to personally congratulate me on the success of our entry in the festival. I was to be sorely disappointed.

'Good morning, Peter.'

'Good morning,' I replied.

'This is for you.' She handed me a long round tube. I shook out a certificate of appreciation from the Singapore Police. It thanked me for all the help I had given them and apologised for any distress I had been caused.

'That's very decent of them,' I remarked.

'Yes… indeed.' The principal moved uncomfortably. 'There is one other matter I've been asked to bring to your attention.' She glared intently at the pencil on her desk. 'The Foreign Recruitment Office has asked me to warn… I mean… inform you that the government will not be renewing your contract for a further term.'

I was dumbfounded.

'We are advising you in advance so you can get your affairs in order and prepare to…'

'Is there a reason for this?'

'Not that I'm aware of, but a reason does not have to be given. I realise this might be something of a shock…'

'A shock? That is the understatement of the year. I thought I was cleared of all that molesting nonsense.'

'I'm sure this has nothing to do…'

I leaned on the desk. 'And I'm equally sure it has a great deal to do with it. My God! Guilty even when proven innocent!'

Suddenly I saw it all. The principal had not spoken on my behalf at the hearing as everybody supposed. She had waited, the cunning old fox, to see which way the decision was likely to go. Then, when she saw that Snake was heading for the gurgler, she promptly distanced herself from the losing side and jumped onto the winning horse.

Once the decision was out and the matter over, she dropped me as deeply in the horse-shit as she could… revenge for destroying her faithful little toady.

'I think you should go away and contemplate your future calmly and carefully.'

I looked down at the woman and shook my head. 'Contemplate my future? You're contemptible!'

'Mr Richards, I will not sit here and…'

I turned and strode from the room.

My emotions were again in turmoil. I was angry, fed-up, sad, humiliated, disappointed and bitter. Two weeks ago I was sailing along, confident and contented. Now I was a cast-off, dismissed with prejudice.

I thought of phoning Shau Wee but I knew that would be a waste of time. I did not want to fight to stay in a country that did not want me. The ministry had not even bothered to inform me personally.

When I arrived in the staff room, Jean leaned over, 'Congratulations, my dear!'

'Didn't you say that before?'

'Not yer medal. On yer expulsion.'

That bloody staff grapevine, I thought. They probably knew the news before I did.

'What'll you do?'

'Return to God's Own, I suppose. Ming Chuan's been wanting to leave Singapore for a while.'

'Good on yer. You'll be pleased to hear that I'm leaving at the end of the week.'

'How come?'

'Not here! Let's go get a coffee.'

Jean was back to her serious voice. We left the staff room and headed for the canteen. On the way we ran into Theresa, whose crestfallen features reminded me of a sad rabbit. I waved her away, unable to deal with her condolences or explanations. The canteen was deserted. I got the coffees and Jean prepared her explanations.

'Rojan and I purchased a quaint wee villa above some famous beach in Penang.'

'Ferringhi?'

'Can't remember. Anyhow it's all planned. On Friday I fly to Scotland, ma dad's health's been failing for a while and ay ken he's no sae guid at the moment.' Jean winked. 'I'll fax ma resignation to MOE on Saturday and fly to Penang on the Sunday.'

'Jean, you're a caution! But what about the tax you owe?'

'Dinny be daft! They'll hae to catch me first.'

We both shrieked with laughter.

Suddenly I remembered Boong-boong. 'Did Josie call you?'

'She did an' it's all been taken care of. Yer ken that Rojan, the auld lump, has always wanted a kid and at ma time of life...' She burst into another guffaw of laughter. 'That wee Thai laddie was heaven-sent. I've arranged for ma lawyer in Scotland to prepare the papers an' we formally adopt the wee fella as we enter Malaysia.'

'Jean!' I threw my arms around her neck and hugged her tightly. 'God, I'll miss you.'

'Nonsense. Yer'll be up to visit us in nae time at all and I've a hankering to fly over an' see your bonny wee paradise wi' aw its mountains and lakes.'

I struggled through the remainder of the morning and after the final bell, stood for a while gazing out over the grounds, beyond the neighbouring park, across the highway and scattered housing blocks, far out to where the PSA building glittered in the distance. Modern, lush, and in its own way majestic, Singapore had established itself as one of the most successful economies and desirable destinations in the world.

I watched the bobbing figures, whose forefathers had left them such an enduring legacy, scatter out of the school in chattering clusters. Two young girls turned, and shielding their eyes from the sun waved up at me. I waved back. Momentarily my vision changed and I saw a dark room crammed full of bright, young Thai faces. How could these two neighbouring worlds be so different? I had come a long way in the past three weeks — Terence dead and my naïvete dead with him. In one way, I was bitter about my new perspective, in another, my faith had been strengthened. It was time to move on.

My musings were disturbed by heavy panting to my left.

'That's a long haul… wah!' Mrs Teo gasped as she paused for a moment on the top step. 'Mr Richards, they said you'd be up here. I had to speak to you… privately.'

'Good afternoon, Mrs Teo.'

'Yes, good afternoon.' She needed time to recover from her exertions, so we both stood and admired the view for some minutes.

'I wanted to tell you that the SAC were sorry to hear about your contract and they wish me to tell you that they will support a direct appeal to the minister.'

I was impressed. 'That's very good of you all, but I need time to think.'

'I see,' Mrs Teo dabbed at her reddening cheeks with a saturated tissue.

'Please express my appreciation to your council…'

'No longer my council, Mr Richards, I'm afraid.'

'Really?'

'I tendered my resignation when I heard you were unlikely to continue.'

I blushed, and then extended my hand and we shook. 'We'd better head down,' I suggested.

'Right.' She pulled out a small slip of paper. 'This is my phone number. You will consider our request?'

'Of course,' I lied.

We parted on the ground floor. I wanted to get away from the place, but then Theresa walked out of the administration corridor in the company of a white-headed gentleman.

'Peter, come and meet our new council member.'

I was trapped. Unable to escape in any direction, I complied.

'Peter Richards, this is Mr de Vere.' She grabbed me and bubbled in my ear, 'That's French, you know! Mr de Vere, this is our English specialist, Peter Richards.'

We shook hands and I recognised the elderly gentleman who had presented the drama awards.

'English specialist? A good title.' He gestured towards the large mural on the far wall, a painting of Sir Stamford Raffles greeting Malay chiefs in early Singapore. 'This must be a good school, with such a feel for history. History is so vital, Mr Richards. It can teach us so much.'

I wanted to move away. I knew the principal was still in her office and I had no desire to meet her again. I also found the stranger's thick, rasping voice disturbing. There was something about him that seemed thoroughly unpleasant.

'I must go to the hospital,' I muttered, excusing myself. The white-haired gentleman nodded and was swept away by an enthusiastic Theresa.

I arrived at the hospital an hour later. When I reached Yan Siang's room, he was lying in a different position and his injured leg looked more comfortable. The bandaging had been reduced. I sat down beside him, took his hand and squeezed gently. There was no reaction. I sat back and gazed at the pale little face. Gradually my eyes closed.

'Hi, teacher!' I was dreaming and the little voice called across my English class. 'Teacher?' There it was again. Suddenly someone squeezed my hand and I opened my eyes.

Yan Siang was staring at me.

'Yan Siang? Yan Siang, my God!' I grabbed the nurse's call-button and squeezed frantically. Yan Siang just lay there, his stare creasing into a smile.

'Hello, teacher,' he said again as a nurse bustled into the room.

'He's awake,' I squawked hysterically.

'We expected it,' the nurse replied. She took his pulse and checked the readings on the surrounding machinery. 'Don't excite him. I'll inform his specialist.'

'Are you feeling better?' I leaned over and kissed his forehead. Then I got a grip on myself and scolded, 'Why so long? I've been waiting to speak to you for days!'

His eyes twinkled.

There was so much I wanted to say, but where to begin? Eventually I just sat back and savoured the moment. Yan Siang closed his eyes. An hour passed.

'He's conscious then?' Josie came up behind me with Boong-boong.

'How did you know?'

'The nurses are all talking about it.' Josie sat down and Boong-boong wandered over to the window.

'Yes, he's come back… to a charge of manslaughter.'

'Isn't there something we can do?'

'Like what? I went back through the evidence yesterday and Tony's right, it's just our opinion against Chia's.'

'If only someone had been there that night. If only someone had seen his father fall.'

'I did!' Boong-boong turned back from the window.

'What?'

'You saw Mr Chang fall… that night?'

'Same same.' He mimed a body falling, and then, 'Boossshhh! On the grass.'

'He was dead?'

'No… no! He come up… all funny.' More miming like a dazed zombie.

'Then?'

'This policeman come. Go and get this… this thing and hit… hit… and hit…'

Josie grasped Boong-boong. 'You were there? Why?'

'Go to see friend.' He pointed to Yan Siang. 'But thing fall. I run behind concrete. Then policemen come. I very scared. Go back… tell no one.'

I stared at Josie open-mouthed. 'It's a gift from heaven. Let's take him to Ling.'

Boong-boong grunted, 'I want speak Yan Siang.'

'Later.' Josie moved him out of the room.

Suddenly Yan Siang's eyes opened again. 'You teach me next year, teacher?'

'We'll have to see.'

His little brow furrowed and he looked at me wistfully. Then his eyes softly closed.

Josie looked around the door. 'Are you coming?'

'Could I borrow your cell phone first?' I moved into the

corridor and found the slip of paper.

'You calling Ming Chuan?'

'Nope.' I put my arm around her shoulder and dialled as we walked down the corridor.

'Hello. Mrs Teo? I think we should meet.'